W9-BXY-699

THE CHERISHED WIVES

Also by Valerie Anand

Gildenford
The Norman Pretender
The Disputed Crown
To a Native Shore
King of the Wood
Crown of Roses

In the 'Bridges Over Time' series

The Proud Villeins
The Ruthless Yeomen
Women of Ashdon
The Faithful Lovers

THE CHERISHED WIVES

Bridges Over Time
Book V

Valerie Anand

ST. MARTIN'S PRESS ❧ NEW YORK

f/Anand

ISBN 0-312-13943-8

First published in Great Britain by Headline Book Publishing

First U.S. Edition: January 1996
10   9   8   7   6   5   4   3   2   1

104922

Sources

A definitive list of the books I consulted when preparing this novel is, of course, not possible. But chief among my sources were:

The Age of Improvement 1783–1867 by Asa Briggs (Longman Group UK Limited, 1959)

Clive of India by Mark Bence-Jones (Constable, 1974)

Coming of Age in the Milky Way by Timothy Ferris (Bodley Head, 1988)

The Eighteenth Century 1714–1815 by John Bowen (Thomas Nelson and Sons Ltd, London, 1974)

England in the Age of Hogarth by Derek Jarrett (Hart-Davis, Macgibbon, 1974)

English Costume of the Eighteenth Century drawn by Iris Brooke, described by James Laver (Adam & Charles Black, 1970 edition)

English Social History by G. M. Trevelyan (Book Club Associates by arrangement with The Longman Group Ltd, 1973)

Guildford, a Short History by Matthew Alexander (Ammonite Books, 1992)

The Herschel Chronicle by Constance Lubbock (Macmillans, New York, 1933)

A History of India from the sixteenth to the twentieth century by Percival Spear (Penguin Books, 1990)

An Illustrated Guide to London 1800 by Mary Cathcart Borer (Robert Hale, 1988)

A Matter of Honour by Philip Mason (Jonathan Cape, 1974)

A New History of India by Stanley Wolpert (3rd edition, Oxford University Press, 1989)

The Oxford History of England edited by Sir George Clark:
   The Reign of George III, 1760–1815 by J. Steven Watson (Clarendon Press, Oxford, 1960)
   The Whig Supremacy, 1714–1760 by Basil Williams (2nd edition revised by C. H. Stuart, Clarendon Press, Oxford, 1962)

Seven Hundred Years of English Cooking by Maxine McKendry, edited by Arabella Boxer (Treasure Press, 1985)

Acknowledgements

I would like to thank the Royal Society for their assistance when I was seeking information on the astronomer William Herschel.

Most grateful thanks also go to Norma Gordon and Barbara Lawrence, who obtained information for me on Robert Clive, and on the history of Guildford, at a time when I was unable to go hunting myself.

Contents

THE WHITMEAD FAMILY

Ninian Whitmead 1640 m. Parvati (Penelope)
(1600-1684)   (died 1648)

Charles Whitmead 1667 m. (2) Christabella Davison
(1642-1710)   née Morris (1639-1701)

1664 m. (1) Louisa Lagrange
(1643-1666)

Henrietta Whitmead
(1665-1742)

Matthew Whitmead
(1665-1743)
1686 m. Deborah Hill
(1666-1740)

Caroline Whitmead 1688 m. Hugh Browne
(1668-1712)   (1666-1717)

James Whitmead (1687-1718)
1709 m. Araminta Cadell
(1688-1743)

Hugo Browne 1723 m. Lucilla Compton
(1689-1749)   (1700-1759)

George Whitmead (1713-1781) 1742 m. Lucy-Anne Browne (1725-1799)

Hugo Harper 1774 m. Mary Logan
(1749-1799)   (1752-1822)

Henry Whitmead (1748-1812)
1794 m. (2) Horatia Miller (1769-1838)

James Harper
(1785-1809)

Richard Harper (born 1775)
1800 m. Jane Merridew (born 1778)

Francis Whitmead
(born 1795)

1770 m. (1) Emma Kendall
(1750-1781)

Sophia Whitmead
(born 1781)

Phoebe Whitmead
(born 1779)

Anne Whitmead
(born 1775)

THE BIRD, MILLER AND KENDALL FAMILIES

Charles Miller 1727 m. Eleanor Bird (1701-1772) (1704-1767)

James Bird 1730 m. Jane Weldon (1702-1779) (1704-1772)
— no issue

Walter Kendall 1722 m. Anne Morley (1700-1777) (1703-1778)

Harry Miller (1728-1790) 1755 m. Catherine Stonely (1732-1786)

Ellen Miller (1730-1791) 1749 m. Ned Kendall

others

Annette Kendall (1723-1790) 1743 m. Thomas Robbins (1720-1784)
— issue

Ned Kendall (1726-1784) 1749 m. Ellen Miller

2 sons

Frederick Kendall (1753-1814) 1778 m. Alice Pugh (1748-1812)
— no issue

Elizabeth Miller (1756-1810) 1779 m. John Ford (1756-1808)

3 sons

Horatia Miller (1769-1838) 1794 m. Henry Whitmead

Emma Kendall (1750-1781) 1770 m. Henry Whitmead (1748-1812)

Francis Whitmead (born 1795)

Anne Whitmead (born 1775)

Phoebe Whitmead (born 1779)

Sophia Whitmead (born 1781)

PROLOGUE
The Bridegroom
1740

Young Mr George Whitmead, as always, had dressed for the occasion in what, according to the latest shipload of arrivals from England, was the very latest mode.

As was the fashion, his grass-green coat with its yellow frogging was tailored tightly at his middle, even if it did reveal the beginnings of a paunch. His white stockings fitted without a crease. His wig, the same pale red as his natural hair, was smooth and neatly rolled.

He was also sweating steadily and unpleasantly, while prickly heat drove pins into his chest and the insides of his elbows and thighs. That he was sitting on a cushion instead of on a chair didn't help, and nor did the warmth from the many lamps by which the Nawab of the Carnatic lit his banqueting hall.

The bearded Nawab himself, Anwar-ud-din, was wearing loose silken robes which were no doubt far more comfortable, and there were times when George suspected that their host's flashing smile contained a trace of the sardonic. To him, the English probably did look odd or even funny, sweltering in their Western clothes.

But one couldn't possibly adopt Indian fashions, no matter how practical they might be. Mr Whitmead surreptitiously scratched his chest, swatted a whining mosquito, pushed aside a sudden, outrageous desire to be an Indian prince and dress for the climate, and agreed with his neighbour, Mr Nicholas Morse, who would probably be the next Governor of Madras, that the channel of water which tinkled through the midst of the hall did indeed create an illusion of coolness even if it couldn't quite produce the reality.

The hall was beautiful. A scalloped archway leading to the open air framed a segment of starry sky and a tree twinkling with fireflies, and within the room the walls and ceiling were a mosaic of delicate paintings and intricate inlaid patterns made from semi-precious stones. The graceful arches leading to other parts of Arcot palace and the lattice, fine as filigree yet made of stone, that formed part of one inner wall delighted the eye as well as allowing for the best possible circulation of the humid air.

One could not, however, spend too much time in gazing. The conversation was too important. They were here at the Nawab's invitation and it was becoming obvious, from the tone of the remarks he was making through an interpreter, that he was delicately enquiring into the chances of getting them to pay more for cotton cloth. He was

3

also hinting, his smile now broad, amiable and ominous, that if they didn't, the rival French concern might.

'Bloody French,' muttered Nicholas Morse in an undertone. 'They're always in the way. They're turning Pondicherry into a major town; it'll rival Fort St George before they're finished. They'll do anything – *anything* – to gain an advantage over us. I think they'd be willing to put themselves out of pocket if it put us out of business.'

'Is there a genuine danger of that?' George enquired seriously.

'I hope not.' Morse wiped his brow and said, 'Thank ye, my man,' to a servant who moved unobtrusively to cool the air for him with a feather fan. Nicholas Morse was a big man, his face a network of small broken veins and his blue eyes always just a little bloodshot. His midriff had long gone past the stage where it could stand the present fashions in men's coats, and he wore his burnt-orange jacket open.

He reached out to the little carved table in front of him and helped himself to a compote of fruit in a dark, rich sauce. 'I wonder if there would be a market in England for some of the more exotic spices in this? I like it, myself, but it makes the steam come out of my ears.'

'If we can ascertain the ingredients, I could take samples back to England and examine the possibilities, sir.'

'Ah. I was forgetting. You're sailing for home soon, aren't you?' Morse said. 'I heard some talk that you were going back to look for a wife.'

'That is my intention, sir, certainly.' George's glance had been momentarily distracted after all. Beyond the stone lattice, he had glimpsed movement. He pulled his gaze away and turned back to Morse. 'I take the view that a man should marry before the age of thirty.'

'You have found no young lady here who might suit you, it seems?' Nicholas Morse said jovially. 'And your family haven't found anyone they could send out to you? I take it, though, that you'll be bringing your new wife out?'

'I think not, sir. The climate of India bears hard on women and I can offer my wife a most comfortable establishment in England. Two, in fact. I have two houses there, one of them with some land attached. My wife would not be alone, since my mother uses my houses and will be glad of her companionship. I shall of course hope to leave my wife with child. A young lady of homeloving inclination, with a preference for England, will suit me best, and of course it is in England that I must seek for her.'

'You have land?' Morse was diverted. 'Well, well. I've known you a good long time and yet I never knew that. Unusual, isn't it? You're a merchant, and so, I believe, was your father. Landowners and merchants aren't commonly the same thing.'

'My father was successful enough as a merchant to be able to afford a modest estate as an investment. He believed that land was the soundest investment of all,' George said. 'In fact, there is a landowning tradition in my family. A branch of the Whitmeads still farms in Essex.'

'You'll have a strange sort of marriage, my boy! I have always been glad I have Mrs Morse with me here.'

4

Mrs Morse was not present at this moment, but had been left in Fort St George, about seventy miles away. George's relations with her were perfectly correct but nevertheless he knew rather more about her than her husband apparently did. She was one of the reasons why he didn't intend his wife to come to India. If Mrs Morse were to become the governor's lady, she would wield a great deal of influence and in George's opinion it wouldn't be of the right kind. When he married, he would see that his bride was properly protected from questionable influences.

He could hardly say that to Morse, however. 'Your good lady seems to deal admirably with the climate,' George said. 'But it is not always so.' He mentioned the names of three young women who had died, two of tropical fevers and one of snakebite, in the past year. 'It would be my considered preference to take no risks.'

A proper enough sentiment, thought Nicholas Morse, but what a ponderous way to express it. He didn't actually dislike George Whitmead, who although he was only twenty-seven had bought his way into the East India Company at Councillor level and proved himself to be able and well conducted – a valuable member of the Company, in fact. But a man of twenty-seven oughtn't to talk as if he were seventy. The Company could do with new young blood out here, Morse decided privately. He'd try to encourage it.

He said no more, but addressed himself to another helping of fruit compote and noted that his fanbearer was murmuring something in his own language to a servant with a sherbet jug.

The servant nodded and departed with his jug, but the exchange probably had nothing to do with sherbet, for a moment later the interpreter at the Nawab's side addressed George.

'Mr Whitmead! The Nawab is interested to learn that you are seeking a bride. Alas, that he cannot help you! Our ladies are the most beautiful, the most faithful, the most devoted in the world, but an Englishman of your rank must marry among his own – that the Nawab well understands. But to encourage you in your bridegroom's mood, he has asked his dancing girls to perform. May the lady that you choose be their equal in her grace and charm. Here they come!'

'At these affairs they usually do, at some point, as part of the entertainment and without any excuse,' said Mr Morse, as the musicians and the little troop of girls in their tinselled silks and their clinking bangles filed in. 'Our Nawab has just chosen a tactful way of warning his guests and his court that their conversations may be overheard and that his servants will report them. He lives a dangerous life, of course. He's technically a usurper. He has rivals.'

George nodded. He didn't want to discuss the Nawab's political problems just then. The thin music, with its undulating scale and the complex rhythm of the little hand drums, had begun, and the bare, henna-painted feet of the girls had started to twirl and stamp. Silk-trousered legs flashed. Gold-edged, diaphanous skirts and veils rippled out; red and blue and hot pink. Slender ivory hands gestured; graceful and beckoning. An audible sigh escaped him.

'I have been told,' said Morse, 'that although Englishmen of your

5

rank do indeed, customarily, marry among their own, there is actually Indian blood in your family, Mr Whitmead.'

'Yes, I believe that is so. But it's too far back to be of any importance,' said George. 'I believe a female forebear of mine was a survivor from a shipwreck, a century or so ago. The details have been lost.'

'You certainly give the impression of being quintessentially English,' Nicholas Morse said.

'It is what I would wish to be,' said George.

His words had a double meaning. He did wish to be perfectly English but he also knew, with regret, that at some level he was not. He found the dancing girls not only agreeably disturbing, but somehow natural, as though they were nearer to his ideal of womanhood than the English girl whom he intended to find and marry.

Except, of course, that one's wife must never make a public show of herself as these girls were doing. She should be more like . . .

He glanced again at the filigree stone lattice. Once more, he had sensed movement beyond it. The lamplight gleamed briefly on gold embroidery, on a jewelled earring. The lattice fragmented her shape, concealing her as a tiger was concealed by its stripes or a leopard by its patterned coat. But the light found, for one short instant, a pair of bright eyes, shyly looking through the filigree screen to see the dancing and the feast.

One of the ladies of the Nawab's own family, of course. He must not appear interested. He drew his eyes away with an effort, and set about making further conversation, on the subject of the French. The Nawab knew all about that anyway and his servants were welcome to listen if they liked.

He had been through all this before. Those glimpses of the women behind the lattice moved him in a deep, powerful way which he could neither describe nor explain. It was like the stirring of some ancient, buried memory.

It was also quite useless. He must go home and marry an English girl and he must keep himself attentive to Nicholas Morse, that rising man. The sherbet jug was being brought round; courteously, he nodded to the servant to fill Morse's cup before his own.

'Thank ye,' said Morse, but in a gloomy tone of voice. Morse, just now, was feeling aggrieved. Regardless of the hovering fanbearer, he grunted: 'Sherbet's a dead bore. I'd sell my soul for wine.'

PART I
The Wife
1742–1748

Art she had none, yet wanted none,
For Nature did that want supply

John Dryden, 1631–1700

Chapter One
The Bride

When, in the October of 1742, Lucy-Anne Browne married her second cousin George Whitmead, the bride's elderly great-aunt Henrietta wished her not only happiness, but power and freedom too.

Lucy-Anne had never been so taken aback. They were the last things in the world she ever expected to possess. She certainly couldn't look for them now that she was George's wife. They had only been married for a few hours and already it had been made clear to her that her life would be passed in his shadow.

On her wedding day, a girl expected to be the centre of attention. The focus of all eyes, the subject of all the admiring whispers, was traditionally the bride. But from the moment she joined him at the altar, the premier position had been somehow claimed by the groom. Immaculate from his smooth wig to his buckled shoes, his vows clearly audible the length of the aisle, his voice dominating the wedding breakfast as he discoursed fluently to his guests on the work of the East India Company, the hazards of voyaging, the marvels of Mughal architecture and the famous people he had met (all with the wide vocabulary and numerous subordinate clauses that betokened a classical education), George Whitmead commanded attention.

Even those who did praise the bride paid more heed to her dress of ivory-coloured Indian silk, with its colossal skirts and lace flounces and its seed-pearl embroidery, than to the sparrow-boned little seventeen-year-old inside it.

At the reception in George's house, one of the elegant modern ones in Hanover Square, she felt lost. It was bigger than her own home near St Clement Danes, where she had been married, and its size was the reason why George was giving the reception instead of the bride's father. This house could accommodate the huge number of guests. She had of course been here before, with her parents, but even then she had found the size of the rooms and the number of servants oppressive. Now, as evening approached, the rooms were like caverns, acquiring shadowy corners as the daylight faded, and the tall, ubiquitous footmen were like guards posted to keep her from running away.

Tonight, when her parents went home, they would leave her here, with George Whitmead whom she scarcely knew – to live with, to sleep with, for always and always . . .

The church ceremony had been early and the sit-down wedding breakfast was over by mid-afternoon. George had provided buffet-style refreshments for the evening and one of her uncles, after handing her to a seat and asking her what she would like to eat, had left her in order to fetch it.

Somehow or other, most of the guests were either dancing or had gathered around the bridegroom, in the next room, and so here she was, the bride, left sitting alone like a wallflower, which made her feel unregarded and conspicuous both at once. She was relieved when an elderly lady, dressed in grey satin and leaning on an ebony walking stick, came over to her. She smiled at Lucy-Anne, who made herself smile back and said uncertainly: 'You ... you are my great-aunt Henrietta, are you not? Father pointed you out earlier, but we have not spoken before.'

'She's your great-aunt and George's too,' Hugo Browne had said. 'She's the twin sister of your great-uncle Matthew, who is George's grandfather. I don't think you've ever seen her before, though you know your great-uncle, of course. Matthew is all right, but Henrietta is decidedly odd.'

She didn't look especially odd, although Lucy-Anne, studying her shyly, saw that her great-aunt was walking evidence that the story of East Indian blood in the family was probably true. Henrietta's eyes were unusually dark and her skin, covered now with a myriad tiny cracks, was the colour of old ivory. The way her iron-grey hair was dressed, not in fashionable curls but swept back and knotted at the nape of her neck, laid bare a delicate, smoothly chiselled bone structure which again made one think of ivory, and which was somehow un-English.

'You've had other matters to attend to,' she said to Lucy-Anne. 'I'm getting on in years, my dear, and I can't keep the late hours you younger people can, so I'm about to retire. But I had to wish you happy before I went.'

Her voice was English enough, with a West Country accent. Hugo had added: 'It was brave of her to tackle the journey from Somerset. She's in her seventies, you know.'

Her wedding gift had been delivered only that morning. 'Oh!' Lucy-Anne exclaimed, suddenly recollecting it. 'I must thank you for your gift. Such beautiful linen and such a charming device embroidered on it, with the blue water flowing under the bridge.'

'It's some sort of Whitmead badge,' said Henrietta. 'Or so my grandfather told me. It was used back in the days of Good Queen Bess. He was born while she was still on the throne, you know, and he could even remember seeing women in ruffs. I had the device embroidered on to new sheets and napkins for you. I couldn't stitch it myself; my eyesight isn't up to it these days. But I've made sure the workmanship is all it should be.'

'I'm sorry about your eyesight,' Lucy-Anne said with genuine sympathy.

'It's the way of the world, my child. But never mind. Your life is ahead of you.' Henrietta's eyes might not be equal to fine embroidery, but they were studying Lucy-Anne just now in a most perceptive manner. 'I feel sure,' Henrietta said kindly, 'that George will take care of you.'

10

'Oh . . . oh yes, I'm certain he will!' stammered Lucy-Anne.

Henrietta leant forward and put a hand on her knee. 'It will be all right,' she said. 'Courage, child.'

The towering footmen were now going around the rooms with tapers, lighting the candles in the wall sconces. Henrietta edged out of the way, but she kept her eyes on her great-niece's face. The uncle who was fetching her some food was still selecting it at the supper table and there was no sign of George, although she could hear his voice beyond an open door nearby, holding forth to someone about the price of cotton cloth. But Lucy-Anne's mother had come into the saloon and was sweeping towards them, glorious in blue satin and diamonds. Henrietta stooped to give Lucy-Anne a kiss and then whispered her remarkable parting words.

'I'm glad you like my wedding gift. I wish you well, my dear, and I wish you power and freedom too; more of them than I have ever had. Goodnight.'

Then she was moving away, quite quickly in spite of her stick. She nodded to Lucy-Anne's mother in passing but did not pause to speak. Lucilla Browne descended on her daughter.

'Was that Henrietta Whitmead? Extraordinary woman. Led an extraordinary life, by all accounts. Spent most of it buried in some unbelievable place called Chugg's Fiddle, nursing a crippled friend, or cousin, or something. Too peculiar ever to get married, I imagine. She's wealthy enough – her father was a regular Croesus – but you'd never guess it to look at her. You look quite bewildered, child. What in the world did she whisper to you, just now?'

'I didn't understand it,' said Lucy-Anne.

'Well, what *was* it?'

'She said she wished me well. And then—' Lucy-Anne's brow puckered in puzzlement '—then she said she wished me something else, too. She wished me power and freedom. It didn't make sense. Women can't have that. Except for Good Queen Bess, I suppose.'

'I told you she was peculiar,' said Lucilla briskly. 'Ah. Here comes your uncle. And here's your bridegroom. Come, child, you look far too serious. What about a smile for George?'

George, arriving in London in the late summer of 1741, had been much occupied. He had taken on the task, on behalf of the East India Company, of investigating the possible market for exotic spices, and he had a number of social introductions to follow up. He had obtained these, he said quite candidly, because he hoped that through one or other of them he might discover a wife.

He did not neglect family duties and made a point of calling on his cousins Hugo and Lucilla Browne, but this was a separate matter. He wasn't expecting to find a bride on that occasion, and nor did he. Lucy-Anne, still only sixteen, a dowdy little mouse who spent most of her time with her governess, either studying in the schoolroom or going out for sedate walks and shopping expeditions, was of little interest to him.

True, she had graduated far enough towards adulthood to dine with the family and to sit in the drawing room for a while in the evening. But

11

she was not encouraged to put herself forward in conversation and, on that first visit, George scarcely registered her existence. He bowed over her hand and assured her that he was her servant but never glanced at her after that. To Lucy-Anne, hesitating on the threshold of the grown-up world, he was just another of its denizens, remote from her in years, experience and entitlements, his face reddened by a foreign sun and his conversation mostly about subjects unfamiliar to her.

At dinner, she sat unnoticeably several places away from him and listened while he talked of far-off places with names like Arcot and Madras and Pondicherry. Pondicherry, she gathered, was infested by the terrible French, who in India as in Europe seemed always bent on doing the English down by political scheming and trade rivalry.

She did observe that he was verbose enough to make some of the other adults restless. The subject of India was eventually exhausted, however, and then he mentioned his quest for a wife and the fact that two introductions he had brought from India seemed after all unpromising. Hugo at once suggested the daughter of a fashionable family of his acquaintance near Portsmouth and offered a letter of introduction. A few days later, they heard that cousin George had gone to visit his country home in Surrey, prior to travelling on to Portsmouth, and she forgot about him.

Until, in the summer just gone, he returned to London still unwed, and once more dined with the Brownes.

By now, Lucy-Anne was out of the schoolroom. Her governess had departed to another position and Lucilla was grooming her daughter for the challenge of the marriage market. Lucy-Anne had been provided with new gowns and hats, a wealth of instruction on how to make conversation in a manner pleasing to gentlemen, and a personal maid who did her best to apply curling tongs to Lucy-Anne's fine, flyaway brown hair in such a manner that it really would curl, and not turn into a frizz.

None of it had made much difference. Lucy-Anne was still as shy as she had been a year ago. She preferred reading, sewing or quiet walks to anything as demanding as riding or conversation; and although she was not plain, she would never turn heads in the street. Her grey eyes were well-shaped but her features were too small and her inches too few. Even dressed fetchingly in a sacque of pale yellow, with blue flowers scattered over it, even curled with tongs and perfumed with rosewater, she failed to impinge. George's bows and declarations of servanthood were to begin with as perfunctory this year as last.

On this occasion there were a number of guests, and George came accompanied by his mother. Lucy-Anne knew Araminta Whitmead and liked her. She was easy to talk to. They sat near each other at table in the panelled dining room and Lucy-Anne was sorry to see that Araminta had a poor appetite and seemed to have grown thin. She asked concernedly after Araminta's health, but was gently hushed.

'I have not been well this year, but that's not an pleasant subject, my dear. Let us listen to George. I have been amazed at him since he came back from India. I have been widowed since George was five, but I can remember his father very clearly indeed and, now, the resemblance is astonishing. James was always so interesting to listen to, and George is just like him.'

George, in fact, was once more holding forth, this time on the shortcomings of England. He had had time to look about him and he was dissatisfied with what he had found. The lawlessness, he said, was a disgrace. In a wild country like India, one might expect bandits to be a hazard of travel, but his coach had been held up on the way to Portsmouth! He had been robbed of his purse, if they could credit it—

'Certainly we can credit it.' Hugo had decided to be amused by George's loquacity. 'How fortunate that you were not hurt.'

—and in addition, in India, he had never experienced any difficulty in finding excellent servants, but in England he had been shocked to discover that things were different.

'Upon my word, they haggle scandalously. I require extra servants when I am home, of course, and I have had to offer the most exorbitant rates of pay imaginable. I am, I may say, quite a generous man and I will spend freely where it is proper, but to throw money down the throats of people who are already housed and fed and largely clothed at my expense truly scandalises me. But if I succeed in marrying before I sail for India again, I shall have to leave a full staff behind, as my wife will need them. I shall owe it to her position.'

'It is not your intention then to take your bride out to India with you?' Lucilla asked.

'No,' said Araminta. 'George wishes – hopes – to marry and then to return to India, leaving an heir in the making, and providing me with family companionship, which I confess I should like. But so far his search for a bride has not prospered.'

'That is true,' George declared. 'The introduction you so kindly gave me, cousin Hugo, in pursuance of which I made my ill-fated journey to Portsmouth last year, came unfortunately too late. The young lady was already spoken for when I arrived there. But even had she not been . . . ah well, I have grown accustomed to another country, and to women who are very different from those of England. You may say perhaps that I have been spoilt. The women of India are so soft of voice and graceful of movement, so aware that for their sex ultimate happiness lies in making themselves delightful to their husbands. Women of the higher sort seclude themselves, taking no part in gatherings where men are present, although sometimes they watch from another room, looking through a latticed screen. Occasionally at such affairs one may catch sight of a face through the screen, or glimpse a jewelled earring or the flicker of a veil . . .'

George was not drinking heavily, but his face had flushed. Unexpectedly, he broke off as if in confusion and fidgeted in a jerky way which caused several people to pause in the midst of eating in order to gaze at him in a fascinated manner. 'What I mean to say is,' he said, 'that by comparison the young women of England, those I have met in Madras and those I have met here, seem bold in their manners and too tall of stature, and lacking in the mystery which is surely the true charm of womanhood. Such was the case with the young lady I sought out in Portsmouth, although she was a good sort of girl, Hugo, and you must

13

not think me insensible of your kind wish to help. But even if she had still been free . . . perhaps the trouble was that she was already twenty-five.'

'And what you seek is someone truly young, who can be easily moulded to your wishes. Someone small of stature and soft of speech?' said Lucilla.

'Quite so. It has taken time for me to realise it, but yes, you have it exactly.'

Lucilla did not glance towards her daughter. But it seemed to the shrinking Lucy-Anne that a shaft of light had suddenly been directed at her, and if Lucilla did not turn to stare, everybody else did, including George. For the first time, he not only looked at her, but saw her.

Nothing was said just then and the conversation passed to something else. But, the following morning, George called upon her father and the two of them were together for a long time in Hugo's study. Then George went away, and Lucy-Anne was sent for.

'Mr George Whitmead,' said her father, 'is interested in marrying you, Lucy-Anne.'

'And,' said Lucilla, 'we think it would be a splendid opportunity for you.'

She was seated in the study's one easy chair, with Hugo, large and protective, standing behind her. They looked as though they were posing for a portrait: *Mr and Mrs Hugo Whitmead inform their daughter of her forthcoming marriage.* It would need a companion portrait: *George Whitmead and Lucy-Anne Browne on their betrothal day.*

'My cousin George has proposed for *me*?' said Lucy-Anne.

'Yes, indeed. What a surprise for you! But a pleasant one, I trust,' said her father with a smile. It was a kindly smile; Hugo had a kindly temperament.

'You and cousin George should be perfectly suited,' said her mother. 'We think so; so does he. You're young and you're quiet – you've always been a good girl; got to say that for you. Someone like you is just what your cousin is seeking. Think we can depend on him to look after you. He's well-to-do; to tell the truth, he's a better match for you than we expected. What do you say?'

'You'll be in very comfortable circumstances,' Hugo said winningly. 'And, since he won't be taking you to India, you . . . er . . . he . . .'

'We wouldn't agree if it meant you going so far. Wouldn't do for you; you're not the adventurous sort. But as it is,' said Lucilla bluntly, 'you won't see all that much of him. Might matter if this was a romantic business, but I didn't bring you up with romantic notions; and how right I was! Let me be frank. You're pleasing enough, child, but you're not striking. Been wondering how best to present you, as a matter of fact, so as to attract the right kind of offers. And now here's an excellent offer before we've even begun! I say accept it. Doubt if you'll ever get a better one.'

'Well,' said her father. 'There we are, then. Er . . . well, Lucy-Anne?'

'I don't know.' She felt quite unable to say anything sensible. Marriage, already? She could scarcely imagine it and still less could she

14

imagine cousin George as her husband. He was grown-up and in spite of her maid and her coiffure and her new dresses, she knew that she was not.

'He's not perfect,' said Hugo, rather anxiously. 'He talks too much! But a man can have far worse faults than that.'

'Well, I . . . of course I will do whatever you think best,' said Lucy-Anne helplessly.

'He will call on you tomorrow morning,' said Hugo. 'You may receive him in the morning room.'

'You'll be his hostess. You can ring for refreshments. I'll tell the kitchen to have lemon puffs and ratafia biscuits ready,' said Lucilla. 'You can wear your yellow silk.'

The following morning, therefore, Lucy-Anne, in buttercup yellow and with her hair curled within an inch of its life, came nervously to the morning room and stood looking down at the top of cousin George's wig as he kissed her hand and said, 'Your servant, Miss Browne,' for the third time.

This time, when he straightened up, he looked straight into her face, and smiled at her in an approving fashion. On her side, she took in that his neck was somewhat thick and that he had pale brown eyes with not much expression in them. She didn't like either of these attributes very much but this was what her parents wanted for her and Lucy-Anne Browne, aged seventeen, couldn't imagine telling them that she had refused him because he had a little surplus flesh and his eyes were the wrong shade.

She could never afterwards remember exactly how the conversation went. She sent for the ratafia biscuits and lemon puffs along with a tray of coffee, and she could recall George clearing his throat and going through a long preamble, explaining that he had obtained her parents' blessing before presenting himself to ask if she would honour him with her hand in marriage, and thereby make him the happiest of men. It was all quite unreal, as though they were taking part in a play.

This was an odd simile to occur to shy Lucy-Anne, to whom the idea of acting on a stage would have been horrific, but it was a good comparison. She had been taught what words to say in these circumstances, and she said them, lines learned by heart. She told him that indeed she was honoured, and hardly knew what to say, but that her parents had told her of his wishes, and that she had their permission to accept his proposal. Then she went with him to the drawing room where her parents were waiting, and stood beside him while he announced that they were now betrothed. She assured them of her delight and then, still performing a part set out for her, she let him kiss her.

The sense of unreality, like a steady river current, bore her on through the betrothal. At her father's suggestion, she and George actually did have their portrait painted, and by a fashionable artist at that, a Mr Thomas Hudson, who posed them just as Lucilla and Hugo had been posed when they told her of George's proposal, with Lucy-Anne seated, back straight, hands on lap, and George standing in proprietary fashion at her shoulder.

There were dinners at her home and George's, shopping expeditions, negotiations with dressmakers. And then came the marriage ceremony itself and the wedding breakfast. The dreamlike feeling did not leave her until that moment when she was left briefly alone in the supper room at the reception. Then it dissolved, to be replaced by the stark fact that she had married George Whitmead, for better, for worse, and for life.

And then she saw great-aunt Henrietta coming towards her, and Henrietta read and understood the panic in her young relative's eyes. Henrietta said that it would be all right and told her to have courage. And finally left her with that strange valediction about power and freedom. Lucy-Anne didn't believe she would ever have either, but although the words were bewildering she found afterwards that they somehow put heart into her. When, presently, she found herself in a bedchamber with George, she was not, after all, afraid.

Though she felt a little depressed. George in his nightshirt, divested of the elegance lent by his fashionable clothes, the largeness and roundness of his stomach and seat distressingly revealed, was a spectacle more embarrassing than exciting. But, sitting up against her pillows, Lucy-Anne smiled at him, and when he got into bed with her, did not draw away, but yielded unprotestingly as he blew out the candles and drew her into his arms.

As he began to murmur endearments and his advances became purposeful, she held fast to Henrietta's encouragement. She found that she needed it. George was experienced but had no imagination. He did not mean to hurt or frighten his bride but apparently had no idea that his efforts might do precisely that. They were to begin with quite as bad as Lucy-Anne's most pessimistic fears. She lay squashed under an elephantine weight and clutched in a bruising grip, while her bridegroom, grunting with pleasure, jammed something hot and hard and apparently enormous repeatedly into the depths of her.

But when, just before dawn, he rolled on top of her a second time, his thrusting this time was merely tedious, something to be tolerated patiently until he had finished. When it was all over and George was once more snoring contentedly with his arm across her chest, she lay thinking that now the worst was over and she need not feel afraid in future. Henrietta had been correct, or nearly. If it wasn't exactly 'all right', it was bearable, and George seemed pleased with her. He had muttered, 'Thank you, my love,' both times, before sliding into sleep.

'Thank you, great-aunt Henrietta,' Lucy-Anne whispered, before she fell asleep herself.

Chapter Two
The Legacy

She was a dear little thing, George decided. He had chosen well. She and his mother already knew and liked each other; Lucy-Anne would be ideal company for Araminta, and Araminta could guide and shelter her when he was away.

She was prettier, too, than he had at first realised. Her wedding gown had been too elaborate for her and so was the very formal, mightily hooped affair of cream and green brocade in which she sat for the Hudson portrait, but in the lighter materials and smaller hoops which were now the latest thing, in her yellow silk, or in her new trousseau dresses of pink and pale green and ice-blue shot with silver, she had surprising charm.

Her inexperience was charming too. Lucy-Anne had travelled very little in the course of her life. She had been taken once or twice to Bath, because it had become very fashionable as a place for taking medicinal waters and they seemed to benefit her father, who had a tendency to bronchitis. But otherwise she had seen nothing of the world outside London.

When, two weeks after the wedding, George closed the town house and shifted his family and most of the servants to his country home of Chestnuts, just beyond the Surrey town of Guildford, she found it all a great adventure. She exclaimed at the amount of transport George required, which included one large travelling carriage for Lucy-Anne, Araminta and their maids, another for the baggage, and two hired conveyances for the butler, cook and maidservants, who set off a day ahead to get Chestnuts ready, and, even at that, George himself and two of the three footmen went on horseback.

'We're like an army on the march,' she said, impressed. 'We just went to Bath in father's coach, with one box of clothes each.'

She exclaimed too at the amount of traffic and at the overloading of the stage-coaches they met.

'The traffic on this route is always heavy, my love, and it's common enough to see passengers clinging to the luggage on the roof of the stage-coaches,' he told her, when at Leatherhead they stopped to rest the horses and take a meal. 'It's the Portsmouth road. Sailors come ashore, go to London to spend their pay, and often enough can only afford to get back to their ships by travelling in the cheapest fashion, which is on the roof.'

'They must be so uncomfortable in this cold weather,' Lucy-Anne said. She had wrapped up well even to ride in a luxurious carriage and

Araminta's thin body felt the cold even more acutely. Her gaunt, middle-aged maid Sarah, herself almost impervious to the weather, had tenderly swathed her mistress in so many rugs and shawls that beneath her hat the elder Mrs Whitmead's hollowed face seemed to be perched on top of a sphere of fur and cloth.

Just for a moment, the sheer schoolgirl innocence of being sorry for hardy sailors because they had to travel in the open air struck George as irritating rather than charming but he knew he was inclined to be short-tempered, and he did not want to upset his bride. 'Sailors are well accustomed to exposure, my dear,' he informed her. 'On board ship, they are often much colder.'

Araminta smiled, but Sarah's expression was slightly disdainful. Lucy-Anne noticed and wondered what she had said that was wrong. Before her wedding day, although her mother had made sure she knew what to expect, she had been nervous of sexual union. But she was used to that now. Far more worrying was the effort of being, doing, saying the right things to please so many people, all older than herself.

Her mother had also told her that she must win the respect of her servants. There was already a feud brewing between the gaunt Sarah and Lucy-Anne's own maid, the plumply pretty Maria. If the two of them really quarrelled, she would have to deal with them. Appalled by the prospect of taking the intimidating Sarah to task, she became so quiet that, when they were back in the coach, Araminta asked her if she were feeling sick.

'No, oh no.'

'You must tell me if you do – at any time.'

'Oh,' said Lucy-Anne, understanding and turning pink. 'But I've only been married two weeks.'

'It can happen within two days. It would please George so much. Let us hope,' said Araminta.

Guildford was crowded. They slowed to a crawl behind a herd of calves being driven through the streets and George, riding up to the coach window, called: 'Market day!'

A distant glimpse of a castle keep, ivy-grown and romantic, looking just like the pictures her governess had shown her during history lessons; some handsome houses in the red brick Queen Anne had made so fashionable; a number of inns. There was a Red Lion, a White Lion, an Angel, and a White Hart. 'Many large functions are held at the White Hart,' Araminta said. 'It is quite a place for society people to meet. I have attended parties there myself, although you will only be able to do so when George is at home to escort you. George feels it best and I agree with him.'

'Oh, of course,' Lucy-Anne agreed. She shifted in her seat, feeling stiff. 'Are we going to stop at all in Guildford?'

'Leatherhead seems a long while ago? But we're nearly there. Chestnuts is only a little way beyond Guildford.'

They were already rattling across a bridge, leaving the town behind, and presently they were climbing, with the horses leaning strongly into their collars.

'We're on what is called the Hog's Back,' Araminta said. 'Only a few minutes now. I'm glad for I do feel much fatigued.'

'You always find travelling tiring, ma'am,' Sarah said, and looked grimly at Lucy-Anne as though it were her fault. Lucy-Anne decided not to notice. How long would it be, she asked herself, before she really learned how to deal with servants?

She was heartily thankful to have her mother-in-law's support. She had known after one day as mistress of the London house that without Araminta's help she would be lost. Mrs Cobham the cook and Fraser the butler were three times her age and Fraser in particular was so august that when he was introduced to her she almost curtsied to him. Furthermore, although it now appeared that some of the towering footmen at the wedding reception had been hired for the occasion, the three who were permanent were not much older than Lucy-Anne herself, and two of the four maidservants were probably younger, which she somehow found even more disconcerting than the seniority of Mrs Cobham and Fraser.

At home, of course, she had given orders to the servants, but she had known them all since childhood, and usually had some kind of mandate from her mother before making any but the most routine request. Being the lady of George's house was different. She blessed Araminta for being there to help her – to say to the cook, 'Mrs Cobham, do remember that Mr Whitmead prefers lamb cutlets to veal,' to encourage Lucy-Anne to explain what her own favourite dishes were, and to call for the inventory of linen and go through it with her, item by item. She couldn't imagine doing any of these things all by herself.

George appeared once more beside the carriage. 'Chestnuts is in sight. The vista from here is generally thought to be a pretty good one.'

Lucy-Anne put her head out. The road was running along the top of the ridge and away below was a wide expanse of woods and farms, fading in the distance into a blue November dusk. The trees were turning now to gold and bronze and glowed through the haze like patches of cool fire.

'You will observe such a view from our very bedchamber in Chestnuts,' George informed her. 'Here's the turning.'

The coach lurched to the left, plunging into a lane so narrow that the trees on either side scraped its sides. Lucy-Anne withdrew her head quickly. They passed through some handsome gates and the sound under the wheels changed from earth to gravel.

Ornamental flowerbeds appeared to either side of the drive, and then they had drawn up in front of a fine-looking modern house of grey stone, flat-roofed and symmetrical, its windows tall, unornamented rectangles, and six stone steps leading up to its door.

Grooms ran out to take the horses' heads and the mounted footmen, swinging quickly out of their saddles, came to open the carriage door and hand the ladies down. Lucy-Anne followed Araminta, and then Sarah pushed her way out, brusquely, ahead of Maria in order to adjust Araminta's shawls and retrieve a rug, which had slipped off.

George also dismounted at once, but turned his attention to the bodywork of the carriage, which had apparently been scratched by the trees in the lane. He was examining it with disapproval, running a finger over it. But Fraser was at the front door, holding it open. 'Come along,' said Araminta. 'Let's go in.'

The house was warm and the candles had been lit against the early dusk, flickering welcomingly in the sconces around the hall and up the wide staircase. Maria took Lucy-Anne's cloak and then, not knowing the house, hesitated. Sarah, very much the senior showing the junior what to do, said, 'We take the outdoor clothes upstairs. Follow me, if you please,' and led her away. Araminta tucked her arm through Lucy-Anne's and steered her through a door on the left, into a sizeable and pleasingly furnished drawing room, with sofas and comfortable wing-chairs, and a harpsichord. More lit candles greeted them, and a fire crackled in the hearth.

Araminta at once sank into a chair beside it, while Lucy-Anne went to the windows. They looked out to both the front and the back of the house. The front she had already seen, but now she had a view of what lay behind it. Peering out at the darkening landscape, she saw a terrace and a neatly scythed square of grass, and beyond this a parterre garden, its paths edged with low box hedges, its flowerbeds shaped into arabesques like the pattern of a carpet. In the distance, an avenue of chestnut trees, no doubt those that had given the house its name, led towards a white marble folly.

The garden occupied what might be called a broad shelf in the hillside and it faced south. In good weather, it would be a pleasant place to walk, she thought. She turned back into the room and found that Fraser had come in with sherry and biscuits.

'Mrs Cobham suggests a hot supper, madam. She proposes chicken soup with vermicelli, and poached eggs on hot rolls. Will that be satisfactory?'

'Er...' Lucy-Anne glanced at Araminta, but her mother-in-law seemed to be dozing. 'Yes, Fraser, I think that will do very well,' she said.

'Thank you, madam.' Fraser withdrew towards the door, but stepped aside quickly as George bustled through it. 'Ah, Fraser! Perhaps *you* know where Stephen Clarke is. I expected to find him here to meet me.'

'Mr Clarke said he would wait on you at ten o'clock tomorrow morning, sir. He felt that you would wish to recover from your journey before discussing business.'

'Wish to recover?' George sounded thunderous. To her alarm, Lucy-Anne saw that something had annoyed her husband very much. The indulgent bridegroom who had complimented her on her dresses, smiled at her naive excitement about the journey, and, if not precisely a sensitive lover, had cuddled her sometimes in bed, had suddenly vanished. 'I have no need to recover from a ride between London and Guildford,' he said coldly. 'I am not quite such a decrepit dotard yet. In India, I ride hundreds of miles as a matter of course and deal with business at the end of it while I have one foot still in the stirrup. Stephen Clarke is not paid to "feel I would wish to recover"; he's my bailiff and he's paid to look after my land and see that the things are done that I have ordered to be done, which they have not. Specifically, the trees in the lane have not been cut back as they should and the bodywork of my travelling coach has been scratched. Oh, very well, Fraser. I'll see him in the morning since the arrangement has been made, though without reference to me, apparently.' He let out a noise which sounded like 'Harrumph!' and was evidently meant to express exasperation, and swung round to leave the room without acknowledging either his mother or his wife. With the idea of somehow mollifying him, Lucy-Anne addressed him.

'Will you not come and sit by the fire? Supper will be here soon. Perhaps there is some simple explanation about the trees and it will all be made clear tomorrow. Surely you must be a *trifle* tired.'

'If I say I'm not tired, I'm not!' said George irritably. Lucy-Anne stared, startled and a little hurt. He paid no attention. 'Now, what's this about supper? The dinner we took at Leatherhead was a sorry affair but it's somewhat soon for another meal. What is to be served?'

'Ch-chicken soup with vermicelli and poached eggs on hot rolls,' said Lucy-Anne timidly.

'Poached eggs? Feeble stuff. Ring the bell and tell them that we will have the hot rolls now, with some coffee, but supper can wait till the usual hour and we will have a choice of cold meats with bread as I prefer. I'll take the rolls and coffee in my study, and probably my supper too. Since I shan't see Clarke until tomorrow, I can at least list meanwhile the matters I want to raise with him.'

He departed, shouting for someone to bring the sherry decanter to the study. Lucy-Anne, whose healthy young appetite had been looking forward to the poached eggs, felt near to tears. Araminta, however, who was now awake, merely said: 'Better ring the bell, dear. We must do as George wishes. I'm afraid he is very put out over Stephen Clarke and the damage to the carriage. You mustn't mind too much.'

George did not appear again that evening. Supper arrived eventually, consisting of cold pheasant with bread and butter, and Lucy-Anne ate it in subdued fashion. Araminta, who seemed by now to be drowning in exhaustion, hardly spoke and ate even less than usual. As soon as the meal was over, she declared herself ready for bed.

'When you wish to retire, my dear, ring and ask for Maria. Sarah will have shown her about the house by now, I daresay. I should have taken you over it, I suppose, but I was so thankful to settle down by the fire, and you will see it better by daylight tomorrow. If you don't wish to go up yet, there are books in the cupboard over there, or you can amuse yourself by trying my harpsichord. But now, my love, I must say goodnight.'

Left alone, Lucy-Anne tried the harpsichord, but was too dispirited to play for long. She rang for Maria instead.

Maria took her up to a spacious bedchamber, also pleasant with fire and candlelight. The fourposter bed, hung with blue and gold brocade, had been freshly made up with crisp sheets. Maria, who had unpacked Lucy-Anne's clothes and put them away, brushed her hair and helped her into her nightgown, and a maidservant arrived with a warming pan to take the chill off the sheets. They wished her goodnight and went away and Lucy-Anne slid between the sheets.

The bed was very comfortable and she would have liked to fall asleep, but with George so cross – and for so little reason! – she dared not. It would be like a sentry falling asleep at his post.

When George eventually came, however, he blew out the candles and settled down at once with his back to her. Lucy-Anne, lying stiffly beside

21

him, was not sure if this was a cause for worry or relief. She did not feel in the least like being bounced on by George tonight, but did his abstinence mean that he was still angry?

George, in fact, was feeling somewhat guilty. The scratches on the coach, Clarke's carelessness in letting the trees grow like that and his failure to be instantly available when his employer arrived were very annoying, but Lucy-Anne was not responsible. He had given way to his short temper and no doubt, after all, caused distress to this soft little kitten of a bride, whom he had undertaken to love and cherish. Poor creature – she had probably wanted her hot supper and he hadn't let her have it. George detested apologising, but he realised that this time he must.

In the darkness his voice spoke: 'Lucy-Anne?'

'Yes?'

'I was a little brusque with you this evening. I must ask your pardon. It is a fault of mine. You must indulge me but not take my irritable nature too much to heart. You did quite right to consider my comfort and order supper; naturally you do not yet know all my habits and preferences. And naturally, in future, you may order what you wish for yourself.'

'Oh – thank you. I will remember in future that you don't care for eggs.'

'It was Mrs Cobham's fault, no doubt. She has not been with me for long enough to know my ways. I have seen that confounded man Clarke, by the way. Fraser sent a boy down to fetch him – he lives at the foot of the hill.'

'What did he say about the trees in the lane?'

'Ah, well. I wanted them cut back as part of a general refurbishment of the grounds here, with an enlargement of the formal parterre garden and the chestnut avenue cut back too, to give a better view of the folly – which perhaps you saw from the drawing-room window. The gardeners I commonly employ had raised their charges, like everyone these days, and Clarke feared that I would consider the cost too high. On the other hand, he did not wish to employ different gardeners without my consent and, since I was to come here soon, awaited my return in order to discuss it with me. I feel that he should rather have written to me, and he should have had the trees seen to at least, but he was doing what he thought would best please me. I have accepted that.'

Lucy-Anne, reassured that he was no longer angry, and lulled by his verbose monotone, was growing drowsy. She stiffened when he turned over, fearing for a moment that she would have to wake up again. It would be such an effort.

But he merely dumped a heavy arm across her, murmured that tomorrow he would show her the grounds of Chestnuts, and then fell mercifully asleep.

The morning brought fine, cold weather and, while Araminta stayed in bed, Lucy-Anne went round the house with George, admiring the handsome morning room, the bookroom, the dining chamber, the study, the small, snug parlour, the well-proportioned bedchambers and, on the topmost floor, the suite which might – one day – be the nursery.

Then, warmly clad, she went downstairs again and into the frosty grounds on George's arm to make the acquaintance, at close quarters, of the parterre garden and the chestnut avenue and the folly.

The latter was actually a large summerhouse with an upper floor, but it was built of white marble, the upper level being roofed by a dome, and its entrance was an oriental-looking scalloped arch, a shape which was repeated in the windows on either side.

'It was built to my instructions while I was still away,' George said proudly. 'I had drawings made in India and sent them to England. The design is based on that of Mughal palaces I have seen. It will be a pleasant place in which to entertain visitors on summer days. If you wish to entertain suitable friends while I am in India, I have no objection, given that they are genuinely suitable. I would not like you to attend public functions of any kind in my absence. Some people – including friends and neighbours whom you will meet – occasionally, for instance, hold celebrations in places such as the White Hart in Guildford and such affairs are so large that there is no knowing whom one may meet there. I must forbid your going to such events without me. But, naturally, you may give and receive private invitations. I hope you will make friends among the wives of my acquaintances. Fortunately, you will have my mother to advise and chaperon you. When I am on the high seas, I shall picture you and my mother seated here, in my airy summerhouse, drinking coffee with your female guests, or embroidering, on sunny afternoons.'

He continued to talk, about the foremost local families. She would shortly meet the Reverend and Mrs Bird from the village of Southdene at the foot of the hill, and there were the Kendalls who owned most of the village of Southdene – 'I own only three or four cottages on this side of it' – and the Millers, who were related to the Birds . . .

Lucy-Anne, trying to take it in but becoming slightly dizzy as a stream of unfamiliar names poured over her, gazed around the folly and thought that it was beautiful, but odd. George, at last breaking off his recital, led her up the narrow spiral staircase to the loft under the dome. The room was circular and bare except for a chair and an old easel.

'There are sliding panels here in the dome,' George said, demonstrating. 'As you see, they afford a view of the surrounding countryside. You may care to come here and sketch. No doubt you were taught sketching as part of your education. My mother used to be fond of it but has lost her taste for it lately. Perhaps you may encourage her to resume it.'

'I think perhaps she isn't very well,' said Lucy-Anne.

'She has been out of sorts this year,' George agreed. 'But she has benefited from being regularly bled and she assures me that country air and simple, wholesome food will soon set her right. I shall not ask her to try out the samples of spices I brought from India! Shall we go down again?'

In London, Matthew Whitmead was down as usual at nine o'clock to take his breakfast of coffee and rusks. He liked to breakfast promptly, he said, because he had kept the old custom of dining at midday. He had no

23

patience with the new fad of dining at three in the afternoon. At this rate, dinner would soon be taking the place of supper and when would people eat their supper? At midnight? Then he would laugh and say that he was becoming a crotchety old man and set in his ways – but at seventy-seven, why not? And he'd still have his early breakfast, Jenny, please.

He didn't expect guests to rise as early as he did, however. His twin sister Henrietta, after staying at George's house until the wedding was over, had now joined Matthew for a visit and the maid Jenny would serve her with hot chocolate and sweet cakes in bed. She was looking frail these days and he was anxious to make her as comfortable as possible. In fact, he wished she'd stay with him for good.

'What's the point of making the journey all the way back to Somerset, Henny? That cottage up there in the Quantocks is too isolated. Why don't you let it and stay here with me? Hugo and Lucilla are just round the corner and the farmland begins not a mile away if you fancy country walking.'

'I'm past long walks,' said Henrietta. 'And I don't like London. But I always enjoy *your* company, Matt. I'll stay till Christmas.'

With luck – all that was needed was a snowfall or some heavy rain, neither of them unlikely in wintertime – the roads would be too bad after Christmas for travelling to the West Country, where they were terrible at the best of times, all hills and bends, apparently designed on purpose to defeat wheeled transport. Even at her age, Henny would have to get from the village of Chugg's Fiddle in the valley up to Broom Cottage on the back of a hired pony. By the time it was again possible for her to get home, Matthew thought as he sipped his coffee, she might have changed her mind.

Yes, with just a little luck, he would get her to stay after all. He'd like that. He'd never seen enough of Henny, all through their lives. His fortunes had kept him in London, where he had prospered as a lawyer. Henny, cast off by their father long ago for refusing the marriage he had arranged for her, had spent most of her life marooned in lonely Broom Cottage, where she had first found shelter with her cousin Eleanor and, later on, been trapped.

The coffee pot was empty and on this frosty morning he felt inclined for an extra cup. He rang the bell, his mind still on Eleanor. She had been dead for years but he still bristled at the thought of her.

It was not of course Eleanor's fault that she had been crippled in an accident not long after Henrietta joined her, but it was very much her fault that she had clung to Henrietta, refusing to be cared for by anyone else, and thus wrecked any chance Henny might have had of marriage. Dying, she had left Henny the cottage and a fair amount of money, but if ever a legacy was earned that one was.

But Henny had come through it with something essential still intact – a humour and a realism which made her the best of companions. Somehow or other, Matthew said to himself, somehow or other I'll persuade you to stay. Perhaps I'm as bad as Eleanor was, wanting to hold on to you, but at least I'll give; I won't take.

Jenny was a long time in answering the bell, which was unusual, for she was a brisk girl as a rule. But when she finally came, she burst into the

24

room rather than entered it, and at the sight of her face, Matthew got quickly to his feet, coffee forgotten. 'Jenny?'

'It's Miss Whitmead, sir, I've just been to take her breakfast to her . . . oh, Mr Whitmead, she's just lying there, with her mouth all pulled down on one side and when I spoke to her, all she could make was a queer sort of noise . . . please come!'

Chestnuts, in its commanding position near the top of the Hog's Back, overlooked the land attached to it as from an eyrie.

'My province extends as far as that cluster of roofs and the church tower that you can see in the distance,' George said proudly, explaining the view to Lucy-Anne as they stood at one of the topmost windows of the house, gazing out over the fields and pastures and woodland which sloped away into the rolling valley land to the south. 'That is Southdene, where my friend Walter Kendall, of whom I have already spoken, is the landlord. St Anne's, the church there, is where the Reverend Bird is vicar and that is where we shall worship on Sundays. It is a fine old church, first founded in Norman times. If your eyes are sufficiently sharp, you may behold a flock of sheep in a field at the foot of the hill. Can you see them?'

'Yes, George,' said Lucy-Anne, who had discovered by now that when George was talking she rarely needed to say much more.

'They are mine,' George said. 'I have a home farm, and one subholding by the name of Upwood – you can see the smoke from their chimney, over there to the east. It is rented by some very decent people. The house just at the foot of the hill, beyond that patch of woodland, is occupied by Stephen Clarke. Can you see a few cottages scattered about just beyond the field where my sheep are?'

'Yes, George. Do they belong to you?'

'They do indeed. My labourers live there, and some of them rear a few vegetables and run some animals on my open grazing land. They are all most respectable and if you wish to visit the women and take them gifts in time of illness or when children are born, I will not object. Most of my cottagers – and indeed Mr and Mrs Ross at Upwood – are Methodist and therefore do not attend church in Southdene, but they have a pastor of their own there and attend prayer meetings. Ours is a well-ordered community.'

'Yes, George.'

'I will leave you now to go on learning about the house. Mrs Cobham is ready to assist you. I wish to ride over and call on Mr Kendall and, since I believe you do not care for riding, I will not ask you to accompany me. I have no particular wish for you to ride. There is a light chaise and pair, should you desire to go out, and I feel that it is a safer conveyance for a lady.'

'Thank you, I should like that. It's true I am not a good horsewoman.'

'I shall hunt, naturally,' George said, 'but I would not in any case wish you to do so. Ladies do hunt, of course. In some parts of India, even Indian women of rank attend the tiger hunts. There is a Hindu province called Rajasthan. I have not been there but it has been described to me, and there such women sometimes ride behind their husbands on elephants to hunt the tiger. But I find it amazing.'

'Yes, so do I!' said Lucy-Anne, earnestly.

'Walter Kendall runs a pack of hounds,' George said. 'During the winter to come I shall be out with him, after the fox, three days a week, but I am happy, my dear, to know that you prefer to stay at home.'

On the following day, George drove her round the estate in the chaise and introduced her to his tenants. The decent Mr and Mrs Ross at Upwood Farm took her into a kitchen where, to Lucy-Anne's mingled disgust and fascination, a dismembered pig's head was boiling in a cauldron, with the snout bobbing over the edge as though the pig were imprisoned there and trying to escape. The couple, who were middle-aged and soft-spoken, gave her home-made cider and then, while George and Mr Ross discussed agricultural matters, Mrs Ross told Lucy-Anne that they had inherited the tenancy from Mr Ross's father but would have no one to follow them as they were childless.

'But the ways of the Lord are mysterious and not to be questioned. It's to be hoped, though, that He'll look on you with favour and grant you fruitfulness.'

Lucy-Anne was excessively embarrassed.

The cottagers were even more embarrassing, in a different way, especially a family called the Craddocks. Craddock himself was not so bad. He was a lean, tired-faced man whose clothes had seen too much wear, but he gave her a smile and wished her happy as if he meant it. His wife and his twenty-year-old son Mark, however, did not. They not only had the thin bodies of those who had known long toil on not enough food, but also hard eyes full of silent comment on satin skirts and the luxury of a two-horse chaise.

They were outwardly polite and showed her and George into the cottage, which was poky and dark and smelt strongly of the hens that kept scuttling in and out. George, enlarging heartily on the virtue of thrift (which he seemed to think the Craddocks practised from choice), was evidently quite unaware of their dislike. Lucy-Anne, on the other hand, was instantly and acutely conscious of it and would have liked to run away.

She would have to get used to the Craddocks; she knew that. She would have to make them respect her, even if they couldn't like her. It was going to be part of marriage to George. The cottages were no worse than the crowded, noisome streets of London, she told herself, and there were pickpockets in London, and thieves who robbed with violence; the Craddocks were far less dangerous.

She said the expected things, asking how long the family had been there – the answer was since the days of Mr Craddock senior's grandfather – and told them that she would always try to be of help to them in any fitting manner within her power.

They didn't look as though they expected very much of her, and Mrs Craddock's eyes were unmistakeably saying: 'Help us? A petted baby like you?' Lucy-Anne was more than thankful when the visit was over.

She was more at home in the domestic world inside Chestnuts, although even here there were challenges to meet. But running a house and the art of entertaining had at least formed part of the education provided by her mother and her governess and she was now discovering how to give orders and conduct conversations.

'Mrs Cobham, we expect the Birds and the Kendalls to dine tomorrow, and probably Mr and Mrs Ross as well.' The tenants of Upwood, it had transpired, were of sufficient social standing to be asked to dine. 'We must decide on a menu. Can we go through the contents of the larder . . . ?'

'. . . please, Mr Bird, Mr Kendall, let us not dispute over the dinner table. Pray let us talk of something else.'

'Thank you, Mrs Cobham. That was an excellent dinner. My husband sends his compliments.'

'Maria, you haven't yet repaired the flounce on my yellow silk. Please make sure it's done this morning.'

I'm learning, Lucy-Anne thought, after surviving her first dinner party. This was nearly a disaster, but not through any fault of hers. George must have known in advance that the Reverend Bird from St Anne's had reformist tendencies while Walter Kendall very definitely had not, and it was George who decided to ask them both. Nor, in any case, could anyone have foreseen that Araminta, who had felt well enough that day to join the dinner party, would suddenly burst out of her shell of gentle compliance, and startle everybody.

James Bird, who was short and bouncy with the bright-eyed aggression of a robin, began the trouble by remarking that, on a recent visit to London, he had been appalled to learn that the already scandalous death rate among pauper children in the workhouses there was rising, and that he also considered the treatment of the lunatics in the Bedlam hospital near Bishopsgate to be outrageous. 'Most men treat cattle better,' he said.

Mr Kendall, who had a large red face and small, knowing eyes, promptly declared that the deaths were God's will and, in the case of the workhouse children, a judgement on the idle, gin-sodden and frequently unwed parents who had put them there. He was backed up by Mr Ross, who maintained that madness was also a judgement, usually on people who had committed sins of a kind unsuitable for discussion in mixed company.

Whereupon Araminta, without warning, flushed an angry pink and riveted the whole gathering by announcing that she had had a mad uncle who had been kept at home in a locked room to preserve him from the horrors of Bedlam.

'It was not a judgement on anything, but a most hideous affliction!' she told Mr Ross indignantly. Mr Ross looked as though he had just been pecked by a sparrow; George, who was slightly drunk and showed no disposition to damp down the quarrel, merely said, 'Upon my word, Mother, I never knew before that you had a mad uncle,' and Mr Bird, following up the advantage with which Araminta had presented him, informed the room that he had visited Bedlam and there seen a girl of only fourteen who had been born witless. 'What kind of sin could she have committed? Hm?'

'You are a man of the cloth, sir,' said Kendall. 'The text that the sins of the fathers shall be visited upon the children should be familiar to you.'

Mr Bird then became really infuriated and began to hammer on the table, while the wives began an argument of their own. It was left to Lucy-Anne to plead with them all to change the subject. To her surprise, they actually did, and Bird apologised for what he called his over-enthusiasm. She was still so distressed by the whole incident that when she led the ladies from the room she caught her skirt in the door and tore a flounce. But, nevertheless, she had performed well as a hostess and controlled the situation.

'My goodness, my dear,' said Araminta afterwards. 'You can consider yourself honourably blooded. You did excellently. Really, what a to-do!'

Lucy-Anne felt, after that, that she had gained a little confidence. But she found, as she had instinctively feared from the start, that it could at times be easier to calm down the most obstreperous guests than to reconcile the opposing parties in servants' feuds.

'Maria, this is very hard for me to say . . .' This was the first reprimand she had had to issue and she was hating it. Her heart was thumping and her palms felt hot. 'The fact is, I have to talk to you about Sarah. It . . . it really won't do for the two of you to make it so obvious that you don't get on.'

'I'm very sorry, ma'am,' said Maria. 'But that Sarah! That room where we sew and iron; she's always going in there and using the iron just when I need to; she does it on purpose, that's what. And she's always trying to tell me 'ow to do my work.' Maria's Cockney accent deepened, as it always did when she was aggrieved.

'I see. Well, Maria, you must still watch your tongue. However, I will get you another iron and you can work in my dressing closet sometimes. Of course, there have never been two ladies' maids in the household before. I expect Sarah finds it hard to get used to.'

'Yes, ma'am,' said Maria, dubiously.

Lucy-Anne, feeling that while taking Maria to task over one matter, she might as well deal with another, took the opportunity to remind her of the flounce which still needed stitching.

'Yes ma'am,' said Maria again.

Lucy-Anne didn't feel that she had dealt with any of that particularly well. Maria didn't seem sufficiently impressed. Still, she had tried. She *was*, gradually, learning.

A lady should have a parlour or sitting room of her own. Araminta, who spent much of her time in her chamber, had had it adapted for this purpose, with easy chairs and a table. When she was downstairs she used the morning room or the drawing room. The little parlour on the ground floor had become Lucy-Anne's domain. Since George was out a great deal, going round his land, hunting or seeing various friends in the countryside, she had much time to herself and often sat in the parlour when working on her embroidery or, sometimes, when going through the household books. Lucy-Anne's mother had taught her how to keep household accounts and, with Araminta's help, she was tackling those at

Chestnuts. She already knew the names of their principal suppliers, and knew how much of this or that would be used in an average week. This task was well within her compass and she did not fear failure.

Only in one respect did she feel a complete failure. At the beginning of December, she was for the second time disappointed of the hope of pregnancy. George was very anxious that a child should be on the way before he sailed for India in the spring. 'It can hardly be said that I have not been a most assiduous husband,' he remarked complainingly, when it once again became clear that, as yet, there were no results.

He certainly was; his assiduousness often left her aching. Araminta said there was no need to be anxious, that Lucy-Anne was still young and these things didn't always happen at once. But she said it to Lucy-Anne rather than to George, which didn't help very much. Sitting in her parlour on that gloomy December day, using the quiet hour before dinner to add up a few tradesmen's accounts, Lucy-Anne wished that George would understand that the disappointment was hers as much as his.

Glancing at the parlour clock, she saw that it was time to go upstairs and change. Once more, they were to have a guest at dinner. She had as yet barely been introduced to George's bailiff, Stephen Clarke, who had been away for some time, seeking information about some kind of new root crop. But he was back now and would dine with them today. She locked her books in her desk and went upstairs, pausing on the way to tap on Araminta's door.

Araminta called her in by name. 'I know your knock now,' she added as Lucy-Anne came to her bedside. 'I even recognise your footsteps.'

'How are you, Mrs Whitmead? Will you be down for dinner? Mr Clarke is coming.'

'I think I'll stay up here, my dear. Give Clarke my regrets. Oh, it's nothing much, just another of my stomach upsets, but I would rather rest in bed today.' Araminta smiled.

Lucy-Anne regarded her with concern. She was surely thinner now than when they left London and the brilliance of her blue eyes did not seem healthy. 'Can I ask them to send you up a tray?' Lucy-Anne asked.

'No, thank you. Just some milk, perhaps.'

Lucy-Anne withdrew to her own room, and immediately discovered that the yellow silk dress, which should by now be lying, neatly repaired, on the bed, was still nowhere to be seen. Irritated, she rang for Maria, who came promptly, but in tears.

'Oh, ma'am, I'm so sorry. I 'aven't – I mean I haven't – done your yellow gown. I can't. There's no more yellow thread in my workbox and that Sarah's gone and changed everything round in our workroom and I can't find where she's put all the thread. I dunno *what* she's done with things and . . .'

Oh no, thought Lucy-Anne, wilting. At this time of the month she was prone to headaches and the first signs of one now throbbed menacingly in her left temple. She massaged it with her fingers. Why couldn't Maria and Sarah make more effort? Well, she mustn't ask Araminta to intervene. She was sure her mother-in-law was ill. She would have to deal with this herself.

'Come with me to the workroom,' she said to Maria. 'And show me where the thread ought to be.'

The maids' workroom was well lit, with windows facing south and east. There was a hearth, where an iron was heating on the fire. There were two tables, two upright chairs and two basket chairs, a tall cupboard and a chest of drawers. Maria went to the chest and began to pull the drawers out, revealing folds of unused fabrics, lengths of lace, packets of dye, boxes of hooks and eyes, buttons and cord, and, in the case of the top righthand drawer, complete emptiness.

'The stores of thread and needle were *here*, in a box. There was plenty, all colours, and now the drawer's empty! What has she *done* with them? I went to her room to see if she was there, but the door was locked and she didn't answer my knock. But she must have taken them; they wouldn't just vanish!' Tearfully, Maria dragged the drawer right out and turned it upside down, as if hoping to find the missing box stuck to the underside. 'Oh, ma'am, I'm so sorry, but it isn't my fault. I can't sew without thread.'

'Oh dear. I wish you'd come to me at once,' said Lucy-Anne. 'There's some cream silk thread in my embroidery workbox. It's downstairs in the parlour. Cream's not exactly the right colour, but it would do.'

'There's no need for that,' said Sarah, stalking through the door. She put a box down, not too gently, on the table. 'The proper thread is here, decently tidied. I took the box away to set it straight. When you want something from it, Maria, you just scrabble about in it and upset everything and all the threads get into tangles. I'm sorry if you needed it, and I'm very sorry, Mrs Whitmead, ma'am, if you have been inconvenienced, but the job needed doing and—'

'Well, really, Sarah, it might have been better if you'd mentioned it to Maria first, or done your tidying here.'

'Yes, why couldn't you do it 'ere?' demanded Maria, snatching up the box. She dumped it in its drawer and rammed the drawer furiously back into its place. 'What did you take it away for?'

'The threads were in such a muddle that I knew it would take some time to sort them out.' Sarah's dignity was regal, her back as rigidly straight as a flagpole. She addressed Lucy-Anne. 'I took them to my room so as to be within call if Mrs Araminta wanted me. She's not well and I wouldn't hear her from here.'

'But why did you lock yourself in and not answer when I come to look for you?' Maria turned in angry appeal to her mistress. 'That's what I'd like to know, ma'am!'

'Maria, please moderate your voice!' said Lucy-Anne sharply.

'Indeed, yes. Behave yourself, girl,' Sarah said. 'I never heard you knock, as it happens. But I was out of the room, attending my mistress, for a time. No doubt that was when you came to my door.'

'You're lying, you spiteful old cat! I heard you moving about in there. You done it on purpose to get me into trouble, that's what you done, an' if your face weren't already as ugly as the back end of a mule, I'd spoil it for you, I would!' shrieked Maria, and made an alarming clawing gesture in the air.

'*Maria*!' Lucy-Anne desperately asserted herself. 'Stop this at once, both of you! Sarah, you shouldn't have just taken the threads away and not told anyone. Please don't do such a thing again.'

'Maria is a slattern. If she knew how to behave like a proper lady's maid—'

'*Sarah!* Be quiet; just be *quiet!*' Lucy-Anne pressed a hand to her forehead, trying to stop its throbbing by force. Pink spots had appeared on Sarah's cheekbones and she radiated indignation, but at least she said no more. Lucy-Anne pulled the drawer open herself and found the gold-coloured thread. 'Maria, come to my room and do that flounce immediately. Not one more word! Not from either of you!'

Leaving Sarah behind, Lucy-Anne marched her maid back to the bedchamber, sat her down to her mending and then, lips compressed, went to her dressing table and set about brushing her own hair. Maria, stitching rapidly, was silent for some time, but kept on giving her mistress covert glances. Twice Lucy-Anne caught them in the mirror and quickly looked away.

'Ma'am ... I'm afraid you're angry with me,' Maria said at last. 'But truly, I couldn't find the thread.'

'I know that, Maria. But you should not have made such a noisy scene with Sarah. Please don't ever again do things like telling Sarah she looks like the back end of a mule.'

In spite of her headache, it was difficult at this point not to giggle. Lucy-Anne was very aware that to be only seventeen was a disadvantage in more than one way. It wasn't only a matter of fearing that other people might think her childish. She *was* childish and knew it.

'It wasn't me that took the box away.'

'Oh, for goodness' sake, Maria. I don't want to hear any more about it.' She overcame the giggles and somehow achieved a severe tone. 'The matter is not to be discussed any further, is that clear? Have you finished? Then help me dress.'

She was glad that George did not put in an appearance until she was ready to go downstairs, having gone to his own dressing room to change. Presently, still feeling vaguely upset, but aware that the yellow gown became her and with her headache much reduced, Lucy-Anne went down to dinner on her husband's arm.

They found Stephen Clarke in the library, standing by the fire with one foot on the fender and his nose in a tome on agriculture. He was a blunt-featured young man who wore his own brown, crinkly hair, usually tied back in a queue for convenience while he was working. For dining with his employer, he had loosened it, brushed it over his ears and attempted to keep it under control with pomade, but it was now falling forward as he read, which he did with impatient, page-flicking eagerness.

He bowed to Lucy-Anne and asked if she were well, but after that turned at once to George and said: 'I had a most interesting journey, sir. If it isn't the best time of year for travelling, the effort was worth it. Ever since I heard from my sister near Bath of the success some of her neighbours have had with these new crops, I have been impatient to find out more.'

'I take it that you have succeeded in so doing?' George enquired.

'I have indeed. The difference which could be made to farming in this

31

country' Or in this part of the country I should say, as it seems that other places are ahead of us. My sister's neighbour got the idea from a visit to Norfolk, where they have been planting turnips for more than half a century! But I am at fault; this must be tedious for Mrs Whitmead. Do forgive me, ma'am.'

'Not at all. I am interested in everything to do with my husband's lands,' said Lucy-Anne. He had behaved just like this when George first introduced him to her, the day after her arrival at Chestnuts. He had begun to talk of estate matters, stopped and apologised for boring her, and then asked stiff questions about her journey until she was so embarrassed that she made an excuse to withdraw. But she couldn't retreat from dinner. Stephen, now, was one more difficult guest, and must be managed. 'I shall be happy to listen,' she said firmly. 'Please go on.'

'By all means, Clarke,' George agreed. 'I myself wish to hear your news. Continue. Mrs Whitmead will not object.'

Clarke was obviously only too pleased to accept this invitation and he was still talking eagerly when they went in to dinner. Lucy-Anne had never heard of turnips before, but by the time dinner was done she could have passed an examination on the subject.

According to Stephen Clarke, the turnip was related to the cabbage, should be sowed at the rate of half an ounce of seed to each hundred-foot row, would be well suited to the lower half of George's ten-acre field and was perfectly suited as winter feed for cattle. A nobleman called Lord Townshend had apparently spent much time and energy urging its use, and claiming that it would revolutionise farming.

'I don't keep cows,' George observed. 'But some of my tenants do. This, I take it, means that more of their calves could be kept through the winter and therefore they would have well-grown bullocks for sale the following season.'

'Indeed, sir. For that reason the turnip is also a most saleable commodity.'

Lucy-Anne's air of bright attentiveness had been somewhat forced to begin with, but Clarke's enthusiasm was undeniably likeable and by this time her interest had become real. She remembered the herd of calves that had blocked their way as they came through Guildford. 'You mean that we could sell turnips to farmers who rear cattle?' she asked.

Stephen Clarke turned to her. 'Yes, indeed we could. You have grasped the issue, Mrs Whitmead.' He sounded slightly surprised.

'It appears to me,' George pronounced, 'that we might consider trying the crop out. I shall want to examine the costs and possible profits in detail, Clarke.'

'Of course, sir.' Clarke gave Lucy-Anne a smile, a genuinely friendly one this time, which included his hazel eyes as well as his mouth. 'I believe, ma'am, that I have not bored you after all and that is a relief. My sister Julia tells me that I am impossible when I begin to talk of things that interest me; I don't know when to stop, she says. Though perhaps it is a family failing. She is married to a clergyman, but he has a great interest in science and astronomy and all branches of modern learning and has taught her to be interested likewise. When Julia talks of planets and

32

constellations, she is quite as bad as I am, I promise you.'

'She lives in Bath, I believe you mentioned, Mr Clarke?' said Lucy-Anne.

'Close to it. Her husband is vicar of St Oswald's, in a small village just on the other side of the River Avon.'

'I have been to Bath with my parents,' Lucy-Anne said. 'My father was taking the spa water for his health. We attended some concerts, I remember.'

'Oh, yes. Bath is becoming a fashionable society centre as well as a spa,' Clarke agreed. 'People repair there now as much for the social life as for the waters, and many fine new buildings are going up these days. When my sister has guests – she has a growing family but she and Edward are hospitable souls – she sometimes takes them to what is called the Pump Room in Bath. One can drink the waters there, listen to music and perhaps catch a glimpse of some famous person or other. Many fashionable people stay in the city and visit the Pump Room.'

George, listening, had started to fidget and make faint harrumphing noises, which Lucy-Anne now knew were a sign of impatience. She turned to him, smiling, and he said, looking past her at Clarke, 'My wife has no taste for society.'

He meant, 'I have decided that my wife should have no taste for society,' but Stephen Clarke, eager and earnest, failed to grasp the nuance and blundered blithely onwards.

'Oh, but have you tried it out, Mrs Whitmead? Can you say you do not like society unless you have experienced it? Surely you cannot say that you do not enjoy balls. All young ladies like to dance.'

He himself was scarcely thirty, but his attitude to Lucy-Anne was very much that of grown man to a very young girl. Lucy-Anne, rendered despondent by her failure to conceive and by the quarrel between Maria and Sarah, wondered sadly if she would ever really become properly grown up.

She was trying very hard to make herself into a good wife for George, but every time she thought she was getting somewhere her youth and diffidence would suddenly get in her way. She wished that she were ten years older, with half-a-dozen children. Perhaps then the servants wouldn't quarrel in front of her and people like Clarke wouldn't address her as though she were a schoolgirl.

Trying to sound adult, she said: 'Well, naturally I like to dance. But I have only attended a few private dances. I have not been to any large balls.'

'But you think you would not enjoy them if you did?'

'I cannot judge, sir. But the question hardly arises. I am married now and my husband will often be away. While he is gone, I shall live quietly here at Chestnuts, except for occasional visits to my parents in London.'

'Quite,' said George. 'My wife could hardly attend public balls or assemblies while I am in India. It would be most improper.'

Clarke seemed to realise that he had been tactless. 'I beg your pardon; both your pardons, in fact. I spoke out of turn. I hope I have not given offence.'

'Not at all. Our situation is uncommon,' George told him. 'My absences will be prolonged. And, naturally, I hope that my wife will in due course have a family to occupy her time.'

'A family certainly does that,' said Stephen, laughing. 'As Julia would confirm. She has five already, the youngest only three months old.'

'Admirable!' said George. 'Eh, Lucy-Anne?'

Her headache was back and a dismal cramp had gripped her stomach. There had been a gibe in George's tone, faint, but there. He was being subtly unkind and it wasn't fair.

'Yes, admirable,' she agreed colourlessly and was glad to see Fraser arrive with the port decanter.

The arrival of the decanter was Lucy-Anne's dismissal. She went into the drawing room, where a coffee tray was waiting. The men did not join her and at last, feeling somewhat neglected, she made her way to her parlour, stitched a little, went up to see Araminta, who had slept and said she felt better, and eventually supped alone and retired to bed, leaving the candles, however, alight.

She wakened as George, entering the room, closed the door after him.

'I am sorry we left you alone,' he said. 'But we went to my study and became very much immersed in business. Supper was brought to us there.'

'Were you talking about the turnips?' asked Lucy-Anne.

'Yes, as it happens.' He was in his night-clothes, but instead of coming to bed he sat down by the dying fire. There was something odd about him. His voice was unusually expressionless and he was avoiding her eyes. 'You seem to have a satisfactory grasp of the subject,' he said. 'Not that you will need to concern yourself much with estate affairs while I'm away; most of that can be left to Stephen. But still, it is right that you should understand something of such things. My mother tells me that she intends to encourage Clarke to make his regular reports to you rather than to her and certainly it is better that you should fill your head with such practical matters, than with nonsense about society.'

'Than with . . . ?'

He turned towards her and she saw that his face was red and his eyes hard. 'What the devil do you mean, Lucy-Anne, by contradicting me like that over dinner?'

'Contradicting?' Lucy-Anne pushed herself up on one elbow. 'But I didn't!'

'You have just done so once again. I object to it, my dear. I object to it very much.'

'But, George, I took great care not to—'

'When I say that you do not care for society, it is your business to accept that point of view. Not to tell some other person that you like to dance, as if you were accusing me of preventing you.'

'But—'

'I have said that when I am at home we will exchange visits with our friends and no doubt you will do a little dancing at times. I have no wish to deny you ordinary amusements. But I hoped when we married that you would be content to live tranquilly in my home, devoting yourself to my interests and not anxious to attract the notice of other men.'

'But I am! I mean, I don't—!'

34

'I am extremely displeased. I am not accustomed to being set at naught like that in my own house.'

'But I didn't!' Lucy-Anne was almost crying. 'I *didn't*!'

'I say you did.'

Lucy-Anne flopped on to her back, staring up despairingly at the blue and gold bed-canopy. He was being so unjust. He had got to be right, apparently, even when he was wrong. Her father had never behaved like that. If Hugo found that he had made a mistake, he just said so, casually. She could make no sense of George. But he had hurt her bitterly.

'Well, well,' said George, after the silence had gone on for some time. 'You are very young, and no doubt you did not mean to give offence. But I must ask you to make me a promise. I wish you to promise that, when I am away, you will not entertain or visit anyone except people of whom you are sure I will approve and that you will attend gatherings only of a private and most respectable nature; and that you will never again embarrass me by contradicting me as you did today.'

'Yes, yes, of course, if you wish it. I promise.'

'Sit up,' said George. 'Give me your word properly. There's a Bible on the bedside table. Put your hand on it and say after me: "I swear by all that is holy . . ."'

It was ridiculous, like a parody of a marriage service. It was difficult to believe that he meant it seriously, but it seemed that he did. While she sat on the edge of the bed, her hand on the calf binding of her husband's Bible, and swore, in the words he gave her, to keep her social life within the bounds he set and never to set her opinions up against his in all her life again, he watched her in an intense fashion which frightened her. It was so out of proportion to the nature of the promises. They were too mundane, too trivial, for such passion.

When it was over, and she had let go of the Bible, he nodded his head in a satisfied way, but his eyes did not soften. Then she discovered that this wasn't the end of it.

'If you keep your word,' he said, 'I shall be content. However, since I have had to speak to you on one matter, let me mention the other which is on my mind, and then the account will be clear.'

Lucy-Anne stared at him in alarm. 'What . . . what account?'

'I was passing through the hallway this afternoon and I could hear the voices of your maid and my mother's, shouting at each other. I could hear them even at the foot of the stairs. You must learn to control the household better. I suggest that you ask my mother's advice; I am sure she can instruct you wisely.'

'I would be glad of your mother's advice.' Her voice was trembling. It was too much. One accusation after another; and she tried so hard to please, so very hard. 'She is not well just now. I will of course seek her guidance as soon as I can.'

'Good. Well, no need to be too downcast. I speak to you only for your own good and you have promised amendment. Go to sleep now. I will come to bed presently.'

He said no more, but sat gazing into the fire. Lucy-Anne lay still, making no further attempts to talk but far too miserable to sleep. For the first time in her life she was making a deliberate effort to look ahead, to foresee the future. Hitherto, it had seemed always to be bounded by some forthcoming event or other – leaving the schoolroom, accepting George's proposal, marriage, coming to Chestnuts. Now she peered into the distant future, trying to imagine what the years would be like as George's wife. It was a bleak vision. She had been very ready to love her husband, but what was the use of loving a man who criticised and magnified tiny faults or even invented them. Who demanded Bible oaths about them! No one could be as flawless as he apparently thought she ought to be.

Her head was pounding. Pressing her brow into her pillow, she cried, but silently, for fear of annoying him again.

She was unaware that George, sitting by the fire, was also unhappy. The scene they had just had was of his making, but he hadn't enjoyed it. He feared he had made too much of too little and had once again failed to cherish his young wife sufficiently.

Sometimes he felt as though there were a second man inside him – a haughty, bullying stranger who on occasion took him over. But he couldn't have his wife's head turned by talk of the society world; he knew more than she did about society and it was full of dangers for innocent young girls. The Kendalls always went to London for the winter and, on his return from India, they had regaled him with all the latest scandals. Lucy-Anne, for her own protection as well as for his honour, must let herself be guided by him. For her own good, she must learn not to set her will against his.

He wanted a peaceful house, too. Surely Lucy-Anne and Araminta could achieve that between them? He would not always be here to watch over things. In three months' time he would be sailing for India.

. And *still* – the angry stranger spoke up inside him, indignantly – and *still* there was no sign of a child.

'He made it all so . . . so dramatic,' Lucy-Anne said in bewilderment to Araminta. 'I felt as though I were taking an oath in a church. And it was all over such little things. I meant no harm at dinner, and the maids – I do tell Maria to respect Sarah's seniority. But . . .'

Araminta, this morning, had declared that she felt better, and had firmly rejected any suggestion that Dr May, the Guildford physician who usually attended Chestnuts, should be summoned. Well wrapped in a very beautiful gold and peacock Indian shawl, she had come down to sit by the fire in the morning room, and Lucy-Anne had been emboldened to mention her bewildering quarrel with George.

'I will have another word with Sarah,' said Araminta. 'I've spoken to her before. I'm afraid that she is causing most of the trouble and I apologise for her. As for George . . . my dear, my father was just the same and so was my husband. They are very jealous of their consequence and one must never trespass on it. Whatever George says, agree with him. It is as simple as that.'

'But I didn't *disagree*. Well, not really.'

'Even that,' said Araminta, 'could be enough, with George. And as for the promise – well, I don't find that as extraordinary as you do. When George goes back to India, he'll be gone a long time and you will be left here with no husband to guide you. It seems to me quite natural that he should want you to promise to live as he would wish, during his absence. It is a pity that he chose to do so just after you had quarrelled, but there – he only wants to protect you, you know.'

Lucy-Anne sighed. It was as though she had been walking on what looked like smooth grass, and put her foot straight through into perilous bog. She had been glad that today he had breakfasted early, before she was downstairs, and then vanished into his study. She was afraid of meeting him in case she once more gave offence by mistake. It seemed to be alarmingly easy

But in Araminta's eyes George's behaviour was apparently quite normal. There was evidently no more to be said. Lucy-Anne changed the subject.

'Shall I ring for sherry and biscuits? Could you take them? It's eleven o'clock.'

'No, my dear, I think I will keep to very bland things for a few days and not too much even of those. But you must have your eleven o'clock as usual. Ring by all means.'

Lucy-Anne rose to do so, but paused, looking out of the window. 'We have a visitor; there's a carriage just driving in. Good gracious! It's great-uncle Matthew, with a manservant!'

'Matthew? But he never travels anywhere, these days.' Araminta was surprised. 'How extraordinary. Well, you had better sit down again. The refreshments had best wait until Fraser brings him in.'

But George, from his study, had seen the carriage draw up and had emerged to greet his grandfather. They heard his voice in the hall as Fraser opened the door and, a moment later, it was George who brought Matthew into the morning room. Lucy-Anne jumped up, an eager greeting on her lips. She did not know her great-uncle very well, but she had occasionally visited him with her parents, and she liked him. Her expressions of welcome, however, died away when she saw that he was dressed in black and that his faded eyes were bloodshot, as though he had been weeping. Araminta, also recognising the signs of grief, half-rose in alarm, pushing herself up on fragile wrists.

'Araminta! Lucy-Anne, my dear!' said Matthew tremulously, and came at once to embrace them. 'I bring sad news. Such sad news. I still can't believe it myself.'

'It's great-aunt Henrietta,' George said. 'Grandfather has driven all the way from London this morning to inform us. It is amazing, since my great-aunt attended my wedding and seemed in perfectly good health then, but . . .'

'Have this chair, father-in-law.' Araminta guided Matthew to a seat. 'What has happened to Henrietta?'

'She's gone,' said Matthew bleakly. 'Jenny found her lying stricken in her bed, two weeks ago. We hoped to nurse her to recovery, but she died in her sleep, before dawn, yesterday morning.'

'Poor soul!' Araminta sank into her own chair again, drawing the beautiful shawl round her as though to protect herself against even the mention of mortality.

'She was seventy-seven. So am I! We were twins,' Matthew said. 'For a great part of our lives we saw very little of each other, but I always knew she was there in Broom Cottage. She was *there*. And, lately, I had begun trying to persuade her to give up Broom Cottage and remain with me in London. Only two days ago I still hoped for her recovery. She had improved a little, enough to speak my name. I didn't send word to you, not wishing to disturb your honeymoon days. I feel . . . forgive me.'

Lucy-Anne pulled the bell. When Fraser came, she said decisively, 'Hot milk for Mrs Araminta, please, some biscuits, and sherry for three, but bring some brandy too,' and saw Araminta nod approvingly.

George, who had taken up a position on the hearth, with his back to the fire, observed: 'It was most thoughtful of you to come yourself to tell us, grandfather, but should you have done so? You must have set out at cockcrow, and at this time of year, with the cold and the muddy roads—'

'It was most desirable that I should come in person,' Matthew said unsteadily. 'I felt it was a necessary courtesy. Henrietta left a will and made me executor. She had told me where to find it – in a bureau in her room. It is very recent; in fact, she made it the day after your wedding, George. Lucy-Anne is a beneficiary. My sister has left me her money, but Broom Cottage and its contents, Lucy-Anne, have been willed to you.'

'To Lucy-Anne? Property has been left direct to Lucy-Anne? Good God!' said George, and Lucy-Anne, looking at his reddened face, saw with resignation that her husband had, once more, taken offence.

It took time and a good deal of the brandy to soothe George out of his ruffled feelings.

'Well, really; I am sorry to say it in your presence, grandfather, especially with my great-aunt so lately departed, but I feel the slight very much. I am Lucy-Anne's husband and her property naturally passes to me; it would have been better simply to leave it to me. The law cannot be flouted, of course, but this amounts to a questioning of its wisdom. It has the appearance of a reluctance to trust me.'

'I believe,' said Matthew, 'that my sister took to Lucy-Anne when she met her at the wedding, and wished to signify this in her will. There was no slight intended, I feel certain.'

George harrumphed. 'If only she had discussed the matter with one of us! If only she had sought the advice of a male relative in what one would think was the proper fashion!'

'Henrietta was of a very independent temperament,' Matthew said. The combination of brandy and disagreement had gone some way towards dispelling the effects of grief and his voice now was both steady and vigorous. 'Her judgement was good,' he said. 'I am quite aware that most members of the family regarded her as eccentric, to say the least of it, but I knew her better than any of you and I can assure you that her understanding was excellent, in matters of business as in all other things. She rarely sought advice; she had no need of it.'

'But, nevertheless, you yourself must feel somewhat surprised.' George emptied his brandy glass and refilled it as if it were liquid sanity. 'No doubt the cottage is of some value and you might reasonably have expected—'

'I am a man of means and I don't need or want Broom Cottage,' said Matthew with asperity. 'If Henrietta had discussed the matter with me I should have told her to do exactly as she liked with her own. I'm sorry to hear you take this attitude, George, and I hope that you will allow your wife to exercise rights of ownership over the cottage because I feel sure that Henrietta wished it, and you have, I trust, been brought up to respect the wishes of the dead – not to mention the wishes of your elders!'

Brought up short, George once more turned an affronted crimson. 'I must beg your pardon, grandfather. I have spoken my mind too freely. Perhaps we should continue this discussion more privately, in my study.'

'We should indeed, but not yet,' said Matthew. 'First, I wish to speak alone with Lucy-Anne. Henrietta was, I think, aware of her approaching end. She made that will, for one thing, and in addition, shortly before she fell ill, she spoke to me about Lucy-Anne. She didn't mention Broom Cottage, but she did say something which I think I should pass on to you, great-niece. Will you walk with me in the garden? I see the sun has come out.'

Neither Lucy-Anne nor Araminta had dared as yet to comment. Lucy-Anne now looked timidly at George, who snorted and said: 'If my grandfather wishes to walk in the garden with you, naturally you must do as he asks. I cannot possibly object. Put on something warm.'

A few minutes later, snugly protected from the chilly though sunlit air by a thick woollen cloak and thankful to be out of George's presence, Lucy-Anne was strolling between the parterre beds, holding the arm of her great-uncle. They went slowly, on account of Matthew's age, but he declined to be led down the chestnut avenue to take shelter in the folly. 'It is pleasant out of doors today, December or not. The air smells sweet after London. Your great-aunt always said that London reeked of smoke.'

'I suppose it does. I'm afraid,' said Lucy-Anne, 'that George is rather cross.'

'Very angry, you mean. He's a generous man in his way,' said Matthew dispassionately, 'and he'll always look after you and see you have all the comforts you want; you can rely on him for that. But he's got a great sense of his own importance. You won't go all wifely and fly out at me for saying so, will you? You must have noticed it yourself, unless you're blind with love. Are you?'

'I ... well ...' stammered Lucy-Anne.

'No, you're not.' Matthew chuckled. 'George has a tendency to get puffed-up. Let's just admit it. It is something you will have to live with.'

'I rather wish,' said Lucy-Anne, 'that my great-aunt *had* just left the cottage to him instead. It would have been more fitting.'

'You mean it would have saved you one of George's sulks. I used to warn his mother to take a firmer hand with those sulks, when he was a boy, but Araminta always was a complete doormat. She agreed with every word my pompous son said and encouraged my grandson to grow up just like his father, except that George is slightly worse. James was never quite so touchy. Now then, listen. I've got something more than a parting message from Henrietta to give you, my child. It's the real reason why I got my old bones out of bed and into the carriage before daybreak today. A message could have waited and the will still has to be proved, but this – well, it was burning a hole in my furniture. I had to bring it at once.'

'Burning a hole in your furniture?'

'Metaphorically, not literally,' said Matthew. 'It is something that should remain a secret between you and me. Above all, I strongly advise you to keep it from George. You can take my advice on this; I *am* his senior in the family, after all.'

'Yes. Yes, of course. But what . . . ?'

'It's simple enough. I am hoping that you and George will accompany me back to London for the funeral, but tonight at least I must stay here. I have brought a clean shirt and my shaving things and so forth, in a box which my manservant will by now have taken to my room. In that box there is also a casket containing five hundred pounds in sovereigns. It's for you.'

'I don't understand.'

'Henrietta was quite a wealthy woman. She was left out of my father's will, you know – on account of a quarrel between them long ago – but your grandmother and I put that right when our father died. There was more than enough to go round, lord knows. My father was very rich indeed. Henrietta's will doesn't mention the casket; except for some provision for an old servant, she just left her money to me. But when I went to get the will out, I found the casket with it, and a letter addressed to me. This one – here.'

From a pocket inside his coat he produced a single sheet of paper. Lucy-Anne read it, holding it in her spare hand as they walked along. It was brief, blunt and autocratic.

My dear Matthew

I am leaving this letter under a casket containing £500 in sovereigns. When I am gone, I wish the casket and the money to be given to our great-niece Lucy-Anne, so that she may have a little more power over her own life than I ever had. Give it to her secretly and try to persuade her to keep it for herself and not reveal it to her husband. He'll claim it if she does. Kindly regard this letter as a codicil to my will but inform no one of its existence except Lucy-Anne.

In loving farewell,
your sister, Henrietta Whitmead.

'More power . . . she said something like that to me at my wedding,' Lucy-Anne said slowly. She handed the letter back to Matthew. 'But in law the money belongs to George. He has a right to claim it. I have to tell him.'

'Confound George. If you let him know about those sovereigns, he'll take them from you. Henrietta wanted you, and I want you, to outwit the law. Hide the money in a safe place and don't mention it. You presumably don't actually wish George to impound it. Now. Have you somewhere where you can keep it?'

'In my parlour there's a desk with a lock, yes, and it has several inner drawers, also with locks. I keep some money in one of them already – for paying the servants. I keep the keys of the desk.'

'And George doesn't poke into it?'

'Not so far. There are two sets of keys, but I have them both and he's never asked for them. And he's going away in March.'

'Well, if you're sure it's secure, lock the casket in your desk.'

Lucy-Anne bit her lip. 'He'll be very angry if he finds out by accident. He'll say I've deceived him. Great-uncle Matthew, I don't need so much money! Whatever will I use it for?'

'Who knows? That is just it. One never knows what will happen in life. My dear child, you aren't going to deceive anyone, not in the sense of telling lies, anyway. You will just not mention the casket.'

'But to George it would be the same thing! Oh, I'm truly grateful to my great-aunt for this kind thought, but surely you see . . . Great-uncle? What is it?'

'We are talking of Henrietta and I find it *impossible* to believe that she's gone, that's all.' Matthew pulled out a handkerchief and wiped his eyes, almost angrily. 'My apologies. And no, I am not putting on a show in the hope that you'll do as I wish for fear of upsetting me further. Come. Let us return to the house. At a suitable moment I will give you the casket, and you will do as you choose with its contents. But if you decide to keep them secret, then you must give George some account or other of what I have said to you this morning. To get you out here, I pretended that I wanted to tell you something Henrietta said before her death. I suggest you tell him that it consisted of some sage advice. Say that she told me she was very glad to see you at your wedding, but feared she was failing and would not see you again, and was anxious that you should never make her own mistakes. She set up her will against that of her father and was exiled from her family for most of her life as a result. Tell George that she recommended you, through me, to conform to his wishes in all things. There isn't a word of truth in any of this,' said Matthew with a naughty chuckle. 'But it will please him, and provide an answer to the questions he'll want to ask.'

'I wish I knew what to do!' said Lucy-Anne in confusion.

'Even if you hand the casket straight to him,' said Matthew cunningly, as they turned back towards the house, 'he might be quite annoyed to learn that Henrietta had left you that as well. Do you know her story? Father wanted her to marry an old, old man. A rich old man, naturally. She refused and he disowned her. At that time, I had no means of helping her. That had to wait until my father died, more than a quarter of a century later. Henrietta became the companion and almost the prisoner of the cousin who took her in. Had she had money of her own, she might have avoided that. I'm only sorry that the five hundred pounds isn't five thousand. Except that five thousand sovereigns wouldn't fit into the casket. It's a pretty thing – made of chased silver, worth a penny or two in its own right. In fact, I gave it to Henrietta as a Christmas gift some years ago.' He drew in the elbow that she held, pressing her hand affectionately against his side. 'It's just big enough for the five hundred pounds. I hope that your secret drawer is big enough for the casket.'

What she was doing was, of course, completely and utterly wrong. Lucy-Anne's hands shook as she slid the silver casket into an inner drawer of her writing desk.

The casket was ornate, but in a delicate fashion, the chasing graceful, and the four small feet elegantly curved. The desk was ornate in quite a different way. It was of French origin – the creation, George had told her, of a famous cabinet-maker called André-Charles Boulle. It was fashionable to collect French furniture and, although relations between France and England were sour and getting worse, the craze still went on.

Lucy-Anne wasn't sure that she liked the Boulle style. Her tastes were simpler, and the desk, with its lavish marquetry and the wealth of gilded bronze arabesques and curlicues which half-concealed the keyholes of its innumerable drawers and tiny cupboards, was anything but simple.

But it was nevertheless practical. The handsome clock on top was the parlour timepiece, and there were drawers for writing paper and a shelf for an inkstand, and André-Charles, catering for customers who were quite likely to want hiding places for illicit correspondence and jewellery presented by their lovers, had provided numerous hidden compartments. Some of them were big enough to accommodate quite a number of letters or bracelets in presentation boxes. There were two or three that could accommodate the casket.

Examining it had been a curious experience. She had never seen so much money all at once before, and was astonished at the weight of it.

If George ever learned of this, Lucy-Anne had no doubt at all that it might well give him apoplexy.

But he had been unfair yesterday, being so angry over so little, and gibing at her over her failure to conceive. Resentment was finding its way to the surface of her mind, sending up sharp shoots like crocus spears.

Great-aunt Henrietta and great-uncle Matthew wanted her to have this secret. All her life, she had obeyed the adult world. She had had no choice, because whether she liked it or not they were always united in their opinions. Now, for the first time, two of them had stepped away from the rest and taken *her* part. It was exhilarating.

Her hands had stopped trembling. She shut the chosen drawer, turned the key in the lock with a positive flourish, and then pulled down the flap that hid the drawer from view even when the desk was open. She shut the desk-lid and locked that too. She stood holding the key in her warm palm.

Right or wrong, she was going to deceive George, without a twinge of conscience.

Chapter Three

The High Seas

'I am far from poor, but nor am I a spendthrift. I agree with Stephen Clarke that the work on the garden should be carried out by a less costly contractor. But I have heard that the man he recommends cuts corners as well as costs. I have left all the details in a letter for you, at home, but I may tell you now that on the way here I decided on a Mr Sanders from Farnham instead. You will have to inform Stephen.'

'Yes, George, of course.'

'You will at all times have my mother to advise you. I will return as soon as I can; if I can find and undertake a duty for the East India Company which brings me back within three years I will naturally accept it. I am sorry that I have to leave you so soon, especially as . . . well, we will say no more about that.'

Lucy-Anne, standing on the deck of the *Winchester*, and shivering slightly as the March wind that ruffled the Thames also cut through her cloak and all the layers of her hooped dress and underskirts as though they were made of tissue paper, wondered whether or not to tell him that she was now a week overdue. But it was too soon. How dreadful if she raised his hopes now, and then had to write and say it was all a mistake. She would write when she was sure, and he would have a pleasant surprise when he was in India. She said, 'I shall miss you.'

Oddly enough, it was true. She did not love George and had often had cause to resent him. His self-esteem and his ability to sulk had hurt her several times now. But he had certainly provided for her with the utmost generosity, and she was growing used to him, and even accustomed to his lumbering notions of lovemaking. Life without him would be restful, comfortable and peculiarly blank.

She had become quite skilled now at not irritating him. With Araminta's advice and connivance, even Maria and Sarah had at last been induced to behave. 'We shall just have to threaten to turn them off,' Araminta had said, looking worn, after another dispute between the two ladies' maids. 'That should do it.'

She was right. The threat had reduced both Maria and Sarah to horrified tears, and since then peace had reigned. Lucy-Anne had followed Araminta's advice simply to agree with everything George said, and he had of late become quite jovial. Yes, it was true. She would miss him.

A sailor came along the deck, calling that the gangplank was about to go up, and that all who were not passengers should now go ashore.

'Oh, George!'

'There, there. The time will soon go. Write often, as I will do, and heed my mother in all things.'

'I do so hope you'll be safe!' To Lucy-Anne, the *Winchester* and her companion ships, moored close at hand, seemed small and cramped and the *Winchester* was definitely smelly. The stench of bilgewater was already drifting up through a nearby hatchway. The red and white striped ensign of the East India Company, flying from the stern, looked more like puny defiance of the elements than confidence in the ship's ability to survive them. 'I'm sure you won't be comfortable,' she said dismally.

'Ah, well. I have long felt that your sex is unsuited to the rigours of travel, but men are more durable. Now, to me, this is as fine an East Indiaman as you'll find on the waves. We're all proud of the *Winchester*. Five hundred tons—'

'Five hun— but how can she float?' Lucy-Anne gasped ingenuously.

'She's floated well enough so far. This is her third voyage. Now listen, my love. Have a safe journey back to Chestnuts, but make sure that the London house is well cared for while it is shut. Give my respectful duty to your parents and to my mother. I wish she had felt up to coming to London to see me off. And now, we must say goodbye.'

She waited long enough on the quay to see the *Winchester* sail. George waved to her as the ship eased her way out into the river, and she waved back. Then he was gone and she was alone with his houses, and his servants, and Araminta. It felt like a heavy responsibility.

George was a fairly good sailor but the winds that year were blustery and the progress of the *Winchester* and her sister vessels southwards through the Atlantic was more like bucketing than sailing.

Nicholas Morse had carried out his plan to encourage more young men to come to Madras. There were young employees of the East India Company on board, clerks – writers, the company called them – going out for the first time, and a seasoned Council member like George naturally wished to impress them. But it was difficult to maintain one's dignity when constantly obliged to shout to make oneself heard above the howl of the wind in the rigging and forced to clutch at adjacent objects in order to stand upright.

On the third day out from the tip of Land's End, Captain Gabriel Steward issued orders that passengers were not to go on deck, and this meant being confined down below where the bilge smell was pervasive. George Whitmead continued to fight off seasickness, but took to his bunk in order to do it and lay there wrinkling his nostrils, uneasily eyeing the bucket which he had put handy just in case, and wishing that after all he had a manservant with him.

Except that he had brought one out last time and the wretched fellow had not only died of fever a week after reaching Madras, but had been seasick all the way, even though the voyage was fairly calm. Throughout most of their association, George had been the one who did the looking after. He had decided to take care of himself this time.

But how he would like someone here now, to give him drinks of water

44

and mop his sweating face. He thought of Lucy-Anne and wondered for a moment if he shouldn't, after all, have brought her too. He had the oddest idea that she might have proved tougher than that disastrous manservant.

A stupid notion, of course. Lucy-Anne was where she should be, quietly guarding his home and awaiting his return. If he ever did return. If that damned wind didn't tear the *Winchester*'s masts off and sink her before she even reached Brazil, let alone India. If . . .

A tap on his door obliged him to sit up. Groaning, he crawled out of his bunk, pulled on a robe and opened the door. One of the young clerks was outside it.

'Can I come in, sir? I wanted to ask you something.'

The ship rolled. Not sure if he could trust himself to open his mouth and speak, George stepped back in mute invitation and the youth, who was large and dark and clumsy, plunged through the door and tripped over the bucket.

'I beg your pardon,' he said, retrieving the bucket and setting it the right way up. George sat down on the bunk and the young man, glancing at his face, said anxiously, 'Are you unwell? I need some advice, but . . .'

When a youth sought an elder's advice, the elder must oblige, even if he were half-dead. 'By all means, my boy. By all means. You're Clive, are you not?'

'Yes, sir. Robert Clive. But if you're not feeling quite the thing, I'll go away again. You weren't at dinner, were you?'

'I eschewed dinner,' said George majestically, 'only because I frequently find the standard of the food on this vessel too unpalatable to tolerate. Sit down on the end of my bunk there, and tell me what it is you need advice about.'

'You think the food is poor too, sir? I have had no previous experience, of course. But I've already come to the conclusion that Captain Steward,' said Clive with vigour, 'is more grasping than a chimpanzee and too mean to spare the cheese for a mousetrap. *That* was what I wanted advice about.'

'Oh?' said George wanly. The mere word 'cheese' made his insides shudder. He strove to compel them into good behaviour. The ship performed an extraordinary corkscrewing movement and he gripped the edge of the bunk with both hands.

'It's quite simple,' said Clive, frowning. His dark brows were very thick and his nose fleshy, and when the frown drew them all together they dominated his face. 'When I set out,' he said, 'I understood that I would have to buy clothes and any other things I needed from the ship's stores – that the captain sells them, in fact. He is a sort of merchant.'

'That is perfectly correct.' The ship had steadied a little. George took a deep breath and wiped his damp temples with his palm. 'A forebear of mine, a Captain Charles Whitmead, was a captain of this line.' Much of the Whitmead money, indeed, had been originally made by the hard bargains Captain Whitmead had driven with his passengers.

'Yes, I see. But,' said Clive in outraged tones, 'I now find that his prices are higher than I was given to understand. Than *he* gave me to understand when I came aboard. I have no great store of either money or clothes with me. When I arrive, I shall earn only five pounds a year as a clerk. I think that Captain Steward is charging rates at will, and that he has no right to do so. What will happen if we are delayed on the way? Such delays are not uncommon – I know that much. Now, sir. Can I insist that the captain should reduce his prices to something more reasonable? To whom should I threaten to report him?'

'*Report* him? A young writer report a captain of the line?' Indignation made George speak emphatically and an invisible hammer instantly struck him above the right eye. Valiantly, he ignored it. 'Such a thing is unthinkable. A captain on the high seas is a law unto himself. Captain Steward can charge whatever prices he thinks he can obtain. They may well be high, but you have no redress, none at all. The practice of economy will do you no harm.'

'Economy's one thing. Penury's another.'

'Well, we have not been subject to delay as yet. Hardly, with this gale behind us,' George said. 'Your fears may never be realised. If they are, you will find that credit is obtainable, although you should keep this to a minimum. I would advise you—'

'I know. I asked. At a rate of interest even more exorbitant than the damned prices are. Fifty per cent!'

The ship plunged anew, this time apparently bent on diving headlong into the ocean. Green water rolled past the porthole above the bunk and the wind in the rigging became a shriek. Clive's lips continued to move but George couldn't hear the words and didn't much care, for terrible things were happening to him. He lunged, just in time, for the bucket, surrendering not only to seasickness but to the shame of having a junior as a witness.

The boy stepped up to him and took hold of his head. 'Just let it go, sir. Just let it go. That's what I've been told to do if it happens to me. Luckily it hasn't, yet. I'm liable to gastric upsets sometimes but not, so far, due to the sea. That's it. Bring it all up.'

His hands were as badly co-ordinated as his feet and his grip on George's head was awkward, but he was trying to be kind. George, groaning, muttered his thanks.

'There's no denying,' said Clive, cheerfully and tactlessly, 'that a rough voyage like this is quite an adventure. I've always wanted adventures.'

It was the duty of the experienced to disabuse the beginner of absurd ideas, even at a topsy-turvy moment like this. George, in the brief interval before another paroxysm seized him, did his best. 'If you're going to be a merchant, my boy, you'll need to work hard and keep your eye on the profits. That's what the Company will expect.'

'I shall look to you to advise me, sir.'

'I'll do my best. Oh, *God*,' said George sincerely, 'has anyone ever died of seasickness, I wonder?'

Lucy-Anne had never felt at ease in the Hanover Square house. She stayed there for only one day further, long enough to give final instructions to the caretaker staff and visit her parents. Then she set off gladly for Chestnuts. In only just over four months, she had, she found, come to think of it as home.

The entrance hall was agreeably familiar. The portrait of herself and George had been hung there, and looked, Lucy-Anne thought, as though it had been there always. She did not care for the portrait overmuch; it was too formal for her taste. She was posed so stiffly, and neither of them was smiling.

The artist had reproduced their features faithfully, however, and this was the only picture of George that she had. The sight of it gave her a rush of sentiment. She stopped short in front of it and Fraser, who had welcomed her at the door with genuine warmth, waited for a moment before approaching her to say that fires had been lit in her parlour and in the drawing room, and also in her bedroom, and that Mrs Araminta, who was not so well today and had been spending it in her room, had asked to see her as soon as she arrived. Lucy-Anne blinked away a desire to cry, which had taken her by surprise, and turned away from George's picture. 'Thank you, Fraser.' She had grown accustomed to Fraser now, and was no longer afraid of him. 'I'll go up at once. See that a tray of coffee is sent up, will you?'

Sarah let her into the room. Araminta was propped up on a stack of pillows and her face was very drawn, but she smiled and held out her hand. 'Lucy-Anne. Did George sail on time?'

'Yes, the day before yesterday, the tenth of March. He sends his farewells. How are you, mother-in-law?'

'Taking care of myself, as you see. I'm glad you're back home again.'

'I'm glad to *be* back. It was a very quick journey, though the weather's cold and windy. I—'

Lucy-Anne stopped. There was an unpleasant smell in the room. Looking about her, she realised that on the floor by the bed was a basin containing evidence of both nausea and diarrhoea. There was blood in it, too. She swung round to face Sarah and saw tears in the woman's eyes.

'Dr May came yesterday,' said Sarah. '"An affliction of the bowel due to the inclement season," he said. The sort of thing physicians say. An affliction of the bowel, because the weather is too hot, too cold, too wet; it's unwise to eat this, or that, at this particular season ... they don't know what they're talking about!'

'Please, Sarah. Don't be so shrill,' said Araminta. Her voice was faintly hoarse. 'I have had a bad turn, Lucy-Anne. I'm glad it didn't happen until George had left. I wouldn't have wanted him to delay his sailing. But I wish he wasn't going to be away for such a long time. It's hard not to worry in case I don't see him again.'

'But of course you will!' Lucy-Anne took her mother-in-law's hand. The thin fingers were burning hot. 'I think you have a fever, though. Didn't the physician give you anything for it? You sound as if you have a cold. Perhaps that's all it is – a bad cold. I have things in my stillroom that might help. Sarah, you know where the key is. There's a horehound brew, for coughs and sore throats, on the second shelf down, beside the door, and a febrifuge next to it. They're both labelled. Please fetch them.'

47

'We've tried all those things, ma'am. It's all no good. She can't keep them down.'

'Then we must get Dr May back!'

'No,' said Araminta.

'But...'

'No. Sit down, Lucy-Anne.'

Frightened, Lucy-Anne obeyed. Her mother-in-law's hollowed, luminous eyes regarded her sadly. 'I'm so tired of pretending,' Araminta said. 'So tired of lying. To George, to myself... I can't be bothered any more. There is nothing any doctor can do.'

'What... do you mean?'

'You're young, my dear. You don't know about these things yet. But my mother died like this.'

From Sarah, there came a sob. Araminta turned her head. 'My water jug is nearly empty, Sarah, and my mouth tastes so foul. Will you get me some water from the well? I'm sorry to ask you to go outside in the cold, but...'

'As if I cared for the cold!' said Sarah with passionate scorn, and took the jug and went.

As Sarah's footsteps retreated, Araminta said: 'I'm very glad indeed to see you, Lucy-Anne. There's strength in you, more than you suppose. I have such a pain in my stomach when I even try to eat, and if I pass anything I bleed and ... I know what it means and I know I must accept what there's no help for, but oh God, I'm so afraid!'

Exhaustion, soft and heavy as a fall of snow, descended on Lucy-Anne but she pushed it away and put her arms around Araminta. 'Oh, Mrs Whitmead, please don't weep so.'

'I can't help it and I need to weep. Let me cry,' said Araminta.

By the time she reached her bed that night, Lucy-Anne was dazed with worry and tiredness. She was not herself feeling very well, and in addition to that, she must, it seemed, look after Araminta, and also cope with Stephen Clarke, who had sent a note up to the house saying that he would wait on her in the morning. She would have to give him George's new instructions. She must read George's memorandum through again and make sure she had everything right.

She fell thankfully asleep between the sheets that great-aunt Henrietta had had embroidered in each corner with a little picture of a bridge across a river, and was frankly relieved to know that she would not be awakened, quite likely in the small hours, by George's weight on top of her, his knees pushing her thighs apart and his tongue searching for hers.

She woke early, put on her dressing robe and went to Araminta's room, where she found Sarah distractedly straightening the bedclothes over a patient who was obviously very ill indeed.

'I'm getting the physician back,' said Lucy-Anne decisively. 'Meanwhile, let's just try that febrifuge of mine again. There is some left, I take it, Sarah?'

'Half of a bottle, ma'am.'

48

'Bring it here. Then send the groom for the doctor.'

Sarah hurried away. Lucy-Anne made her mother-in-law as comfortable as she could, trying to conceal her own distress. Giving way wouldn't help. Irritation presently replaced sorrow, however, since Sarah failed to come back. Eventually, Lucy-Anne went to the stillroom to find her.

She heard the wrangling voices even before she reached the door. She pushed it open and Maria, clutching a small jar, turned to her instantly for support.

'Ma'am, one of the maids – Polly – 'as a bad cold and Mrs Cobham asked me to get something for it from the stillroom, and I see there's things been used while we've been away and more than that, bottles have been moved about and—'

'I've had to come here for things to help Mrs Araminta. What if I did shift a bottle or two about? I had to pick them up to look at the labels, didn't I? If I didn't put them back *exactly* as they were before, the world'll hardly come to an end—'

Lucy-Anne boiled over into fury. 'How dare you? How dare the two of you quarrel like this when Mrs Araminta is ill? The moment my husband is out of the house, you go back to your old ways, it seems. I will not put up with it. Maria, I once threatened to turn you off. I may do it yet, so take care. Sarah, go at once and send the groom for Dr May and tell him to say it's urgent and he's not to come back unless the doctor's with him. Then go at once to Mrs Araminta. Maria, take that potion to Polly and tell her to stay in bed – I don't want her sneezing all over the rest of us. Then attend me in my room; I have to get dressed ready to interview Mr Clarke this morning. Are you going, Sarah, or do I have to see the groom myself?'

Both the maids, looking horrified, fled to carry out their errands. Lucy-Anne carried the horehound and the febrifuge to Araminta and coaxed her to take them, staying with her until a subdued Sarah returned. Then, militantly, she went to her room where a very anxious-to-please Maria was waiting for her.

While Maria did her hair and helped her into a hooped sacque, Lucy-Anne preserved a tight-lipped silence but presently relented, partly because anxiety and anger had made her feel queasy. 'I'm not going to turn you off this time, Maria, but I want no more of this trouble in the household. We have more important things to think of – mainly Mrs Whitmead's illness. Sarah is with her now. While I am downstairs, you will fetch and carry for her and Mrs Araminta as required, and you will do so willingly. You understand?'

'Yes, ma'am.'

'Good.'

Ignoring the queasiness as best she could, Lucy-Anne presently went down to breakfast and cautiously tackled a roll and a cup of coffee. But she found it best to take the meal slowly, and by the time she had finished Stephen Clarke had arrived.

'I asked him to wait in the parlour, madam,' Fraser said. 'But would you prefer to see him in the master's study?'

'No, the parlour will do very well. I'll come now.'

She had dressed plainly, with no jewellery beyond a single strand of pearls and her wedding ring. A white linen cap partly hid the brown curls so carefully constructed by Maria. The effect was to be one of dignity and propriety, with nothing frivolous about it.

Five minutes into the interview, she knew that she had been wise to come, so to speak, wearing armour. Stephen Clarke was going to be awkward.

There he stood, his crinkly hair tied back in its workmanlike fashion, and his hat respectfully in his hand, but his brown coat with its patched elbows said that he was too busy for parlour manners and had presented himself only as a courtesy, and if the hazel eyes were kindly enough, it was the half-impatient kindliness of an adult humouring the pretensions of a schoolgirl. And the first thing he did was question her instructions.

'Mrs Whitmead, I can assure you that before Mr Whitmead left Chestnuts, we talked at length about the final plans for the grounds. Mr Whitmead had had several new ideas and we went into those in detail before deciding on a contractor, which was of course why the decision wasn't made until it was nearly time for him to leave. But it definitely *was* made, and Mr Frederick Palmer of Guildford was chosen on my recommendation as being the most economical.'

Lucy-Anne, seriously regretting the coffee and the roll, seated herself in front of her writing desk, and then regretted that too, because she must now look up at Mr Clarke, which was tiresome.

'I don't doubt what you say, Mr Clarke. But my husband thought it over on the journey to London and changed his mind. It seems that he had heard an adverse report of the work of Mr Palmer. He told me that he would prefer us to hire Mr Sanders from Farnham. He will not be at all pleased if I have to write to him and say that you refuse to carry out his orders.'

'There's no question of my refusing to carry out his orders, providing I am sure that they genuinely are his. Where were you when he told you this?'

'On the deck of the *Winchester*. But that is hardly important. My husband—'

'Forgive me, Mrs Whitmead. But that must have been a moment full of emotion, and ships' decks are windy. Are you sure you did not mishear him? We did consider Sanders; he may simply have mentioned that we did so, and—'

'—*my husband*,' said Lucy-Anne, raising her voice, 'wrote all his instructions down in a memorandum which he left for me to study at my leisure. I very much regret that I am obliged to prove to you that what I say is true, but the letter is here on my desk.' She produced it and handed it to him. 'You may read the paragraph for yourself. There it is – the second on the page.'

Clarke took the memorandum, scanned it, folded the paper and handed it back to her with a slight bow.

'I must ask your pardon, Mrs Whitmead.'

Lucy-Anne took a deep breath. 'Mr Clarke, I am aware that to you I must seem very young. But I am not entirely foolish. There is of course much that I do not know and must still learn. But I would not tell you that I am passing on instructions from my husband, unless I were sure that they really were his instructions.'

There was a brief silence, while Stephen Clarke visibly wondered whether to be chagrined or not. Then, to Lucy-Anne's immense relief, his smile shone out – the friendly smile she had glimpsed during the discussion about the turnip crop.

'No, I see that. Can I,' he asked engagingly, 'make a new start? I'll begin by hiring Sanders immediately. Was there anything else?'

'Nothing of immediate importance.' She was thankful that that was over, but she didn't feel any better. A giddiness had set in and she couldn't see Clarke's face clearly. If she didn't get out of this room soon, something dreadful would happen. 'If you will forgive me, Mr Clarke, my mother-in-law is ill and I should go to her. But perhaps you would call on me again at the same time the day after tomorrow? If you pull the bell,' said Lucy-Anne, holding off disaster by the exercise of will-power she hadn't known she possessed, 'you can ask for refreshments before you leave, if you would like them. Please do so. I don't want you to think me discourteous, even though ... I'm so sorry, Mr Clarke, but I really must ... must get back to ... Mrs Araminta ...'

She got out of the room. She climbed the stairs. They felt as though they were melting under her feet. She reached her bedchamber and fell rather than lay down on the bed. She came to, to find Maria was peering worriedly down at her.

'Ma'am, whatever's wrong?'

Lucy-Anne sat up cautiously. 'I think I fainted.'

'But you've never done that before! Oh, ma'am, are you ill? It's not the same as what Mrs Araminta's got, is it? When the physician comes to see her, had you better see him too?'

'Perhaps I had.' Lucy-Anne smiled. 'But I haven't got Mrs Araminta's illness. Far from it! You needn't worry, Maria. Oh, surely you've noticed? I'm more than a week late.'

'A baby? Oh, my dear. George will be so pleased. So I'm to be a grandmother. I hope, oh, I pray to God,' said Araminta, 'that I live long enough to see the child born.'

Chapter Four

Running Aground

'I pray to God that I may live long enough to see the child born.' Never, thought Lucy-Anne, stumbling through the nightmare days that followed, never before was a prayer so unwise. Long before her own waistline had increased enough to prove that a new life lay beneath it, it was clear that Araminta's life was ending, and in pain so horrific that Lucy-Anne, who had grown to love her mother-in-law, now learned that there were circumstances in which one might pray for the death of somebody one loved – circumstances in which death was the only kindly thing to wish for them, and in which they too prayed aloud for it to come.

It did not help that her pregnancy was difficult. As her changing body fired off one chemical salvo after another, she reeled through bouts of nausea and faintness and a continual desire to curl up and sleep and be free of the burden of Araminta's sickroom.

For the burden was huge, remorselessly filling the nights as well as the days. Lucy-Anne and Sarah and Maria took turns as best they could, watching by the bedside, desperately offering water, milk, broth, wine, as long as Araminta could swallow any of it, holding her hands when the pain overwhelmed her, crying with her.

Dr May, large, compassionate and nearly as helpless as they were, came and went, shaking his head, but did at least provide them with laudanum, some of which they managed to get into Araminta's system to hush the anguish. But often her inability to accept anything by mouth defeated them and then she would lie on her side, weeping hopelessly, continually drawing up her knees to her stomach as if trying to ease herself by a change of position, as if trying to curl up and return to an imaginary womb.

The sickroom stank and Lucy-Anne repeatedly had to flee the room, ashamed of her weakness, but afraid for her child. The unborn were vulnerable; what if she harmed her baby by exposing it to such loathsome influences?

In between times, somehow, she ordered meals, checked accounts, told Mrs Cobham to buy extra candles ('We use so many, because we must keep Mrs Araminta's room lit all night') and received the reports on the estate that Stephen Clarke made each week. He informed her that Mr Sanders was competent and that repairs had been done to the Craddocks' cottage roof. He persuaded her not to press for the rent on another cottage because everyone in it had been ill and unable to pick the vegetables and make the butter that provided most of their income.

'But they're honest and they'll catch up; it's worth showing consideration to good tenants like that.' He showed her bills for seed and fodder and horseshoes and a new plough, and told her that the first turnips had been planted.

'The turnips are a very interesting experiment. I shall make every effort to see that it succeeds. Is there any word from Mr Whitmead yet?'

'Not yet. But it hasn't been very long. I have written, of course.'

'How is Mrs Araminta?'

'No better, I'm afraid.'

'Yes.' Clarke studied her thoughtfully. 'I imagine you might well be.'

'How do you mean?'

'I mean you might well be afraid. Serious illness is always frightening, and above all when the person is someone you depend on as I feel sure you depend on Mrs Araminta. The care of Mr Whitmead's property is a considerable weight for you to carry. Something similar happened to my mother, when I was about ten. She was left a widow, with no one to advise her and an estate – smaller than this but still quite a responsibility – to administer.'

'What happened?' Lucy-Anne asked.

'She was swindled by a bailiff,' said Stephen dryly. 'Then she ran up debts and there were some bad harvests. In the end, she sold up to pay off various loans, and bought a small house in Farnham. She was fairly happy there, but it must have seemed strange to her. She died some years ago.'

'I'm sorry. Is that why you became a bailiff yourself?' Lucy-Anne asked. 'So as to be an honest one? Is that why you want me to wait for the Milners' rent?'

'I've never thought of it in that way before.' Stephen was surprised. 'I went into it because I'd learned something about it as a boy and I felt drawn to it – I had a gentleman's classical education but I've always preferred practical things. I'd sooner read account books than Latin. But yes, perhaps I did choose my calling partly to make up for that damned – oh, I beg your pardon, Mrs Whitmead.'

'It's quite all right,' said Lucy-Anne, amused for the first time in weeks. She had graver matters to worry about than a stray swear word.

In the midst of it all came the news from London that great-uncle Matthew had died, though with merciful quietness, in his sleep, without even a warning illness. Lucy-Anne grieved for him and because she could not attend his funeral. But even if she had felt equal to the journey, she couldn't have left Araminta. On the day that great-uncle Matthew was buried Lucy-Anne was on duty in the sickroom, washing Araminta and with Maria's help changing yet another set of horribly soiled bedlinen, while Sarah, exhausted after being up all night, snatched some sleep. The burden could not be put aside, even for another death.

But the end was coming. Stephen Clarke, a restless sleeper, often woke in the small hours and had several times looked up at Chestnuts, on the flank of the hill, and seen the gleam of the candles in Mrs Araminta's room. But when he found himself awake at three on a late April morning and glanced out at his employer's house to see lights not in just one window but in half a dozen, he knew that some new crisis had broken.

Such domestic affairs were hardly the bailiff's business, and although Mr Whitmead was away, his wife was scarcely alone. She had Fraser and Mrs Cobham to turn to, both of them mature and sensible, and a staff of active footmen and maids, plus Silas the coachman and a couple of grooms to run whatever errands were required. Even the most conscientious and sympathetic bailiff could legitimately go back to sleep. If he had a devout turn of mind, he could say a prayer for poor Mrs Araminta before doing so. No one would ask more of him and if he offered more it could even be thought intrusive.

Stephen Clarke was well aware of all this. But young Mrs Whitmead had begun to impress him. She had amused him at first. She was so young and inexperienced that she seemed like a child pretending to be a woman. But since then he had watched her learning how to fill her new position, forcing herself to grow up, and he had found himself admiring her.

But despite all her efforts, she was still young, and vulnerable. She might even be in the family way. Mrs Ross at Upwood Farm sometimes talked to the maids at Chestnuts and she thought so; he'd heard her saying as much to her husband. Servants were all very well, but had Mrs Whitmead anyone to help her who really felt for her as an individual and not just as their employer's wife?

No, he couldn't possibly turn over and go back to sleep. He got out of bed, reaching quickly for his clothes. Presently, lantern in hand, he was hurrying out of the house. The night was very dark, with ground mist drifting through the patch of wood on the lower slopes of the hill. It was the hour when people most easily let go of life. He made haste through the wood, cut through the garden and knocked on the back door of Chestnuts.

The knock was answered by a fully dressed and tearful Mrs Cobham.

'Mr Clarke!'

'I saw the lights. Is it Mrs Araminta? And can I do anything – ride for the doctor, or be of use in any way?'

'The grooms are both out now, scouring Guildford for Dr May,' said Mrs Cobham. 'They went hours ago. He must be out on a call somewhere else, not that it matters. There wasn't a mortal thing he could have done if he had been here. No point in you going after them or him, not now. But it was kind of you to come. Come in. The mistress will appreciate it, I'm sure. Mrs George Whitmead, I mean. She's the only mistress now. Mrs Araminta . . .'

Mrs Cobham's voice faltered. Stepping into the kitchen, Stephen put a hand on her stout shoulder and found it uncharacteristically shaking.

'Half an hour since. Oh, dear God.'

'Steady, now, Mrs Cobham. Perhaps . . . well, from all I've heard . . . Mrs Araminta herself may . . . have been glad.'

'I know that. I keep telling myself that. But the end was— I'm just putting together some hot soup that Mrs Whitmead's asked for. "You sit there in the drawing room and I'll fetch it to you," I told her. We've sent the maids to bed. I had to give Sarah a dose of laudanum, she was in such a state. They've had a terrible time. We all have. Fraser's well-nigh dead on his feet.'

'Mrs Cobham?' Lucy-Anne spoke tremulously from the door. She too was dressed, but haphazardly, with no hoops under her gown, and a fringed shawl thrown anyhow around her shoulders. 'Who is it? I heard voices . . . Mr Clarke?'

'I saw the lights,' Stephen said briefly. He glanced sidelong through the door into the pantry and saw Fraser slumped on a chair, his head propped against a doorpost. He was asleep. 'Sit down, Mrs Cobham. I'll see to the soup. I'm quite useful in the kitchen. It comes of doing for myself. I think a drop of brandy would do Mrs Whitmead no harm – or you, either. Where is it kept?'

'There's a decanter and glasses in the dining room,' Lucy-Anne said. 'Yes, bring it. We'll all have some.'

'Go back to the drawing room, Mrs Whitmead. Mrs Cobham and I will see to it all.'

Brisk and wideawake, Stephen assembled decanter and glasses, stirred the soup and virtually willed it into bubbling, filled a bowl, found a spoon. He did not want any himself and Mrs Cobham shook her head at it. 'I couldn't. Turned me right up, tonight has. But it's a good thing Mrs Whitmead wants some. She's eaten nothing since dinner and not much then. All this trouble isn't good for her.'

'Is she expecting, by any chance?'

Mrs Cobham nodded vigorously. 'She is indeed and now, just when a young wife needs peace and quiet, she has all this to put up with. I'm that sorry for her.'

It was no wonder that the lights in Chestnuts had attracted his attention when he woke, for in the drawing room, every single candle was lit but no one had thought of closing the curtains. The night stared blackly in, at a room where a small fire had been hastily kindled in the hearth, and where the social rules had gone overboard, for Stephen and Mrs Cobham stayed to keep Lucy-Anne company, as though the drawing room were the most natural setting in the world for the bailiff and the cook-housekeeper; and Lucy-Anne, sitting exhaustedly by the fire with one hand resting protectively on her stomach, was obviously glad to have them.

'Where is Fraser?' Lucy-Anne asked as Stephen pulled a small table near her and placed the soup and a glass of brandy on it.

'Asleep in his pantry.' Stephen filled two more glasses. 'We thought it best not to disturb him.'

'No, I'm sure you're right. Oh, what a night! We couldn't get hold of the doctor, but he couldn't have helped her anyway. If you saw an animal suffer like that, you'd put it down.'

'There was no mercy for her.' Mrs Cobham sat clutching her brandy glass as if for support. 'She couldn't lose consciousness. She suffered and suffered all the way to the very edge of death. She cried to God to let her go and he wouldn't . . . he wouldn't . . . she was so gentle and harmless. What had she ever done to anyone . . . ?'

'Mrs Cobham,' said Lucy-Anne, 'for goodness' sake drink that brandy. You need it.'

Mrs Cobham obeyed, and almost at once tilted her head against the back of her chair and fell asleep like Fraser.

'She was very fond of my mother-in-law,' said Lucy-Anne in a low voice. 'She has been up and down the stairs about a hundred times today, trying to help, asking if Mrs Araminta needed anything, or if I did. She—'

Her voice cracked. Hurriedly, she sipped at her glass and began to spoon soup into her mouth. Stephen said nothing, but let her recover herself undisturbed and quietly swallowed his own brandy. When she had finished, however, he said: 'You should get to bed, Mrs Whitmead. Forgive me if I speak too boldly – but you should at present be taking care of yourself, should you not?'

Lucy-Anne laid her spoon in the bowl. 'You mean I'm increasing, as the saying goes?' she said, trying to smile.

'I've heard so, yes,' Stephen said.

'Well, it's true enough. But I can't go up yet. When the grooms get back they'll probably have the doctor with them. He'll have to have a glass of something after riding out so far. I can't go to bed till I've seen him.'

'I came to help if I could,' said Clarke. 'Well, I can do this for you. I'll sit up for him. Here.' From a side table he picked up a branched candlestick holding two lit candles and handed it to her. 'You go upstairs now. Leave the doctor to me.'

'Thank you.' Lucy-Anne took the candlestick and dragged herself out of her chair. 'You're sure? You must be tired too. You've had a day's work.'

'Not like yours, I suspect, and I've had some sleep already. Yes, of course I'm sure.'

'You're very kind.' She moved towards the door and he opened it for her. There were more candles in the sconces of hall and stairs but there was no sign yet of dawn and between the pools of light the shadows were dense. A little wind shivered through the house and made the yellow flames flicker. Lucy-Anne stopped and turned to him. The pupils of her eyes were wide, so that her eyes seemed to be more black than grey.

'What is it?' Stephen asked.

'I can't go up the stairs,' Lucy-Anne whispered. 'Not in the dark. She's up there, lying on her bed. All that pain is still in the room.'

'I'll light you to your door. Are there lights in your room? And a supply of fresh candles?'

'Yes.'

'Keep them burning until daybreak, and use all the new ones you want.' She still looked scared, so much so that it was all he could do not to put comforting arms round her. Since this was out of the question, he offered practical help instead.

'Someone should watch by her. It's a good old custom and I approve of it. I'll sit beside her until the doctor comes, or else until dawn. Will you feel safe then?'

'You must think me so foolish,' Lucy-Anne said. 'But I would, indeed I would. I'm very grateful.'

She climbed the stairs with Clarke protectively behind her, dispelling the fear from the shadows, and pointed out Araminta's door. 'It's there. And thank you, Mr Clarke.'

Once in her room, she followed his advice, lighting fresh candles which would not gutter out before daybreak. Then she changed into her nightgown and crept into bed.

Stephen Clarke must think she was a very poor thing, to be afraid of the dark because Araminta's torment was over and she was lying up here in peace. Tomorrow she would feel ashamed. But just now she was too tired to worry about it, and anyway it could have been much worse.

He didn't know – and he must never, never know – how, down there in the drawing room, the concern in his eyes had made her long to throw herself into his arms. For that one moment, another image had actually blotted out the horror of Araminta's death.

George had forbidden her to attend public balls or assemblies, no doubt fearing that in his absence she might be drawn to other men. But the greatest danger was here, in his own home. In that moment, in her mind, she had seen herself holding Stephen Clarke and being held by him, not in mere kindness, but in love; and she had longed to know what that brown, crinkly hair would feel like beneath her fingers.

Robert Clive was in George Whitmead's eyes a somewhat brash youngster, and George Whitmead was in Clive's opinion much more pompous than a man of only thirty was entitled to be. But Clive wanted to know more about the life that lay ahead of him and George Whitmead took pleasure in instructing his juniors, and the fact that Mr Clive had held Mr Whitmead's head while the latter gave way to seasickness had created a curious sort of bond.

Also, they were both lonely. There were no other passengers of George's status, and although Clive was technically travelling in the company of a cousin and two friends, all setting out, like himself, to be writers to the East India Company in Madras, they were in one of the companion vessels. The two clerks who were aboard the *Winchester* were brothers who preferred each other's company to his.

'Accommodation on these ships is so limited. One of us had to travel separately from the rest and we thought it best if I split up from my cousin,' Clive said. 'Then if one of us should be lost at sea, the other might survive and the family be less afflicted. We tossed to see who should travel alone, and I lost.'

Normally, an established merchant and a Councillor of the East India Company like George, and a mere clerk whose employment with the company had scarcely begun like Robert Clive, would not have been much in each other's company even in the cramped conditions aboard ship and even if they had been kindred spirits.

As it was, however, they found themselves quite often seeking each other out. Clive asked questions and George answered them; George invited his young friend to an occasional game of cards. Over dinner they were companionably rude about the standard of the cooking, and from time to time, when the weather permitted, they sauntered together on deck.

The weather frequently didn't permit. As they buffeted their way towards the equator, the *Winchester* and her companion vessels continued to meet storms and contrary winds. One ship, though fortunately not the one containing Clive's cousin William King and their two friends, was lost on the shoals of Cape Verde. As the little fleet began to forge its way across to Brazil in search of the winds that would carry it eastwards again round the tip of Africa, the mood on all the vessels was serious and, although Clive displayed no sign of fear, he was obviously impatient with their slow progress and the long confinement on the *Winchester*. During this part of the voyage, he and George both grew short-tempered, sometimes with each other.

'Young Mr Clive may do well in the end, I do not say otherwise,' said George to Captain Steward, on a day when he and Clive had actually had an argument and parted in a mutual huff. 'But he must learn to apply himself. He thinks only of such things as freedom and adventure. He did not care for being informed that he is as yet just a restless boy, but he is.'

'He's bloody awkward with his feet and elbows,' said Steward. 'Can't walk into a cabin without knocking into something. Good thing most of the furniture is bolted down. He'd be a menace in a lady's drawing room.'

Clive on his side had sought out one of the livelier seamen as, for the moment, better company than George, and was complaining that Mr Whitmead was such a prosy lecturer that it would be a pleasure to push him overboard.

'He's spent half the morning solemnly warning me that I have too many romantical notions, and that in Madras everyone has to work for their pay, through the heat of the day regardless, and Councillors like himself often sort cloth with their own hands. In Madras as in London, he said, cloth is cloth, and it is hard work and respect for one's elders that leads to success. For God's sake! One of the reasons I wanted to come to India was to get away from all the pomposity you find in England. The older men there all want to keep the younger ones down. And from what George Whitmead says, it'll be no better in India. Bah!'

'But you spend a lot of time talking to him,' said the seaman shrewdly. 'I've seen you walking with him on deck, time and again. Why'd that be, if you don't like him?'

'Well, he can be interesting,' Clive conceded. He frowned, dark brows drawn together. 'It's a strange thing,' he said, 'but I sometimes feel that, secretly, he isn't as prosy as he tries to appear. When I get him to describe India – not the work of the Company, but India itself – his manner changes. He won't admit it, but I think he loves the place.'

They had put their disagreement behind them within a few days. George still wanted the pleasure of imparting information and Clive was still greedy to acquire it. As renewed gales once more drove the passengers into the smelly heat below decks, instructive conversation again proved useful as a way of passing time.

'Before I left London,' Clive said, as they sat on in the dining saloon after one of the *Winchester*'s indifferent meals was over, 'I heard that the French East India Company was becoming a serious challenge to English interests. Is that true, Mr Whitmead?'

'The French are a constant trouble to us,' George agreed, rather loudly, so as to be heard above the wind. The gale was worsening and, somewhere above them, orders were being shouted to shorten sail again. 'While I was in England,' said George, 'I heard that there was a new Governor-General in charge of the French trading company, a man called Joseph Dupleix. He is said to be very able. But I also heard that he does not wish to provoke any conflict with us, which is heartening.'

The ship rolled heavily. Glasses and plates jiggled against each other. Damp cloths had been laid to discourage them from sliding far, but one plate still fell off and shattered on the saloon floor. Clive shot out a hand and, deftly for once, stopped a second from following it.

'Dupleix's attitude,' said George, 'suggests that he does not think that in such a conflict the French would prevail. A very proper conclusion for them to reach! They lack the resources that we possess – sea forces in particular. It is hoped that we shall in due course drive them out—'

The ship shuddered. There was a reverberating thud and the rolling unexpectedly ceased. But a flurry of shouting broke out overhead, and Clive shot to his feet.

'Wait!' said George sharply. 'We should do nothing until we receive the captain's orders.'

'We're *aground*! Come on, Mr Whitmead. We've got to get on deck! If the ship's holed . . .'

George, galvanised, got up. Side by side they flung themselves across what was now a steady but weirdly slanting floor towards the companionway. At the foot of it, George pushed in front. 'I don't believe we are sinking. Let us remember our dignity. Elders first, young man.'

Clive was obliged to climb out of the hatch behind George, his urge to speed blocked by Mr Whitmead's well-padded rear end. They emerged at last into a driving wind laden with cold spray. Someone was bellowing orders to lighten ship by jettisoning cargo, and sails were being brought down with a rush. The *Winchester* was lodged on a sandbank, within sight of the eastern coast of Brazil but quite beyond hope of reaching it. She was listing heavily while the waves broke over her hull and swirled dangerously along the sloping deck.

Clive ever afterwards believed that it was George's ponderous talk of captain's instructions and letting one's elders go first (however slowly) that kept him from leaving the saloon fast enough to see, before it was too late, that among the items of cargo a couple of frightened sailors had rushed to throw overboard were several pieces of the passengers' luggage, including a box of his own clothes.

Clinging grimly to the rail and watching while his belongings sank into the Atlantic, Clive wondered whether George Whitmead was after all quite lacking in imagination or – really, it seemed more probable! – was slightly crazy.

Chapter Five
The Barren Vista

'I'm sorry, Sarah.' Lucy-Anne spoke as kindly as possible and wished the parlour fire hadn't lately taken to smoking. It undermined one's dignity to have a fit of coughing in the midst of a difficult interview like this. 'I've given you time to look for another situation, but since you haven't found one why not accept the post Mrs Bird has suggested, with her sister-in-law? It may not be exactly what you want . . .'

It certainly wouldn't be. Once, when dining at the Birds' vicarage with George, Lucy-Anne had met Mrs Bird's sister-in-law. Mrs Miller was a commanding woman who took pride in being 'most particular' and 'keeping up the household due to her position', but, as her position was that of wife to a Farnham gentleman of good breeding but modest means, her employees had to put up with modest remuneration, and worked hard for it. Few of them stayed long, and vacancies were frequent. The post offered to Sarah was that of maid both to Mrs Miller and to her eldest daughter. Double duty was never a sinecure.

But it was a post. 'I'm grateful to you, ma'am, for interesting yourself in me.' Sarah stood there, twisting her hands together just as she had done three weeks ago when Lucy-Anne first told her that she must leave. 'I'll do as you say; I've no choice. There's no place for me now that Mrs Araminta is dead and buried. There are times when I wish that God in his mercy would call me so that I could be dead and buried too. It's no joke, ma'am, to be growing older and have no certainty of a roof over one's head in old age.'

'Oh, come now, Sarah! You're not old yet and when you are – surely you've family you can go to?'

'I've no family, ma'am. I don't know who my parents were. I was a workhouse brat.'

'Sarah!' The fire belched smoke again and Lucy-Anne flapped an exasperated hand to waft it away. 'You mustn't call yourself names.'

'I'm not,' said Sarah flatly. 'That's what the overseer at the workhouse called us. We were just brats, hardly worth feeding, that's what he used to say. Half of us died before we were old enough to be apprenticed. I was lucky; I was strong, and when I was put out to a trade, as a sempstress, I got a decent mistress. Most orphan apprentices are no better than slaves, but my mistress taught her girls properly, reading and writing too, so later on I could work myself up to be a proper lady's maid. But where I'll be when I'm old . . . back in the workhouse, as likely as not.'

'I'm extremely sorry,' said Lucy-Anne inadequately.

But sorry or not, she couldn't keep Sarah any longer, couldn't even consider finding her other work in the household. In George's absence it seemed impossible to stop her from constantly criticising Maria. Grief for her mistress, and jealousy because Maria now had a secure job while she had not, had made her worse, and Maria could not be blamed for sometimes answering back. In the interests of peace, Sarah must go.

'I shall give you an excellent reference, I promise,' Lucy-Anne said. 'Perhaps you will find a post you like better, later on.'

'Thank you, ma'am,' said Sarah, while her hands went on twisting with tension and her eyes burned with resentment at Lucy-Anne's power over her – Lucy-Anne, who was not yet eighteen and was settled for life in a comfortable home.

'Oh, hell,' said Lucy-Anne to the air, after Sarah had gone, and was surprised at herself. As a girl at home she would never have dreamed of using such language.

The next task of the day was not much pleasanter than dealing with Sarah. One of Sarah's complaints against Maria was that the girl flirted with the footmen and, however rude and tactless Sarah might have been, the accusation had substance in it. Lucy-Anne had herself seen Maria and the youngest footman, Percy, snatching a kiss.

Maria, then, must be summoned and warned. 'Now, if Percy is courting you honestly, I've nothing against it,' Lucy-Anne said. 'But I don't want any scandals in the house. I shall speak to Percy, too.'

'Oh no, ma'am, please don't do that! I'd be that embarrassed. Percy don't mean anything. I know he ain't – isn't – serious.'

'If you know that, then I advise you not to encourage him. All right, Maria, off you go.'

She let Maria get well out of sight and then spoke to Percy anyway. When a chastened young footman – candidly warned that if he led Maria into trouble he would find himself marrying her whether he liked it or not – had gone back to his work she sat down at her desk, where two letters, as yet unopened, awaited her attention.

There seemed, she thought as she took up her little paperknife, to be no end to the things the lone mistress of Chestnuts had to do. George, with all his talk of cherishing her, had never envisaged this. He had thought she would have Araminta to help her.

But Araminta was in the churchyard of St Anne's at Southdene and Lucy-Anne must do without her. Lucy-Anne wondered where George was by now. Well into the south Atlantic, according to the itinerary he had given her. She felt uneasy about him, which worried her because feelings like that had a habit of proving to be right.

Her father had once told her that this knack of sensing things at a distance ran in the family. She wondered if George shared it. Certainly, he had the fox-coloured hair that was another family characteristic, capable of missing a generation and then reappearing. Her father had it too, although in Lucy-Anne it was muted to a faint patina when her own brown hair was freshly washed. Would her child have the Whitmead hair, or the Whitmead sixth sense, she wondered.

Shifting her position in order to ease an aching back, she took up one of the letters. She knew as soon as her fingers touched it that here was more trouble.

In fact, both the letters were trouble. The first was from the housekeeper who was looking after the town house with the help of a handyman and a maidservant. The handyman had taken to drinking gin and making unwanted advances to the maid and was suspected of pilfering. The housekeeper was empowered to hire and dismiss but did not know what to do with a hefty man who did not appear to know what the word *dismissed* actually meant.

The second letter was from a Taunton lawyer, to whom great-uncle Matthew had delegated the task of administering Henrietta's estate. Henrietta's will had provided for a monthly payment to an elderly servant called Dotty Larrimore. Dotty was still living in Broom Cottage, and the lawyer now wished for instructions about both Dotty and the cottage. Was the building to be sold or let, or was it to be left as it was with Dotty as caretaker? The will had also required that Dotty should be 'looked after', which presumably meant that if she had to leave the cottage somewhere else should be found for her.

Lucy-Anne sat for some time, trying to think it out. Should she go herself to the West Country? She didn't feel strong enough, although she supposed she could get to the town house and, since she was now George's representative, she supposed she must. Very well, she would go to London, but write to the Taunton lawyers with her instructions. Only, what should they be?

She didn't think she could sell the cottage without George's consent, and anyway what was to be done about this woman Dotty? Once again she longed for Araminta's advice. Well, she couldn't have it; she must decide for herself. In her mind, one thing at least slowly clarified. She didn't want the cottage sold. It had belonged to great-aunt Henrietta, and she felt a fondness for it without ever having seen it.

It could be kept and let, of course. Perhaps the tenants would take Dotty on as their servant . . . but how old was Dotty? 'I really ought to go and see for myself,' Lucy-Anne said aloud. 'But if I can't, then someone must go in my stead.'

Well, of course, there was Stephen.

Since the night of Araminta's death, she had avoided Stephen Clarke's company as much as possible. Of course he had no idea what shocking images had invaded her mind that night, but he had seen her in a moment of weakness and fear and it would be wise to keep her distance until the memory had faded, for both of them.

Clarke apparently felt much the same and kept his regular reports brief and formal. His announcement that the turnip planting was finished, and that Mr Ross was interested in trying the crop, was delivered from the far side of the room, in the monotonous tones of someone reading an exceptionally dull lesson in church. The news that a tree overhanging the lane had become unsafe and should be felled came over like something learned by rote.

He reported weekly, on Monday mornings, and never before had she sent for him in between. He came promptly, however, and Lucy-Anne handed him the letter from Taunton. 'Would you read this through, please? Then I'll explain why I needed to see you.'

He scanned the letter in his rapid way and then, going instantly to the kernel, said: 'You have to decide whether to sell or let, and there is also an aged servant whose future is your responsibility. Have you decided what to do?'

'Not entirely.' Lucy-Anne moved her chair to avoid another gust of smoke from the fire. 'I want to let the cottage but I don't know what to do about Dotty. She might stay on as a servant, going with the let, so to speak, but I don't know what her state of health is. If she stays on, we must make sure the tenants treat her well. My great-aunt would expect that. I want you to go to the West Country, call on the lawyers and see Dotty, and advise me on what is best.'

Stephen Clarke nodded. 'You will not object if I ride aside to Bath for a day or two and call on my sister? I see Julia very rarely.'

'Oh, by all means.'

'Thank you, Mrs Whitmead. I'd better keep this letter for the time being. I can leave tomorrow, if you like. I'll send word of my progress, of course.'

'Yes. I shall be in London for a few days, but I imagine I'll be back before your first letter arrives.'

'Oh? Is there trouble in the town house?' Lucy-Anne looked at him in surprise, and he said: 'I talk to Percy sometimes. His parents live near your town house and know the housekeeper. They wrote to him that a manservant there has turned out dishonest.'

'Dishonest and aggressive,' said Lucy-Anne, and passed the other letter to him.

He perused it as swiftly as the first and then laid it on the desk. 'Mrs Whitmead, if you wish, I will come to London with you and give you my support in dealing with this. I can ride on to Taunton after that. Are you intending to have this man taken up for theft? It may not be easy to get evidence, if he has disposed of what he took.'

'I don't want him hanged. I just want to get rid of him. I'll take a footman, of course. But,' said Lucy-Anne, knowing that any of the footmen would be adequate support and that she was simply yielding to the chance of Stephen's company, but unable to help herself, 'I would like the matter dealt with by myself and someone senior in my husband's employ. Thank you.'

'Not at all, Mrs Whitmead. And while you're out of the house,' said Stephen, 'you could get the chimneys swept.'

The journey was unpleasant. The weather was grey and windy and she felt ill all the way, so much so that they rested a night at the George Inn, south of London Bridge, instead of attempting to complete the whole drive in one day. Even so, the road seemed interminable. In the future there would be a more convenient bridge into London; despite the howls of rage from the City, which feared that it would lose business if people coming from south of the Thames had an alternative to London Bridge, a new bridge was being built, at Westminster. But as yet it was still a mass of scaffolding and half-raised piles, and to get George's lumbering four-horse carriage to Hanover Square meant an excursion via the City and then a westward journey through the congested streets of the ever-expanding town.

Trying to use the widest route for as long as possible, Silas took the coach along the Tyburn road and discovered too late that the death-cart, accompanied by its usual raucous and enthusiastic crowd, was on its six-weekly journey to the Tyburn gallows. He reined in to let it pass. Lucy-Anne peered out at the baying mob, some of whom were waving gin bottles while others peddled crudely printed doggerel about the condemned man. Amidst them all, whores not only touted for business but conducted it, backed up against any convenient wall. Lucy-Anne had seen such processions before, but always hated them. She couldn't see the death-cart itself and didn't want to. Even the thought of it was too much. To the alarm of Maria and the footman, she threw up out of the carriage window.

But Stephen had ridden on ahead to warn the housekeeper at Hanover Square that she was coming and once there she found her room in readiness and light refreshments waiting. The house was blessedly secluded from the racket of the Tyburn road – quiet and soothing. The trouble in the servants' quarters at least hadn't penetrated to the drawing room. She rested in the afternoon, took supper and retired early. She rose next day feeling considerably better and, with Stephen and a footman to back her up, more than equal to dealing with the handyman.

George had a study in this house too and Lucy-Anne sat at his desk in order to interview the offender, while Stephen and the footman, Arthur, stood behind her. At that hour in the morning the man had not had time to get what the housekeeper called his usual skinful and, judging from his bloodshot eyes and his evident dislike of the sunlight through the window, had a bad hangover. He hadn't shaved, either.

Lucy-Anne castigated his habits and appearance at length, before informing him that he was not the kind of employee who was suited to the house of a gentleman like Mr George Whitmead and telling him to be out of it before midday. He attempted to bluster, but Lucy-Anne stared at him with a hauteur she had never before known she could achieve, and Stephen said levelly: 'I believe some small articles have been missed from the house. Mrs Whitmead does not wish to be vindictive, but I think you should not provoke her.'

Lucy-Anne thought of the mob she had seen on the way into London, and turned her instinctive shudder to her own purposes. 'The penalty for theft,' she said, 'is the gallows. A thief was hanged yesterday. We passed a crowd of people going to watch. They were enjoying themselves so much.'

'Admirable,' Stephen Clarke said afterwards, when the objectionable handyman had slunk out of the house. 'You were quite admirable, Mrs Whitmead.'

Lucy-Anne glanced at him in surprise and then smiled.

'When I first came to Chestnuts,' she said, 'you took me to be just a schoolroom miss, playing at being a lady. Do you remember?'

'Mrs Whitmead! I hope I never said anything to suggest...'

'No, you didn't. But it was obvious enough to annoy me, if you recall,' said Lucy-Anne. 'And you were right – then. But since then... I think I've become older.'

'Perhaps by too harsh a route.' Stephen's voice was kindly. 'That was a bad time for you, when Mrs Araminta died.'

There was a brief pause, during which the memory of that night filled the room.

But it was not to be mentioned in words.

'I must instruct you further,' said Lucy-Anne, 'about Taunton and Broom Cottage. I believe that the cottage is actually some distance from the town...'

A visit to London meant an opportunity to call on her parents. Hugo and Lucilla were pleased to see her and more pleased still to hear that she was expecting a child, but were somewhat disturbed by her description of Araminta's passing and the difficult handyman. 'Got to take care of your health,' Lucilla said. 'I'm the last woman to make a to-do over what's natural, but you've got to be sensible too. When you're home again, make sure you rest.'

Lucy-Anne, putting aside the recollection of being sick out of the coach window, assured them that she felt perfectly well. But when she set out for Chestnuts once more, reaction set in. The so-called merry month of May was thoroughly disgracing itself. It was cold and overcast, and the journey began in heavy rain. This ceased later, but between Leatherhead and Guildford the carriage stuck twice in mud. Lucy-Anne began to feel queasy again. She was thankful when at last they turned down the lane and Chestnuts came into view. The horses were muddy to the hocks and the wheelers, which were growing elderly, were obviously tired, but they all pulled valiantly towards their stable. 'Nearly home,' said Lucy-Anne, thinking of hot chocolate and a rest on her bed.

Maria, peering from the window, said, 'Ma'am, whatever's that, sticking out of that chimney there?'

Lucy-Anne also peered out, craning her neck. 'I can't see... oh, yes I can. It's a sweep's brush, Maria. Well, I did tell Mrs Cobham to have the chimneys swept.'

At the front door, to her bewilderment, Lucy-Anne was met by Mrs Cobham and Fraser together, both of them anxious of face. The maidservant Polly was for some reason hovering behind them, exuding a curious, aghast excitement. 'Now, what in the world...?' said Lucy-Anne.

'We are very sorry, madam.' Fraser was mindful of his dignity. 'We had expected everything to be finished before you arrived, but...'

'Yes, indeed, Mrs Whitmead. Oh dear, and you'll be needing some hot food, but just at the moment... Polly, go and see if the drawing room is fit for Mrs Whitmead to sit in, at least...'

'There's no need to upset yourselves,' said Lucy-Anne. Fraser and Mrs Cobham looked more as if they had committed a crime than obeyed orders to carry out a commonplace if messy domestic duty. 'I'll go up and rest on my bed – or is my bedchamber under sheets as well?'

'Well, yes, madam, but they could be taken away in a trice. It isn't that. But it's cold and just now we can't light any fires. At least, Mr Hayes says we can, but I don't feel somehow that we should . . .'

'Why not? Fraser, whatever is the matter?' Lucy-Anne, with Maria at her heels, walked into the hall and looked round her. The house was cold and draughty and the chequered tiles of the hall were a mass of sooty footprints, as if a dozen chimney sweeps had been dancing there. 'Mrs Cobham, Fraser, just what is going on? It isn't just that the sweep's come, is it?'

'It's nothing that you need to trouble yourself with, madam,' said Fraser, just as Lucy-Anne's footman came up the steps with a couple of boxes. '*Arthur!* Don't put Mrs Whitmead's boxes down in all this muck. Put them in the porch! I don't know what Mr Whitmead would say if he were here—'

'Fraser, I demand to know—'

The door of the parlour opened, to reveal a room shrouded in old sheets, and a chimney sweep, so thoroughly sooty that his face appeared to consist only of eyes and teeth, came out. Since Mrs Cobham was between him and Lucy-Anne, he failed at first to notice the mistress of the house and informed Mrs Cobham that there was no luck in there, missus, and he was blamed if he knew where the little bleeder had got to.

'Please, Mr Hayes!' said Mrs Cobham, horrified.

Lucy-Anne stepped past her. 'I am Mrs Whitmead. I have just arrived home. I want to know what is happening in my house. Will you be good enough to tell me, Mr . . . er . . . Hayes, is it?'

'That's right, missus.' The sweep grinned and pulled a filthy forelock. 'Mr John Hayes, at your service, and very sorry to be inconveniencing you—'

'Have you lost something?' asked Lucy-Anne, 'Or someone?'

'I regret to say that such is the case, madam,' said Fraser, getting in before the sweep. 'But I'm sure that all will shortly be well. It is the reason, however, why Mrs Cobham and I feel that at the moment we can light no fires in the house—'

'Wouldn't do him no harm. Scorched feet might teach him to watch what he's doing in future. Begging your pardon, missus. Lost my boy, that's what,' said Hayes crossly. 'Stuck somewhere, that's what he'll be. I knew he were growing and I oughter turn him off and get a younger one, but, there, I'm that softhearted—'

'D'you mean,' Maria broke in, 'that you've sent a boy up into the chimneys to 'elp you clear 'em and he's got lost?'

'That's about it, begging your pardon for the upset. Last chimney of all, too. Wouldn't surprise me if the little bugger's just gone off to sleep up there; lazy as they come, these workhouse brats are. I'll half-kill him when I get him down—'

He broke off short. Somewhere in the house, muffled as though by layers of wall, was a quavering moan. Maria clutched at Lucy-Anne's arm. Lucy-Anne whitened. 'Is that him?'

'That's upstairs, that is.' Arthur cocked his head.

'Then we'll go up and see if we can make out just where. Come with me,' Fraser ordered.

They vanished up the stairs. The sweep turned back into the parlour and the others followed him, Lucy-Anne's high heels catching in the folds of the sheeting. Piles of soot lay in front of the hearth and brushes lay on the floor beside them. The sweep put his head up the chimney and shouted. The moan came again. Gooseflesh rose up on Lucy-Anne's arms. It was the voice, unmistakably, of a child.

'How old is he?' she asked.

'He would be perhaps ten, ma'am,' said Mrs Cobham. 'It's hard to tell.'

'Push yourself back and down! Come on, come out of there!' bellowed the sweep. 'I'll have your hide for this, you stupid little basket! Come *down*, I say!'

There was a distant knocking and a voice, which sounded like Arthur's, echoed hollowly in the flue. In response there was a scrabbling and a gasping sob. A shower of soot came down. There was another sob, fading out in a choking cough.

'He's trying to breathe soot, poor thing!' Maria exclaimed.

'You shouldn't be here, Mrs Whitmead.' Mrs Cobham was alarmed by Lucy-Anne's blanched face. 'You don't look well. Let me take you into the drawing room and—'

'I've got to stay. They're my chimneys. Oh, for the love of God!' cried Lucy-Anne, as a retching whimper full of desperate misery and fright drifted down. 'It's as if the house itself were crying. Get him *out* of there!'

'I'm trying, aren't I?' The sweep twisted his head at an impossible angle, in an attempt to peer up into the darkness. 'He's stuck by the sound of it. You stuck or just lorst your way, you little perisher? Answer me!'

The only reply was another agonised whimper. Arthur and Fraser came hurrying into the parlour.

'Madam, we think he's got himself jammed in a chimney behind the one for the big guest room. We can get at him easily enough – at least, I think so,' Fraser said. 'But it will mean making a hole in the back of the guest-room chimney.'

'We can't do that!' cried Mrs Cobham, scandalised. 'Knock the house about just for a sweep's climbing boy?'

Lucy-Anne put a hand on the mantelpiece to steady herself. She felt almost too tired to stand but she wasn't going to give way. 'By all means,' she said. 'Knock the house about. Do whatever needs to be done, but get that child out quickly.'

It took longer than they expected, since tools had to be found and the wall between the flues proved very resistant. The whimpering went on for a time while they were working but fell silent before they reached the boy. When he was at last lifted out, the limp, filthy body was quite dead.

Lucy-Anne gazed, appalled, at the signs of death by suffocation, the cyanosed face under the dirt, the mouth and nostrils choked with soot and vomit. She looked, too, at the ragged breeches and jerkin which did not hide the jutting ribs and stick-like limbs, and at the smears of blood where he had struggled against the imprisoning brick. Beside her, Maria was in tears.

'What was his name?' she said to the sweep.

'Name? Lord save you, missus, I just called him brat. That's what we allus call the pauper boys.' The sweep regarded the corpse with more exasperation than pity. 'And now I'll have to get another one. Still, he was growing, like I told you, so I'd have had to get another soon, anyways.'

'And if he'd lived, what would have happened to him? When he was too big to go up chimneys any more?'

'Oh, assistant to a sweep somewhere – not me, I don't need one. But some do. Could of done all right, in time, given a bit of luck. Now I'll have to bury the little halfwit.'

'No.' Lucy-Anne had now reached such a point of exhaustion that she seemed to be standing aside from herself, and her own voice sounded as though it came from a distance. 'We'll be responsible for that. Fraser, have word sent to Mr Bird. Explain. And someone wash this poor child and lay him out – in my parlour, that'll do—'

'But Mrs Whitmead. There's no need—'

'Don't argue, Mrs Cobham. Will you all just do as you're told! And now, please, will someone go and make my room ready for me? I want to rest.'

When she awoke next morning, she was feverish. At some time during the restless day that followed, with Mrs Cobham and a worried Maria anxiously hovering around her with medicines and enquiries over whether they should send for the doctor, she noticed that she had a pain in her stomach.

In the evening, she found that she was bleeding.

A summer day, full of sunshine and birdsong, was the wrong sort of day for writing such a letter as this, but Lucy-Anne, sitting at her desk in the parlour, looking out on the parterre garden which under Mr Sanders' skilled hands had bloomed into curving patterns of bright colour, knew that it had to be done. Her mother had said so very firmly. The brief pregnancy was proof that Lucy-Anne was capable of starting one and George, said Lucilla, had the right to know of it.

Reluctantly, Lucy-Anne dipped her pen and began.

My dear George

I hope all is well with you and that this letter will reach you soon after you arrive in India. What manner of voyage did you have? I think and worry about you constantly.

I must tell you that shortly after you left I found that there was hope of an heir for you. But since then, God has decreed otherwise. I was sadly unwell and Mrs Cobham sent for my mother, who kindly came to me to help me. But I have now recovered and my

69

mother has gone home. My father is not in good health, by reason of the bronchial humours from which he suffers so often . . .

She paused, realising that she had no idea how George would feel about the lost baby. Would he be grieved for the waste of a small life? Concerned for Lucy-Anne? Or angry that his hopes had come to nothing? She didn't know, but feared that anger was the most likely. That was a depressing thought. She dipped the pen again and passed to the next item. Unfortunately, this too was likely to annoy him.

At the present time, Mr Clarke is away in Somerset. Great-aunt Henrietta's lawyers wrote asking if Broom Cottage should be sold or let. I did not think I could sell without your consent and there is also an old servant of great-aunt Henrietta's, still at Broom Cottage, for whom, as you know, we must provide, under the terms of our great-aunt's will. I sent Mr Clarke to discover how best to achieve this. Unfortunately, a difficulty has arisen . . .

Dotty Larrimore was in her seventies, according to Stephen's first report, but she was still active and was violently opposed to leaving Broom, having known no other home since she was fourteen. 'Let the cottage,' said Lucy-Anne in her reply, 'but on condition that the tenants keep Miss Larrimore on. Please stay in the neighbourhood until you are sure all has been satisfactorily settled.'
Stephen's next letter, three weeks later, was exasperated.

I have now found suitable tenants twice over, for Broom Cottage. But neither could tolerate Miss Larrimore. It seems she wants everything done and kept as it was when Miss Henrietta Whitmead was alive and resents newcomers as intruders. She made their lives a burden to them with her complaints and both sets of tenants withdrew within a week. But she becomes hysterical at the suggestion that she should leave Broom Cottage. It is distressing to behold. May I respectfully suggest that for the time being the cottage should be left as it is, with Miss Larrimore in occupation to look after it?

Lucy-Anne had already written back agreeing, but she knew without asking that George would want to make money out of Broom Cottage and would not be much impressed by Dotty's hysterics. But she wished to fulfil not just the provisions, but the spirit of her great-aunt's will and could see no other way of doing so.
She raised her head, hearing a knock at the front door. Fraser's footsteps crossed the hall and there was a murmur of voices. Lucy-Anne laid down her pen. That was Stephen, surely. But he wasn't alone; there was another man's voice, deeper than Stephen's, and a woman's laughter. Then Fraser was at the parlour door.
'Mr Stephen Clarke is here, madam, accompanied by his sister and brother-in-law, Dr and Mrs Harper. Dr Harper is a clergyman. I have shown them,' said Fraser, faintly disapproving, 'into the drawing

70

room, as Mr Whitmead always requested me to do when they called.'

The disapproval, as Lucy-Anne well understood, was because, although Stephen Clarke was of sufficient status to be invited to dinner now and then, he was still only the bailiff, but a clergyman and his wife were guests of importance. Fraser's tone suggested that it was a little inconsiderate of them to be related to a mere bailiff, and that he hoped the latter wouldn't get above himself.   •

Lucy-Anne read the unspoken message and for the first time since that dreadful day when she had seen the body of the chimney sweep's boy brought out of the wall, and her own baby had started to die, she wanted to giggle. She checked herself, however, capping the ink-bottle in a brisk manner. 'I'll join them, then. Arrange some light refreshments, if you please.'

She found Stephen in conversation with a tall man in clerical dress. Edward Harper had an apparently grave face, which nevertheless had attractive laughter lines at the corners of the eyes. And on the sofa opposite was the most charming lady Lucy-Anne had ever seen.

Charming, not beautiful. Julia Harper had never been a beauty. She was in her early thirties, a square, solid lady, with the same blunt features as Stephen's, and an incipient double chin. She had large, capable hands and large feet in stout black shoes which did not go with her light sacque of cream cotton scattered with pink rosebuds.

But Julia's hazel eyes too had laughter lines at the corners and the eyes themselves were bright with friendliness. She rose as Lucy-Anne entered and, before Stephen could begin his introductions, cut in with: 'My dear Mrs Whitmead! Stephen has told us all about you. We are here on a visit to him – a little holiday for my husband, who is the hardest-working man one could ever imagine – and I am so happy to have the chance of meeting you.'

It wasn't that Lucy-Anne lacked female acquaintances. George had introduced her to a fairly wide circle of ladies. Some, like good-natured Mrs Bird, she liked; some, like Mrs Miller and Mrs Kendall, who were stiff and full of self-consequence, she didn't; while Mrs Ross, though amiable enough, couldn't be cultivated because she was the wife of a tenant. None of them, anyway, was under forty and none of them could she truly call a friend.

Julia would be here only for a short time. But Julia was of the breed which can maintain friendship across time and distance; Lucy-Anne knew it instantly, and knew too that friendship was on offer. Her hope of a child was gone and, until George returned, could not be renewed. In the barren vista ahead of her, she would need friends.

'And I,' said Lucy-Anne with sincerity, 'am so happy to have the chance of meeting *you*.'

Chapter Six

The Cottage and the Fort

It took a week to refloat the *Winchester*, and then such a contrary gale arose that it was all they could do to keep the ship from being blown back across the Atlantic. Four months passed before they could get her into Pernambuco for the repairs she so badly needed.

The Brazilian shipyards proved to be run on the principle of getting things done *mañana*. Yes, yes, the timber, the extra workmen, the new canvas, would be coming tomorrow. The new mast would be ready tomorrow. All would be done, senor, tomorrow, *mañana, mañana* . . .

The delay had made young Mr Clive so restless that while the ship creaked her way into her Brazilian shelter it was impossible to keep him off the deck, bad weather or no bad weather. 'You'll end by falling overboard,' prophesied Captain Steward gloomily. 'You're clumsy enough when the deck keeps still. I'll have to keep an eye on you.

He kept his word, to good effect. When Clive duly fulfilled expectations, lost his footing and toppled into the sea, it was Captain Steward who personally threw him a rope and dragged him back on board.

'Can't let you drown,' said Steward, as Clive rolled dripping to his feet. 'You owe me money.'

'I'll soon owe you more,' spluttered Clive, feeling his wet hair. 'I've lost my wig. I'll need another.'

In Pernambuco he was no less restless and George took him to task.

'You should make up your mind to pass the time in some improving fashion,' George pronounced. 'I can teach you some words of Indian dialects, my boy, if you want to learn. I may say I have made quite a study of such things, which is not just in the common way among Englishmen in India. Although Portuguese will be of more use to you in the work of trading. It is widely used even by the Indians, who cannot always understand each other's tongues.'

'I'll learn Portuguese,' Clive decided, and did.

'Fifteen months. It's taken us fifteen damned months to get here,' George Whitmead said, leaning on the rail of the anchored ship and staring across the Madras Roads to the land. 'This is June 1744. We ought to have been here last September. I daresay there will be a whole budget of letters waiting for me, that got here on ships which had a less eventful journey.'

'Letters from Mrs Whitmead, I expect, sir,' said Clive. Standing on the rail at George's side, he gazed at the coast with interest. 'I still don't quite understand why you didn't bring her out with you.'

Because George had helped him with his Portuguese, they had continued to spend time in each other's company during the long, dull days in Brazil and on the tedious voyage since. Their conversation, gradually, had become nearly as free as though they were of the same generation. George's description of his domestic arrangements had puzzled Clive a good deal.

'I told you why I didn t bring her, my boy,' George said. 'I want to protect her from the roving eyes of young bucks like you, and also from the sorry example set by certain ladies in Madras.'

'Indeed, I remember you saying as much, sir. But the more I think about it, the more strange it seems. There are young bucks in England, and plenty of ladies with questionable morals. Here, at least, she would have her husband by her side.'

'Oh, she is well guarded, I assure you. My mother is there to watch over her and they have the society of respectable local families. She promised me that she would not seek diversion beyond those boundaries and I have no fears for her.'

Clive was inclined to feel sorry for the unknown Mrs Whitmead. 'But you will miss each other,' he said.

'Marriage is not the whole of a man's life,' George said. 'I accept that, and so must she. In India, most ladies of standing live in seclusion. This is true among both the Mohammedans and the Hindus. I am inclined to think that we could learn something from them.'

'Yes, you have already described many of the customs of Indian society. But I must say I find the idea of a society in which female company isn't freely available quite appalling.'

'Exactly,' said George. 'And now you see why I am so anxious to protect my wife from male attentions.'

'I didn't mean necessarily to sleep with, sir. I meant to talk to, to dance with, to drive out with, to share dinners and musical evenings with.'

'You won't be deprived of such things in Madras,' George assured him. 'And my wife won't be deprived of them in England, either. But, in my opinion, she will be safer there.' He lost interest in the subject. 'Well, the sun's come up. It's time they got us ashore. You do know what you're looking at? That is Fort St George – my namesake fort. You will observe the battlements on the walls surrounding it. The church spire you can see beyond is St Mary's, where we shall worship. Most of our accommodation, as well as the Company's offices and warehouses, lies within the fort. On the north side there is a local town of sorts, with every kind of person crammed into its streets. They are even more noisome than the streets of London.'

'I believe I can smell something now.' Clive lifted his face to the breeze. 'It's strange. It's a mixture of the sweet and the rotten. I don't recognise it.'

'You will smell that everywhere,' said George. 'Dung and jasmine, rubbish and sandalwood. When you go home again, it will haunt you.'

Clive turned to him, a smile lightening his dark face. 'You *do* love the place, sir. I have thought so before.'

74

'Love it?' George snorted. 'It is a place in which to work, to make money, nothing more. But the smell lingers in the memory; I grant you that.'

Clive leaned over the rail again, once more gazing fixedly at the shore. George let out an admonishing harrumph. The boy looked eager, expectant, as though the fort and the yellow beach lined with palm trees and the dusty plains glimpsed beyond were positively exciting. Ah well. He'd learn.

George detested the process of landing. It involved a small rowboat which bounced crazily through the surf of the shallows between the anchorage and the shore, and then an undignified piggyback ride up the steep beach, clinging to the shoulders of one's boatman. That Clive appeared to enjoy it all was just one more sign of the lad's immaturity. At the top of the beach, however, there was for Clive and the other clerks only a noisy reception by Clive's cousin and the various friends who had travelled on one of the *Winchester*'s sister ships and had got to India first.

For George, Councillor of the East India Company, there was ceremony. He had brought no servant with him, but his Indian servants had been paid retaining wages and had awaited him in the Company bungalow on which he had kept up the rent.

While Clive and his companions waited for the boats to bring the luggage, which they would then have carried to their crowded hostel, George's personal man Ahmed produced bearers with orders to collect the sahib's luggage for him, and led his master away to the rickshaw that would take him at once to his well-swept and spacious bungalow.

Here, there was lukewarm water ready in which he could sluice off the sweat of travel, and he could smell food cooking. Once washed and dressed in clean clothes, he settled down in a chair on his verandah until the meal should be served, and Ahmed brought him a brandy and the expected package of letters which had overtaken him while the *Winchester* lay on her sandbank and languished in a Brazilian shipyard.

Ten minutes later his peace of mind was gone, lost in a flood of grief and fury.

His mother was dead. She had been dead for more than a year and he hadn't known, although the letter bearing the news had been sent off immediately after her burial.

And the one thing that might have comforted him, the coming into the world of another generation, had been briefly promised and then lost, and that was worse than if it had never been there at all. It was as though fate and Lucy-Anne had conspired to torment him.

For, according to the next letter, which bore a date in the previous June, he had after all left his wife with child, and she had miscarried. And on top of *that* – was there no relief to be found anywhere? – no profit could be made from the cottage Henrietta had left him because his wife had handed it over – rent-free! – to a crotchety old servant of Henrietta's! The only thing that had apparently gone right was a successful turnip crop!

He gulped his brandy down and bellowed for pen, ink, paper and more brandy. His servants, scuttling about to fetch them, wondered among themselves what had upset the sahib so. He'd been all right when he arrived.

At the end of August 1743, Mrs Kendall drove to Chestnuts in a chaise and, over the coffee that Lucy-Anne at once sent for, announced that her eldest daughter was to be married in early November and that Lucy-Anne would of course be invited. 'It will be over six months since poor Araminta's death.'

The words 'poor Araminta' were faintly condescending; Mrs Kendall had first-class health herself and regarded it as a sign of superiority. 'I do hope, dear Mrs Whitmead, that you will be present. There will be a ceremony at St Anne's in Southdene, and a private reception at our home, and three days after that the groom's family are to hold a big celebration of their own at the White Hart in Guildford. You will receive an invitation to that, as well.'

'How very kind,' said Lucy-Anne, non-committally, and paid a call of her own, next day, on Mrs Bird.

'What should I do? You see, George asked me to promise . . .'

The oath that George had made her swear was a heavy weight on Lucy-Anne's mind. The prospect of a life in which there was nothing at all, perhaps for years, except embroidery and books and gardening, a few quiet social events and consultations with Mrs Cobham and Mr Clarke on household and estate matters, was hard to bear.

But the exacted oath had left a mark on her; George had been so intense about it that it seemed to be branded on her mind and she felt obliged to put every offer of diversion, no matter how unexceptionable, against some invisible standard – a standard which, moreover, Araminta had approved.

'What promise is that, my dear?' Mrs Bird asked. When Lucy-Anne told her, she shook her head gravely. It emerged that, like Araminta, she thought the promise reasonable. 'There are so many temptations out in the world, my dear, and – let me be frank – a young married woman, who is thought to have a certain kind of knowledge, is more at risk than a young girl. Your husband may have seemed overbearing, but I am sure he meant well. His knowledge of the world is superior to yours, don't forget. I think you can attend the ceremony and the private reception with perfect propriety. You can come with us. But you had better decline the big affair in Guildford.'

'But if I were with you and Mr Bird then, as well . . . ?'

'We would be only too happy, of course. But, my dear, one should keep one's promises in full. I think you should not go, especially if the White Hart has already been mentioned to you as a place which you should only enter in your husband's company. If you are worried that the Kendalls might be offended, you can make the excuse that you feel that as your mother-in-law is only a few months dead you would not be quite correct in attending so large a gathering.'

Lucy-Anne therefore contented herself with going to the marriage service – in a new gown which, although lavender for half-mourning, was still as elegant as any in the church. On the day of the White Hart gathering she stayed at home and wrote to Julia, sounding as light of heart as possible. 'I am being such a model of propriety, believe me . . .'

Over her friendship with the Harpers, it was possible that she had not been a model of propriety. It was quite possible that she had breached her promise by becoming the close friend of people George had not officially approved, even though he had met them and even though Edward Harper was a clergyman. It was also true that, even if the acquaintance didn't break the terms of the promise, the Harpers' relationship to George's bailiff might make them ineligible.

But on this matter, she had defied the shackles George had placed upon her. She was without husband or child; she had lost Araminta; she had found no truly kindred spirit among the other women of the locality. She needed Julia's friendship too much to forgo it, oath or no oath.

Later on, she came to believe that during the days when her bereavements were still raw she might well have succumbed to some illness or other and simply died, if Julia hadn't been there.

At the beginning, the Harpers had stayed a month with Stephen. They had brought with them two of their five children – the eldest, Stevie, who had just turned five, and the youngest, the baby Julian.

'I've left Annette and the twins with my sister-in-law in Taunton,' Julia said. 'This is not just a frivolous holiday for us. My husband has had influenza very badly. It's an unusual time of year for it, but he has been very tired. He works too hard and too long. He does much extra work for the poor and there aren't enough hours in the day for him. We thought it would be more restful not to bring the entire family.'

Lucy-Anne feared at first that even a family of two would be a painful spectacle for her, but when she saw them, with their broad-spoken West Country nursemaid, they were enchanting. 'While you are here, do please come to see me often,' she said to Julia. 'You and all your family.'

For the most part, this meant Julia and the children, because Edward Harper spent much of his time out on the estate with Stephen, regaining his strength in the open air. But Julia, sensing Lucy-Anne's need for companionship, came to Chestnuts on most afternoons, with or without the children, to walk with her in the garden, or sit with her, sipping lemonade, embroidering or simply talking, on the terrace or in the drawing room, or, sometimes, in the Indian folly.

When Edward did accompany his wife, he proved himself to be a well-informed man who did not treat Lucy-Anne as a child but talked interestingly of church work and political affairs and also of astronomy, which, as Stephen had once said, was a hobby with the Harpers. Lucy-Anne's sphere of knowledge began to expand.

She had not known before that the earth was part of a solar system containing six known planets – 'although more may exist. We have a telescope in our garden and Edward has an ambition to find a new planet,' Julia said.

She did know that there was conflict between the English and the French in India, but she hadn't known that in Europe several rulers were locked into a complex territorial squabble; Frederick II of Prussia, who had only recently acceded, was attacking French possessions and King George II of England was even now setting off to support him with English and Hanoverian troops, in the hope of thoroughly trouncing England's old enemy, France. It could affect events in India, Edward said, but in what way would depend on who prevailed. The French no doubt had hopes of the Jacobites, the supporters of the dispossessed Catholic King James II and his son.

'But there they hope in vain. The Jacobites and their incessant plots are a nuisance, but nothing worse.'

When it was time for the Harpers to go home, they invited Lucy-Anne to accompany them for a visit. 'You're still not strong, after your sad loss,' Julia said. 'I can tell. But the spa waters may restore you.'

'But...' Lucy-Anne began, and then stopped.

'But?' asked Mr Harper.

She had not mentioned the promise to the Harpers. On the verge of doing so, she veered away. Instead, she said, 'I'm in mourning. I shouldn't go on, well, jaunts.'

'But this would be for your health,' Edward said. 'And you would be staying at our parsonage. We should be most careful to respect your mourning, naturally. I have met your husband and I can't think that he would really object. You must write to him about it, of course.'

'You had better ask Dr May to recommend the waters,' Julia said. 'I think you really do need a change of scene. You are too pale and too thin. We would take the greatest care of you.'

She was deceiving them and she knew it. But she could not bear to part with Julia so soon and her weak health was no pretence. She had had two colds in quick succession, and she was constantly tired. She was apt, too, to have fits of weeping. She would go to Bath, if Dr May agreed, and never mind George. She had a right to defend herself against illness.

The doctor was enthusiastic about the waters. 'The very thing, Mrs Whitmead. Indeed, I often encourage my patients to visit spas. If you have the opportunity of going to Bath in suitable company, I heartily urge that you should do so.'

It did not occur to Lucy-Anne, that time, to ask Mrs Bird's opinion. Three months later, when the question of the wedding reception in the White Hart arose, she wondered if she had avoided turning to Mrs Bird by instinct, in case the advice of that admirable but punctilious lady wasn't what she wanted to hear. By default, she let Mrs Bird suppose that she had had a dispensation for visiting Bath.

She wrote to her parents to tell them where she was going, left full details with Fraser and Mrs Cobham, and set out, half-shocked at her own temerity, and half-exhilarated. She also decided not to write to George.

The Harpers lived beside Edward's small church in a hamlet overlooking the city of Bath from the hill on the other side of the River Avon. The vicarage was plain and square, but it was built of the lovely local stone, of a subtle shade between dove grey and pale honey. Its garden was large though untidy. The Harpers had some private means as well as Edward's stipend and were not poor, but they had certain limitations nevertheless, and did not employ a gardener. The only part of the garden that was properly weeded was the vegetable patch. 'We have to look after that,' Julia said. 'We eat the vegetables. But a wild garden is better for children to play in.'

'Come and see our own plaything,' Edward added, and took Lucy-Anne into what appeared to be a garden shed but turned out to be where he and Julia housed their telescope.

It was a three-foot reflector, Edward told her, and then, seeing that this didn't mean much to her, explained that it gathered light by means of a curved mirror. 'The old refractors used a curved lens but they had to be bigger and that made them unwieldy. The weather's clear and we'll be skywatching tonight. Would you care to join us? There's a full moon, which is worth seeing. It will mean sitting up late, but you may find it interesting.'

'Yes, please, I should like that,' said Lucy-Anne.

She said it mainly to be polite, and several times had to swallow a yawn as she sat drinking coffee with the Harpers after the children were in bed, waiting for the long summer dusk to fade. Because of the fatigue she had suffered since her miscarriage, she had found the journey very wearing.

But when she looked through the eyepiece of the telescope, at the craters and mountains of another world, she forgot her malaise as she became filled not only with astonishment but with exhilaration. It was like an escape. To look at it was to leave her own narrow life, her loss, her grief, George's strictures, behind her. Chestnuts, she decided at once, must have a telescope of its own.

Next morning, accompanied by Julia, she went to Bath and solemnly drank the waters in the Pump Room, where she could watch Bath society, even if she took no part in it. The waters tasted terrible but after three days of this regime, whether because of the spa springs or the change of scene, she was feeling very much better, more energetic and interested in life as she had not been for a long time.

'Would it be possible,' she asked the Harpers, 'while I'm in Somerset, to visit a cottage I own in this county? I expect you know of it from Stephen. It's called Broom Cottage and it's in the Quantocks, near a village called – believe it or not – Chugg's Fiddle.'

Certainly Stephen had told them about Broom Cottage, Edward said, and yes, of course she could visit it. The following week, the Harpers took her there.

The cottage stood alone on a hillside above the village, and it was necessary to leave their hired carriage at the foot of the hill and walk up, after arranging for their bags to be brought up on a pack-pony from the village. But, on reaching Broom, Lucy-Anne was both surprised and impressed.

The word 'cottage' had to her meant a place like the dark, poky dwelling inhabited by the Craddocks, with hens running in and out of the door. But Broom, though thatched and gabled in true cottage style, had big, well-lit rooms. Its limewashed stone walls had a cleanly air, and within them were some unexpectedly fine pieces of furniture.

It transpired that great-uncle Matthew's will had required several valuable items to be sent to Broom Cottage after his death, thus enhancing the worth of Lucy-Anne's legacy. Lucy-Anne, admiring a superb walnut bureau and a set of exquisitely carved dining chairs, considered having them transferred to Chestnuts but decided against it. They looked at home where they were.

Besides, Dotty Larrimore had become fond of them.

Dotty was ancient, whiskery of chin, and lame, and it soon became clear why the tenants had found her impossible, although that was not the way Dotty herself put it.

'They was the end, ma'am; they wasn't to be tolerated. I'm here to look after this place for the Whitmead family, I told 'un, and look after it I will. No, I said, no, you *can't* shift all the furniture round in the parlour; Miss Henrietta'd never have the bookcase where the sun'd fall on it directly like that; it might hurt the bindings. And then the next lot wanted meals at all hours. I wasn't having that, ma'am. Miss Henrietta wouldn't have liked it.'

Lucy-Anne felt considerable sympathy for the luckless tenants who had been confronted with Dotty's proprietary quirks about Broom, but she could not feel angry with Dotty. The old servant was both endearing and pathetic. With Lucy-Anne, the great-niece of her beloved Miss Henrietta, she was quaveringly anxious to please, all curtsies and 'yes ma'am's, and her eyes filled whenever Henrietta was mentioned. Lucy-Anne's arrival in person made her anxious in case it meant that new plans were being made for Broom, which might compel her to leave it.

She begged to be allowed to stay there. 'It's been my home nigh on sixty years and I can't see myself nowhere else,' she said, stroking the bureau, which certainly owed its present high gloss to her polishing.

Within twenty-four hours, Lucy-Anne had promised to let her remain there for life as its caretaker, with an especial duty to look after the furniture. She went away with her ears full of Dotty's effusive gratitude.

A month later, Lucy-Anne returned home with her health sufficiently improved to offset most of her twinges of conscience over whether or not George would have approved the trip. Such twinges as remained she dealt with by adhering very carefully to her promise in all other respects. But she exchanged regular letters with Julia and was glad to do so. Her father had recovered his own health and her parents visited on occasion, and from time to time she entertained people from the circle selected by her husband. But when she needed advice or a confidante it was Julia to whom she turned.

When George's first letter arrived, unexpectedly, from Brazil, with the alarming news that the *Winchester* had run aground, Lucy-Anne at once wrote to Bath, expressing her fears for the rest of the voyage, and was glad of her friend's calmly sensible reply that George was obviously unharmed and that the next news would surely be of his safe arrival in India. There was something very reliable about Julia.

Stephen Clarke was there, it was true, living at the foot of the hill, running the farms, coming when necessary to discuss estate business. But she must be careful with Stephen. It would be easy to depend on him too much. Far too easy to walk forward one day and simply go into his arms.

She almost did just that on the day late in 1744 when Julia's prophecy was fulfilled and a letter came from George to announce that he had reached India. Stephen, arriving to make his weekly report, found her reading it at her desk. Lucy-Anne looked up, taken by surprise and unable to hide her expression, and he came forward in concern. 'Mrs Whitmead? Have you had bad news?'

'No, oh no.' Lucy-Anne tried to laugh. The laugh almost turned into a sob and she startled both of them by producing a sound like a whinny. 'My husband is safely in Madras now. That's splendid news. It's just that . . . just that . . .' She must control herself. In a flat voice, she said: 'Just that I fear he doesn't approve of what I've done with Broom Cottage. He thinks it should be let. And now I've given my word to Dotty Larrimore that the present arrangement shall last for the rest of her life!'

'Is that all? But my dear Mrs Whitmead, by the terms of your great-aunt's will you are obliged to take care of Dotty. It would be difficult to make any other arrangement, Dotty being as she is. Please don't look so worried. I will write to Mr Whitmead myself and explain matters.'

'No, I must do that.' Here was a new cause for distress. She didn't want Stephen innocently telling George that she had been to Somerset. George was so obviously ready to be made angry. 'But thank you, Mr Clarke.' She fought off the tears. She would write to Julia and tell her the rest. She couldn't tell Stephen. She put the letter down, folding it to hide the dreadful paragraph dealing with the loss of the child.

. . . I learn with great regret that you were not able to sustain the child with which I had indeed hoped to leave you, and trust that this was not due to negligence on your part. Knowing how long it must be before we have hope of such another, and knowing that we have both been sadly bereaved by my mother's passing, it behoved you to take the greatest care. I am gravely displeased by this news.

Oh, was he indeed? And what did he think it had been like for her, lying there in the grip of that awful, useless pain, while what would have been her baby – hers as well as his! – was squeezed bloodily and remorselessly out of her? She realised that Stephen, obviously aware that she was in deep distress over something she could not tell him, was asking – intending to be tactful – if there were any news of Mr Whitmead's return.

If George were to walk through the door now, she would want to kill him. 'Oh no,' she said, still flatly. 'He didn't get there until last June! He has only been there six months. Well, Mr Clarke. What have you to tell me today?'

And then, while Stephen talked of crops and rents, she sat grasping the edge of her chair, to keep herself from getting up and simply going to him for comfort, telling him all about it and asking for his sympathy,

81

as naturally as though she were his child, or his lover.

She did write to Julia and followed Julia's advice, which was to compose a loving and apologetic reply to George. 'I expect he wrote in the heat of the moment and has long regretted his harshness,' Julia said. It was a consoling thought and Lucy-Anne did her best to believe it.

In the course of the next year, she went on living carefully as George had prescribed. While the Kendalls and the Millers went to London regularly and came back full of accounts of balls and concerts, Lucy-Anne stayed quietly at Chestnuts.

She purchased the telescope she had promised herself and had it set up in the folly; on the Harpers' advice she bought some books on astronomy. As a hobby, it was a change from embroidery and it was certainly harmless. She improved her performance on the harpsichord, brewed medicines for the stillroom and took drives in the chaise. She paid and received sedate calls, gave and attended small dinner parties. But she stopped visiting her parents and did not encourage them to visit her. Lucilla had taken to asking, in almost accusing tones, when George was coming home to perform his conjugal duties. Lucy-Anne didn't know the answer and didn't know, either, what she felt about the idea of George's return. She preferred not to be forced to discuss it.

Her one piece of self-indulgence was Bath Spa. She took the waters, and stayed with the Harpers twice more before the spring of 1746 when Julia came to make a short stay with Stephen. She was calling at Chestnuts when a further letter arrived from George, announcing that the news from Europe, of the continuing war and the worsening of Anglo-French relations, had indeed had its echoes in India. The French Governor-General, Joseph Dupleix, had not wanted war with the English in India to begin with, but the rumour now in the air was that this might change.

'We all consider this a likely and desirable state of affairs.' George's handwriting was spiky and aggressive and a little disjointed, as though he had been in a state of excitement as he wrote. 'It may perhaps allow us to clear our trading rivals out of the way. We have heard that an English naval squadron is on its way to attack French shipping off the Indian coast . . .'

'Suppose there is fighting and he's killed!' Lucy-Anne exclaimed.

'Life is full of dangers,' Julia told her. 'Men risk their lives in war. Think of the Jacobite rising there has just been in Scotland, when the Young Pretender tried to land. He has escaped, but many of his supporters did not. There was terrible slaughter at Culloden, and they say that many more will die on the gallows before all is done. Women risk themselves in childbirth and all of us are vulnerable to disease. We can only keep our hearts up as best we can, and pray. Lucy-Anne, my love, we can't control our fortunes, much as we would all like to. Yours wouldn't be among the worst, even if something were to happen to George. You will be provided for. You'll never be on the parish or in the workhouse.'

'I know that!' For the first time ever, Lucy-Anne met Julia's eyes with something near to antagonism. 'For once, Julia, I'm not sure you really understand, though you should. I told you about that unkind letter. Believe me, I have tried to be a good wife to George. I *want* to be a good wife. Or I did want to. But now...'

'Don't say any more,' said Julia, almost sharply.

'I must,' said Lucy-Anne. 'It's burning me within. I can't forget that letter. Part of me worries about George as a wife should worry over a husband in danger, but another part is wishing that—'

'*No*, Lucy-Anne. Don't say it.'

'I've got to say it! Part of me wishes that he would get in the way of a cannonball so that I could be free of him!'

'You don't mean that, Lucy-Anne.'

'I don't altogether mean it, no. But—'

'You don't mean it at *all*,' said Julia fiercely, and put her arms around her friend, as Lucy-Anne burst into tears.

The day was not only hot but sultry, the air as thick as a horsehair blanket. Against the even blue of the Indian sky, the battlements of Fort St George, which were coated in a cement made of burnt seashells, were outlined in a gleaming and horrid clarity which revealed every wrecked crenellation and threatening bulge where French cannonballs had hit them.

Governor-General Joseph-François Dupleix had taken the poorest possible view of English attempts to abolish his shipping. This was his reply. Off the coast, where, over two years ago, the *Winchester* had anchored, a French naval squadron now patrolled and although its commander, Bertrand La Bourdonnais, had behaved with courtesy since Fort St George surrendered, and had agreed that those within might ransom themselves, somehow or other the business did not look like ever being concluded.

Soldiers under the direct command of Governor-General Dupleix had joined the matelots on guard inside and outside the fort, and those within it, under a form of large-scale house arrest, were constantly and uneasily aware of them.

But nevertheless, although the East India Company's operations in Fort St George were at a standstill, social life of a kind went on. There were no more morning rides outside the fort, and no more palanquin trips into the bazaars of the town, but those ladies who had not been sent to safer places at the start of the siege still called on each other, gentlemen met to play cards, and, since food supplies were once more getting in, Governor and Mrs Morse went on entertaining people to dinner. 'We owe it to ourselves,' Morse had said, 'to behave as if everything were normal.'

Today, the dining room was superficially as usual – quiet and a little dim, the sun excluded by the stone lattices, the double doors open to allow the air to circulate. Everyone in the room was carefully and correctly dressed and the cooking was as excellent and the servants as soft-footed and deft as ever.

If, privately, they thought their employers looked absurd, sweating in their tight clothes, or noticed how often Governor Morse's wineglass was being refilled, they gave no sign of it. Nor did those who understood English appear to notice how very far from normal the conversation was. It was on the conversation that pretence had foundered. Tongues apparently had minds of their own.

'Has there been no reply, still, to our representations to Dupleix?' George Whitmead wanted to know. 'I am persuaded that if only he would use his authority to insist that La Bourdonnais completes the agreement we have made with him, we could be on our way south to Fort St David within the hour.'

'How I wish we could be,' sighed Eliza Walsh, who was young and pleasure-loving, and considered the loss of the morning rides and the palanquin trips to be extremely serious. 'Oh, to be free again.'

'Free but destitute,' remarked Clive grimly. He was seated further along the table with his cousin William King and a number of friends, including John Pybus and John Walsh, the two who had travelled out with King. Eliza, who had followed them out, was Walsh's sister. Their young cousin, a freckle-faced youth called Edmund Maskelyne, also a recent arrival was sitting opposite Eliza. The little group, with its brother and sister and its two sets of cousins, had become so tight-knit that now, if one were invited anywhere, they all were.

Which did not prevent them from having their little semi-serious disputes.

'Robert thinks we should have fought on,' John Walsh remarked, wickedly, with the intention to provoke.

'Do you, Clive?' Morse asked.

'Well, I do.' Clive eyed Walsh with pugnacity. 'Edmund and I were saying only this morning—'

'Oh, Mun is a hothead and so are you!' Walsh tended to be waspish. 'I beg your pardon, sir,' he added to Morse, 'but these wild young ones...! Mun and Robert both know perfectly well that we couldn't afford to hold out. Our naval forces had fled and we were outnumbered, three to one at least.'

'But I have to agree,' said Morse gloomily, draining yet another glass of wine, 'that destitute may well be the right word. It looks as if we shall all be precisely that. La Bourdonnais wants everything but the clothes we stand up in. And that's the cause of the delay. He and Dupleix are quarrelling over the spoils. It's seeped down to their men; haven't you noticed their officers cutting each other dead? Dupleix wants the ransom divided between them and La Bourdonnais thinks that, since he was the one who overcame the fort and negotiated the terms, he's entitled to all of it.'

'It will amount to a severe loss, for us and for the Company,' said George Whitmead seriously, mopping a wet forehead. He always did perspire heavily and today the heat was exceedingly oppressive.

'We've lost our dignity as well,' Clive muttered under his breath, to John Walsh. George heard him.

'One must not undervalue money, Robert.'

'I don't, sir. Far from it. But there are some things—'

'I've often heard you complain that your work is dull, but though shooting French seamen from the battlements is no doubt more amusing than counting cloth bales, wrangling with Indian merchants and adding up figures in ledgers, these tedious tasks are the ones that make money and that is what counts.'

'Robert does get bored quickly,' said William King with affectionate malice. 'He put a pistol to his head once, out of weariness with the tedium of life.'

Mrs Morse looked horrified and Eliza cried, 'Oh, surely not!'

'It's quite true,' said Clive. 'I have never understood why suicide should be thought such a sin. One's life is one own, and if it becomes intolerable – why then, one has the right to end it.'

'That is a shocking thing to say. Most irreligious. Harrumph!' exclaimed George.

'He's only showing off,' said King. 'Stop it, Robert! The pistol wasn't loaded.'

'It probably wouldn't have gone off if it had been,' said Clive. 'It was one of those terrible Turkish flintlocks that can't be relied on. It wouldn't fire when I tried to shoot a Frenchman with it from the walls. But I can't afford a better one. I'm by no means indifferent to money, Mr Whitmead. I'm in debt to my father – he sent me money to pay off Captain Steward – but a debt to one's father is still a debt. Now, I shall be beholden as well to Governor Morse here because he is paying my ransom. I can't pay it myself. Indeed, that is one of the reasons why I wish we had fought on longer, even if it is not the only reason.'

'Let us not wrangle,' pleaded Eliza. 'It's too hot.'

'Stifling,' Mrs Morse agreed. 'It lacks even the suspicion of a breeze. There was no cool breeze yesterday evening, and that is very rare.'

'It makes people irritable,' her husband said. He nodded towards the window lattice. Beyond it, French voices had been suddenly raised in an angry exchange. 'That will be Dupleix and La Bourdonnais squabbling yet again, by proxy—'

He stopped. The wished-for breeze had suddenly risen, lifting the edge of the white napery on the table and stirring Eliza's ringlets. But it was icy cold. In the act of wiping his forehead again, George lowered his handkerchief and said, 'Upon my word. That made me shiver!'

Morse rose to his feet. He had taken a great deal of wine and wasn't entirely steady as he walked across to the window to look at the sky above the battlements. 'The sky's growing murky,' he said. 'There's a storm on the way.'

Before the dinner party had ended, the sunlight had vanished, and word had come that the French fleet was on the move towards deep water. The chill breeze blew for a time and then died away again, leaving an intense, hot stillness behind. As he left the Governor's residence to walk through a livid twilight to his bungalow a hundred yards away, George found it hard to breathe. The very air seemed scanty. His legs ached and he was swept by alternate sweats and shivers. He felt as though he were coming down with a fever. If not, this was going to be the storm of the century.

Before he had traversed even the short distance to the bungalow, he realised that it wasn't a case of one or the other, but of both. He found Ahmed already closing shutters and lighting candles. He longed to lie down, but the stuffiness inside the bungalow was unbearable, and instead he clambered up the stair to the flat roof. The French bombardments had obligingly made a hole in the battlements close by and through it one could catch a glimpse of the sea.

The world was holding its breath. Above an ocean unnaturally smooth, the sky was indigo and the palm trees that fringed the beach were eerily green against it, as if luminous. The French ships had long since vanished into the darkness where the horizon had been.

He saw the approaching hurricane before he heard it – a foaming whiteness racing towards him across the sulky Madras Roads. Then came the noise, a distant but increasing roar which resembled nothing he had ever heard in his life before, not even on board the *Winchester* in a gale.

The palm trees bent double. An instant later they vanished, as a huge sea rolled in and almost casually swallowed them. At the same moment, the daylight went out as if snuffed.

'Sahib!' Ahmed was beside him. 'You must come down, Sahib. Big storm; you are not safe up here.'

George started to walk towards the stair. The roof seemed to have become amazingly wide. Ahmed put a hand under his elbow. Then everything dissolved in a roaring confusion made partly of the elements and partly of the blood pounding in his head. When he came round again, Ahmed was depositing him on his bed in his candlelit room. Despite the closed shutters, the candle-flames were streaming. The house was wrapped in a wind that howled and tore at it like a vast, invisible jackal. From somewhere close at hand came the crash of falling stones. It was followed by a savage swish of rain.

Ahmed pulled a light coverlet over his master's shivering form, and George closed his eyes. His head had begun to ache horribly, but he had had these fevers before. One eventually recovered. A thought occurred to him. 'Such a pity,' he remarked aloud, 'that the storm didn't come before we surrendered. It's got rid of the French fleet rather too late.'

Had it come sooner, it might have saved Fort St George, the Madras trading post, for the English. As it was, the hurricane merely put an end to the quarrel between Dupleix and La Bourdonnais, by coming in, as it were, on Dupleix's side. Without his fleet, La Bourdonnais was unable to pursue the argument. He withdrew and Dupleix arrived in person and triumph to inspect his captives with his own eyes.

In the grey stickiness which had succeeded the hurricane, on the parade ground in the midst of the fort, Governor Morse waited grimly to receive his conqueror.

He was not without moral support. Except for George Whitmead, who was ill, the Company Councillors were beside him. Most of the lesser employees were assembled behind them, and also on parade were the officers and soldiers of the garrison, drawn up in fairly tidy ranks. Morse wished that the word *fairly* could be omitted.

Young Mr Clive (whom Morse rather liked, although he tripped over the furniture rather a lot and was sometimes more outspoken than a lesser employee ought to be) had once complained that the commander of the garrison was too old and that most of the men looked to him like ex-felons who had taken the king's shilling for the sake of regular meals with a chance of rape and pillage. The annoying thing was that young Mr Clive might well be right.

Just now, the soldiers, like everyone else, were showing signs of restlessness. They had been waiting in the heat for nearly an hour.

But at last there was a stir. Mrs Morse and several other ladies, including Eliza Walsh, all very carefully dressed in hoops and satins and shady hats, came out on to a balcony overlooking the parade ground and stood gazing towards the gate. There was a distant noise, hard to identify. In the gate-arch, a sentry saluted and came to attention as a squad of soldiers and an army band marched in. The noise resolved itself into the sound of kettledrums. A mounted guard, bearing the French flag, clattered in after the foot soldiers and the band.

Joseph Dupleix, the French Governor-General, rode in majestically on the heels of the guard. His mount was caparisoned in scarlet and gold and Dupleix himself was a glittering figure in a uniform freely embellished with gold and silver lace. He rode at ease, elbows relaxed on the arm-rests of his howdah, while a turbaned mahout perched in front of him did the work of controlling his gigantic steed.

'Good God!' said somebody. 'The man's arrived on an elephant!'

'I believe he makes a habit of it,' said Morse. 'Dupleix is reputed to go in for vulgar ostentation.'

He glanced around, expecting to see his own disapproval reflected on other faces, and on most of them it was. The exception was Clive, whose expression was not in the least disapproving. 'Well!' said the look in young Mr Clive's dark eyes, 'this is something like! This is more fun than sorting bales of cloth and entering figures in ledgers. This is seeing life!'

'This is outrageous,' said Governor Morse. He brushed at the gold frogging on his coat as if the words he had just heard had somehow contaminated it. Or, possibly, as if he had to give his hands a harmless occupation to keep them from throttling the French Governor-General. 'It is *preposterous*, sir!' He heard his voice slur and regretted the fact that before this interview, in what had been his own main reception room and had now been claimed by Dupleix, he had fortified himself with brandy.

He attempted to speak plainly. 'There was an agreement with Bertrand La Bourdonnais . . .'

The Councillors and employees who, once more, were present in support of their Governor, muttered their assent. Dupleix, however, smiled. The Frenchman's face was candid, almost chubby, with well-opened eyes and an amiable mouth, but it was deceptive. The man was formidable. His voice was cold and his clothes, beautifully cut in the European fashion but made of the most exotic Indian silk and brocade, said clearly that he had power and wealth and enjoyed them. As if, thought Morse bitterly, the kettledrums and the elephant hadn't said so already, and louder.

'La Bourdonnais was not authorised to make any such er . . . *pacte* with you, m'sieu.' Dupleix was multi-lingual and his English was adequate if idiosyncratic. 'The pacte is – you would say – null and void. In due course, M'sieu Morse—'

'Governor Morse.'

'. . . In due course, M'sieu Morse, I will dictate my own terms. They will not be ungenerous, considering the provocation I have had. I did not seek war with the English here in India, and regret that your Hanoverian government thought fit to harass my shipping in these waters. I hope for better relations' – he pronounced 'relations' as though the word were French – 'in future. Now that England once more has a Catholic king, who is in debt to France for *le secours*—'

'*What* did you say?'

'We are aware, m'sieu, that the grandson of your King James the Second has overthrown the Hanoverian dynasty in England.'

The reaction to this was not what he expected. The Councillors and employees gathered with Morse had been looking as dejected as a defeated enemy should and the reminder that back in England the government which had supported them had been routed should have sent their spirits plummeting by several further degrees. Instead, they laughed. Dupleix's eyes narrowed.

'Ah, yes. We heard about that,' said Morse. This time he determinedly kept his diction clear. 'All the bells in Pondicherry rang for joy, did they not? You were misinformed, however. *We* have had accurate news. The Pretender's forces were wiped out in Scotland, at a place called Culloden, and the self-styled Prince Charlie is back in exile. The Hanoverians remain in power – permanently, I trust.'

'Indeed?' Dupleix recognised the note of certainty, and cut his losses cleanly and without visible effort. 'However, it makes no difference; not to you. You may regard yourselves as my prisoners. I have done you the *honneur* of attending you today in my own person and you may be well assured that all proprieties will be observed towards you. I must ask you, Governor Morse, and your Councillors, to make ready, *s'il vous plaît*, to travel now to Pondicherry. Every respect will be shown to the ladies. My wife is already preparing to receive Mrs Morse as her personal guest.'

He indicated a tall Indian, robed and turbaned, who was waiting one pace behind him. 'This is my deputy, Ananda Ranga Pillai, who will attend to your travel arrangements on my behalf and of whom you may ask any questions you wish. He has a list of your Councillors and will make sure that you are all here—'

'We are not,' said Morse, aggressively. 'Mr George Whitmead is ill with malaria. He can't travel.'

Dupleix bowed. 'I am a civilised man, m'sieu. Mr Whitmead may follow the rest of you when he has recovered. As for the East India Company employees and the garrison, I have no wish to incarcerate them in this heat. I shall require from each man an undertaking that he will not take up arms against us until he has been ransomed. They must then leave Fort St George. The fort, M'sieu Morse, is now a French possession.'

He took their compliance for granted. From the moment when he was borne so triumphantly on to the parade ground of Fort St George, with his charisma surging in front of him like a bow-wave, he had made Governor Morse look like an inebriated schoolboy.

Robert Clive, standing among his friends, studied the two leaders and, although he liked Morse personally, nevertheless found himself longing with all his heart to push the governor out of the way and step into his place. Dupleix would dwindle then. Young Mr Clive, clerk of the East India Company on a salary of five pounds per annum, believed that he was capable of making him dwindle, and clenched his fists with frustration because he couldn't put it to the test.

'We're getting out of here,' said Clive with passion, thumping himself down on the end of George's bed. 'And without taking any damned oaths, either. I'll give him oaths!'

'He is bad taste personified,' William King agreed, propping a hip on a windowsill. Pybus took the only chair while the cousins Walsh and Maskelyne sat down on a spare charpoy. 'I wouldn't,' said King, 'give Dupleix a fright at midnight, let alone a promise not to take up arms. I've every intention of taking them up as soon as I can lay my hands on some!'

'I saw his elephant,' said George. 'I was watching from my window. A most impressive display of power, it must be said.' His tone suggested that, like Clive, he found Dupleix not only infuriating but also slightly enviable. 'It will not be easy to avoid taking the oath, however. Or not easy for you. It is not required of me. As a Councillor, I shall soon be moved to Pondicherry and will have to ransom myself. I have staved it off so far by pretending to be too weak, but I cannot keep it up for much longer. But Dupleix will have that oath out of you young men, for sure. I gather he has said he does not wish to lock anyone up in this heat, but if you do not swear then lock you up he will. You'll stifle.'

'I said we're going to get out of here,' said Clive. 'My God, no one could dislike Morse – he was very kind to me when I was homesick after I first got here – but sometimes he's too easygoing for his own good. He entrusted our garrison to a commander aged seventy – *seventy*! No wonder we couldn't hold out! He's finished now as Governor and I'm sorry for him, but I'll be even sorrier for us, unless we escape. To get back to the point: are you well enough to join us, Mr Whitmead? And do you wish to do so?'

'The answer to both questions is yes,' George said. 'But how can it be done?'

'Well, as to that,' said Walsh, 'Mun here . . .'

'. . . has an idea,' said Edmund Maskelyne smugly.

'Charcoal,' said Edmund, putting down his booty on George's bed. 'That'll darken our faces. Sandals with thongs between the toes, some of those loose kurta shirt-things and some white turbans from the servants' quarters. Whew! The washerman came in to empty the laundry basket, just as I was putting it all in a bag.'

'What did you do?' enquired Pybus with interest from where he sat reading, cross-legged on the charpoy.

'That washerman wears very loose sandals,' said Mun. 'They go slap-slap as he walks along. I heard him coming and got out of another door just in time. Anyone would think I was a thief!'

'From the servants' point of view, you are,' said King.

King, on the plea that he had been sleeping badly and ought to conserve his energy, was stretched out on George's bed. George himself was up and, with Walsh, was going through another pile of clothing. 'Ahmed has been helpful,' he said. 'I wasn't obliged to steal these. We should have enough for us all, now. I have spare pairs of black stockings if anyone should require them. There are no signs that the French are suspicious, I trust? You seem to be visiting me quite freely.'

'Robert has arranged for us to take the oath tomorrow,' said Mun with a grin. 'Thus allaying suspicion if they had any. But I doubt if they did. I fancy they think that escape is impossible.'

'I hope it isn't.' Clive had come quietly into the room. 'I've been on the roof, surveying the scene. Dupleix's soldiers are all over the place, as usual, of course. Now, listen, all of you. We could be shot if we're caught, so we have just got to make sure that we aren't. There's something we must all remember. There is more to pretending to be Indian than simply smearing charcoal all over our faces and wearing our servants' clothes. We must walk as they do, make their kind of gestures. And we ought to get used to the sandals. I hope we don't have to wear them all the way to St David's Fort – it's more than a hundred miles off. With luck, we'll get horses somewhere. I have some ideas about that. But I think we should put our disguises on and have a little practice.'

'Good lord!' said King. 'Need we go that far?'

'Attention to detail,' said Clive, 'can make the difference between failure and success.'

He had changed. George, sorting their disguises into sets of kurta, turban and sandals, paused and considered Clive thoughtfully. Life in St George's Fort had probably started the alteration. Dining at the Governor's residence, taking responsibility for large sums of money, dancing with ladies of fashion, making love to the ladies of the town, and (on his own admission) twice having to be treated for diseases caught from them – all these were maturing influences.

But the process had recently accelerated. Even a few days ago, the boy of the voyage out, that uncertain mixture of hot temper and diffidence, the clumsy youth who had fallen over buckets and stumbled overboard from the *Winchester*, had still been there, in a modified form. His final disappearance, giving place to a young man of presence and physical co-ordination, seemed to have happened overnight. Clive had entered the room just now as softly and smoothly as a pacing cat.

He was also, George saw, actually enjoying this adventure. A perilous escape from an enemy-held fort, complete with disguises and a risk of getting shot was far more to Robert Clive's taste than the everyday work of warehouse and office. His eyes were bright and his bearing jaunty.

'In time to come,' he informed Walsh, 'I may well have a more glittering future than you and if I do, it will be because I go in for attention to detail.'

'Why, you . . . !' King sat up, a glint in his eye. Clive grinned. King

90

leapt. The others, except for George, gleefully joined in the tension-relieving scrimmage that ensued.

George afterwards wondered whether Clive had actually provoked it on purpose, for the tension was considerable. They couldn't leave until nightfall. When the wrestling match was over, Clive found them things to do, such as trying out not only their stolen footwear but all the rest of their disguises too and – because stockinged feet wouldn't easily accommodate the toe-thongs of the sandals – cutting off the toes of their stockings and putting charcoal on their feet. But the wait was so nerve-racking that before evening came Clive himself had succumbed to a bout of nervous stomach-ache and diarrhoea.

'Absolute silence as we go out,' Clive said in a low voice. 'We're not all that convincing close-to. I wish King and Pybus didn't have blue eyes. Still, it's nearly dusk. Mr Whitmead, I can see your gun-butt. You must keep it hidden. I wish we all had guns. How did you manage to hide yours when the French came round confiscating them?'

'Ahmed put it in a cooking pot and left it in the kitchen,' said George.

'Oh, well. It wasn't worth my while to hide mine,' Clive said. 'It's unreliable. The French are welcome to it; it may kill one of them one day, by failing to kill an enemy. Now then. The most dangerous thing will be if anyone speaks to us. Who among us knows any of the Indian tongues? Mr Whitmead does, I think, sir?'

'Some Tamil and some Hindustani,' said George. 'But only a few words of the local Telegu and in these circumstances none of it would be of much use, for although I might understand what was said, I would sound like an Englishman if I answered.'

'Well, all I know,' said Clive, 'are *chalo* and *jaldi*, which are Hindustani for "let us go", and "be quick". How about the rest of us?'

A rapid check revealed that between them they could manage 'come here', 'go away', 'let us go', 'be quick' and 'be quiet' in Hindustani, and not much else, and none of it with the authentic accent anyway.

'Very well,' said Clive. 'Now, the place where we're most likely to be challenged is, obviously, the gate. The guards may be French, Indian, or Portuguese and we won't know until we get there. If we are challenged, we answer in Portuguese. Indians often use it among themselves if they don't speak each other's dialect. It won't matter if we speak it badly because we're not pretending to be Portuguese ourselves. But whatever happens we mustn't be overheard speaking English. Well. It's time.'

'*Chalo*,' said the irrepressible Mun.

Ahmed was waiting in the entrance hall. 'All the other servants are in the kitchen, Sahib. We all wish you good success. No one in this house will betray you. I will go to the door ahead of you and see that all is safe.'

They waited, standing back, until he signalled to them. As they passed him, George muttered, 'Good man,' and pressed a small bag into Ahmed's hand. 'There's six months' pay for you and all the others. And get them away to their homes before the French come prowling round.'

'It is arranged for, Sahib,' said Ahmed softly.

He had chosen a good moment for them. French soldiers were

roaming about the paved square within the fort, but no one was nearby or looking their way as they stepped out and began to saunter towards the gate. No one was interfering with the movements of servants. Ahmed had a family in the town and had been visiting them as usual and George expected that all his servants would be able to disperse in good time, out of the fort and into the town, before anyone started to ask awkward questions.

But Ahmed and his fellow servants were genuine Indians. For six imposters, the gate was a serious hazard. 'Don't walk so fast,' Clive muttered. 'We're not supposed to be on an urgent errand. Look humble and shuffle a bit.'

'In these damned sandals, we can scarcely do otherwise,' growled George, a little too loudly.

'Shush!' said Clive peremptorily.

The sea breeze of evening had sprung up and the air was cooler now. Dusk was falling swiftly and when they passed into the shadow of the arch it blessedly swallowed up the tell-tale blue of King's and Pybus's eyes, and conveniently concealed the presence of black stockings and charcoal.

They never did find out whether the guards were Indian or European because the guards took no notice whatsoever of the little bunch of Indian servants in their loose clothes and scuffling footwear. Pybus made a subservient hand-to-forehead gesture as he went by, earning a bored nod from one of the sentries, and then they were moving out into the open, free.

All six straightened instinctively. 'But keep moving,' said Clive quietly. 'Keep pretending. Even in the town, we must take care. They all know that the French are in possession here, and there have been rewards offered for the recapture of anyone who tries to escape.'

'Ah. I thought they might do something of that kind,' said George. 'I didn't give my servants six months' pay out of pure generosity, I assure you.'

'It was a wise move, sir,' Clive said. 'But please keep your voice down. Once we're out of the town and across the bridge there, we can just melt away into the countryside. There should be a moon later on.'

They tramped on, into the town, with its familiar combination of smells that George had once described to Clive as 'dung and jasmine, rubbish and sandalwood'. The place was still wide awake. Men dressed like themselves were strolling about; a cow wandered along past a row of stalls which were still doing business by the light of torches thrust into holders on poles, and a stray dog with jutting ribs was slinking hopefully in the shadows near a booth where kebabs and puris sizzled over a charcoal fire. 'I'm hungry,' said Mun.

'There's a village within two hours' walk, where we can get food and take some rest,' Clive said, keeping his voice low. 'The people there have always been friendly to us. With luck, we'll be safe with them and we may get horses there, or mules, at least.'

'I can see the bridge,' murmured King.

'And,' added Mun a moment later, 'there's a whole gang of Indians dawdling across it.'

'We'll draw more attention to ourselves if we hesitate,' Clive said. 'Come on.'

They went forward, warily. The Indians who were strolling across the bridge towards them were a party of young men. They carried torches to light their way, and were laughing and talking as they came. They had probably been to some kind of celebration, for the torchlight shone on clean clothes and ornamental belts. And also, more discouragingly, on dagger hilts jutting above the belts. The torchlight, indeed, was a menace in its own right.

'Step aside respectfully when we meet them,' whispered Pybus. 'Keep back from the light.'

They followed his advice. Once again, to their relief, they found themselves ignored. The young men were concerned with their own conversation and a group of shabby servant-wallahs did not interest them. As the last of them went by, Clive grinned at Mun, murmured, '*Chalo*,' and signalled his companions on again.

'One could justly suppose,' George murmured, 'that there is something in the theory of divine Providence. We have been miraculously fortunate tonight.'

'*Quiet*. Sound carries,' whispered Clive.

And this time, it had. Behind them, a voice called out sharply. They ignored it, walking steadily on, but as they stepped on to the bridge torchlight and swiftly running feet overtook them. They swung round. Clive was swearing under his breath.

Four of the young men had turned back to accost them. The leader, a slender, haughty youth whose belt had not only a dagger but also a pistol thrust through it, rattled off some words. 'I don't understand you,' said Clive in Portuguese. 'What is the matter?' He hit George in the ribs with an elbow. 'What is he saying?'

'God knows. He's speaking Telegu,' growled George, also in Portuguese.

The young man, dark brows meeting in a frown of suspicion above a proud hawk-nose, rattled out a further spate of his own language. One word flickered ominously from the midst of it. It sounded like 'English'.

An excited babble broke out among the rest. Several of them pushed nearer and the light danced perilously over the faces of the escape party. The charcoal had been applied with great care and withstood the test. But, with a shout of triumphant discovery, one of the Indians pointed at King. They did not need to know his language to understand what he was saying. He was announcing to the world that one of these tongue-tied Indian servants had *blue eyes*.

The French had undoubtedly been promising rewards to anyone who apprehended escaping captives. By the look of it, they had been none too particular in specifying that such captives should be taken alive, either. The young man with the gun snatched it out, pointed it at Clive and without hesitation pulled the trigger.

There was a feeble click as the gun refused to fire. Its owner turned dusky red and cursed in his own tongue. Two others sprang forward waving torches and daggers but Walsh and Mun, moving in unison as though they were twins instead of merely cousins, stopped them short, knocking the torches aside, kicking a dagger out of a lunging hand and punching its owner very hard on the jaw. He fell backwards. Clive snapped, '*Run!*'

They wheeled and tore across the bridge, ears on the stretch for gunshots, backs quivering with the expectation of bullets in the spine. But there were no bullets and no pursuit. As they reached the far bank of the river and veered aside into the night and the shelter of the roadside trees, they glanced back. Their young assailants were standing where they had left them, outlined in torchlight, gathered around their leader, who was still staring furiously at his useless firearm.

'On!' panted Clive. 'Don't stop. Don't make a noise either. Keep among the trees.'

'You know,' said George, 'when that young man pulled out his pistol, I observed that like yours, Robert, it was of Ottoman design. Those Turkish pistols do most certainly seem to be untrustworthy. I am inclined to wonder—'

He broke off short because Clive had seized him in a powerful grip and clamped a hand over his mouth.

'God in heaven, do you ever stop talking? One more word from you, Mr Whitmead, and I'll personally break your neck.'

'May I remind you,' said George coldly, wrenching himself free, 'that you are addressing a Councillor of the East India Company?'

'Councillor! You're a windbag, sir! A badly designed pistol was all that stood between me and oblivion just now, thanks to you! Now let's get on!'

They moved on again, keeping in the shelter of the trees that lined the straight dust road. Above them the sky was jewelled with stars and the good-natured Mun, embarrassed by the argument, tried to distract them by pointing out constellations, revealing for the first time that in England he had a brother who was an astronomer and that his sister Margaret also pursued it as a hobby.

Clive occasionally responded, but George did not. Under cover of charcoal and darkness, his face was still suffused with indignation. His recent illness was also making itself felt. Suddenly, he needed all his energy for the simple task of putting one rather shaky leg before the other. He could no longer spare any for talking.

But he was thinking. When Clive so unceremoniously stopped him, he had been about to say something himself on the matter of badly designed pistols. He had been going to say that there really ought to be a very lucrative market in India for properly made handguns.

Chapter Seven
The Opportunist

'I think that's the end of scanning the heavens for tonight,' said Julia, as Saturn disappeared behind an inexorably advancing bank of cloud. 'It must be very agreeable for an astronomer to live in a place like India where the skies are clear for months at a time. We will go indoors and enjoy some coffee before we retire.'

'What a spectacle Saturn was,' said Lucy-Anne. 'I have heard you speak of its rings but to see with my own eyes was . . . was breathtaking. Your telescope is a marvel; it's only three feet long and yet it's so powerful. I must replace the one at Chestnuts with one like this. I sent Fraser to London to buy mine, and told him not to spend too much money on it, and he came back with one which he said he'd got secondhand. I've been quite satisfied with it up to now, but it's so enormous and clumsy and still doesn't show me the heavens as yours does. I'm changing my mind about it.'

'Yours is a refractor, is it not?' said Edward Harper as he led them out of the viewing shed and locked it behind him. 'So was the first telescope I had. But when I found out how much better reflectors were, I lost no time in replacing it. This one was an extravagance, but Julia talked me into giving in!'

'You work very hard. You more than earn the right to one harmless indulgence,' said Julia, laughing.

'I had this one made for me,' Edward said. 'If you wish, I could arrange to have one made for you. They're not a particularly new invention – Sir Isaac Newton made the first one, back in the last century – but making them is still quite costly. I could find out how much it would be now, though. It's the mirror which sends the price up. It's made of an alloy of copper and tin, which is a somewhat difficult material to handle.'

'I expect I could afford it. Yes, please enquire for me,' Lucy-Anne said. 'My refractor gives spurious colours. I soon discovered that, and it's irritating.'

'And the genuine colours are quite splendid enough,' said Julia. 'You've never been here in winter, Lucy-Anne, but, at home, do you ever brave the cold and go out to the folly in the winter months? Have you ever seen Sirius through a telescope? It looks blue-white when you observe it with the naked eye, but considered through a telescope—'

'It flashes with every rainbow hue you can imagine. Yes, I have certainly seen it,' Lucy-Anne assured her eagerly. 'I've looked at that mysterious bright patch in Orion, too. I have been in correspondence with the Royal Society, did I tell you? I obtain news of the latest subjects of study, and it seems that these strange luminous patches among the stars are exciting much speculation.'

'You enjoy your astronomy, do you not?' said Julia, as they entered the candlelit kitchen and she went to stir the fire and brew the coffee. She moved softly, for it was nearly midnight and the maids and the children were asleep elsewhere in the house.

'Very much,' Lucy-Anne said. 'It is something to think about and make plans about but not to worry about, and that is such a blessing.'

'An acute way of putting it, if I may say so,' Edward observed. 'You do a great deal of worrying, I suspect.'

'I suppose I do.' Lucy-Anne sat down at the table and gazed at its scrubbed pine surface, a little embarrassed. 'I am sorry. I don't mean to complain. I know very well how fortunate I am compared to – well, poor people. I never thought of that when I was a girl, but since I have known you, and Mr and Mrs Bird at home, and since I saw that little climbing boy die, I have realised that I really must *not* complain. But, yes, there are things I worry about and I am very grateful to you for letting me visit you sometimes and for introducing me to astronomy. I find it a welcome distraction. I think it does me quite as much good as the spa waters!'

'There's no need to apologise,' Julia said. 'Even with Stephen's help, I imagine that controlling your husband's estate is not always easy, and you must be constantly wondering how your husband is. Is there still no word of his return to England?'

Lucy-Anne shook her head. 'According to his last letter, when the French seized Fort St George he escaped, along with some others, including a young man he met on the voyage out, Robert Clive. They reached a place called Fort St David and the French attacked that too, but were driven off.'

'It looks as though the French are now determined on seizing all our share of the Indian trade for themselves,' Edward said seriously. 'It is to be hoped that they don't succeed.'

'They haven't as yet,' said Lucy-Anne. 'It seems that this Mr Clive volunteered for military service as soon as he got to St David. My husband says he is not properly respectful towards his seniors, and will never make a good merchant, but nevertheless showed great courage and promise during the defence of Fort St David. The English also had some support from one of the Indian princes – my husband calls him the Nawab of the Carnatic – who sent men to help them, led by his son. It appears,' said Lucy-Anne, 'that this son, who is called Mohammed Ali, rode to war on an elephant, and would not dismount even though the French guns were pointing at him, by which my husband was much impressed. Then some of Mohammed Ali's men got close to the French and shot some of them with handguns, but many of the guns failed to go off because they were of a poor Turkish pattern. Mr Whitmead is now arranging for some handguns of good English make to be shipped out to provide the Nawab's army with better weapons. It is private trading – nothing to do with the East India Company – and all the profits will be his. In fact, his letter sounds almost excited and he does not seem much concerned about the activities of the French, or even the loss of Fort St George. He sounds as though he is prospering and expects to prosper still more before long. But there is not a word of his coming home.'

'I feel sorry for Lucy-Anne,' Julia said, as she and Edward settled down together in bed. 'She is a wife and yet not a wife and that isn't easy for any woman, even one in comfortable circumstances.'

'It was a very great shame that she lost the baby,' Edward said. 'She likes children. I saw how well she soothed little Julian yesterday when he fell over.'

'She has a good heart. I noticed, at our last visit to Stephen, that her tenants respect her. She shows them consideration and she told me herself, making a little joke of it, that she has learned not to visit them wearing satin skirts.'

'She has sense,' Edward agreed, drowsily. 'I approve of the way she has turned for occupation to the things of the mind rather than to empty social occasions. I must say George Whitmead is a most extraordinary man, to leave his wife alone so long. I have only met him once – when we visited Stephen just after Mr Whitmead last came to England, before he was married. I must admit that I didn't take to him. But there it is, Julia. We can hardly make George Whitmead come home and meanwhile Lucy-Anne lives in every comfort. It is as well that she has the grace to realise it.'

'At least,' said Julia, also sinking towards sleep, 'she isn't taking lovers. Some would, in her position.'

War might simmer, but Fort St David, among its wooded hills, its access to the sea guarded by English shipping, and a ferocious hedge of cactus and aloes defending it from intruders on the landward side, had twice repelled a French attack, and for the time being felt secure.

The simmering produced, as it were, the occasional bubble. A call for help had gone to England. An Indian interpreter was discovered to be in the pay of Madame Dupleix and was hanged. A scandalous rumour was abroad to the effect that while ex-Governor Morse was drowning his sorrows in wine, Mrs Morse had taken the commander of the English naval squadron as a lover. It was said that Madame Dupleix, who had coaxed her husband into handing back some of Mrs Morse's sequestered valuables and thereby made friends with her, was now trying her hardest to convince Mrs Morse that a French triumph was only a matter of time, in the hope that this depressing news would be passed on to the commander and would undermine his resolution.

Meanwhile, Robert Clive had at last turned his attention back to trade, concerning himself on the Company's behalf with gold thread and haberdashery. And George Whitmead had ploys of his own. One of these days, he really must go home to England and make another attempt to get himself a son, but not, he decided, until certain opportunities here had been exploited to the full.

Obtaining two hundred good quality European pistols, without having to send to England for them, proved not too difficult. East India

Company captains often had crates of speculative merchandise in their holds. Delivering them, however, was more complicated.

Mohammed Ali was now back at his father's base in Arcot. In the past George had journeyed there from Fort St George, and if only he could have gone via Fort St George now it would have meant only a sea voyage and then a sixty-mile ride inland.

But St George was now in French hands and he must go overland, on an unfamiliar route. It was Clive, of course, who turned out to know all about it and produced maps. 'What do you want to go to Arcot for? It's a long hot ride and there's always the risk of running into the French on the way.'

'I've executed a little commission for Mohammed Ali,' said George. 'We owe him a favour, you know.'

'Don't get lost,' said Clive, with a grin.

He didn't get lost; nor did he encounter any of the French. But Clive was right about the journey being long and hot. It was also slow, the pace of the horses held down to the pace of the pack-mules. When at length, very tired after a long day's travel, George and his hired escort came through the surrounding hills to Arcot, the place startled him. He hadn't been there for a long time and he had forgotten how disconcertingly Indian it was, and the curious way its mighty pagodas with their elaborate carvings always jolted him under the breastbone, as though somewhere in his not entirely English bloodstream a memory of such things lingered.

As a merchant, he was always slightly ill at ease when pursuing an interest that didn't make money, but he allowed himself to do a little sightseeing in Arcot, and enjoyed it. He had nothing else to do, in any case, because he was forced to stay in the town for several days. First of all it took nearly a week to obtain an audience with Mohammed Ali, in order to present his goods. Then, although he was finally admitted to the citadel, he got no further initially than the entrance to the palace. Here, the guns were whisked out of his possession by a minion and he was sent away without seeing Mohammed Ali or receiving any pay. He was to wait for a further summons, he was told. It was another three days before it came.

He was collected by an English-speaking messenger who took him, on foot, to the citadel and, this time, on into the palace. He followed his guide across a courtyard and along an arcade of fretted arches. He was here on business concerned with firearms, but nevertheless a sudden rattle of gunfire, accompanied by a chorus of shouts, made him jump. In this rich, quiet setting with its dozens of courteous servants, such sounds were out of place.

They turned through a further arch and then out into the glittering sunlight of another courtyard. The smell of gunpowder hung in the air. An interested crowd of Mohammed Ali's soldiers were standing at the sides of the paved square, and in the middle of it was Mohammed Ali himself, pistol in hand. George stopped short and gasped. The pistol was aimed at a blindfolded man bound to a post and wearing a coat which, though richly embroidered in silver and gold that flashed in the sunlight, was unquestionably European.

Mohammed Ali glanced round, grinned at George with a flash of superb teeth in the midst of a thick dark beard, turned back to his victim and fired. The figure jerked. George stared at it, horror prickling his scalp beneath his wig. Then, slowly, he took in the absence of blood.

'Lifelike, eh?' said Mohammed Ali cheerfully. 'I have dressed it like Joseph Dupleix. But it is waste of a good coat, isn't it?'

George produced a handkerchief, wiped his perpetually damp forehead, remembered himself, and bowed before saying in a fairly steady voice: 'Is that one of the guns I supplied? It seems to work as it should.'

'I have been putting a number of your guns to the test.' Mohammed Ali draped an arm round George's shoulders and took him to inspect the target. At close quarters it could be seen that the figure was stuffed with straw and that the wide blindfold hid a face made of painted paper. The exquisite coat was peppered with blackened bullet-holes.

'So far,' said Mohammed Ali, 'all have fired, to my entire satisfaction. You have my thanks. Come.'

Signalling to his officers to dismiss the men, he swept George on to a terrace and into a shadowy room furnished with divans and low tables. Servants came to offer fruit juices and sherbets, and a dignified secretary, who had apparently been waiting for them, came forward with a small coffer which he opened before presenting it to George.

'Your payment,' said Mohammed Ali casually. 'Count it – yes, here, before me. Assure yourself that it is all correct. I am very happy with the guns. I shall require some more. You are leaving soon for England, so I hear.'

This time George managed not to jump. He hadn't even told Lucy-Anne that he was thinking of coming home. He had mentioned the plan, verbally, to only one or two close associates. Some of the servants in Fort St David were presumably being paid twice, once by their English employers and once by the Nawab, to report what the English were saying in private.

Life in India was never simple. Always, it seemed to be intricately patterned, the quarrels of the English and the French and the rivalries of the Indian princes interlinked and curving into each other like the carvings on the pagodas or the filigree of a pierced screen, and one never quite knew what the carvings were trying to tell you, or who it was that moved, so intriguingly, beyond the screen.

And how he would miss it, the subtlety and the unexpectedness of it, when he went home.

'I am hoping to return to England for a while, yes,' he said cautiously.

'To get more guns?'

'I could send for those without going in person. But I have a wife in my own country and as yet we have no son.'

'No son? You are ambitious to have one only? A man should have ten sons, my friend, or a dozen, or ten dozen if he can.'

'One must then worry how to provide for them all.'

'Ah, yes. They may quarrel and kill each other for their inheritance,' agreed Mohammed Ali casually. 'Life is full of difficulties, alas. One must balance one thing against another.' He took a long drink of sherbet. 'So, he said, 'when you reach England, you will send me some more fine guns from there. When you come back – you are coming back?'

'Most certainly.'

'When you come, if the guns are good, I will reward you well. Send all you can, as quickly as you can,' said Mohammed Ali. 'There is more war to come. Among my people, and between yours and the French; and the one fire will enflame the other. May God hold off the conflict until your guns reach India.'

Chapter Eight
Blood-Red Berries

Somewhere in the years between seventeen and twenty-two, Lucy-Anne had learned how to wear fine clothes without being overwhelmed by them. To welcome her husband home, she had put on a gown in the newest fashion, made of shell-pink and pale green brocade, with a skirt opening in front to reveal a shell-pink underskirt. Her hair was dressed high, in a sophisticated style, and powdered. Her reflection in the mirror told her that she looked well.

But it also reminded her that in one respect she had scarcely changed at all. The waist of the dress was cut very small but she had needed little tight-lacing to get into it. She was as slight as when she was first married.

In five years of matrimony, most women put on a little flesh. But most women had had two or three pregnancies. George's letters had become amiable again, but when he came face to face with this thin, sophisticated, childless wife, what would he think of her?

As Maria, remarking that her mistress looked lovely, really lovely, took away the mantle that had protected the shoulders of the brocade dress from the hair powder, Lucy-Anne realised how nervous she was about George's homecoming, and not only because she had no child to show him. She had kept her promise to him, at least as long as he didn't decide that the friendship with the Harpers and the visits to Bath contravened the terms of it, but what if he did?

There was also a formidable list of decisions she had taken, of necessity, during his absence. She had been as careful as possible with money. The personal allowance that George had arranged for her was generous, and she had been able to buy her two telescopes with it, leaving Henrietta's silver casket untouched. But the bill for having the folly at Chestnuts cleaned and some ivy removed had been paid from estate funds and both she and Stephen Clarke thought it somewhat steep. There were also such minor matters as the slightly disrespectful attitude of the new groom, Jacob, and the modern pattern of the new chairs in the drawing room. George, as she well knew, was capable of having strong feelings about minor matters.

Well, she had done her best. If George were displeased, she couldn't help it. If *only* he didn't interfere with her friendship with the Harpers.

Maria was glancing out of the window. 'There's a carriage just turned the corner, ma'am.'

'I'd better go down,' said Lucy-Anne.

Fraser stepped out into the hall just as she reached the foot of the stairs. 'A happy day, madam, and long-awaited.'

'Yes, indeed, Fraser.' It occurred to Lucy-Anne, for the first time ever, that she knew next to nothing about her butler. He was simply Fraser, a middle-aged man with portentous manners and thinning sandy hair who opened doors and announced callers and kept the rest of the servants organised.

She had no idea what family he had; she didn't even know if he had ever been married, although something settled in the shape of his mouth and the lines around his eyes suggested that he had. But she also knew very well that he would prefer her not to enquire. Fraser believed that there should be a distance between employer and employed. She knew, from occasional nuances in his voice, that he didn't altogether approve of her link with the Harpers, because they were related to Stephen Clarke. But he would never say so openly.

'Open the front door, would you, Fraser?' she said. 'Let Mr Whitmead see us waiting for him as he steps out of the carriage.'

'I had had the same thought, madam. Mrs Cobham is just bringing the rest of the staff out into the hall. The weather is rather cold. May I suggest that you yourself remain just inside the door, rather than out on the steps?'

When George descended from the carriage, therefore, Lucy-Anne's first sight of him for nearly five years was from a distance. She saw a man in his thirties, with a reddened face, a fox-coloured wig, not powdered, an expensive green coat which, for all its elegance, was somewhat strained across a thickening middle, and a very marked air of self-consequence.

Nothing in her moved towards him with glad recognition. She could recall standing on the deck of the *Winchester* and minding that they were to part, but she couldn't connect the man now stepping on to the pavement below with that remembered emotion. The memory of that bitter letter had come between.

Her returned husband might as well have been a total stranger.

Fortunately, no one expected her to embrace him passionately in the presence of Fraser and the staff, least of all George himself. He greeted her formally, bowing over her hand, and then they walked sedately, side by side, into the drawing room. Lucy-Anne asked after the voyage; George asked if she were well. She took the opportunity to say casually that her health had not always been good, but that she had found the waters at Bath of benefit and formed the habit of visiting the place. She had gone there again only this summer, she said.

Dinner was announced. George talked throughout the meal, mainly about the struggle between the English and French East India Companies, and then, just as the table was being cleared, Lucy-Anne's parents arrived. 'We felt we must welcome our son-in-law home,' Lucilla said. 'Though we won't stay too long,' Hugo added, and embarrassed his daughter by whispering in her ear: 'You'll be like lovebirds again and perhaps that will make up for all the years apart.'

Before long, however, further visitors, in the shape of three of George's London business contacts, presented themselves. George, enjoying his audience, repeated most of the things he had said at dinner and went on to plan further meetings with his contacts, at which, Lucy-Anne gathered, they would discuss rare spices and firearms. The evening went on longer than expected. Night had fallen before the visitors took their leave.

Then, at last, Lucy-Anne and George, returning once more to their drawing room, realised that for the first time, they were alone, without as much as a footman within earshot.

'I am pleased to find you now in good health,' said George, at precisely the same moment as Lucy-Anne said that she was so glad that his ship had met with no delays. They stopped, confused.

'I have been away a long time,' said George.

'Yes. It has been . . . long.'

'It's growing late. Shall we go upstairs?'

He took a candle from the table and lit their way up. Maria was waiting in case she was needed, but Lucy-Anne shook her head and Maria, with a curtsy, withdrew. The luggage had been unpacked, except for one box, which George now opened himself.

'I gave orders that this should be left for me to attend to,' he said, putting back the lid. 'This contains my gifts. Now, Lucy-Anne, what do you say to this? Or this? And this is for your mother. I didn't interrupt our gathering today to present it to her, but I will visit her tomorrow and give it to her then. Will she like it, do you think? And I thought this for your father . . .'

He had brought beautiful gifts – a shawl of blue silk with red and gold embroidery for Lucilla, brocade coat material for Hugo, and, for Lucy-Anne, three exotic shawls, gloves of silk and fine leather, a fan of peacock feathers, necklaces and earrings of gold and lapis lazuli and filigree silver, and a skein of gold embroidery thread.

'They're wonderful,' Lucy-Anne said, trying a lapis necklace on, and draping one of the glorious shawls around her shoulders. 'I had no expectation of such things. What am I to say?'

'There is no necessity to say a great deal,' George told her. He came to her, removed the shawl and unclasped the necklace. 'There might however be something you could do.'

'And what might that be?' Lucy-Anne enquired, aware that she was being consciously flirtatious, but not knowing how else to answer him. This man was her husband. He had been unkind in the past, but that was long ago. At this moment of reunion she should be able to put the past aside. She ought, surely, to be feeling warmth, affection, or desire . . . or something. But there was nothing. Nor had George himself shown affection; he had not hugged her or admired her careful toilette. She was apparently just as much a stranger to him as he was to her. She made herself smile at him, but when he took his wig off he looked so unfamiliar that she might as well have been confronting a burglar. It was all she could do not to panic.

But he needed her help to get out of his skin-tight stockings and she needed his to get out of her stays. Freeing each other from these constraints did something to ease their mental constraint as well. Once inside the darkness of the drawn bedcurtains, Lucy-Anne began to hope that it would vanish entirely. Her body at least had vivid memories of George's lovemaking. She lay squashed under his weight, smelling his sweat, and the intervening years at last began to be bridged. She had grown accustomed to him before and would soon grow accustomed again.

Perhaps she would do better even than that, for now, within her, his efforts were for the first time producing a small flicker of pleasure. She concentrated on it, trying to coax it into a genuine flame. George cleared his throat, evidently about to speak, and she smiled, thinking that even in bed he couldn't stop talking.

'I am disappointed in one thing,' he said. 'I must own that I am sorry not to be greeted at home by a little son. I trust that before I sail again you will once more be with child, and that this time matters will come to a happier conclusion.'

He spoke quite gently, but the note of accusation was unquestionably there. She wanted to cry out that it wasn't her fault, that she hadn't been able to help it, and who was to say that the child was a boy, anyway? But the pain of this unprovoked attack was too great. It went through the pit of her stomach like the stab of a physical knife, leaving her stiff and speechless. The tiny, hopeful spark of pleasure had been extinguished, and she knew it would never return.

George noticed nothing. His movements and his breathing quickened and she realised that his mind was now engaged entirely with his own mounting sensations. He had spoken as he thought and didn't even know what he had done to her. Inside her, he came with a thud which she felt, and then withdrew and rolled aside. He pulled her close and nuzzled at her. Presently, he fell asleep.

They travelled from London to Guildford through a winter landscape of bare trees and bleak skies. As the horses plodded up the hill on to the Hog's Back, George gazed with disfavour at the chilly western sky and longed for India. There, too, the sun at rising or setting might be orange and distended, but always it spoke of heat, past or to come, unlike that lugubrious apology for a sun now sinking into a bank of cloud beyond Farnham.

He found the sight of it so repellent that he closed his eyes. He was tired, anyway. He had spent the entire week since he returned in a whirl of business – meeting people, negotiating the purchase of this and the sale of that.

He had also entertained innumerable contacts to prolonged dinners, from which he had excluded Lucy-Anne on the grounds that all the conversation would concern business, which would bore her. She had eaten alone in her parlour and passed her evenings alone, but had had instructions to be awake when he came to bed, however late it was, because then he would make up for his seeming neglect. She hadn't seemed to mind. She had been gracious, a little aloof perhaps, but perfectly amiable. She was sitting quietly opposite him now and, just before he closed his eyes, she had given him a smile.

George, in fact, was once more feeling somewhat guilty about Lucy-Anne, just as he had when he first brought her to Chestnuts. He was not in the habit of self-criticism but he knew that he had in the past week been neglectful. It was not Lucy-Anne's fault that England was so damnably cold, and not her fault either that she was so damnably English. His first thought, when he walked through his front door and came face to face with the wife he had once considered a dear little thing, had been: oh God, how insipid those pastel colours are; how tediously correct she looks, and how dull. Where are the pliant shoulders, the sidelong glances, the smooth dark braids, the tawny skin, that would truly entice me?

That night, within the curtained bed, he had *almost* managed to blend his fantasies with reality. Invisible in the darkness, she had felt almost right, her bones small and fragile, her skin smooth. But her response was so poor. He did not want, at that moment, to remember the lithe, uninhibited girls he had at times resorted to in the Madras brothels, but couldn't stop himself. Lucy-Anne's body did not move to meet his but merely lay passive beneath him, and his nostrils missed the sandalwood with which the brothel girls scented their skin.

Subsequent nights were no better. Lucy-Anne was simply no longer what he wanted, and she hadn't (it was unjust, but the bitterness still welled up in him) even been able to compensate for her limitations by giving him a son.

But – behind his closed eyelids, he took his feelings in hand – she hadn't been a failure in all respects. She seemed worried about various things she had arranged in his absence, but on the whole she had done quite well at the business of controlling his properties, even though she had been deprived of his mother's advice. Of course Stephen Clarke had been there to do most of the work and no doubt, where there were shortcomings, some of them were his. A woman and an employee – they were bound to make mistakes. No doubt they would be relieved that he was now back to take charge. He would not be too critical. That, perhaps, would make up to Lucy-Anne for his remoteness last week.

He really was drifting off to sleep now. As he nodded off, he decided that when next he came to England he would bring his wife some soap perfumed with sandalwood. His final waking thought was: how soon can I decently sail for India again?

Lucy-Anne had done her best to wrestle with her feelings. Everyone had faults, and George's besetting sin was tactlessness. He saw things only from his own point of view. He had been deeply disappointed over the loss of the baby, and he had simply blurted out what he felt, not realising the grief he would cause her.

As for those lonely dinners during the week they had spent in London – he had surely decreed them only in order to protect her from the boredom of endless talk about money and merchandise. It was absurd for her to refine so much upon them, to feel so slighted. He had always made up for it in bed afterwards hadn't he?

Oh yes, certainly. The answer rose angrily up in her mind. He wanted a son! He cared nothing for his wife.

No, that wasn't true. Look at the generous presents he had brought her. And look how good-humoured he had been over such things as the expensive repairs to the folly and Jacob's smirk and the new chairs (which she was sure were not really to his taste).

He hadn't even censured her for visiting Bath, beyond remarking that it was odd that she hadn't mentioned it in her letters. She hadn't yet mentioned the Harpers, though sooner or later she knew she must; she hoped that this revelation too would pass off smoothly.

But even if it didn't, even if he forbade the friendship, that was nothing compared to the things some women had to suffer. The world was full of women who were unhappy because their husbands were parsimonious or violent, or simply because of poverty. The Birds and the Harpers, who all did so much charity work, had told her a great deal about the hidden world of misery all around her, and some of it she had observed for herself. She had seen the sweep's boy, and talked to Sarah, and she had once called at Upwood Farm to find Mrs Ross nursing a black eye and a badly sprained wrist, because Mr Ross, whom Lucy-Anne had till then quite liked, was apparently liable to beat his wife up when he was in drink. She also knew quite well that none of the cottage people had enough to eat, considering how hard they worked. The world, in fact, was full of people who would have sold their souls to change places with Lucy-Anne.

But she lectured herself in vain. The fact remained that she now disliked her husband and would be both pleased and relieved when in due course he sailed off again to India.

She also knew that, although George had never injured her physically or even threatened to, she was rather afraid of him. But she was married to him, for better or worse, till death did them part, and there was nothing to be done but to keep relations as pleasant as she could while George was at home.

So she was quiet and compliant, smiled frequently, and as soon as they returned to Chestnuts, offered to arrange a homecoming dinner party for him. George was pleased with the notion and she sent out invitations – to the Birds; to their relatives the Millers, including the Millers' twenty-year-old son Harry and their handsome eldest daughter Ellen, who was now nearly eighteen and out in the adult world; and to the Kendalls, including their eldest boy Ned, who was twenty-one, was going to become as red-faced and conventional as his father, and was looking for a wife. The Millers and the Kendalls were hoping that Ned and Ellen would make a match of it and it had been tacitly agreed in their circle that invitations would include them both whenever possible.

Since that first, hair-raising dinner party at which Walter Kendall and James Bird had quarrelled, with Araminta fanning the flames, she had avoided having the two families to dine together, but she had by now discovered that although they didn't entertain each other except on such major occasions as weddings, funerals and christenings, they could and did meet in the homes of mutual friends without always arguing, and even when they did fall out they managed it without hard feelings afterwards.

Kendall did not own the St Anne's living, which was in the hands of the bishop, and had been heard to admit that if he had he wouldn't have appointed Bird, but nevertheless, in a curious, argumentative way, the two men liked each other.

They had, in any case, both been George's friends since before he first went to India, and George wanted them there. 'I shall try to keep the conversation harmless,' Lucy-Anne said to him, and was rewarded by seeing that she had amused him.

She took trouble with her table, making sure that the napery was freshly laundered, asking George what dishes he would prefer, and then consulting for one whole morning with Mrs Cobham on the menu. When the time came, George, dressed for the occasion in a much-embroidered coat of tawny, with his wig fashionably small and his shirt excessively frilled, gave his wife his arm to lead her to the table and Lucy-Anne, wearing her pink and green brocade and with her hair once more piled and powdered, took her place, smiling on her husband and her guests.

'We are to begin the meal,' she told them, 'with a sweet chestnut soup. I thought it would be a pleasant compliment to the name of the house. Mrs Cobham tried it out last winter, with great success.'

'Except,' said George, quite roguishly, as Fraser and Polly put the tureens on the table, 'that the trees which give our house its name are horse chestnuts. I pointed this out to my wife when she did me the honour of discussing the dishes with me, but she says that horse-chestnut soup is out of the question.'

'It would be something of a tax on your cook's skill.' Charles Miller was an amiable enough soul. He helped himself, tasted and gave a nod of enjoyment. 'Horse chestnuts are poisonous! But this is delicious. I congratulate Mrs Cobham.'

'I feel sure that Mrs Cobham had the benefit of Lucy-Anne's advice,' said Mrs Bird in her kindly fashion. 'Lucy-Anne is very knowledgeable in culinary matters. She is skilled in making preserves and brewing medicines, too. Mrs Harper has remarked to me how much she admires such a talent. Will we be seeing the Reverend and Mrs Harper here again before your husband leaves us? My husband enjoys Edward Harper's conversation so much.'

'I shall try to keep the conversation harmless,' Lucy-Anne had said, with Walter Kendall and James Bird in mind. It had never occurred to her that the goodhearted and correct Jane Bird would be the one to hurl a cannonball into their midst.

But here it was, the subject of the Harpers, tossed across the table without warning and without any privacy either in which to face George's disapproval if he felt like disapproving. Lucy-Anne did not know how to reply and put off doing so on the pretence that her mouth was full. George answered instead and not encouragingly.

'Reverend and Mrs Harper?' No roguishness now; his voice was sharp. 'Who are they? Do you mean Clarke's sister and her husband, Mrs Bird?'

'Why, yes.' Mrs Bird, aware of having somehow said the wrong thing, gave Lucy-Anne a puzzled glance.

'You have been seeing something of the Harpers, my dear?' George enquired of his wife.

Mrs Bird had meant no harm. The Birds, Lucy-Anne thought bitterly, were always easy together and had no notion of the curious quagmires that surrounded herself and George. Also . . . It suddenly struck her that the excuse of ill-health, which she had given as her reason for going to Bath, amounted to another quagmire. It was perfectly true, but the cause of it was mostly the miscarriage which had made George so angry.

But there was no avoiding the subject now. She swallowed and, adopting a casual tone, said: 'Yes, Mr Clarke introduced them to me some time ago. In fact, when I go to Bath to take the waters, they are kind enough to let me stay with them in their parsonage. I was glad of their offer, because I was anxious to find the kind of quiet lodgings that you would approve, my love, and theirs is a most well-conducted household. It's well outside the town, too.'

'I see them when they visit Clarke,' Mr Bird added. 'Harper does wonderful work among his poorer parishioners.'

'An aunt of mine, with severe rheumatism, derived great relief from the medicinal baths at Bath,' remarked Mr Miller. 'We used to make a joke of its name and say that Aunt Meg was going to Bath, meaning that—'

Ellen Miller, who would one day be as commanding as her mother, said, 'Oh, *Father!*' and Mrs Miller coughed. Mr Miller's voice trailed away, lost between the disapproval of his wife and daughter and George Whitmead's frown.

'I recall that when I first came home you made some reference or other to visiting Bath,' George said to Lucy-Anne. 'You had been unwell, I believe? And the waters were helpful, so you made further visits?'

'Yes.' There was a saying about grasping nettles. Lucy-Anne decided grimly to grasp this one and be done with it. 'In the first months after you sailed, I was far from well. Your mother's last illness was most distressing and I suffered a sad loss of my own, too.'

Of *my* own. George undoubtedly thought that the miscarriage was his loss alone and it was time he understood otherwise.

'But the waters were amazing,' she told him. 'I was astounded at the change they brought about. However, I am often pulled down again in the winter – as my father always is. I have come to the conclusion that a yearly visit to Bath is a great help in avoiding illness.'

'But you have been staying with my bailiff's sister and brother-in-law?'

'The Harpers. Yes,' said Lucy-Anne. She looked at George's face and looked away, shrinking within herself, her calm facade about to crumble. His brow was thunderous.

'I can scarcely,' said George, 'think it desirable for you to become a friend, on equal terms, of my bailiff's sister. How many times have you stayed with them?'

'F . . . four,' said Lucy-Anne in a low voice.

'*Four?* In spite of the fact,' said George, dropping his voice to a deep, sad note, 'that you gave me your promise, your solemn word, to make social visits only to the households I chose?'

'It wasn't quite like that. I mean, the physician said . . .'

'And you never saw fit to inform me? Let alone to seek my permission?'

He was rebuking her in front of guests and servants. The Millers and the Kendalls were listening with unashamed interest, and if Fraser (who was carving at the sideboard), the two footmen (who were standing by the wall) and Polly (who was now handing crisp rolls round) were pretending not to hear, their ears were certainly just as stretched. She hadn't finished her chestnut soup. She considered plunging her face into it and drowning herself.

Stout little Mr Bird saved her.

'But of course you were informed, my dear fellow. I wrote to you myself, on Mrs Whitmead's behalf. You were after all a long way off and an exchange of letters would have taken months, perhaps more than a year, but Mrs Whitmead was ailing and in need of a course of treatment immediately. She asked us if we thought it would be proper for her to go, and I not only took the liberty of assuring her that it was surely in order if her doctor advised it, but I undertook to write to you and explain. Did you not receive the letter? It's true you didn't reply, or not to me. I took it that perhaps you had written to your wife.'

'I most certainly didn't receive your letter. Lucy-Anne has never spoken of it.'

'It was so long ago,' said Lucy-Anne, nervously, but following Mr Bird's blessed and unexpected lead. 'Do you know, I had quite forgotten it. I think that originally I just took your silence for consent. And, indeed, I cannot think that you would object if you knew the Harpers well.'

'That is very true.' Mrs Bird joined in splendidly in support of her husband. 'Mr Whitmead, you forget! Edward Harper is an Anglican clergyman with some private means and is a man of station. He and his wife are very fit company for your Lucy-Anne. Stephen Clarke is a sensible man, not at all presumptuous, and his connection with Julia hardly signifies.'

Mrs Miller here observed with dignity that she and her husband had met the Harpers once or twice and had not hesitated to allow Ellen to meet them too, and Harry Miller commented that he had come across Mr Harper once when out riding, and that Harper had struck him as good enough fellow. Walter Kendall also nodded and then produced a backhanded testimonial of his own.

'Harper's got a lot of reformist notions – always wanting to help the poor and so forth. Does nothing but encourage them to expect to live at other people's expense, in my opinion. But he's respectable enough. He's like Bird, here. Your mad reformist ideas put me out of temper often enough, Bird, but I'll share a dinner table with you at any time. You're not what I call sound, but you come of a decent family and so does Harper. As a matter of fact, a cousin of mine was at Oxford with him.'

'Quite,' said Mr Bird. 'Surely, George, you remember what the Harpers are like. I know you've met them at least once. I hope you will not wish Lucy-Anne to end the acquaintance. The spa waters are assuredly of value to her and it is far more proper for her to stay in the house of a clergyman than to spend money on hired lodgings and be all the time among strangers.'

George looked nonplussed and Lucy-Anne held her breath. Her husband considered the matter in silence while the next course was brought in. 'I will not forbid the connection,' he said at last, with an air of magnanimity. 'Nor the visits to Bath, if they are genuinely for your health, my dear.'

'Oh, yes, they are. Most certainly. I find them so invigorating!' Lucy-Anne exclaimed.

'But you must be careful that no harm comes of it, and alter your arrangements should the least awkwardness result. There are other spas, after all. No lady can be too careful in her choice of company.'

'Mr Harper is more of a gentleman than I am,' Bird assured him. 'He never loses his temper with Kendall!'

Charles Miller and Mrs Bird laughed. Ned Kendall, who had been strategically placed beside Ellen Miller, whispered something into her ear and made her laugh, too, and both sets of parents regarded them benignly.

'Harper's fond of all these new sciences that everyone's so excited about these days,' Kendall remarked. 'Can't see what use most of them are, myself. Even if you do know how far it is to the planet Saturn, what of it? Can't grow crops in a lot of empty space and Whitmead here can't sell it to the Indians. But Harper's quite an interesting talker, I'll give him that.'

'Oh yes!' Lucy-Anne seized on the new topic with relief. 'The Harpers have interested me in astronomy.'

'Astronomy?' George turned to her in surprise.

'Yes, indeed.' Lucy-Anne rushed on. 'You have not yet been into the folly, have you? The weather has been so cold since we came back from London. But, when you do, you will find that I have a little telescope there, on the upper floor. It is all immensely interesting—'

'Really? A friend of mine in India, an Edmund Maskelyne, has a brother who is an astronomer,' said George. 'And a sister who also regards it as an amusement. The Harpers introduced you to it, did they?'

He could scarcely hold that against them. As a pastime it was about as unexceptionable as a pastime well could be and George knew it.

He did not know that a little less than a century ago, under circumstances which certainly couldn't be called unexceptionable, his grandfather Matthew and his great-aunt Henrietta had been simultaneously conceived in an observatory. His instinctive suspicion was based on something quite different. His wife's attention ought to be fixed on him, on George Whitmead. He did not want her eyes raised to the remote heavens and gazing out beyond him to an infinity where he was nothing.

But he could hardly say that. It would sound quite ridiculous. He knew that sometimes, unintentionally, he did sound ridiculous and that it undermined people's respect for him. There had been that occasion when young Clive had virtually attacked him, just after their escape from Fort St George. He never quite understood how these things happened, but he had begun to be careful.

He changed the subject, and for the rest of the dinner they all conversed about local affairs – the success of the turnip experiment, Mr Kendall's new hunter, and how well the eldest Kendall girl looked since her marriage and what a good thing it was for young people to be settled in suitable marriages, early in life.

***

'Thank you,' said Lucy-Anne quietly to the Birds, as they were taking their leave. 'You . . . you didn't really write to my husband, did you?'

'No. And I'm not sure,' said Mr Bird candidly, 'that we did right today, but I have to say that I felt a little troubled for you. It looked as though there were some kind of misunderstanding and I didn't want George to be angry with you. Certainly not when it was Jane who brought the Harpers into the conversation! My thanks for conspiring with me, my dear Jane. I was afraid that you wouldn't. You are honest to a fault at times.'

'Well, it *was* my fault,' said Mrs Bird. 'Quite innocently, I caused embarrassment. And I must say I think George is not quite reasonable. I take it, Lucy-Anne, that you were afraid to write for his consent in case it was refused. Well, if you had asked me, I would have told you that you *must* seek his consent, but I also think George could well have left it to your parents, or to friends such as ourselves, to advise you on such matters and certainly we would not have discouraged you from the Harpers' acquaintance. Are they likely to come to Guildford while George is here, by the way, Lucy-Anne? You didn't say.'

'I think not.'

'Just as well,' said Bird. 'The less said the better now, I fancy. Here comes George. Once again, Mrs Whitmead, my congratulations on a most excellent dinner . . .'

How wonderful, Lucy-Anne thought enviously, how wonderful to be so comfortable with one's husband, so frank and yet so friendly. The Harpers had the same kind of comradeship. Would she, could she, ever have it with George? She knew the answer. No.

Crunching across a frosty garden in search of holly and ivy with which to decorate the house for Christmas, Lucy-Anne was tired. George was exhausting. Determined to get her with child again, he was allowing her little sleep at night, and during the day she had to tread with constant care.

While he was away she had grown used to giving orders, but he had made it clear that, now that he was home all decisions, even the smallest ones, were his. She had even had to ask permission to put up evergreen garlands, although it was a long-established custom in most houses.

He had decided to sail again in March. Lucy-Anne was secretly but unashamedly counting the weeks which must elapse before she could be free of him.

The crisp frosty air had woken her up a little. There was a clump of holly bushes beyond the parterre garden, and she found the energy to tackle her task quite briskly. It took some time, for the stems were tough and the prickles perilous.

She had nearly filled her basket, however, and was ambitiously attacking a particularly obstinate stem, because the berries it bore were so thick and brilliant, when Stephen Clarke appeared, taking a short cut through a side gate, across the garden in the direction of the house. Seeing her, he paused and took off his hat. Stephen never wore a wig when he was working, and never used powder at all. His wiry brown hair almost

111

crackled with vitality. 'Good morning, Mrs Whitmead. Holly for Christmas?'

'Yes, indeed.' Lucy-Anne, sawing vigorously, pricked herself on a holly leaf and stopped to suck her hand. 'I shall want some ivy too. There's some on the oak tree at the end of the garden, I think.'

'Yes, plenty, but you'll find it even harder to cut than that holly. Your knife isn't sharp enough. I'll bring the ivy in for you, if you wish. Well, this is a happy Christmas for you, with your husband home. You and Mr Whitmead have only had one Christmas together so far, I believe – for goodness' sake,' said Stephen with impatience, as Lucy-Anne abruptly renewed her onslaught on the holly, 'why aren't you wearing gloves? Look at you, your hand is bleeding. Here.' He took the knife away from her and cut the holly himself.

'You're not wearing gloves either,' said Lucy-Anne. 'These prickles are like cats' claws – oh, now *you've* scratched yourself.'

'I'm used to it. Outdoor men always are. Here.' Stephen freed the berry-laden branch and held it out to her. 'Please excuse the bloodstains on my thumb.'

'My fingers are just as bad,' said Lucy-Anne, laughing. 'We're both shockingly gory. Look, isn't it strange? The blood exactly matches the berries.'

She had taken hold of the spray of glossy dark green leaves and scarlet berries, but somehow Stephen had forgotten to let go. They stood there, motionless, their fingers touching, while a little trickle from Stephen's scratched thumb ran down on to Lucy-Anne's pricked forefinger and their blood mingled.

Their eyes met. For an unbelievable moment Lucy-Anne thought they had done so with an audible clash. There was a long, sparkling silence, until Stephen said lightly: 'Long ago, men sealed vows of brotherhood by mingling their blood, and I believe that, even now, some savage peoples maintain such customs, for the marriage bond, as well as brotherhood.'

Lucy-Anne snatched her hand away and thrust the holly hurriedly into her basket. 'I must go indoors. Were you coming to see Mr Whitmead?'

'I was, but it isn't urgent. I'll fetch your ivy. When next you see Mr Whitmead, would you mention to him that Silas has been talking to me about two of our carriage horses – the pair he uses as wheelers on the travelling carriage, Piper and Flute. He says they're getting too old and should be retired to light duties and replaced with a younger pair.'

'I'm sure he's right.' Lucy-Anne hoped he wouldn't notice that she was trying not to gabble. 'Tell him I will raise the matter with my husband.'

She was almost running as she made her way back to the house. She didn't know exactly what had happened; on the surface, nothing had happened at all. But she was trembling as though she had just found a tiger prowling in the garden, and she was full of lightness, as though her limbs were made of air. Arriving dizzily at the back porch, she sobered herself with an effort. Leaving the holly basket there, she hurried indoors, calling for hot water to be brought upstairs, and sped up to the bedchamber, loosening her mantle as she went. George, in riding dress, was examining the set of his coat in front of the mirror. He turned as she came in.

'Ah, Lucy-Anne. I am about to go out round the farms—what have you been doing? You seem flurried.'

'Do I?' Oh dear, was it as visible as that? 'I've been walking fast in the cold,' said Lucy-Anne. 'I've only been cutting holly. I met Stephen Clarke and he'll bring the ivy. He gave me a message for you. Apparently Silas thinks that we ought to replace Piper and Flute because they're getting old. I said I was sure he was right; I expect you've noticed how they strain on the hill up from Guildford. I said I would tell you and—'

George regarded her with raised eyebrows. '*You* said you were sure he was right?'

Standing there like that, Lucy-Anne thought irrelevantly, with his eyes wide and his mouth pursed, he looked just like a frog. But an alarming frog. He exuded anger. She found herself stammering. 'I . . . yes . . . shouldn't I have . . . ?'

'Have you seen yourself in a mirror? Look at yourself!' George caught her arm and pulled her to the dressing table. A transfigured Lucy-Anne, flushed and untidy, her dress hem dark with damp, her brown hair, not yet powdered for the day, curling wildly and adorned with a couple of holly leaves, and stars unaccountably in her eyes, looked back at her from the glass. The hand which at once came up to remove the leaves was smeared with blood and she knew, if George did not, that not all of it was her own.

'You resemble a gipsy!' George barked. 'And so you're sure Silas is right? Carriage horses are costly, my dear. You make very free with my substance, upon my word. You should have told me that Silas wished to see me and left the rest to me instead of sending him messages saying that *you* thought he was right, as though you could speak for me.'

'But . . . but those horses *are* old. I only agreed with what Silas had said!'

'If you are unable to see that you have just tried to usurp my authority, then I despair of you, Lucy-Anne.'

'But I haven't tried to do anything of the kind! George, that isn't fair. While you've been away I've had to . . . to decide things. But now, when you're home, I mustn't even utter a casual opinion? It's rather difficult!'

He might as well have been deaf. 'Please don't stare at me in that offensive manner. Tidy yourself,' said George. 'Wash your hands, call Maria and get yourself properly dressed. I'm gravely disappointed in you. You should understand how to give orders in my absence and surrender authority gracefully to me on my return. Make a resolve to behave more correctly in the future.'

'I have not behaved *in*correctly!'

'Have you not?' George knew nothing of that extraordinary moment by the holly bush, but something in the spectacle of Lucy-Anne, dishevelled and mysteriously excited, had made him want to work himself into a rage. 'Junketing about to Bath without my permission, all because you were unwell—and why were you unwell? Because you had lost my child!'

'I knew this would happen. I knew you would sooner or later fling that at me. You've made comments already, even in bed, on the very night you came home! I'm aware that I lost the baby. It was my baby too!'

'Don't answer me back. Why did you lose it? I have never asked you, but now I would like to know.'

'I can't tell you.' Lucy-Anne was furious, and oddly buoyed up, as though the encounter with Stephen Clarke had intoxicated her. 'Often enough there's no apparent reason for these things. I think it was the chimney sweep's boy.'

'The what?'

'A sweep's climbing boy was killed in our chimney the day before it happened. It distressed me.'

'A climbing boy?' George dismissed this with a gesture as if he were swatting a mosquito. 'Rubbish. Depend on it, you were careless in some way. Had you been junketing while you were with child? Had you? Tell me!'

'I paid a brief visit to the town house, yes. I had to go, to dismiss an insolent servant.'

'You went to London?' George turned scarlet. 'At such a time, you left the shelter of your home in order merely to get rid of a servant? Why didn't you send Fraser? So that was it. Now I see! Instead of staying quietly here as you know I would wish—'

'I also wanted to see my mother!' shouted Lucy-Anne. 'I wanted to talk to her about the baby. I needed to see her. Is that so hard to understand? I tell you that if it hadn't been for that sweep's boy—'

'Pah! Sweep's boy! And now you shout at me like a madwoman. I am appalled. I came home, my dear, determined to approve of your efforts on my behalf and to excuse any mistakes. You must not suppose,' said George, with chilly loftiness, 'that I am indifferent to the fact that it was hard for you without my mother's presence. But this ill-mannered conduct is quite beyond excuse. I dare say your upbringing has been faulty. I was much surprised, I recall, when your great-aunt Henrietta favoured you by leaving you a legacy in your own name. I should have been warned by that, that you had been encouraged to believe too much in your own consequence.'

'Oh, this is so unjust. You make so much of so little!'

'Do you call the loss of the child *little*? No, spare me your weeping. It will do you no good.'

'So I mustn't be angry and I mustn't cry. Am I allowed to feel anything at all? It *was* my child, too. Why can't you realise that?'

'Nor will I put up with sarcasm. I'm going out now. I cannot say when I shall be back.'

'I think I should tell you,' said Lucy-Anne to his back as he stumped towards the door, 'that I have just missed my second course in succession. I am probably with child again. Perhaps I shall succeed in bearing it this time. Provided that I'm not intolerably upset!' George did not turn round or stop. 'I could do,' she said miserably, 'with a little cherishing.'

He walked out of the room.

Chapter Nine
Horsehair and Bright Silk

He was gone, leaving Chestnuts in January on the excuse that he had business to complete in town before he sailed and that Lucy-Anne could not accompany him because even the short journey from Chestnuts to London might harm her delicate condition. She was, he said, on no account to travel away from Chestnuts until after her delivery.

'After that you may if you wish continue to take the Bath waters. I have spoken to Dr May and it appears that they may be truly valuable to you. And I would rather give you permission to go than fear that you may be deceiving me behind my back.'

He spoke in a tone of sad despair, as though she had deceived him incessantly, in a thousand different ways, and he had given up trying to dissuade her.

Lucy-Anne did not know whether she was thankful or heartbroken to see him go. She resented his behaviour, but he would be gone a long time and she was his wife. She would have liked them to reach some kind of understanding before he left. But, despite even the new pregnancy, George had never softened. She had mortally offended him by answering back and that was the end of it. He put up a pretence of normality when they were with other people; the Christmas revels had been merry enough on the surface. But in private he had scarcely addressed a word to her since the quarrel, and when, in bed, she once or twice tried to put her arms round him, he lay in her embrace like an unyielding log.

Once, she attempted to mend things by saying she was sorry for the quarrel, but he walked away before she could finish the sentence. When he kissed her goodbye on the doorstep of Chestnuts, the kiss had looked affectionate, but his lips hardly touched her skin, and his last words to her were an exhortation to take good care of herself, and the hope that when he returned he would find himself the father of a son. That, it seemed, was all he wanted of her.

When the carriage had disappeared around the curve of the lane, Lucy-Anne was the first to turn away and go indoors.

She went up to her room, telling Maria not to disturb her until she rang, and lay down on the bed. She was glad he was gone, she said to herself. She didn't want him. She wouldn't miss him. But the whole world seemed cold and empty.

No one would think it strange if she stayed in her room for a while, not after she had just seen her husband off to India. But below-stairs they would know all about the quarrel; servants always did know things like that. She would not feed their tendency to gossip. However much she wanted to go on hiding, she must not. She must behave as though nothing were unusual, and she must take care of the child she carried.

She allowed herself to spend the rest of that day in her room, but the following morning she rose and breakfasted as usual and went to George's study, where he had left a memorandum for her of matters he wished seen to while he was away. The first item was a note to the effect that he had told Mr Clarke to see that Piper and Flute were retired. It was worded as though George had been the first to notice that they were ageing. 'Oh, really,' said Lucy-Anne in exasperation.

Nothing on the list was actually urgent. She dropped it back on George's desk, roamed restlessly from room to room for a while and then, since the weather was mild for January, decided to stroll in the garden.

Once out of doors, her feet took her, apparently of their own choice, past the holly bushes, out of the side gate and then down through the wood below Chestnuts, to emerge close to Stephen's cottage, where she stopped short, astonished at herself.

What on earth was she doing here? Calling on Stephen? She had been to his house before, of course, but only when the Harpers were there. Otherwise, it was always for Stephen to come, hat in hand, to Chestnuts. She was still standing there, in a state of bewildered indecision, when the back door opened and Stephen came out.

'Mrs Whitmead! I saw you from the kitchen window. Were you coming to see me? Can I offer you some coffee?'

She followed him through the kitchen door, which in itself made the visit different from any other, for she had hitherto always entered through the front door and gone into the parlour to sit in ladylike fashion with Julia.

The kitchen turned out to be a cramped place, its pinewood dresser and its wooden table both too big for it, and the easy chair beside the hearth much too bulky. Yet it had a welcoming air. The red-tiled floor was clean and the fire bright, and the cushion on the easy chair was encased in a cheerful knitted cover which Lucy-Anne thought she had seen Julia making. A pot in the fender gave off a pleasant smell of fresh coffee.

Stephen had been writing a letter at the table. He picked it up and handed it to her. 'Did you come about the carriage horses by any chance? Your husband told me to replace them. This is a letter to Mr and Mrs Miller. I hear they may be selling a pair.' He smiled. 'Rumour has it that now that Miss Ellen is engaged they want some extra cash to help with the expenses of a big wedding. Am I speaking out of turn if I say that the whole world knows that Mrs Miller always wants to look more affluent than she is?'

'Not at all,' said Lucy-Anne. 'The whole world *does* know it. Sarah didn't stay with them long. She was hard-worked and underpaid. I understand she is now settled with a lady in London, and will have a pension for her old age. I'm glad. I understand these things better now I've come to know Julia and Edward. I must thank you for that.'

'If Sarah is safe, I'm glad too,' Stephen said seriously. 'Life can be hard for the Sarahs. They're fed and housed as part of their wages, but you can't put bits of your dinner and tiles off someone else's roof aside for the future. But I'm forgetting my manners. Do, please, sit down. That easy chair is quite comfortable. You must have seen the horses I'm considering – they're those matched greys the Millers often use in their chaise. They're six and seven years old respectively, saddle broken as well as harness trained, and from what I hear the price is acceptable.'

'I'm sure you've gone thoroughly into everything. I didn't come about the horses, as it happens. I came—'

Lucy-Anne stopped. The fire whispered. 'I don't know why I came,' she said lamely. 'I wanted to walk in the open air and I just found myself here.'

Stephen took two cups and saucers from the dresser and stooped for the coffee pot. 'I made this ready for you. I caught sight of you as you came out through the side gate and I wondered if you were coming to call on me. Here.'

'You made coffee for me?' said Lucy-Anne. As she took the cup from him she was careful not to let their fingers touch. 'How ... how hospitable.'

'Well, if you hadn't come after all I could always have drunk it myself. I ... Mrs Whitmead? Mrs Whitmead, what is it?'

He caught the cup back just in time, before Lucy-Anne's shaking hand spilt it. He set it down on the table. Lucy-Anne, her head averted, was struggling against tears and losing the struggle. 'I don't know what's the matter with me. I'm sorry. I'm sorry.'

'Mr Whitmead only left yesterday. No doubt you feel very strange. I expect—'

'No.' Lucy-Anne could hardly speak. 'No. It isn't that. I ... I ... he ...'

Stephen pulled a straight chair close to her and sat on it. 'Can you tell me what's the matter? Or should I not ask? Perhaps I shouldn't – only, you seem so upset.'

'You were there at the Christmas feast, weren't you?' Lucy-Anne could not look at him. 'Didn't you notice anything? Not *anything*?'

'I thought I sensed a constraint in the air. But since then I have heard that you are again with child. Surely your husband is pleased about that?'

'Oh, yes.'

'Then why are you so unhappy?'

'I'm not unhappy.' Lucy-Anne spoke slowly. This time, she met his eyes. 'I'm *angry*. Yes, that's what it is. I scarcely knew it myself, until now. I'm so very angry.'

'What about?'

'*Because* he's so pleased over the child. He has told me to be very careful and make sure I don't lose this one. He wants to come back and find himself the father of a son. I'll be failing in a task he has left me, if I miscarry again and I daresay if it's a girl instead of a boy that will count as failure, too. I'm here to provide his son – nothing else. I watch over his property while he's away, but when he's here I'm usurping his

117

authority if I have as much as a thought of my own. How was it usurping his authority just to say that I agreed with Silas . . . ?'

It came out, in jerks – the whole bitter story of the quarrel, the weeks of Arctic coldness, of her efforts to apologise. 'I still don't know what I did that was so wrong! I said I was sorry, for the sake of peace, but I was lying. I had nothing to be sorry *for*. And I wished him a safe journey and I didn't mean a word of it!'

'Oh, come! You'd hardly want his ship to sink with all hands. What about the poor seamen?'

Lucy-Anne almost laughed, but lost it in a hiccup. 'You're trying to divert me.'

'You say you didn't come to talk about carriage horses. But you came, all the same,' Stephen said. 'Was it for comfort, and perhaps in the hope that I would . . . divert you? Or,' he said, taking her cold, shaking hands in his, 'did you come for love?'

They migrated into the parlour almost without noticing it, their arms around each other, the coffee abandoned. The parlour was stiffly furnished, with a little gateleg table, several small, prim chairs and one battered horsehair sofa with stuffing oozing from its seams. He established her on the sofa and went to put a taper to the fire, which was laid, but not lit. When he had it burning he came to her and they sat for a while, embracing. Grey eyes and hazel asked wordless questions and their tightening arms gave decisive answers.

Only one exchange was in spoken words.

'Could it hurt the child?'

'I didn't tell George until I was sure. In that time, he . . . well, it came to no harm then.'

And that should have killed it if anything could, Lucy-Anne thought savagely. Night after night, lumbering on top of her, driving himself in and out, George had hammered the receptacle of his seed from inside and outside alike. Anything that survived that must be strong.

'I will be careful,' Stephen said.

He was careful. Lying in his arms on the ancient sofa, her fingertips at last discovering the precise texture of his crinkly brown hair, Lucy-Anne marvelled at his gentleness, his care and his skill. In the act of love his impatience was reined in, changed into a quivering, controlled strength which he knew how to direct. She had not had the least idea that she could be brought, like this, to long for the man's entry, for George had never wasted time on preliminary caresses. She arched and stretched, yearned against Stephen and then wanted him, *wanted* him . . .

Even with George, she had, just once, known faint beginnings of pleasure. But, when Stephen at last entered her, she learned what its exultant heights were like, and its triumphant end.

'When you get home,' Stephen said, letting her out of the kitchen door, 'go straight to the stableyard and tell Silas that I am writing today to Mr Miller about his pair of greys, and that he is to hold himself ready to come with me and inspect them. Say openly that you called on me, to make sure that your husband's orders were being carried out. Then if anyone saw you, either coming or going, they won't wonder about it.'

'I mustn't come here again like this. I dare not.'

'I shall wait on you in the parlour at Chestnuts in two days' time. We will talk further then,' said Stephen.

'Admirable, Mr Whitmead,' said Mohammed Ali, sitting cross-legged on a divan with the contents of a crate of handguns spread out around him – lethal metallic objects in odd conjunction with vividly embroidered silk upholstery. 'You have done excellently, and more quickly than I hoped for.'

'I would have got the guns to you even sooner, but no ship sailed before March,' George said.

'No matter, the guns are here. How we need these weapons. My father, you know, is under challenge from a rival member of our contentious family. I fear that the French and the English may soon take sides in the matter, which can only cause the quarrel to grow worse.'

'This is merely a first delivery. A further hundred guns will follow soon.'

'God was kind to me when he put you in my way,' said Mohammed Ali. He favoured George with his magnificent white smile. 'And now I am going to be kind to you. You have been paid in money, but I said I would reward you well for this service and I meant more than mere gold. One moment.'

He clapped his hands. Through a door at the far end of the audience chamber came a dignified Indian manservant, leading a small female figure dressed in crimson silks, in the style of a dancing girl. Her head was bent and she hung back a little, as if shy. The manservant brought her to Mohammed Ali, who took her hand and laid it in that of George.

'This is Sita,' said Mohammed Ali. 'She is yours, Mr Whitmead. I wish you joy.'

PART II
The Mother
1748–1752

Is it, in Heav'n, a crime to love too well?
To bear too tender or too firm a heart . . . ?

Alexander Pope, 1688–1744

Chapter Ten

Catastrophe

'I'm not expecting any callers this morning, Fraser,' Lucy-Anne said. 'I'm going to the folly to sketch the view through the window and write up my notes on last night's telescope observations. I don't wish to be disturbed and I'm not at home unless there's an emergency.'

But before going out to the folly she must of course call in at the nursery to see her son Henry. She found the nursemaid Agatha knitting, seated in a patch of late September sunshine, while the wet-nurse placidly suckled her own tiny daughter at one breast and George's heir at the other.

Lucy-Anne made the proper enquiries, wishing that she could love him more. He was a good baby and she could hardly complain that he had given her trouble either during her pregnancy or during the birth itself. She had had toothache in the seventh month, and the extraction of a crumbling molar was far more painful than her labour. George had never expressed any preference about his son's name and Lucy-Anne had named him after great-aunt Henrietta. At only six weeks old, Henry Whitmead was gaining weight exactly as he should, and he ought to make her very proud and fond.

But already his head had developed a pale red fuzz and his face had acquired a marked resemblance to George's face, and love refused to grow. She did her best to make up for it by taking the utmost care of him. She had interviewed half a dozen young mothers from local farms before selecting the wet-nurse. She had rejected one for tippling gin, two for being grubby, one for being ill-natured and one for looking consumptive. This girl was healthy, good-tempered, reasonably clean and didn't drink. She was also rather stupid, but one couldn't have everything and it probably wouldn't affect the milk.

The girl gave her a slow smile and said, in her country voice, 'He do be takin' his vittles like a real good 'un.'

'That's good news.' Lucy-Anne patted her son's head, smiled at Agatha and the wet-nurse, promised to return in the afternoon, and went out of the room with a sense of a duty fulfilled.

With that, she was free. Rejoicing, because she was slim and light again, with her milk dried up and her breasts comfortable once more, she fetched her sketching gear, sped down the stairs, and out of the back door.

Watching her as she went across the grass, Mrs Cobham remarked to Fraser: 'The mistress is in looks. That flowered gown suits her; she's

123

like a young girl again in it. It isn't my place to say so, but if you ask me, Mr Whitmead can be a heavy burden. He was in a sulk all those last weeks he was here, Lord knows why. Maria says the two of them hardly spoke a word to each other in private, and she saw Mrs Whitmead crying more than once.'

'Nevertheless,' Fraser said, 'it would have been better if he'd stayed longer. They'd have settled their difference, whatever it was, given time. A young woman shouldn't be left so much alone and who's to know what a man may get up to, out there in India, half a world away?'

The folly was not locked. Lucy-Anne stepped inside and found the key, as she expected, in the keyhole on the inner side. She locked the door after her.

It was a warm day, but here, within the marble walls, the air was cool. She climbed quickly to the upper floor. One of the sliding shutters had been pushed back to let in a shaft of sunlight in which dust motes danced cheerfully. The light gilded the floorboards; touched the telescope on its stand, the little table where her notebooks lay along with some old landscape drawings, and the easel, on which she quickly propped her sketchbook.

To one side of the floor was a pile of rugs. Lying on them, relaxed, hands linked behind his head, was Stephen.

'At last!' Lucy-Anne threw herself down beside him. His hands slid apart and he opened his arms. 'Welcome home, my darling. I brought the rugs safely, you see. I crept in with them after dark last night. In case you have visitors who want to see the folly, I've found them a hiding place under the floorboards.'

'Oh, Stephen. It's been so long.'

'I know. Too long. Come closer.'

They had come together six or seven times in the spring, snatching their chances as best they could: in Stephen's parlour, in the wood close to his house, twice here in the folly (very uncomfortably on those occasions, since they didn't then have any rugs) and once, insanely, in Lucy-Anne's parlour when Stephen came to report on the work of the estate.

That time, they had loved in furious haste, flinging themselves at each other, pulling frenziedly at each other's clothes, rolling over with Lucy-Anne on top, to couple immediately, with no pause for leisurely caresses. Not that it had mattered. They'd been ten days apart and they were ravenous.

But after that Lucy-Anne's rapidly increasing waistline began to make her clumsy, and her desire faltered. At their next meeting, in the wood, they were uneasy.

'Shall we leave it now until afterwards?' Stephen had asked. 'I'll wait. What a meeting it will be!'

'Perhaps it would be best,' Lucy-Anne agreed.

'I thought the time would never pass,' she whispered now.

'The sketchbook,' said Stephen, as caresses and mutual disrobing blended into each other. 'Is it primed with enough convincing pictures?'

'Yes. I made one sketch to work from and I've sat up in bed for the last three nights copying it, with variations.'

'Maria doesn't share your room?'

'No, she sleeps next door. I've been very careful, about everything.'

'Care is necessary,' Stephen said. 'Before, you were already safely with child by your husband. But if you were to become pregnant now—'

Lucy-Anne sat up in alarm, pulling herself out of his arms. Her eyes were wide with horror.

'I never thought of that! I've thought only of coming back to you. I've been longing for it so. Oh God, does that mean . . . I suppose it does . . . we mustn't . . . we can't—'

'Hush, hush. Of course we can. I would never have asked you to meet me here like this otherwise. Let me show you. You can trust me, you know.'

Every time she was with Stephen she learned something more. The caresses she was giving and receiving now had been utterly unknown to her until he taught them to her. Then he was in her and she was rising splendidly, as her tower was built on the sure foundation he had laid.

She cried out in disappointment when he slipped away from her. Aghast, poised and abandoned on an excruciating pinnacle, she watched his seed pumping out between his fingers on to the floor. 'I've lost it! Oh, Stephen—'

'No, you haven't.' He was on top of her again, his fingers deftly working for her. 'Lie back and wait. Yes? Is it yes? Is it?'

'Yes! It is! *Stephen* . . . !'

However, Lucy-Anne asked herself when they were lying, curled together, half-asleep on their bed of rugs, however would she endure it if – when – George came back again? How could she bear lovemaking in which there was no desire on her part, and the man did nothing to encourage any?

She looked up into Stephen's face. 'Your eyes are such a magical colour. Did you know? They're dark in some lights and green in others, but when I look right into them, like this, I see that they're brown in the middle, round the pupil, and greenish-grey at the edges. I could look at them for ever.'

'And yours are grey, a strong grey, with a darker rim and very clear whites.'

'We can never have a child,' Lucy-Anne said inconsequentially. 'I wonder which one of us it would resemble, if we could?'

'Lucy-Anne . . .'

'Yes, Stephen?'

'I love your name. I love – just saying it. Lucy-Anne, Lucy-Anne. Why did your parents call you that, with two names put together? It is so pretty, and unusual.'

'My mother wanted me called after Queen Anne, for whom she has an admiration, and my father wanted me called after my mother. Mother's name is Lucilla. She said it would be confusing to have two Lucillas in the house, and he said, well, let us shorten it to Lucy, and then – so Mother told me – while they talked about it, they kept on saying the two names, and suddenly it struck them that Lucy and Anne, put together, sounded musical. And so I was christened.'

'They chose well. It's bewitching. Lucy-Anne, Lucy-Anne.' He sat up, eagerly. 'Lucy-Anne, my darling, my love, why don't we run away together? I could find a position somewhere else, a long way away and you could be with me as my wife. We could have a child then.'

'What?' Lucy-Anne also sat up, startled.

'I said,' said Stephen, laughing, 'why don't we run off and make our lives together? I'd look after you, better than George.'

'But we can't!'

'Why not?'

'Well, there's Henry for one thing. I couldn't take him away from his inheritance. If I did, George would hunt us down and take him back. He'd come home especially to do it. He'd find us, too.' Lucy-Anne had gone very pale. 'In fact, I think he'd find us even if I left Henry behind. I know George very well. I think he would still come after me and God alone knows what he'd do to me. Or you. It's a lovely dream, Stephen, but it's only a dream. It can't come true.'

'But it could! If you could bring yourself to leave Henry – could you? Would you? – and if we went far enough away and used different names—'

'Stephen, we *can't*. Oh, my darling, don't let's quarrel. Please don't let's quarrel.'

Stephen lay back with a sigh. 'All right, my little love. But think about it sometimes. Don't you long for us to be together, free of subterfuge, living openly as man and wife? If you change your mind, tell me.'

'I'm sorry,' said Lucy-Anne sadly, and thought it wiser not to tell him that the idea had filled her not with longing, but with panic.

George's first letter arrived early in the new year. It was amiable enough in tone, and mainly concerned affairs in India.

> ... I am on excellent terms with Prince Mohammed Ali, but I am constrained on occasion to wonder whether the Indian rulers with whom we deal realise to what extent we and the French use them as if they were stalking horses, in order to pursue our own hostilities.
>
> At the moment, we are upholding the rights of Mohammed Ali's father, the Nawab Anwar-ud-din, while the French support a rival contender by the name of Chanda Sahib.
>
> In addition, the Nawab's overlord, the Nizam of the Deccan, has died this very month and now there is rivalry between his second son Nasir Jang, and his grandson, Muzaffar Jang, who both seek to be Nizam after him. We uphold Nasir and the French uphold Muzaffar.
>
> I personally suspect Joseph Dupleix of wishing to extend his power across as much of India as he can. I certainly think that he

intends to drive us out completely. We must be on the alert for Dupleix's next move.

But you need have no fears for my safety. All is calm enough where I am, which at the moment is Fort St David. I have rented a bungalow there . . .

Lucy-Anne, reading the letter, tried to picture the bungalow, which he described in the next paragraph. It had a verandah, apparently. Perhaps he had written the letter there, after the day's work, when the air was cooling down.

It was true that he had written it in the evening, but not in his lodgings or on a verandah.

A mile south of the fort was a little Indian town. Here George had rented another house, a small, cramped affair by his standards, but a continual marvel to Sita, who had never had a home of her own before.

Here he had installed Mohammed Ali's living gift, with a servant of her own to clean and cook, so that Sita should have nothing to do but care for her hair and her skin, and spend the money he gave her on saris and veils and ornaments, and practise the dancing with which she sometimes entertained him before they went to bed.

She knew nothing of his language but he knew enough of hers to talk to her if he wished. Not that they talked very much. Their principal form of communication was physical.

And astounding.

In all other matters, Sita was utterly gentle and pliant, doing everything she was told, accepting every arrangement made for her. But in bed she knew far more than he did, and she used her knowledge, with authority and without hesitation, for his pleasure. Repeatedly, she left him reeling, trying with his not very subtle mind to grasp at the paradox of a yielding which was also guidance, a surrender which was also a silken conquest, turning him from pursuer to a most willing and astonished captive.

Lucy-Anne, waking suddenly and thankfully from a dream in which George's face, huge as a full moon and distorted with fury, had filled the sky, pushed back the bedcurtains and found the February dawn just breaking. As she had done every morning for the last ten days, she sought the answer to a question and was met by the same terrifying answer.

She was now ten days overdue.

'You sent for me, Mrs Whitmead,' Stephen said, closing the door behind Fraser as the butler withdrew from the parlour. Stephen's voice was correctly formal but his eyes smiled a lover's greeting. It faded as he took in her pallor. 'What is it?'

Lucy-Anne sat down slowly in the chair beside her desk. 'There's no easy way to say it. Stephen . . . I believe I'm expecting your child.'

He didn't answer at once. She looked up into his face. It had become very dear to her and more familiar than that of George. She knew exactly how the flesh was moulded over the bluntness of cheekbone and

127

brow, had so often stroked, with an affectionate finger, the broad strong nose and the chunky outline of the jaw. She knew and loved the way he smiled, the corners of his mouth not turning upwards but contentedly indenting themselves. She knew the wiry, vital texture of his hair. She had delighted, often, in the eagerness, the enthusiasm in his hazel eyes.

At the moment, they were full of the utmost horror. 'Oh, my God,' said Stephen.

'You . . . we . . . we were so sure it couldn't happen.'

There was sweat on his forehead. 'If, just once, I wasn't quick enough . . .'

'I trusted you,' said Lucy-Anne blankly.

'In God's name, I'm sorry. What else can I say? Are you certain? When should you have . . . ?'

'Ten days ago.'

'And that couldn't happen otherwise?'

'It never has, not since I was sixteen or so.'

'Well, I'm here.' He knelt down by her chair and took her hands. 'I won't abandon you.'

'I don't know what to do,' said Lucy-Anne. 'I'm so frightened. If . . . when . . . George finds out . . . how can this be hidden? I can only pray that my parents will take me in, because if they don't I'll probably end up begging in the street, trying to keep myself and the child out of the workhouse.'

'You will not. Didn't you hear me say I wouldn't abandon you?' Stephen gripped her hands tightly. 'At least George is in India,' he said. 'We have time to play with.'

'But we haven't – that's just the point. I was sick this morning, after I'd drunk my chocolate,' said Lucy-Anne. 'I had to pretend it was something I ate at dinner with the Millers yesterday. I hardly ate anything as a matter of fact. I sat there talking to Mrs Miller about Ellen's wedding and to Mr Miller about how well the horses we bought from him have turned out, and I felt as though I wasn't real. I was mouthing words that had no meaning. The only thing that's real is terror.'

'There's no need for that. There's one obvious way out.'

'What's that? I've heard there are things a woman can take. If I could find out—'

'Not that!' Stephen was appalled. 'There are things a woman can take and things a woman can do, yes, but they're dangerous. You could kill yourself as well as the baby. Do you think I want that on my conscience? No, no, *no*! Don't you remember what I said to you, not so long ago, in the folly? Why can't we go away together? Once we're among strangers, who's to know you're not really Mrs Clarke, my wife, expecting my child? We could be a family. Oh, why not, Lucy-Anne? You can't shake your head now, surely? What other alternative is there? Isn't it the obvious answer?'

'No! No, it is not!' Lucy-Anne jerked her hands away. Only the fear of being overheard kept her voice down.

'But why not?' Bewildered, Stephen rose to his feet and stood looking down at her.

Lucy-Anne tried to collect herself. 'Because everything I said the first time still holds. I can't leave Henry. A mother shouldn't abandon her child. Henry has the right to be cared for by me. I can't take him away either; he also has the right to his home. And, as I told you before, George would find us anyway. It's no use. You think you're offering me a shelter but it isn't; it's like . . . like a room with a window that doesn't fit and lets in the wind. I can't do it, I tell you!'

'And what of our child? Our son, our daughter, has the right to live with its parents. You can't just say no, Lucy-Anne. You say you can't leave Henry,' said Stephen resentfully, 'but he'd be safe enough, with his nurses and his inheritance. You can't leave him, you say, but apparently you're prepared to poison our baby before it's born! I love you, Lucy-Anne. I'm ready to devote my life to you and any child you give me. But do you, have you ever, really cared a damn about me?'

Lucy-Anne put her face in her hands, unable to bear his eyes. If she went away with Stephen she would be committing herself to a man on whom she had no legal claim. If he felt at any time like deserting her, there was nothing to stop him. A wife could appeal indignantly to her family, to her in-laws, for help. But a mistress could not. George might not love her but he had supported her and – provided he never found out about this – always would. As his wife, she had standing in the world. She could not, dared not, abandon her security, not while she still had it.

It was quite impossible to say any of this to Stephen. 'I do love you,' she said into her hands. 'You should know that. But this . . . I feel like an animal in a trap. I want to scream and hammer on the walls with my fists, but to run away with you isn't the answer. Oh, can't you understand? I can't do that. Don't ask me again.'

'I see.' Stephen was silent for a moment and she thought, sick with wretchedness, that he had gone into a sulk, like George. But she had misjudged him. 'I can think of one possibility,' he said at length. 'I'd trust Julia, and Edward too, with any secret. I think I should send for them. They'll think of something.'

As he left the house by the back door he heard a noise from beyond the stableyard gate and turned his steps that way. In the yard he found Jacob, that disrespectful young groom, embracing Lucy-Anne's maid Maria, although Maria was protesting, twisting her head away and trying to get out of his arms.

'What do you think you're doing?' said Stephen, intervening with a strong hand on the back of Jacob's coat. 'Can't you see the wench is objecting?'

'I meant no harm. I only wanted a kiss.' Jacob looked after Maria's hastily retreating form and grinned. 'She'd have come round in a minute. She always does.'

'So it isn't the first time?'

'No, that it ain't,' said Jacob unrepentantly.

He was probably telling the truth. Maria was a pretty wench, if you liked them dark and slightly plump, and she had a flirtatious manner. Jacob had no doubt had some encouragement.

But to have the maid going the way of the mistress would be just too much.

'I'd take care if I were you. It's always a mistake to get a girl into trouble,' Stephen snapped, and strode wrathfully on.

Chapter Eleven

The Bargain

'Stephen has told us everything,' said Julia quietly. 'Well. What are we to say?'

'It was kind of you both to come so quickly,' said Lucy-Anne nervously.

'Stephen's letter was persuasive,' said Edward dryly. 'Very wisely, Stephen, you didn't put any incriminating facts in writing, but *dire need, advice and assistance urgently required, please come at once* were phrases more than sufficient to have us hiring a chaise the very next morning. But the nature of your need comes as a severe shock.'

They were in Stephen's parlour, Lucy-Anne perched tautly on the edge of one of the prim chairs, Stephen, in his brown working clothes, sitting just as tautly in another. His blunt features wore the expression of a chastened schoolboy. Julia and Edward were side by side on the horsehair sofa. Julia was majestic in a formal gown of dark blue and Edward was in full clerical dress. They were sitting, thought Lucy-Anne unhappily, in judgement.

She regarded them as friends. It hurt to see those judicial expressions on their faces.

'One hears of things such as this,' said Edward gravely. 'Among fashionable people in London it is apparently almost accepted that once a married woman has provided her husband with a lawful heir it is in order for her to take lovers and even produce children who are not entitled to the name they bear, as long as there is no open scandal. But I never looked to see such things in my own family.'

Neither Stephen nor Lucy-Anne made any reply. The room was silent except for the ticking of a clock.

'What you have done,' said Edward at last, 'is very wrong. You, Stephen, have betrayed your employer's trust. And you, Lucy-Anne, have betrayed your husband. What did he ever do to you, to deserve such a return? No doubt you have been lonely. But you have also been kept in luxury. There are poor women in my parish – widows, and wives whose husbands have lost their livelihoods (a common story these days) – who would be grateful for a fraction of the good things you take for granted as your right. They are ragged and thin and they live in fear of the workhouse, but they would look on both of you with scorn. And you expect us to rescue you from the consequences of your immoral behaviour.'

'You don't understand!' Stephen came to life. 'She *has* been left on her own for years at a time, and the estate is a weight as well as a luxury.

And when he *is* here . . . oh, what's the use? I keep trying to tell you, but you won't listen.'

'These things are explanations. But they are not excuses,' said Edward Harper.

'I don't think you do understand,' said Lucy-Anne in a low voice. 'But that doesn't matter now.' She looked down at her hands, linked on her lap. They were trembling. Every now and then, she thought, she had begun to turn into a grown woman – when she was controlling the estate, when she was making love with Stephen. But each time this nascent growth was checked – by George coming home . . . or by this present calamity – and suddenly she was again in someone else's power, thrust back into the humble, pleading slough of childhood.

But she was *not* a child. She was carrying one, and for that child she must fight, and she must find better weapons than tears and pleas.

She addressed Edward. 'You spoke of the workhouse,' she said. 'I have seen workhouse children, in Guildford, in London. I've given money to charities that try to help them. My mother-in-law's maid, Sarah, was a workhouse child and she was one of the fortunate ones. In this very house one of the less fortunate ones died. I told you about it, Julia. I mean the sweep's climbing boy. He came from a workhouse. I know I ought not to burden my parents; my mother has just written to say my father is ill again. But if I can't find a way to have my baby secretly, and then find someone to give it a kind home, then it too may end up as a pauper. I may have done wrong but my baby has not! I won't let it go to such a fate! I'd rather . . . I'd rather kill the infant and myself!'

'Lucy-Anne!' Stephen said in horror.

'I didn't know I was going to say that,' said Lucy-Anne. 'But I mean it. I will not let your child and mine go to a life of hunger and poverty. I will *not*!'

'Hysteria won't help,' said Julia solidly. And your sudden death, Lucy-Anne, would scarcely benefit your father! Now then, listen to me. We are not in favour of throwing helpless newborn infants on the parish, either. Edward toils hard at home, finding foster-homes for orphans and foundlings. We have already decided to do what we can. To begin with, I have seven children at home now and one more will hardly be noticeable. I can take in an orphaned nephew or niece. The child will be well cared for; that I promise.'

'God bless you, Julia.' Stephen let out a sigh of relief.

'You'll do that? Yourself?' Lucy-Anne was hardly able to believe it.

'Yes. But we still have to find a way for you to have the baby secretly and that is much more difficult. However, we discussed it last night and we think it can be done. Provided—'

Julia stopped, looking at her husband. 'There is a price,' said Edward. 'I am sorry to sound like a merchant in a marketplace but our help can't be given for nothing. You must realise that.'

Lucy-Anne's mind went instantly to the hidden drawer in her desk. 'I have some money.'

Edward shook his head. 'If you choose to contribute to your child's upkeep, we will accept. But I wasn't talking about money. I am a minister of the Church and I can't condone an adulterous affair and neither can my wife. If we are to help you, then you and Stephen must give an undertaking that your affair is over. Permanently.'

Across the room, Lucy-Anne and Stephen looked at each other. For one dreadful, shaming moment, Lucy-Anne understood how they must look to the Harpers – not a pair of tragic lovers whose passion was great enough to lift them above such crude terms as adultery, but a woman who hadn't enough strength of mind to endure loneliness but instead had consoled herself with her husband's bailiff, and a man who had taken advantage of another's weakness, partners in a squalid liaison who were trying to escape ruin by appealing to the charity of the virtuous.

Yet the love had been and still was real. She had a sudden, awful illusion that the floor between Stephen and herself was widening. He was being withdrawn into an infinite distance, a remoteness as final as death. She saw his face and the sorrow in it, and knew that for him she was being similarly drawn away beyond his reach. Their eyes met, in mutual misery.

'Well?' said Edward Harper. 'Will you give us the undertaking?'

Stephen made a sudden movement but did not speak. Lucy-Anne said slowly: 'If we must, we must. But we aren't as wicked as you think; please believe that. Stephen warmed me when I was dying of cold. I'll never forget that.'

'It would be best,' said Julia, ignoring all this, 'if Stephen found employment somewhere else. If he stays here there could be too much temptation. Stephen, you should be gone before Lucy-Anne returns.'

There was no question of refusing. They both knew it. Stephen won't even be here at the foot of the hill, Lucy-Anne thought in panic. I shan't even see him now and then. Oh, God. Aloud, she said. 'Before I return from where?'

'Broom Cottage,' said Julia.

The Harpers had actually worked out comprehensive details already.

'You will travel to Bath ostensibly to take the waters as in the past,' said Julia. 'You must leave Henry at Chestnuts with Agatha and the wet-nurse. From Bath you will go straight on to Broom Cottage. You'll have to put up with Dotty, of course, but that can't be helped. It doesn't matter about Dotty knowing – you're her landlord and besides, she has a past of her own. She told me about it, once. She never leaves the cottage nowadays, anyway. No one else in the district knows you by sight – you've only been there once before, briefly. You can take another name and masquerade as a young widow.'

'But I shall be expected back here after a month or so,' Lucy-Anne said. 'How can I stay away longer?'

'After about five weeks,' said Julia, 'you will write to Chestnuts announcing that you are about to return. We'll send the letter from the vicarage. Tell Fraser to see that the house is ready for you.'

'Then, a day or two later, I shall write to Fraser, explaining that you are ill and that you are to stay on with us until you recover,' said Edward. 'There is an illness which involves a recurring fever, over many months. That is the malady from which you had better suffer.'

'You are probably thinking,' said Julia, 'that for a man of the Church and a vicar's wife we are very willing liars. If so, remember that, like you, we know the child is innocent. To protect a child, we are prepared to lie and in our prayers ask God to understand.'

'What about Maria?' said Stephen in a very practical voice. 'She can't be left at Chestnuts; it would look odd. You'll have to dismiss her when you reach Bath, Lucy-Anne.'

'Oh, poor Maria. I can't do that!' said Lucy-Anne. 'She hasn't done anything wrong.'

'Evil spreads,' said Edward. 'Always, it spreads and touches the innocent. This is an example of it.'

'It may not be necessary to sacrifice Maria.' Julia was less inclined to moralise. 'Lucy-Anne, can you trust Maria? Could you take her into your confidence? You ought to have a friend or a maid with you at Broom Cottage, someone of your own.'

'I think I could trust her,' said Lucy-Anne.

She would make sure of it. Maria came from a poor and overcrowded home which had no room for her now. She wouldn't want to find herself out of work without the reference which was so precious to any unemployed servant. 'But I won't tell her until we reach Bath,' Lucy-Anne said. 'We should be well away from here first.'

Julia nodded. 'When the child is born, I'll take it and find a wet-nurse for it and you can come home. The shorter your absence is, the better. You must leave here, though, before anyone has noticed anything. Are you having much sickness?'

'No. I was afraid I would but it has only happened once or twice and seems to have passed now. I was the same with Henry.'

'Good. When do you think the child is due?'

'About the end of October.'

'If you can delay until May is under way, that would be best, but don't risk starting speculation. Now, are your parents likely to rush to Bath to see you if they hear you're ill?'

'From what my mother says in her letter, my father has been ailing all winter and has now had another attack of bronchitis,' said Lucy-Anne sombrely. 'I doubt if they'll be eager to travel.'

'You'd better visit them very soon,' Julia said briskly. 'You won't be able to do so later. Also, you may as well lead as active a life as possible.'

She did not actually say, 'nature may solve your problem for you', but she meant it.

Having kept the Indian merchant waiting long enough to convince him that he was lucky to be seen at all, George condescended to have the man brought in.

'Here is your pay for the last consignment of turmeric,' he said, handing it across the desk. On returning to Fort St George he had rented a bigger house and also applied for a better office with more costly furnishings than before. It had been a wise move. The merchant's alert dark eyes were taking it in, and the man was obviously impressed.

'Would you,' George enquired, 'be able to handle a regular order for twice that amount at a time? And can you obtain rice in bulk?'

'I can obtain all foodstuffs, Sahib. Turmeric, rice, Bengal beef...'

'There are some valuable contracts to be had with my company. I can put good business your way if you're interested.'

The merchant studied the portly Englishman who chose to conceal his hair under that extraordinary and hideous ginger wig and decided that, despite these eccentricities, the size of the office and the value of the silver inkstand on the polished desk were evidence that their proprietor could probably deliver what he promised. He asked for details.

'But of course,' George said when he had given them, 'to ensure that these contracts are granted to you, I may have to ... er ... offer inducements to certain individuals. I must also give up some of my time. Time is money, as the saying goes...'

The merchant nodded understandingly, and offered to pay a modest brokerage fee. George pursed scandalised lips and suggested a much higher one. The merchant gasped that this was an attempt to bankrupt a poor sales-wallah who had nine children to feed. They settled down to haggle.

The merchant was good at haggling, having learned the art as soon as he could talk. He embarked on the process with confidence.

And made the depressing discovery that George Whitmead did it even better.

The war with the French was over. Back in Europe, peace had been negotiated; in India, Madras had been handed back to the English, Fort St George along with the rest. George was relieved. 'Playing at soldiers is all very well, but you know my views. The real business of life is commerce,' he had said to Robert Clive.

'I enjoyed playing at soldiers,' Clive retorted, albeit wanly, from the bed where he was recovering from a severe bout of fever, complicated by dysentery. '*And* I did well out of it. You ought to approve of that, Whitmead.'

He had indeed done well. True, the expedition to oust a minor Indian ruler to the south of Fort St David and replace him with another contender had been only marginally successful and they had ended up making peace instead with the existing ruler of Tanjore. But he had paid the English off handsomely and Clive had distinguished himself. Returning to the civilian world, he had found himself promoted. He was Steward for the Company now, entrusted with the task of buying in all supplies for Fort St George and Fort St David, from lamp-oil and meat to furniture and silver plate, and drawing an excellent salary for it. The days of clerking at five pounds a year were far behind.

George, however, was not impressed. 'You're getting a good income now but it's a miracle you're here to spend it. On your own admission, all that campaigning in the heat caused the fever which put you in that bed and the campaign itself was very dangerous. But while you, my boy, were galloping to and fro on the plains, nearly getting your head chopped off by enemy swordsmen, I have been trading steadily, and profitably. That's the way to riches, young Clive. I shall be living like a prince before you will.'

That conversation had been some time ago. Clive had gone north to convalesce in the relative coolness of Calcutta in January, and George's private trading ventures were meanwhile growing in a most satisfactory manner.

But all his profits couldn't be saved or ploughed back into business. When he finished interviewing the merchant it was time to leave the office and go home, but he had some personal matters to attend to first. He had ordered some gifts for Sita and arranged a fitting for an outfit of his own, an exotic Indian suit consisting of a coat and turban in cloth-of-gold and a set of silk pantaloons. It looked odd on him, but Sita would like it, and since he had started the fittings the rich Indian fabrics had begun to fascinate him.

At Fort St George, just as at Fort St David, he had placed Sita in a house in the town. When he reached it she did not come running to meet him, because he had taught her to do otherwise. What George liked was to catch a glimpse of her through a latticed window, and to see her draw her veil over her face and slip away out of sight as he came near. He liked to enter the house and then search for her.

This time she gave him a delightful chase, flitting from room to room, letting him catch only the most brief and intriguing glimpses, so that he was red in the face and breathing hard when he finally caught up with her, and it was some time before he gave her the presents he had brought.

When at length he did, he lay on the bed, propped on one elbow, and watched indulgently while with joyous exclamations she drew out lengths of silk and a rope of real pearls. 'Oh, they are beautiful, so beautiful. Thank you, thank you, George-ji.'

What he felt for her was not really love. He never thought of her when he was away from her, any more than he thought about his house or his servants. Like them, she was always there when he needed her; that was enough. When the time came to leave her, he would send her back to Mohammed Ali's harem and go without glancing back.

But meanwhile he took pleasure in her beauty and in her delight when he gave her presents, and hugely enjoyed having his fantasies enacted.

He took great care to see that she did not have children. They would spoil her gracefulness and, besides, children of her blood would snare him as Sita herself could not. He did not want, one day, to go home to England and know that he had left sons behind to grow up in a Mughal court, to become, in all probability, cannon-fodder in Mohammed Ali's army and never to see or hear of their father again.

He did not know if Sita wanted children, but deliberately hadn't asked. There were men who said they would do anything for the women they loved, but George was not among them.

Just before Clive left for Calcutta, George had called upon him, and when they were settled in a shady room with glasses of brandy, Clive had amazed him by saying, 'Whitmead, old fellow, have you ever been in love?'

'In love?' George had almost choked on his brandy. 'I can hardly approve of such excessive emotions.'

'You visit a lady in the town, don't you? Oh, don't look so surprised. Everyone knows about the bungalow you rent. It's all right! No one would ever mention it to your wife, even if she were here. Now, that's odd. I always thought you'd bring her out to India eventually, but you never have. Are you in love with your lady in the bungalow instead?'

'Certainly *not*. A man has . . . needs,' said George primly.

'But are they only the needs of the body? Isn't there more?'

'I really fail to understand what you're talking about, Mr Clive. I am well aware that you yourself have had many amours in the town. Why marvel at mine?'

'I shall give mine up when I marry,' said Clive. 'And I expect to have my wife here with me. If Mrs Whitmead were here, would you give up your bungalow lady?'

'It won't arise. My wife is content to remain in her home and I am content to have her there.'

'You might as well be one of these Indian nawabs, keeping their womenfolk in harems.'

'There is in my opinion a wisdom and a propriety in providing a safe home for one's wife, and expecting her to stay in it. I do, perhaps, impose what you would call an Indian attitude on Mrs Whitmead, but I believe it is better for her.'

'Impose a . . . ?' Clive stared at him. 'You know, from things you've said, I've sometimes got that impression, but I didn't really believe it. To hear you say it, right out like that, is pretty startling.'

'Really?' said George coldly.

'Oh, please don't take offence. Have some more brandy. I meant, Whitmead, that it must be a little difficult for your wife. She's English and she lives in England; it's a different society. If you mean what you say and from things you've occasionally told me – yes, now I think about it, perhaps you do – she must be living an odd sort of life, full of restrictions that don't apply to her friends.'

'Nonsense. She has her social circle, of families I approve, and she has my houses to live in and certain permitted excursions – she has indifferent health and I allow her to visit a fashionable spa from time to time. She also has my son. What more can she need?'

'You worry me, you know, old fellow,' Clive said. 'The Mughals shut their women away because they regard them as property and the Hindus control theirs because they despise them and consider them inferior beings. Oh, I know you think I take no interest in Indian customs, but I hear things from my own lady friends. I know how their men treat them. But we don't think of women in that way, and so we should treat them differently, too. Don't you agree?'

'I think we should guard and protect them, for their own good, and I also consider that you're being extremely impertinent. The only possible excuse you can make is that you're in love and wish so much to talk about the relationships between men and women that you don't even realise that many men would call you out for some of the things you have said, or implied.'

'No, they wouldn't. They know I'd win. Even as a convalescent,' said Clive. He grinned. 'You are acute sometimes, Whitmead. Yes, I am in love.'

'Harrumph.' George allowed himself to be mollified. 'Have I met the lady?'

'No, and believe it or not neither have I. She hasn't set out for India yet. But I am going to write to her and plead with her to come. Edmund Maskelyne,' said Clive, 'has shown me a portrait of his young sister Margaret. I've never seen anything so enchanting in my life.'

Lucy-Anne had left to visit her parents the day after that interview with the Harpers. She had been away a fortnight. She had hoped that, somehow, it would help. But now here she was, back in her little parlour, and here was Stephen, being announced by Fraser, and nothing had changed.

'Two weeks,' she said, as Stephen closed the door. 'I thought the gap would make you seem less dear, less part of me, but it hasn't and I can't bear it. Why have you come?'

'How did you find your parents?' Stephen asked gently.

'My father still has bronchitis. He's far from well and my mother is so worried. She's hardly like herself. I can only be thankful they know nothing of my trouble. *Stephen*. Why are you here today? I didn't send for you.'

'I have some news.' Stephen's voice was carefully steady. 'I have heard of a situation in Wiltshire and Edward has given me a recommendation. I have to go away, you know. Edward says that if I don't leave Chestnuts as soon as possible he will find it necessary to inform George of what has taken place. He'd do it, too. My brother-in-law seems to be an unworldly scholar, but there's a hard, unyielding rectitude under the surface.'

'I know.' Lucy-Anne's hands were clasped tightly together. 'I think ministers have to be like that.'

'Yes. Well – I just came to tell you.'

Her hands were clasped so tightly because it was the only way she could stop herself from reaching hungrily out to him. Her fingertips wanted to trace the blunt contours of his face and feel again the crinkly texture of his hair. They must not. If she touched him again, she wouldn't know where to stop. She couldn't speak.

Watching her, Stephen said, 'I'd like to ask you, once again: will you come with me?'

His face was so eager, and surely, surely, it was trustworthy. But the whole fabric of her life, her whole place in the world, were the stakes. She dared not gamble.

'I love you,' she said at last. 'But no, I can't do that. I've told you why – and on top of all the rest, there's my father. He's been very ill and he's barely begun to recover. I was shocked when I saw him. What would it do to him if I ran away? I must *not* upset my parents.'

'But, Lucy-Anne, I love you.'

'I love you too. I *do* – but oh, can't you see . . . ?'

'I see that it's over,' said Stephen. 'Not just because Edward Harper has ordered it, but because you want it to be over. Very well. I'll give you a written report on the condition of the estate before I leave. You'll find that helpful for my successor and I suggest you set about finding one. I'll be gone in a couple of days. I don't suppose I'll see you again.'

'Please,' said Lucy-Anne. 'Can't we part kindly? I could ring for sherry and we could—'

'Drink a farewell toast? How banal.'

'Oh, Stephen, don't be cruel.'

'You are the one who is being cruel,' Stephen said. The tell-tale glistening in his eyes brought stinging tears into Lucy-Anne's. 'I meant it when I said I loved you,' he said. 'It's an ordinary sort of love, because I'm an ordinary sort of man. But it's love. If I stay any longer, I shall break down. Goodbye.'

She let him go. As he closed the door again behind him, she sank into a chair and hid her face against its brocade and let the tears run freely at last. She would never know now whether she could have trusted him or not.

But the risk was too great. Even the thought of it made her shiver. She would be safer in Broom Cottage.

Chapter Twelve

The Cottage

Lucy-Anne had expected to be miserable in Broom Cottage. Instead, for five astonishing months, she was happy.

She had also been afraid, very afraid, of meeting the Harpers again, but when she reached Bath in May they greeted her kindly. Stephen was in Wiltshire, keeping his side of the bargain. 'It is the future that counts now,' said Julia to Lucy-Anne. 'No more reproaches. We have promised to take care of you, and we will.'

The following day, in the most matter-of-fact way imaginable, Edward and Julia took her to Broom Cottage, where they unblenchingly established her as Mrs Roberts, a widow whose matrimonial home had passed to a stepson she disliked, leaving her obliged to set up house elsewhere. 'Thoroughness is a virtue,' Edward Harper said. 'And that applies even to deception, once one has decided that it is right to enter into it.'

He and Julia knew the vicar in the curiously named village of Chugg's Fiddle, in the valley below Broom. They introduced her to the Reverend Vine and Mrs Vine, vouching for her with such assurance that Lucy-Anne began almost to believe that she was really Mrs Roberts and that Lucy-Anne Whitmead had been only a dream.

Within a week she had adapted herself to a serene routine in which there were no subterfuges beyond simply answering to her new name. The cottage was a beguiling place, full of reminders of great-aunt Henrietta and great-uncle Matthew. Henrietta's name was written inside many of the books that were to be found in every room; the well-polished walnut bureau that now stood in Lucy-Anne's bedroom had come from great-uncle Matthew's house, as had the beautifully carved chairs that now stood around the dining table. Lucy-Anne, who had expected to miss Stephen agonisingly, found that here he was scarcely even real.

For company, she had Maria and Dotty, and a maidservant called Joan. Dotty was now very frail and a year ago, on the advice of the Harpers, who visited Broom now and then, Lucy-Anne had instructed that a maid be employed to help her. Joan believed in the Mrs Roberts story but the others knew the truth. Maria, when informed, had shown no signs of being scandalised.

'Happened to an older sister of mine, it did,' she confided. 'My mam just counted the baby as one of hers, like Mrs Harper says she's going to do for this one. I know my place and I've never commented, ma'am, but it wasn't fair, you having to live like a widow when all the time you're a wife. And even when Mr Whitmead was home ... well, it's not my place to say anything, but I don't blame you for liking Mr Clarke. I always thought he was a nice-looking fellow, and kind. He stopped that Jacob from making a nuisance of himself to me. If you're wondering will I stay with you, well, the answer's yes, I will, and I won't talk out of turn, neither.'

'Thank you, Maria,' Lucy-Anne said gratefully. 'I appreciate this, believe me.'

'You're s'posed to have a fever, Mrs Harper says,' said Maria cheerfully. 'Two of my brothers died with fevers. Their hair got tangled and dirty with sweat so we cut it short. We'd best cut yours before you go home, to look convincing.'

Dotty was even more therapeutic. Her frailty included deafness and the reason why the owner of Broom Cottage was skulking in it under an assumed name was conveyed only with difficulty. Lucy-Anne and Julia both discovered that the gravest news lost some of its seriousness if it had to be delivered in a series of shouts.

When it took five exhausting minutes to convince Dotty that they were not inexplicably insisting that Lucy-Anne was a lady, but were trying to say that she was having a baby, Lucy-Anne found herself laughing. It was the moment when light-heartedness came back into her life.

When Dotty finally understood she put a gnarled finger alongside her nose and said conspiratorially, 'But to Joan you'd best just be Mrs Roberts. She'm a bit young for this sort of secret.' And this time the Harpers laughed too.

It presently emerged that when Julia had implied that Dotty herself had once been in trouble, she was quite right.

'Have you tried gin, missus?' she asked, sidling up to Lucy-Anne when the latter was exploring the garden. 'Or jumping off a table? Worked for me, it did.'

'It's a little late for that now,' said Lucy-Anne, in the loud tone that had the best chance of getting through to Dotty, and tried to imagine what Fraser and Mrs Cobham would have said if their mistress had suddenly taken to swigging gin or bounding on and off the furniture. Once more, laughter bubbled up.

The peaceful summer passed. Lucy-Anne was supposed to be in mourning for the non-existent Mr Roberts, but she exchanged quiet visits with Mr and Mrs Vine, and by them was introduced to the local midwife, and to Dr Anderley, a pink-faced man with white sideburns and a short temper, who was the local physician. She met him at the vicar's house, and the short temper was demonstrated at that very first meeting, when Mr Vine chanced to remark that the treaty of Aix-la-Chapelle, which had made peace between the English and the French, had been a blessing for the East Indian trade, since England had got Madras back.

This was correct, as Lucy-Anne had gathered from George. She had also grasped that many people resented the fact that in exchange England had had to return the French fortress of Louisburg, which guarded the St Lawrence and had been seized in the first place because the French had for years used it as a base from which to plague English shipping.

Dr Anderley turned out to be one of these resentful folk, and indicated this by shouting, turning from pink to crimson, and thumping a small table with his fist so angrily that it broke. To make matters worse, his outraged tirade on this 'monstrous giving-in to they Frenchies' was in a Somerset accent so broad that he was quite hard to understand. Lucy-Anne hoped that she wouldn't fall ill while she was at Broom and that her baby would be born without his assistance.

Maria made forays of her own into the village and apparently formed friendships there with a couple of village girls and the Vines' maidservant. They gave her company on her afternoons off and kept her in good spirits. Lucy-Anne, free of all anxiety, slept well and usually went to bed early; but sometimes, by means of taking a long afternoon rest, she was able to stay awake after dark and then she would go into the garden with a book of star-charts and look at the night sky through the telescope, which she had brought with her.

Maria was now well accustomed to this curious hobby and was almost as good as Lucy-Anne at telling planets from stars. Sometimes they argued about it, standing in the dark garden, with a lamp by which to read the chart. Then they would come indoors, giggling, and Joan, who obviously thought that they were a little mad, but endearingly so, made hot chocolate for them.

Had her great-aunt Henrietta, Lucy-Anne wondered, lived a life similarly easygoing and happy, full of important trivialities? Sometimes she almost imagined that Henrietta's spirit still lingered here, a friendly guardian presence.

The Harpers brought news from the outside world, including letters from George, forwarded on from Chestnuts, accompanied by concerned enquiries from Fraser about Mrs Whitmead's health. Lucy-Anne concocted suitable replies about her recurring fever. Edward Harper, who had undertaken to find a new bailiff for Chestnuts, did so, and went with the man to install him. They arrived opportunely, just in time for Harper to stop Fraser from hoisting his ageing frame aboard a stage-coach and travelling to Bath to visit his sick employer.

'What a narrow escape!' Maria gasped.

The letters from George spoke of affairs in India. Things were quiet, but in a letter which had travelled at unusual speed because George had somehow managed to send it with a diplomatic courier via the Mediterranean, he wrote that the English harboured the deepest suspicions of Joseph Dupleix's intentions for the future. The peace negotiated in Europe might not hold in India. Anwar-ud-din, the Nawab of the Carnatic ('Lord, what names they have!' said Maria, to whom Lucy-Anne read part of the letters aloud), whose favour was so important to the Company's Madras interests, had been killed by a pair of pretenders backed by Dupleix 'and they have granted Dupleix forty-two villages not far from Fort St David. The French have so much land near the fort that they are almost in a position to cut off communication with the rest of the country.'

The English, it appeared, were supporting the Nawab's son

143

Mohammed Ali. But no one was unduly worried, all the same. The real business of life, trade, was continuing despite these annoyances. George remarked in satisfied fashion that his wild young friend Robert Clive looked like settling down at last to a life of commerce, which showed a modicum of sense, although the boy had fallen in love with a portrait of somebody's sister, which did not.

There was no word of George coming home. Lucy-Anne looked thankfully at the very English hills of the Quantocks, where the heather and moor grass, purple-brown and golden, the vivid green of the bracken and the deep green of the woodland made a gentle patchwork under a July sky, and thought that India was a long way off and thank God for it.

The idyll lasted until the beginning of October, when Lucy-Anne was almost the same shape as the bulging ripe plums that Maria and Joan had harvested from the orchard at the end of the garden.

She and Dotty joined in to help stir the saucepans of plum jam which filled the house with sticky-sweet smells. Once the jam was safely in the larder, plans were set in hand to harvest the apples next.

'They'm best left awhile if 'ee want 'em sweet,' Dotty said across the dinner table. They were all, as usual, eating in the kitchen. 'Problem is getting to 'em afore the starlings do. And afore the weather changes.'

Maria glanced at the window. The morning had been sunny but cloud was blowing up now, and a blustery wind had begun to comb the moor grass on the hillside above the cottage. 'The weather's changing now. It's colder.'

'Mrs Roberts is mighty quiet,' said Dotty. 'And a bit peaky-looking. My eyes are sharp if my ears ain't. You feeling quite the thing, Mrs Roberts? 'Ee've been settin' there, leaning yur head on yur hand and not sayin' a word, this last half hour.'

'I'm just tired,' said Lucy-Anne. 'It was stirring all those jam saucepans. I'll lie down this afternoon.'

'I'm worried about her.' When Lucy-Anne was resting on her bed, Maria rejoined the others in the kitchen. 'I could swear I heard her crying last night. She's been happy all this time, but now I think something's wrong.'

'Remembering her husband, perhaps. How long ago was it that Mr Roberts died?' Joan asked casually, scouring pans while Dotty dried them. 'Can't have been all that long.'

At first Maria and Lucy-Anne had experienced a jolt whenever Joan, the only member of the household who didn't know the truth, spoke as though Lucy-Anne were really Mrs Roberts. But they were used to it now.

'That'll be it, I expect,' said Maria. 'Something's brought him to mind again.'

But there had never been a Mr Roberts and somehow Maria did not think that it was Stephen Clarke either. The wind whined round the house and she looked uneasily towards the window. Unease changed at once to relief.

'Well, what a surprise. Here's Mr and Mrs Harper!'

They were on foot as usual, and Edward was leading a pony with their bags slung over its back. Joan ran out to meet them, helped them settle the pony and then brought them into the kitchen. 'Mrs Roberts is resting, but we'll tell her 'ee's here. Will 'ee take some coffee?'

'It would be welcome,' said Edward Harper. 'The wind is sharp. But don't wake Mrs Roberts. We have news for her, but it will keep until she wakes up of her own accord.'

'I haven't been asleep. I . . . I was restless and then I heard your voices.' Lucy-Anne, a loose wrapper drawn around her, came into the kitchen. Maria hurried to give her a chair. 'How are you both? I'm glad to see you.'

'We're glad to be here,' Julia said. 'The journey was a little tiring for me.' She smiled at the question in Lucy-Anne's face. 'Indeed yes, an eighth child, believe it or not. I had thought that Frances would be the last but God has decreed otherwise.'

'But should you have come at all, in that case?' asked Lucy-Anne, as Joan handed the coffee. 'It's *very* good to see you, but if you are finding travel tiring, you need not have undertaken it. I do very well.'

'There was need,' said Edward quietly. 'We both felt that Julia should come with me. The fact is, this is not just a social visit. We have distressing news to break to you.'

'We're so sorry,' Julia said. 'So very sorry.'

'What news?' Lucy-Anne raised a hand and pressed it against her face. 'Tell me quickly! Is it George? Or . . . ?'

Stephen? But she stopped short of uttering his name.

'It's your father, Lucy-Anne,' said Edward Harper.

'M . . . my father?'

'Yes. Lucy-Anne . . . I am *very* sorry . . . he passed away, three days ago. We have a letter for you from your mother.'

The Harpers, deftly, took Lucy-Anne and Maria into the parlour, separating them from Dotty and Joan. Once there, Edward handed Lucy-Anne the letter. 'I thought it best that we should be out of Joan's hearing,' he said. 'We can be easy now, or as easy as possible in the circumstances.'

Lucy-Anne sat down to read the letter. There were two sheets, across which Lucilla's large, looped handwriting slanted wildly, in an obvious appeal for help and support. She knew at once how completely her strong-minded mother had given way to grief.

'His chest complaint grew worse,' she said dully, as she finished reading. 'In the end – she says – he couldn't breathe at all. He choked to death.' She looked up at the Harpers, who were standing anxiously in front of her. 'I wrote to say that I was recovering and would soon be well. My mother says . . . she says . . . can I travel now? Can I get there in time for the funeral? She needs me. But I can't go to her – can I?'

'No,' said Edward quietly. 'No, you can't. We shall have to pretend that the news caused you to have a relapse.'

'But I ought to be there! I *want* to be there. I want to help my mother and I want . . . oh, how can I bear it? I won't be able to say goodbye to him! Oh, if I hadn't been ill – my mother could have sent for me sooner and I could have seen him while he was still alive! Oh, God!'

'Think of it,' said Edward, 'as part of the price. We asked a price when we offered you our help; now God is demanding payment, too.'

'But he's making my mother pay it too!' Lucy-Anne burst out. '*And* my father! He must have wanted to see me!'

'Gently, my dear. You mustn't distress yourself like this,' said Julia. 'You could harm yourself or the child.'

Lucy-Anne, tearfully raging, ignored her. 'Why do I, why should my father and mother, have to pay like this when George doesn't have to pay at all? Why am I supposed to be so wicked when no one ever criticises him? He just left me, left me on my own, and when he did come home he was hateful. Julia knows some of it; I told you some of it, Julia! This is unjust, unjust and so is God. I hate God!'

'Lucy-Anne!' Edward was scandalised.

'You're overwrought.' Julia, wife of a vicar, had only one view of a wife's duty. But she was gentle as she helped Lucy-Anne up. 'Let me help you upstairs. You should rest.'

'I can't rest!' Lucy-Anne's hand was once more pressed against her face. 'I can't sleep! I haven't slept for three nights past. I've got such dreadful toothache!'

She had had a tooth drawn when she was pregnant with Henry and the memory was far more terrifying than the memory of her labour pains. 'I can't go through that again, I can't. It will be all right. I've got some remedies. There's some laudanum in the house.'

'But, Lucy-Anne!' Julia protested.

'It's a front tooth and I'll look hideous if I lose it. I mustn't spoil my looks, now must I?' said Lucy-Anne, with unconvincing gaiety.

But during the night Maria found her mistress crying again and pacing the floor and called Julia.

'It's like a thin white whistle, right down through the tooth into my jaw, and if it goes on, I shall go mad!' Lucy-Anne wailed.

'Sit down. You'll only make it worse, stamping about like that. Maria will bring you some more laudanum, but meanwhile I'm going to send Edward to the village for the doctor,' Julia told her decisively. 'He does the tooth-drawing round here, I believe.'

'No! No, I can't—'

'You must and will,' said Julia.

Edward Harper was already awake and getting dressed. 'I've got to go down the hill, haven't I? Why do emergencies always happen at night? Where does the doctor live?'

'I expect Joan knows,' Julia offered.

'Then she'll have to come with me,' said Edward tersely. 'Is she up? If not, wake her. And tell her to bring a lantern.'

Joan knew the way, but the walk down the hill in darkness and a strong wind took some time, and Dr Anderley, who had only just got into bed after another night call, was not co-operative. Leaning irascibly out of his bedroom window he demanded in his broad West Country voice, to know why Lucy-Anne couldn't wait until morning. 'She won't die. Volk don't die of toothache.'

146

'Oh, if you could see her, you wouldn't say that! Please come, please!' Joan pleaded.

'Ee'll zee me at Broom after breakfast,' said the doctor, and slammed the window shut. Edward Harper promptly handed the lantern to Joan and set about hammering on the door with his fists. The doctor, dressed but furious, opened it two minutes later. 'All right, all right. Zo I'll goo and zaddle my mare. Calling volk out of a night for a tooth; I never hear the like! Why didn't the zilly bitch call me avore in the daytime?'

'You will not call Mrs Roberts names,' said Edward Harper grimly. 'Nor waste time saddling your mare. Let the poor beast rest. We'll get there quicker if we go straight up on foot.'

'Oh, I zee. You be willin' to let my 'orse rest, but not the poor bloody doctor!'

'The mare didn't choose you for an owner, but you chose to be a doctor,' retorted Edward. 'Now come *on*.'

Dotty was hovering impatiently at the kitchen door when the three of them arrived. 'Thank God 'ee's here. I've been a'watching that lantern a'comin' up the hill, and praying it was you and not a will o' wisp. Poor Mrs Roberts, she'm mortal bad. The babby's started!'

Lucy-Anne afterwards remembered that night as a darkness shot through with pain, like flashes of an intolerable, blazing light.

Dr Anderley was efficient even when angry, but his efficiency was almost the most terrifying thing about him. Oblivious to his patient's panic-stricken eyes and streaming tears, he sat her in a chair, told Edward to hold her head, demanded a spoon, opened her mouth, and vigorously tapped each of her teeth in turn with the spoon-handle. Then he grunted, produced a pair of slender pliers from his bag and with astonishing speed and deftness extracted not one tooth, but two.

'In a while, 'ee'd have been in as much trouble again, if I hadn't done that,' he informed Lucy-Anne as she wept and spat and bled into the basin presented by Joan, who was herself weeping in sympathy. 'Rotten as bad apples, both o' they teeth.'

'They're both in front.' Lucy-Anne moaned it out indistinctly through a bloody froth. 'What will I look like?'

'Stonehenge, like as not,' said Dr Anderley unsympathetically. 'Ever zeen it? Up on Zalisbury Plain it be; great tall grey stones with gaps in between. Oh, hush your noise. Which do 'ee want – gaps in the teeth or toothache for the rest of your life? Got no other choices, let me tell 'ee. Now, what be all this Dotty's zaying about the babby coming?'

'It is,' said Lucy-Anne, and with that the pulsing pain in her ploughed and harrowed mouth blended with the clenching in her belly into one gigantic agony, in which she no longer knew what she was saying or doing, and couldn't understand the exhortations of those around her, but was helplessly dependent on them as they lifted her and carried her to the bed.

She was being attended by Dr Anderley after all. It was he, three hours later, who delivered Stephen's son.

She swam back to the world to find that day had broken. She was still in pain, but it was not physical. Her body was at ease; there was little to be felt even where the two teeth had been. The distress was in her mind, an aching grief which she felt too weak to examine. She turned her head and found Julia sitting beside her.

'Ah, you're awake. How do you feel?' Julia put a hand on Lucy-Anne's forehead. 'You're cool; good. You have a son. About three weeks early, I think, but he seems strong though he's small.'

'Where . . . where is he?'

'Downstairs with a wet-nurse. Dr Anderley sent a girl up from Chugg's. He's a competent doctor even if he does frighten one half to death. I've never,' said Julia with feeling, 'known anyone so rude. But Edward paid him, with a bit extra, because you're here and so is the child and both of you in good order, it seems.'

'Can I see him – the baby?'

'It might be better not, or not yet. I will always be your friend, Lucy-Anne; we both like you even though . . . well, you know what I mean. That means that we'll meet, and you'll see your son occasionally. But you have to learn to think of him as mine and perhaps you should put some distance between yourself and him before you see him.'

Lucy-Anne had thought she was too weak to sit up, but now she came upright instantly. 'I *must* see him. Please!'

'Are you sure?'

'Yes!'

But when she was holding him, it was dreadful. He was so beautiful, far more beautiful than Henry had ever been.

But it was Henry whom she must love, if she could. This new son was not for her.

He looked unbelievably like Stephen.

Gently, but inexorably, Julia took him back. 'I shall tell him, when he is older, that Stephen is his father,' she said. 'But I shall never tell him his mother's identity. I think you ought to name him, though. What would you like to call him?'

'It can't be Stephen; you already have a Stephen. And you have a Julian too, so I can't call him after you either.'

'I also have a little Edward.'

'Call him Hugo,' said Lucy-Anne. 'After my father,' and then identified the grief to which she had awoken. At one and the same time, she had lost her father and her son.

But there was one more thing she could do for her son, and for the Harpers who were giving him his future. She asked Julia to fetch Edward, and said: 'I once mentioned to you that I had some money, and you said, Mr Harper, that if I wished to contribute to my child's upkeep, you would accept. If you look in that bureau behind you you'll find a silver casket in the top drawer, with five hundred sovereigns inside it. Take it.'

'Five hundred . . . ?' Julia blinked. 'How on earth did you acquire that?'

'It's a great deal of money,' said Edward.

'Great-aunt Henrietta left it to me. Not in her will; in a letter to great-uncle Matthew. He delivered the money to me secretly and I've had it by me ever since.'

'And you never told George?' Julia asked.

'Great-uncle Matthew told me not to. Oh, *Julia*. You're helping me to hide Hugo from George, but you have scruples about a legacy which was sanctioned by my great-uncle? He was George's grandfather and he still thought I should have my five hundred pounds to myself!'

'Over the baby,' Edward said, 'we felt we had to help you, even if it meant committing deception. You are our friend, Stephen is Julia's brother, and Hugo is a defenceless infant. But needless deception is another matter. However, we take your point.' He went to the bureau and found the casket, Having glanced inside, he closed the lid again. 'Do you want us to take all of it?'

'Yes, please.' Lucy-Anne was growing drowsy.

'You're sure? Lucy-Anne, we are not that well off but we are not so poor either. We can manage without this.'

'No. Children have to be fed and clothed and I would like my son well educated. It isn't right that . . . that he should be a burden on you.'

'I see.' Edward frowned, thinking it out. He and Julia seemed to exchange a silent communication. Then he said: 'We'll give you back the casket as a keepsake of your great-aunt. And, if you are sure it is what you wish, the money shall be used for Hugo.'

'It will be used for no other purpose,' Julia said. 'We promise.'

Chapter Thirteen
The Knife in the Heart

Fraser, welcoming Lucy-Anne at the front door of Chestnuts, looked older. There were new lines in his face, lines which deepened in concern when she smiled at him and he took in not only her cropped hair but the gap in her front teeth. With the utmost correctness, however, he said only that he was glad to see her home. 'We have all been worried, madam.'

'That was kind of you. I'm relieved to be safely back, too,' Lucy-Anne said.

It wasn't true. She had been fond of Chestnuts once, but now it was a cold place, full of the memory of George's unkindness, and empty of Stephen's love. In Broom Cottage she had been free of them both, but here she would meet them at every corner.

And she had left her newborn son behind.

Her last glimpse of him had been a swaddled shape in Julia's arms, while Julia held up one of his tiny hands and made it wave goodbye. He was one of the Harpers' children now. Henry, who could be heard roaring somewhere upstairs, must henceforth be Lucy-Anne's only child.

She hoped to heaven that Julia would come safely through her new pregnancy. It was, after all, her eighth, and although she seemed in good health Edward had gone to the length of reassuring Lucy-Anne about her baby's future if by any chance Julia were not there after all to mother him.

'He will share whatever arrangements I make for our own children. He will be well cared for, I promise. I hope all will go well, but Julia is nearly forty now and God's decisions sometimes seem harsh. One must be prepared.'

'I will pray for a happy outcome, for all your sakes,' Lucy-Anne said, and cried that night for Hugo, who so badly needed a mother.

She had visited her own mother on the way home, piling renewed sorrow for her father on top of sorrow for her son. As a result, in her black mourning garments she would have looked convincingly wan even without her lost teeth and the short hair which had been Maria's inspiration. As she entered the hallway she glanced up at the portrait of herself and George. The contrast between her appearance as a bride of seventeen, and her appearance now, was horrifying. She told herself dryly that her story of a prolonged sickness shouldn't be hard for anyone to believe.

She went first to see Henry. He had not forgotten her and the arms of one small child could, she found, console one a little for the absence of another. But he looked more than ever like George. She feared that he was going to grow into his father's double.

Later, she went to her little parlour. It seemed so familiar that she might never have been away. She went straight to the Boulle desk and unlocked the secret compartment.

Edward Harper had kept his word and given her back the silver casket. She had unpacked it and brought it to the parlour with her and now she slid it back into its old place, pleased to see it there. The bare compartment had been too much of a reminder of her lost son. Just as the whole parlour was a reminder of Stephen. He had stood on that rug, sat in that chair. Made love to her on that floor . . .

Tomorrow she must meet his replacement, must interview a stranger who would stand where Stephen had stood, and she must try not to mind.

But one could get used to the most surprising things. The fact was, Lucy-Anne sometimes thought, that since she married George she had spent most of her time pretending – to be a competent chatelaine when actually she felt like a schoolgirl; to be a meek wife when she had learned to be a competent chatelaine; to be a respectable matron when she had a secret lover; to be widowed Mrs Roberts when she was actually fallen Mrs Whitmead.

Living in Chestnuts without either Stephen or little Hugo, unable to grieve for them or even to speak of them, was just another pretence. She found that she could endure it, having served a hard apprenticeship.

In a dreadful, twisted fashion, the loss of her father did indeed help. If she sometimes cried at night and had red-rimmed eyes in the morning, no one was surprised. Once she even overheard Mrs Cobham remarking to Fraser that the mistress was taking her father's death hard; but it was to be expected, she was obviously that pulled down after her long illness.

What kind of woman have I become? she asked herself. What the world sees, and what I really am, are two different things. And what I really am the world would condemn.

But that real, hidden, Lucy-Anne was made, perversely, out of all that had been best in her. If only, she sometimes thought drearily, George had loved her and let her love him back. All that power of loving had been dammed up in her and gone stagnant, like a pool with no outlet.

Acquaintances came to offer their condolences for her father's death – the Millers, the Kendalls, the Birds. Christmas came. She organised a Christmas Eve dinner for the servants, and herself spent Christmas Day quietly with the Birds at Southdene, attending their church in the morning.

January arrived, and February. The Millers called again, very pleased and proud because their daughter Ellen, now Mrs Ned Kendall, had given birth safely to her first child, a daughter, Emma. 'Such a little beauty. She is going to be fair; her skin is like alabaster.'

152

Lucy-Anne tried not to feel jealous of Ellen, who had not had to conceal her pregnancy or give away her child.

The weather was raw, with dismal mists which often hung about all day. She fell ill with influenza and discovered that Dr May had retired and that his replacement, Dr Graham, was young and full of new ideas. He scandalised Mrs Cobham by insisting that the sickroom windows should be open to admit fresh air.

Whether because of the fresh air or in spite of it, she was slow to recover and it was March before she was herself again. The weather was still gloomy. On the first morning when she felt well enough to get up at her usual time, she looked out of the window at the grey and misty landscape and suddenly rebelled. It was time to stop pretending, time to make the imitation real. Time to begin again.

Today, for the first time since her illness, she was to receive a report from Mr Cottrell, the bailiff whom Edward had found for her, who now lived, with a wife and two children, in Stephen's old cottage. As she entered the parlour she made a conscious effort to brush aside the ghost of Stephen, and succeeded. When Mr Cottrell arrived she greeted him pleasantly and found that she could at last look on him not as the man who had taken Stephen's place, but simply as Mr Cottrell, bailiff, forty years of age, weather-reddened and with a loud voice which, indoors, he kept down with a visible effort.

There was a good deal to discuss this time. Mr Cottrell was less inclined than Stephen to be patient with tenants who got behind with their rent, but he was able and experienced at his work and made his employer's interests his own. He was of the opinion that the size of the Whitmead sheep flock could with advantage be increased – 'wool is extremely profitable, Mrs Whitmead,' he informed her, in tones probably audible at the far end of the garden – 'and then there is the matter of Craddock.'

'Craddock?'

'Yes, the man who had the cottage at the other side of the home farm. He has just died – ah, you have been unwell yourself, of course, Mrs Whitmead, and no doubt you were not informed. I am relieved to see you recovered,' boomed Mr Cottrell, 'for this influenza is a most diabolical thing. Craddock fell ill with it and it turned to a congestion of the lungs. His son – who is in his twenties – wants to take over the tenancy. He is engaged to marry, but he is willing to let his mother continue living there. I recommend that we should agree, but what is your opinion?'

'Oh yes, I'm sure you're right. Mark Craddock is a hard worker and he was born in that cottage. I doubt if we should do better by looking for someone else.'

'Good, then that is settled. Mark Craddock can inherit the tenancy. Returning to the matter of the sheep, I have heard of a new breed . . .'

A smooth, easy interview, Lucy-Anne thought, and then found herself quelling a giggle, the first for months, as it occurred to her that it was a good thing Stephen hadn't had a voice like Mr Cottrell's, or they would never have been able to keep their love affair secret. 'Darling, I

153

love you' would sooner or later have been declared to the whole house in a bellow.

Mr Cottrell, walking home, decided that after all he would stay in his post. He had found Mrs Whitmead very difficult at first, a curious mixture of the very vague and the slightly hostile. But today she had been quite different; it was as if, for the first time, she were actually thinking about the business in hand. Perhaps it was just that at last she had recovered her health. An undulant fever and then an attack of influenza were enough to make anyone seem distracted.

Later that morning, the day having brightened, Lucy-Anne walked through the garden to the folly. She had been there several times since her return, but not to sketch, nor to look at stars through her telescope. On returning from Broom she had simply thrust the telescope into a box-room and left it there, and all she had done with the folly was walk round it and remember being there with Stephen.

She had, in fact, mooned round it. There would be no more mooning. She examined it inside and out, pulled up the floorboards under which Stephen had once hidden their rugs, discovered dry rot in the cavity and decided that the upstairs flooring had better be replaced. After that, she'd reinstate the telescope.

Leaving the folly, she locked it decisively behind her, returned to the house, went to the nursery and played with Henry for an hour. Then she went downstairs to the drawing room, summoned Fraser and Mrs Cobham and announced that she wished to return the Birds' Christmas hospitality.

'Although I am in mourning there will be no harm, I think, in entertaining them to dinner. They have been very kind to me. I think I should ask the Millers too. Mrs Cobham, if you could suggest some suitable dishes . . .'

'She's coming back to herself again,' Fraser said, when he and Mrs Cobham were back in the kitchen. 'I thought she never would. I hear from Maria that they nearly lost her, when she was in Bath. I've been afraid she might go into a decline on us.'

'She gave me a shock when I first saw her, after she came home,' Mrs Cobham agreed.

Mrs Cobham had learned very young that if you wanted to keep your place you'd better not gossip about your employers. She had therefore kept certain thoughts to herself. But when Lucy-Anne came home looking so ravaged, it had given Mrs Cobham a shock for more than one reason.

Mrs Cobham, in fact, had been harbouring some suspicions which she now saw were quite unworthy. The fact was, a woman in a certain condition had a certain look. There was a lustrousness about the eyes and a gloss on the hair, and before Lucy-Anne went off to Bath she had exhibited those signs. She had been away for about the right length of time, too, assuming that she'd delayed as long as she could before she left. Mrs Cobham could even have put a name to the man. That Stephen Clarke had made himself scarce all of a sudden at about the same time, hadn't he?

But Mrs Cobham had now changed her mind and was infinitely

thankful that she hadn't said anything to anyone. The details of Lucy-Anne's illness, as related by Maria, were most graphic, and anyway one couldn't imagine a respectable vicar like Mr Harper being party to such a deception. Besides, Mrs Whitmead's hair had been cut short, which was a sure sign that she'd had a genuine and persistent fever.

As for Stephen Clarke, well, it seemed now that he hadn't made himself quite as scarce as all that, but if he were still interested in Chestnuts, it wasn't on account of Mrs Whitmead . . .

Lucy-Anne, in mourning for her father, had been living very quietly, but would have done so in any case. George expected it and from now on she must take more care than ever to live as he would wish. She could never go through all this again.

According to the Kendalls, who went so often to London, it was now the fashion there for women of position to make a great to-do over getting up in the morning. They would hold court in their bedchambers, receiving callers, admirers and dressmakers, and even having musicians in to entertain the visitors. But George would certainly be horrified by such things and Lucy-Anne herself on the whole preferred to wake quietly and prepare her mind for the day without distraction.

However, when she was expecting guests to dinner she did expect Maria to be on hand to dress her hair, which was now a satisfactory length, and to tighten her stays and help her into the elegant confection of pale grey brocade which she had chosen to wear.

That on this occasion she had to sit in her wrapper and ring her bell three times before Maria appeared did not please her.

'Where on earth have you been, Maria?' she said impatiently. 'My guests are probably having their horses put to at this moment. You're not ill, I hope?'

'I'm very sorry, Mrs Whitmead. I know I should have been here. It was just—' Maria, oddly ill at ease, bobbed a curtsy in lieu of further explanation and said: 'I've brought a letter up with me. Mr Fraser went into Guildford this morning and collected it at the post office. It's from Bath. It's from Mr and Mrs Harper, like as not.'

'From Bath?' Lucy-Anne forgot about getting dressed and reached for the paperknife she kept on her bedside table. 'It's the end of March. Mrs Harper must have had her baby by now. There may be news about it. Yes, it's from Edward Harper. Ah. Mrs Harper is safe and well, thank goodness. But, Maria, where *were* you? It's not like you to be so tardy.'

'I was writing a letter myself, Mrs Whitmead. I wanted to get it finished. I couldn't catch Mr Fraser this morning but Mrs Cottrell called on Mrs Cobham and said she'd take it for me if I'd hurry. She's going into Farnham later and—'

'All right, Maria.' Lucy-Anne was scanning the rest of Edward's letter as she spoke. 'I don't want all the details. I'd prefer you to deal with your correspondence on days when I'm not having guests. However, you've never done this before, so I'll say no more about it. I . . . oh, dear.'

'Is it bad news, Mrs Whitmead?'

'Well, it could have been worse. Mr Harper put in the very first few lines that his wife is safe. But she has been ill and in danger. She had a little daughter two weeks ago, and it was a difficult delivery. The baby died when she was four days old. They called her Amelia. The gravestone will have on it *Amelia Harper, born and died March 1750.* How very sad.'

'My mam lost her ninth and her tenth like that,' Maria said. 'What she went through,' she added confidentially, 'was almost enough to put me off marrying, I can tell you.'

'I must write back today,' Lucy-Anne said. 'Almost put you off marrying, did you say? You've never given me that impression. Didn't Steph— Mr Clarke once have to rescue you from Jacob?'

'Ma'am . . .'

'Yes, Maria?'

'That letter I was writing . . . it's gone off now. So it's on its way and there's something I've got to tell you.'

'I can hardly believe this. How . . . how long has it been going on?' Lucy-Anne was glad she was sitting down. If she tried to stand, she didn't think her knees would support her.

'I'm sorry, ma'am. I was afraid it 'ud upset you. Nothing's been going on, in any wrong sense, honest.'

'I'd hardly be in a position to criticise if it had,' said Lucy-Anne bitterly. 'But please tell me how it . . . how it came about.'

'Well, it come about in the first place because Mr Clarke was concerned for you, ma'am. I never told you, because he said I wasn't to, and so did Mr Harper when I spoke to him about it, but Mr Clarke came to Chugg's Fiddle while we were in Broom Cottage. He had an errand down that way for his new employer – buying a bull, he said – and he lodged in Chugg's a'purpose and waylaid me when I was visiting friends there. He wanted first-hand news of you. Well, we talked. He was there a week. Afterwards, he wrote to me, still asking about you to begin with, but later . . .'

'I've never been much of a hand at writing,' Maria said. 'My mam got a lodger of ours to teach me and some of the others our letters because she said that way we might better ourselves, and I've been glad, because I wouldn't have got a post as a maid without it, would I? But when I come to you, I could just about write down what goes into making a pot of hand lotion. But working for you I've learned more, because you're fond of books and you've shown me things in them that interest you, and got me to read aloud . . .'

'Are you telling me that in my employ you learned to write much better, so that you were able to correspond with Mr Clarke?'

'More or less, ma'am. Well, since we've been back here he's come to Farnham two-three times and we've met. And, well, it's been me he was thinking about. He knew you were all right and anyhow – well, I said, I'm sorry if it upsets you. But all that's in the past, isn't it, ma'am? I mean, there's no reason why he and I shouldn't . . .'

'Quite. You're not upsetting me,' said Lucy-Anne. 'I was simply astonished, that's all.'

With a monstrous effort, she kept her voice steady. Not upset? She was in torment. All the demons she thought she had driven out, the memory of Stephen and the love and longing and desire she had fought so hard against when first she came back to Chestnuts were awake and clawing her once again.

But even to Maria, who knew the truth of what had been, she mustn't show it. At this very moment the proper relationship between them was being distorted, for it was simply not according to the natural order of things for mistress and maid both to love the same man.

But it would be a thousand times worse if they quarrelled over him. She, Lucy-Anne, had no rights in Stephen. He was a bachelor and perfectly free to court Maria, and Maria was perfectly free to accept his proposal.

And if she, Lucy-Anne, came face to face with him tomorrow, would he be likely to want her again? It was astounding how those missing teeth aged her.

She was still holding the paperknife and she gripped it very hard, a symbolic act because she must now insert another, invisible knife into her heart, and twist it.

'You had better get on with getting me dressed,' she said. 'Maria, Chestnuts is to all intents and purposes your home. Naturally, you will be married from here.'

Chapter Fourteen

The Rising Star

'As you see,' said Captain Robert Clive to the Indian emissary at his side, 'we have put Arcot fort into a good state of repair. It was sadly dilapidated when we marched in.' He paused to let the emissary's interpreter transmit this, and then added: 'I'm really not surprised that your men marched *out* when they saw us coming. I cannot understand why they allowed so much deterioration to take place.'

'We were quite shocked.' The officer who was accompanying Clive was his old friend John Pybus. 'When we arrived,' Pybus said, 'the towers were in such a condition that at first we couldn't get cannon up to the top of them.'

'We have cannon up there now, of course.' Clive paused at the foot of tower with new, unweathered stonework at its summit, gleaming pinkly above older, duller stone. 'The first one we put there burst, as you no doubt know . . .'

The emissary nodded stiffly. He had an ascetic face and a fastidious curl to his mouth, and the curl now became more noticeable. War was not a joke but these English sometimes behaved as though it were, which excited his disdain. His master was Raza Sahib, the son of Chanda Sahib, who was the preferred French candidate for the position of Nawab of the Carnatic. Clive had used the first cannon for three days in succession to interrupt Raza Sahib's daily council with his officers. On the fourth day the cannon had exploded, spectacularly, and Raza Sahib, who had been cursing the unknown spy who had told Clive of his routine and calling down anathemas on Clive himself, briefly decided that the Almighty had declared in his favour. But . . .

'. . . but we have replaced it,' Clive said pleasantly. 'I will show you. If you would care to follow me . . .'

'Allow me,' said Pybus, opening the door with alacrity.

The emissary spoke rapidly to his interpreter. 'We believe,' said the interpreter, 'that your men, Captain Clive, number only just over three hundred, counting both Angrezi – your pardon, I mean English – and Indian sepoys. Also, the walls of Arcot are a mile round and they are breached in two places which as yet you have *not* repaired.'

'Ah yes, the breaches. They are nothing.' Clive waved a careless hand. 'They are easily defensible, even with our modestly sized garrison – that is assuming they are still there when the attack comes. Repair work proceeds apace. Shall I lead the way? It's a lengthy climb.'

The heat had been bad enough even in the open air at the middle of the fort, where the surrounding walls reflected the sun's rays fiercely into the centre. But in the stuffy air within the tower it was worse. The steps snaked upwards between curves of warm pinkish-brown stone as though taking them through the digestive system of some fevered monster, and even the emissary and the interpreter in their loose robes were sweating heavily when they emerged at the top. Clive and Pybus, formally clad in red coats and high cravats, were scarlet in the face as well as saturated.

From the top of the tower they could see and smell the fetid moat below. The air quivered silkily in the sun and the distant hills were as unsteady as reflections in water. The tower also afforded a bird's eye view of the place where the biggest breach in the wall had been made, and the temporary but still efficient rampart of rubble that had been thrown up to fill it.

'And this,' said Clive, smiling grimly, 'is our replacement cannon. An eighteen pounder, you may observe, and new.'

It was also the only cannon he now had, but he saw no need to say so.

The emissary contemplated it in silence, and then studied Clive's face. Few traces of boyhood now remained there. Clive's features had become commanding, the lower lip thrust upwards by strong muscles which compressed the mouth into a downturned crescent, the dark eyes very steady. The emissary was the older man, but that face made him feel younger, which irritated him.

He took heart, however, from the sight of the sweat pouring down the enemy's temples. 'My master,' he remarked, 'has cut the water supply. If you still have any water left, it will run out soon.'

'No, you may tell him that we have another reservoir,' Clive said, in a reassuring tone as though Raza Sahib were likely to worry if he had not. The water in the second reservoir was actually very dubious and he had over a hundred men ill with varying degrees of dysentery. Indeed, he had had an unpleasant attack of diarrhoea and stomach pains himself. But the sick quarters were another item not included in this tour of inspection. 'Our supplies of food are also ample,' he said.

'And our guest must also visit our ammunition stores,' said Pybus suavely. 'Next, I should say. Shall we go down?'

'Ammunition?' said the emissary as they moved towards the door to the steps. 'Raza Sahib has reason to believe that while we were driving you from the streets of Arcot your ammunition must have become sorely depleted.'

'Not at all.' Clive started down the steps, talking over his shoulder. 'As you will see for yourself in a moment.'

A few minutes later, back at ground level, Pybus threw open the door of a large shed. Emissary and interpreter glumly surveyed the boxes of ammunition, piled from floor to roof in orderly tiers. Empty boxes, far fewer of them, were tumbled in a heap in one corner.

'As you see, we are amply supplied for the foreseeable future,' Clive said.

The emissary made no further comment. In silence he accompanied them back to Clive's office. Refreshments were awaiting them.

'Your escort are ready to accompany you back to the Nawab's

palace,' Clive said. 'You will take the answer that by now you must have foreseen. My compliments to your master and my thanks for his kind offer. But there will be no surrender, and we will continue to withstand siege.'

The emissary glanced at the interpreter and nodded.

'If you refused Raza Sahib's terms,' said the interpreter, 'there is a further message to deliver. As you were told when we first arrived, he is impressed by your valiant defence of Arcot and is happy to offer you honourable surrender and a very large and valuable gift. But if you refuse then he promises to attack, and if he does so not one man of you will survive his onslaught. For all your courage and all your ammunition, you are only a few hundred, against his ten thousand.'

Clive watched the emissary consume the fort's very last supply of sherbet and said: 'Our present small numbers are misleading. We expect reinforcements at any moment. To be precise, six thousand Marathas tribesmen under the banner of Mohammed Ali, and a further force under English commanders, from Madras.'

'And that is your last word? You wish me to repeat what you have said, to Raza Sahib?'

'Precisely,' said Clive.

'We're in for it now,' Pybus said when the emissary had gone. 'If Raza Sahib really does bring up those ten thousand men . . .'

'Well, he won't take us by surprise. I have spies enough to make sure of that. And the reinforcements really are on their way,' said Clive. 'There's no need for apprehension. We can hold out, and we will.'

'I'm not so sure.'

'You mean,' said Clive, his eyebrows drawing together, 'that you think I should have surrendered?'

'No, of course not. But I do wonder if we should ever have tried to hold Arcot. We made a fine gesture when we marched into the place, and we succeeded to some extent in doing what we meant to do – to draw off the attention of the French and their pet Nawab from Mohammed Ali. Dear God,' said Pybus, letting himself be sidetracked, 'what a state of affairs! The old Nawab gets attacked by a rival and killed in battle; the French uphold the rival; we uphold the old Nawab's son – and now you and me and three hundred and twenty men look like getting put to the sword, and for what? Why are we getting involved in Indian politics? Personally, I'd have left Chanda Sahib and Mohammed Ali to fight it out without us.'

'And if Chanda Sahib had won, we'd have a Nawab full of gratitude to the French and pouring money and land and trade concessions into their laps. Where would we be then? Taking Arcot was Mohammed Ali's idea,' said Clive. 'And he's not only my personal friend, he's friendly to the English altogether. He's the man we want as Nawab. Besides—'

'I know,' said Pybus. 'At least taking Arcot wouldn't be dull! And it isn't. Unfortunately.'

Clive leant back in his chair, hands behind his head. 'I'd like to call in my other officers and share a bottle or two with you. It's a sad state of affairs when we haven't a drop of wine in the fort. We haven't even got the makings of a dish of tea. But there is one thing. I think it may all be over, one way or another, in a few days. The enemy have just started a religious festival, did you know?'

'Mohurrum? That mourning fast they have for the death of the Prophet's grandsons? Yes, I know.'

'It will end on the 13th of November, in eight days' time. By then they'll all be in a state of religious exaltation.' Clive's tone was grave but there was a gleam in his eyes. 'I have a feeling about it.' he said.

'Captain! Captain Sahib!'

The quiet voice near his ear and the pressure of his Indian servant's hand on his shoulder brought Clive out of a dream. It vanished as soon as he woke; he thought it had had something to do with England, and with that intriguing portrait of Mun's young sister Margaret. He brushed it out of his mind and sat up. There was no visible sign of dawn although he could feel that it was not far off. Always, if he chanced to be awake when day approached, he could sense, like a deep murmur just below the edge of hearing, the first stirring of this huge and populous land.

The only light in the room came from a candle which the servant had put on a low table. In the shadows the man's face was no more than a glint of eyes and teeth. Somewhere in the distance was a confused noise.

'They are coming, Captain Sahib. A little ahead of the time our spies estimated. It is a very great array. They cry the names of the Prophet's grandsons as they come.'

Clive swept his mosquito netting out of the way, swung his feet to the floor and was at once seized by a griping of the bowels which made him curse and double up. 'Damn this stomach-ache. Why can't my guts behave? If the men saw this, they'd think I was frightened.'

'I think not, Captain. Many of them are the same, as you know.'

'I'm always having this trouble, with or without bad water.' He straightened himself angrily and caught up his coat from the foot of his bed. 'My boots,' he said tersely, 'and my sword.'

The servant was right; it was a very great array. Clive, driving his gripes into retreat by sheer willpower, joined John Pybus and two other officers on top of a tower. From there, warily, keeping their heads down, they watched the enemy advance steadily through the town, filling the streets and the alleys and the gaps between the houses and pagodas like an armed flood.

The populace hid in their houses or clustered nervously on their roofs to watch them pass: warriors with flaring torches, a marching column of French troops in resplendent uniforms, troops carrying scaling ladders and dragging guns on wheeled carriages and, dimly discernible by virtue of the torchlight, the lumbering shapes of elephants, with heads which seemed strangely distorted.

With the advance came a medley of sound: the names of the Prophet's grandsons, Hassan and Hussein, constantly shouted as a warcry; the trumpeting of the elephants; the call of bugles and a pounding of drums from the French troops; and a wordless, ugly roar of murderous intent.

'They've got iron devices of some sort fastened to the heads of their elephants,' Clive said. 'I think they're going to use them as battering rams. A pity the gates of the fort are only made of wood.' He glanced along the walls extending on either side of the tower. They were lined with crouching figures. 'Are all the gunners in position?'

'They are, Captain. Some of them have got up from their sickbeds. They say it doesn't matter what happens at their rear ends as long as they can still use their hands,' Pybus said. 'I've placed a loader behind each musketeer as you ordered, to allow continuous fire.'

'Don't open fire until the ramming actually begins. We haven't got as much ammunition as all that. On the other hand,' Clive said thoughtfully, 'if we could, so to speak, reverse the elephants . . .'

On the other side of the fort, at the makeshift rampart, firing broke out. 'That's Bulkley at the northwest breach,' Pybus said sharply.

'As expected. The moat's low there. Bulkley knows what to do.' Clive's gripes were trying to return, but he had no time for them now. Ignoring the pain, and clenching his sphincter muscles, he peered once more over the edge of the wall as the gate below suddenly shook from the impact of an elephantine ram. He drew back quickly and gave orders.

A few moments later the gunners on the walls had exchanged their heavy muskets for light firearms and opened fire, aiming at the elephant – but not with the intention of killing it. The beast, its hide scored by grapeshot, veered away from the door and stampeded back towards the town, knocking down and trampling on the soldiers behind it. Pybus threw his hat in the air and cheered. A musket ball from somewhere carried the hat away and Clive yanked his friend down.

'There's a time for rejoicing and this isn't it. It's too soon. They've a lot more elephants and we've a hell of a lot more fighting ahead of us.'

'Ya Hassan! Ya Hussein! Ya Hassan! Ya Hussein!' The warcries rose through the gunsmoke and the gunfire boomed and clattered. Dawn was near. There was a glint of gold on the summits of the pagodas. Another elephant, poor beast, was pounding at the gate and there went the chatter of the light arms that would drive it away. And up went its trunk as it trumpeted in pain, turning in hatred on the puny humans who had driven it into this hell of cordite and uproar and terrible stinging shot. The hoarse screams of soldiers who couldn't get out of the way in time and fell under its huge feet rose to join the rest of the din. They gave Robert Clive an uneasy feeling in the pit of his already afflicted stomach.

Death was rarely kind and an elephant's foot was probably no worse than a musket ball through the belly, but although he had given the order to fire on the elephants with this outcome as his intention, he found that outcome loathsome.

Half an hour later, however, he was feeling better. For the defenders, the noise was almost the worst of it. He had lost four English soldiers and two of the Indian sepoys had been wounded. But one scaling ladder after another had been overturned before anyone could reach the top. Broken ladders and human bodies, smashed by the fall and run through by splintered rungs, lay in a confused mess around the fort.

The commander of the enemy force that had attacked at the northwest breach was dead and his men had fled. A party that had tried to attack the other breach, to the southwest, by raft, had panicked and retreated after only a handful of shots had been fired at them. Despite its small number of defenders and its breached defences, the fort still stood.

The French troops seemed to have done very little. According to one of Clive's spies, their commander had been against the attack in the first place.

John Pybus, his face grimed with smoke and oozing blood from a cut on his temple, came to his captain's side.

'Captain Clive, I think—'

Clive had cocked his head, listening. 'I know. But I can't believe it. We've only been fighting for an hour!'

'Here comes the sun,' said Pybus, awed.

The sun rose, swiftly, uplifted clear of the hills in a blaze of light. And the noise was subsiding, ebbing like a tide. The foe was receding away through the scarred houses of the town.

'We've done it,' Clive said. '*We've done it.* We've held Arcot, the capital of the Carnatic, for Mohammed Ali. Now what will history say of me, Pybus?'

He'd be a great name in future centuries; he knew it. This, his bones insisted, was just the beginning. He was only twenty-six; he had years and years ahead in which to consolidate his place. Joseph Dupleix had had ambitions to be a ruler in India, had ridden about on elephants and kept the state of a king. One day Clive, too, would keep royal state and ride an elephant, and into the lap of the girl he meant to marry he would toss diamonds and rubies and gold.

He would do it in the service of the East India Company and he would serve the Company well, but a king he would be, in all but name. And despite the hardening of his face, he was still young enough to grin at the thought of poor old George Whitmead, who also liked state and dignity and was never going to get it through keeping his head down over his ledgers.

A man's friends, however, rarely saw him in a heroic light.

'It's possible that that tour of the fort you gave to Raza Sahib's emissary helped to depress the enemy's spirits,' Pybus said, 'but if history finds out that three quarters of those boxes of ammunition you showed the fellow were empty containers stacked with their opened sides away from him, history will probably say you were crazy!'

George Whitmead, waking in Fort St George on the morning after the battle at Arcot, found that the malaria from which he had been suffering for the past week had subsided, though he still felt too shaky to conduct any business. This was a pity, since he had several lucrative deals on hand involving betel nut, salt and tobacco, which he did not intend to export to Europe, but hoped to sell on to Indian customers, for instant payment and without any transport charges.

But by evening he did feel well enough to receive callers. One of them was Thomas Saunders, the current Governor of Madras, who arrived with the news that Arcot had withstood attack and that its reinforcements had reached it.

Thomas Saunders wasn't normally a talkative man, but this time he was excited enough to be almost voluble.

'Robert Clive has earned the title of hero, I have to admit it. I didn't think highly of him when I first came – to be frank, I took him for a young hothead. I only put him in charge of the Arcot expedition because cooler heads refused it. I wonder at myself for agreeing to it at all, but I am now persuaded to think that when I let him convince me I perhaps glimpsed more in him than I myself knew.'

'He owes you much for the support you gave him,' George said. 'But for the men and arms you sent with him and the additional help you despatched after him, he must have failed.'

'Well, he could hardly have marched into Arcot and held it with no men or arms at all. That would be asking rather much. You dislike him, Mr Whitmead?'

'No, no, by no means. But he's young,' said George, 'and in my opinion too little prepared to be guided by those wiser than himself.'

'And yet he has succeeded brilliantly this time, on the strength of his own judgement. Ah well. I'll leave you to finish recovering from your fever. Don't return to business yet. Give yourself a little time. These malarial attacks pull one down badly.'

Left on his own, George decided to take the governor's advice. He would not work tomorrow. Instead, he would visit Sita. In her cool room, behind the latticed windows which he had specially and expensively installed, was another world. In George's opinion, Clive *was* a hothead, crazy as a Bedlamite. He, George, was glad to be himself, a reasonable, sensible man. Sita would soothe and pet him and treat him like a prince and he wouldn't have to go to war to conquer his princedom.

PART III
The Mother-in-Law
1765–1781

And yet I am – I live – though I am toss'd
Into the nothingness of scorn and noise,
Into the living sea of waking dreams. . . .

John Clare, 1793–1864

Chapter Fifteen
The Lost Fantasy

In the opinion of George Whitmead's colleagues in Calcutta he was going home in triumph, and at a succession of farewell dinners they said so.

'You've picked the right moment, old fellow. Nothing's going to be the same now that Clive's back with this new Company policy he's hellbent on inflicting on us . . .'

'When one thinks of the amount he gets every year from the Nawab of Bengal, one wonders how he has the nerve. Twenty-seven thousand pounds a year, that's what Mir Jafar granted him. And now he's virtuously telling us that our modest efforts at private trade are illegal. That's doing it a little too brown. You're getting out with your pile at just the right moment.'

And so he was, George thought grimly, as he leant on the rail of the ship and watched the east coast of India glide past. He was leaving India to avoid conflict with Robert Clive. The clumsy, tactless boy who had blundered into his cabin on the *Winchester* long ago now virtually ruled the East India Company. Having, as it were, learned his soldiering in the affairs of the Nawab of the Carnatic, he had finally demonstrated his military gifts by getting involved in those of the Nawab of Bengal. In fact, the appalling behaviour of the present Nawab's predecessor had fairly presented the East India Company to him on a salver.

Clive had married. Edmund Maskelyne's sister Margaret had come to India, proved as lovely in person as she was in her portrait, and Clive, having wooed and won her, had taken her back to England, where he hoped for a future as a solid member of society and a member of Parliament.

Only to be recalled to India as the only man capable of dealing with the situation when the French made another push for mastery. He was therefore on hand when the Nawab of Bengal quarrelled with the English at Calcutta, arrested nearly seventy of them and thrust them overnight into a small, fetid room in which all but about twenty of them died of suffocation in the heat of the Indian darkness.

Clive had deposed the Nawab, replacing him with Mir Jafar, the present incumbent, whose gratitude amounted to that enviable £27,000 per annum. George was not one of those who believed that Mir Jafar was grateful not only for the removal of his predecessor but also for his murder while he was a prisoner. The former Nawab had almost certainly been killed by Indians, for Indians, and probably on Mir

Jafar's orders. One might dislike many things about Clive, said George Whitmead pompously, but he didn't go in for having people assassinated. On the contrary, he was at times too easygoing and apt to say things like: 'Imagine what it would feel like to die in such and such a way.'

Still, he had certainly put paid to the old Nawab, and he had also dealt decisively with the French in Calcutta. The British dominated the province now. It was more important these days than Madras.

And then Clive went home once more, only to be sent out again because the Company management in London apparently considered that their employees in India were celebrating their triumph by diverting too much of the available business profit away from the Company and into their own pockets.

Clive had reappeared in India with a Company mandate to clean up what he chose to call corruption and showed no signs of being easygoing about that. George Whitmead, who had once patronised him and lectured him on the importance of attending to his ledgers, had been summoned to his presence and warned that the very remunerative private trading operations he had built up so industriously through the years, in betel nut, salt, tobacco, firearms, foodstuffs and several other commodities, must cease immediately.

He thought of the hours he had spent, sweating and scratching his heat rash while he pored over figures and balanced prospective investments against likely returns – of the long arguments with vendors and customers, hammering down the prices asked by the one and extracting the highest possible payments from the other – and his thick hands tightened in fury on the rail.

He had been very happy in India. These last few years he had been able to afford a style of life that was little short of princely. Now he must go home, to grey English skies, to expensive English servants, to a wife who had long since ceased to attract him and a son he scarcely knew. He had seen Lucy-Anne only twice since that icy parting when Henry was a baby. He had made himself pleasant enough to her. But she was losing her teeth and he could hardly bear to look at the result, let alone sleep with it. His few efforts to do so had been unproductive and it was fortunate that his one and only child, Henry, appeared to be healthy.

He supposed he would get to know Henry now. The boy was seventeen and old enough to be a companion. At the time of George's last visit to England, five years before, he had been noticeably like his father in looks and he had been gratifyingly respectful. He supposed he could look forward to seeing Henry again.

But Sita he would never see again. He had sent her back to the protection of Mohammed Ali, Nawab of the Carnatic. In Mohammed Ali's zenana she would be safely and luxuriously housed for the rest of her life. George had given her lavish gifts of jewels and clothes before she left; she would have great prestige among the other women. He did not know if she would miss him.

He was grateful to her for being so good about their parting. Sita was a perfect woman, no longer young, but as slender now as when he first knew her; full of passion when a man wanted it; quiet and accepting

170

when he wished only for peace; and, above all, willing to create for him his favourite fantasies.

He would carry with him, all his days, the image of the graceful, elaborate stone lattice that filled her window and the glimpse of her veiled head, her exquisite profile, moving beyond it.

As he stood there at the rail a most extraordinary feeling burgeoned inside him, an ache which swelled and grew until it pressed the breath out of his lungs and pushed the moisture into his eyes.

He did not know if she would miss him but, by God, he would miss her. For a moment the habits of thought by which he had always lived quivered and stretched apart. For the first time he understood that there were other ways to think and feel than those to which he was accustomed. There could, if he chose, be a different George Whitmead...

But he could not hold the vision. It was one with the pain within him, the pain of Sita's loss, and the anguish was too great. He drew back, denying them both, and inhaled a thankful breath as the world returned to normal and the hurt sank away. Did women feel like that when they gave birth?

He had no idea that he had, in a sense, come near to giving birth, to another George Whitmead, a man who loved Sita and was grieving for her.

What he felt instead was that he had recovered his sanity. Sensible men like himself, men who possessed the dignity, if not the title, of a prince, didn't go in for unreasonable emotions. They certainly didn't shed tears because they wouldn't see a thirty-five-year-old dancing girl again.

The new recruit to the Nawab of the Carnatic's zenana was no threat to any of the young favourites. No matter that she had kept her shape and still had black hair and a smooth complexion. She was only five years short of forty and by their standards she was old.

They were inclined, indeed, to pity her because she had no children and wasn't likely to have any now. Then, when the word went round that the man she had been with, the one who had so unaccountably failed to give her any offspring, had been one of those strange creatures, the English, they became inquisitive. They gathered round her like a flock of starlings and pelted her with questions.

'The Angrezi, what was he like? Their faces get so red; was he red all over?'

'No, no, that's what the sun does to their skin. They're pale, under their clothes.'

'And how would you know that, Mina?' enquired several voices in an amused chorus.

'Yes, but are the Angrezi different from Indian men?' the girl called Mina persisted. 'Is it true that they are bigger all over, in every way?'

'Yes, tell us!'

'Tell us!'

'I don't know what other Angrezi are like,' said Sita slowly. 'I only had the one. But he was strange, oh, so strange.'

171

'In what way? How was he strange?'

'He didn't behave as though I were real. To him, I was ... I don't know how to explain. He had pictures in his mind and I acted them for him. To him, there was no girl called Sita; there was only the reflection of his dreams.'

'Did you mind leaving him?' Mina asked.

Sita shivered. 'No. No, I am glad to be here. He was an Angrezi man but he liked to pretend he was a prince, an Indian prince. I was not real to him, but he was not real to himself. He used to say he was a practical man, but it wasn't true. He was all dreams and imaginings and he did not know where they ended and the real world began. I was beginning to be afraid of him.'

England, London, Hanover Square. His son Henry was away at school and wasn't there to welcome him. But Lucy-Anne was waiting. George greeted her as best he could, without warmth, striving for resignation in lieu of it.

It was five years since he had last seen either England or his wife, and he hadn't liked them much then. Now it was worse. It was winter and so bitter that the Thames froze over the day after his ship docked. And Lucy-Anne had lost two more teeth.

Sometimes George Whitmead tried to look back, to that time, nearly a quarter of a century ago, when he came to England to find a wife and fixed upon his cousin Lucy-Anne because she was so biddable and gentle. How in the world had that large-eyed schoolroom miss, so lacking in knowledge of the world that the sight of the Portsmouth stage-coach was something to marvel at, turned into Lucy-Anne at forty, so stout that her stays creaked when she walked, her mouth a repulsive graveyard in which the few remaining teeth leaned awry like ancient tombstones, and deep lines of pain and discontent scoring the little face which once had been so sweet.

It wouldn't have been so bad, thought her husband with distaste, if she had accepted age gracefully and gone in for an unobtrusive style of dress. Instead, she had chosen to brazen her ugliness out. Lucy-Anne, in fact, had decided that if she couldn't be beautiful she would look fantastic instead. In accord with the latest fashion, her hair and her face were copiously powdered, and her clothes were confections of brocade and satin in startling shades of pink and purple and peacock, with falls of lace everywhere and enormous hoops.

He thought of Sita in her gleaming silks, walking under a brilliant sky, through some terraced garden in Mohammed Ali's palace, where the sunlight sparkled on the white and pink stone walls and on the splashing rill which refreshed the air with the scent of water. Lucy-Anne made him shudder.

An attack of depression could sometimes trigger an attack of fever. After reaching London he was ill for a week, and they had to delay their journey to Surrey. When they did finally set out he was still shaky and headachy and the cold weather made him so shivery that he went to bed as soon as they arrived at Chestnuts.

He woke next morning, however, feeling somewhat better. He

stretched in the big bed, glad to be in it alone. At his last visit he and Lucy-Anne had mutually agreed to occupy separate rooms, and it was a relief. The sight of his wife, especially if she happened to smile at him, would have put him off his breakfast. He sat up and rang for his manservant.

Some people brought Indian servants back to England with them, but George had chosen Timothy Barker instead. Barker was an ex-soldier who had been wounded in one of Clive's Bengal campaigns, and on being invalided out of the army with a permanent limp, had taken up work as a valet. He had wanted to come home to England and George needed a man. Barker was efficient if unsmiling and was in the room before the sound of the bell had died away. He had a towel over his arm and was carrying a jug of hot water.

'I heard you stirring, sir, and went down for your shaving water. I have asked them to make you a dish of tea.'

'Good. Get me shaved and into riding dress, Barker. I'll breakfast and then take a ride round the farms. I understand a new hunter has been bought for me. I'll try it out.'

'You will be hunting this winter, sir?' Barker enquired, setting deftly to work with soap and razor.

'Naturally. It's expected of one in my position.'

'Did you hunt in India, sir? My previous employer was a great one for chasing the jackal.'

'Indeed, yes, I often rode to hounds out there. To many of my friends there the pursuit of the jackal was only an imitation of English foxhunting, but I must say that I enjoyed the runs on the open plains. To me the English fox will be a substitute for the jackal, not the other way about. Ah. I think that is someone with my tea.'

The someone was a maid, one he hadn't seen before. But many of the Chestnuts' staff had changed since his last visit home. Silas was dead and Jacob was coachman now. The footmen were all different and so were the maids. Mrs Cobham was still here, but her back was developing a hump and, when she came to welcome him home, George had noticed that her feet were flat and that her walk was turning into a shuffle.

Fraser too was gone. 'I wrote to you,' Lucy-Anne had said, 'but the letter probably reached India too late, after you had left. He was found dead in bed one morning. He's buried in Southdene churchyard. It's curious. I never knew anything about his family until after he was dead. It seems he was a widower. He had no children, but he had a brother-in-law and a brother and sister of his own. They all came to the funeral and I put them up. The sister, a very decent sort of woman, said she had a son who could take Fraser's place. He was in a manservant's position in London but was looking for a better-paid post. So our new butler, Ames, is Fraser's nephew.'

George had met Ames last night. He seemed to know his work and was correctly deferential, but to have the front door of Chestnuts opened by a dark, lanky young man instead of the dignified Fraser was just one more indication that the whole of George's world was changed.

When he was dressed he dismissed Barker and spent a quarter of an hour looking through some of his Indian souvenirs. He had brought home, among other things, his Indian suit, with the gold coat and turban and the silken pantaloons. He stroked the material nostalgically. He had worn it, so often, when visiting Sita. It was as if a little of her essence clung to it.

Sita. What was she doing now?

Grey and heavy as the sky outside, depression descended on him once again.

The new hunter was a good horse but George did not enjoy his ride. The sharp air, which so many of the English in India pined for, had no appeal for him, and the grey sky felt like a weight on the top of his head. His property seemed to be in good order, but he had been away so much that his tenants no longer recognised him and merely stared as he went by instead of touching caps or curtsying, which annoyed him.

He rode on, leaving his own land behind and cutting across a stretch of farmland belonging to the Kendalls. There had been changes here. Fences had appeared where no fences ever were before, and Kendall had surely trebled the size of his sheep flock. He had also, apparently, ploughed up several acres of land which had formerly been rough grazing. He must have a talk with Cottrell soon, and one with Kendall as well.

He turned for home. As he rode back, he could see Chestnuts above him on the hillside. *Home* wasn't the right name for it, he thought. It was just a house, sitting on a cold hill in a cold, unfriendly land, and inside it were servants he didn't know and a wife he had never loved. He had better get Henry back from his school; it was high time the boy left, anyway. He might feel better when Henry was home.

He needed something to make him feel better. All the improvement to which he had woken had vanished. His head was aching fiercely again, and behind the ache, like a veiled head glimpsed beyond a screen, moved the image of Sita.

He felt like going back to bed, but he wanted to see Cottrell first, and sent for him. The bailiff had altered very little. He was as red of face and loud of voice as ever and apparently as active. He wore a businesslike unpowdered wig, and his hands had the hardness of a man who rode in all weathers with the leather reins rasping his palms, personally hoisted himself up ladders to examine the thatch on cottage roofs, and checked the quality of turnips and ears of corn by examining them with his fingers.

'You'll want to see the account books, Mr Whitmead. Mrs Whitmead gave them to me before she went to London to meet you. They're in good order and I doubt if there'll be many queries, but if there are, and I can't answer them, I've no doubt Mrs Whitmead can.'

George was sure of it, but had no intention of allowing Lucy-Anne in on these conferences again. Let her keep to her household affairs or her peculiar astronomy. Extraordinary, that a woman should want to look at stars. Clive's wife Margaret had similar interests, though in her case it was less surprising, because one of her brothers was an astronomer –

174

was in fact the current Astronomer Royal. It had been odd, and somehow irritating, to find that Lucy-Anne had actually corresponded with both Nevil Maskelyne and Margaret Clive on the subject of stargazing. It was as though she had somehow intruded into George's world. Clive and his family, to George, meant India, and India meant...

Sita. He did not want Lucy-Anne even to brush the edges of his other world, the one that enclosed the dream in which he was a prince and Sita his subject.

'It will not be necessary to trouble Mrs Whitmead,' he said coldly. 'Now, the first thing I want to know is, what crops and stock are at present the most profitable...'

Half an hour later he studied the figures he had written in a notebook, and said: 'The turnips have been a very great success. We should increase the crop even it does mean bringing more land under cultivation. And we should certainly run more sheep. I rode across the Kendalls' land this morning and I see that he has both enlarged his flock and put more land under the plough. Kendall appears to be ahead of me in farming methods. His new fences will be a nuisance when we're all out hunting, but one can't have everything.'

'Enclosing the land is the fashion nowadays, sir,' Cottrell agreed in his hearty tones. 'We have in fact increased the size of the Whitmead flock once or twice. But Mrs Whitmead was against taking it any further, or putting crops on additional land. It would mean reducing the amount of grazing your cottagers have for their pigs and cows. It would particularly affect the Craddocks. They make most of their living from the cows they run on the common. Mrs Craddock has a regular stall at Guildford market for butter and cheese, and they sell bullocks for slaughter each spring.'

'Mrs Whitmead was against making this excellent investment for fear the Craddocks would be upset?'

'Well, not only the Craddocks, sir. The other cottagers also use—'

'Upon my word, Cottrell!' George had flushed. 'You amaze me. One would expect a woman to be soft-hearted but you are supposed to be a man of business. I had assumed that you would see that Chestnuts in all respects kept up with its neighbours. If the Craddocks' cows are so profitable – and by the sound of it they are – let them pay an economic rent for the grazing rights. Otherwise, what use is that land to me? I have obviously been away far too long!'

'I doubt if the Craddock family could afford full-scale rents, sir.' Mr Cottrell was not actually raising his voice, but it reverberated through the room nonetheless, making George's temples thump. 'They have only a few animals; it is scarcely a herd. Apart from the cows, they have only a vegetable patch and some chickens. Mrs Whitmead persuaded me—'

'Evidently! But I am now at home and I wish to persuade you otherwise.' George cut him short. 'Let the Craddocks profit from my example and plant turnips. The cows could eat those, perhaps. Now, let us draw a rough plan of the estate and see where the new fences should go...'

Chapter Sixteen

One Woman to Another

The news that George was coming home for good had arrived three months ahead of George himself and Lucy-Anne had had plenty of time to accustom herself to the idea. But it hadn't helped. From the moment she read the letter that brought the news she had dreaded the prospect, and the reality was just as bad as she had feared.

She had grown so used to controlling her own life. It was true that, as Henry grew up, he had shown a tendency, when home, to challenge her authority, but so far he had been away at school most of the time and no real conflict had arisen. For the most part she and Cottrell ran the estate in what was now an amicable partnership and, in their own opinion, ran it well.

But all that was now in the past. George was here. He had made it clear from the moment he set foot on English soil that from now on he would take charge of everything – the estate and the lives of his wife and son. Henry had been whisked home from school and he now joined the regular conferences between George and Cottrell, while Lucy-Anne was excluded. What little she now gleaned only reached her because Mr Cottrell's voice was so very loud and so easy to hear even from her parlour, if she left the door open.

She didn't at all like the sound of some of the plans under discussion, but she knew it would be a waste of time to try to talk to George. He would be at best indifferent and at worst furious. When he first came ashore his up-and-down glance had taken in her garishly fashionable toilette and the contrast with her ravaged face, and his curling lip had told her what he thought of them, and of her.

No. Lucy-Anne now must find her satisfactions in other things, such as dinner parties, embroidery, astronomy, and the visit she hoped to make to Bath in the summer, as long as George didn't object. He seemed to accept that she went there for her health and since his return she had actually pretended to ill-health once or twice to prepare the ground for her next expedition to take the medicinal waters.

Bath was important to her, for Julia was there. And so was Hugo.

Watching him grow up, without ever being able to acknowledge that he was her son, was both anguish and joy, but she could not imagine life without it. Hugo was sixteen now, leggy, hazel-eyed, quick-moving, with a lock of hair for ever falling forward into his eyes and a habit of brushing it impatiently away. He was becoming so like Stephen that sometimes Lucy-Anne experienced a shock at seeing him. It was not that she still loved Stephen. She had exorcised him from Chestnuts and from her heart on the day when he married Maria, and Lucy-Anne, having arranged a lavish wedding breakfast and bought a resplendent gown for the occasion, made the discovery that good food and fine clothes could be a comfort and even a substitute for lost love.

Stephen was dead, these last four years, and when she heard of it she felt surprisingly little.

Yet sometimes she looked at Hugo and felt momentarily confused, as if wondering what kind of love to feel for him.

Not that it mattered, for the only affection she could show Hugo had to be the same as the affection she gave all Julia's children – that of a kindly aunt. Hugo knew Stephen had been his father but he would never know his mother's name and in that lay most of the anguish.

But it would be a far greater anguish if she were prevented from seeing him. To protect herself she must please George as far as she could.

So she kept her conversation away from estate matters, discussed menus with Mrs Cobham, walked in the garden, drove in the chaise, played the harpsichord, began on a scheme to embroider Henrietta's pretty device of a bridge over a river on to some new bedlinen, read books and continued to study the stars.

Because George didn't wholly approve of the astronomy either, she took care not to let it irritate him. Years ago – just after Hugo's birth – she had had the folly repaired and had put her telescope back into it. Now she removed the telescope to one of Chestnuts' attics, leaving the folly for George because he liked to go there by himself sometimes. Probably it reminded him of India.

But her new life was dull, if less responsible, and it was a break in the monotony when, in the second week of May, Ames came to say that Mrs Craddock had called at the house and asked for her.

Lucy-Anne was in the morning room, using its excellent light for the benefit of her embroidery. 'Mrs Craddock, Ames? You mean Mrs Deborah Craddock, Mark's wife?'

'Yes, madam. She asked for you personally and I requested her to wait in the hall. I was not sure if you were at home.'

'Oh yes, I think so.' Lucy-Anne set her work aside. 'Bring her in, Ames.'

Deborah Craddock was no longer very young, but numerous pregnancies had had little effect on her somewhat angular figure and she followed Ames into the morning room with a businesslike step. Most cottagers' wives would have gazed in wonder at the furnishings, but the intricately patterned Indian carpet, the candlesticks upheld by gilded cherubs, the cabinet full of green Sèvres porcelain and the glossy table made of Brazilian rosewood made no impression on this one. Deborah bobbed a very correct curtsy, but her eyes were direct and full of resentment. They were greyish-blue, set in sloping sockets which looked as though they had been thrust into a slant by the high cheekbones below.

Deborah's face was asymmetrical – the angle of cheekbone and eyesocket not quite the same on both sides, the long chin just a little out of true. The result was uncomfortable. There was attraction there but also some incalculable menace. It was a long time since Lucy-Anne had been the shy bride who was intimidated by the elder Mrs Craddock's unfriendly stare, but at close quarters she found she could withstand Deborah's only with difficulty.

'Please have a seat, Mrs Craddock,' she said, 'And tell me how I can help you.'

Deborah, ignoring the offer of a chair, answered the question without wasting words. 'Your husband wants to put fences all round where we graze our cows and plough the land up or stick sheep on it. So then we'll have nowhere for the cows. Will you talk to him and get him not to?'

'Good gracious.' Lucy-Anne had overheard enough of Cottrell's remarks not to be very surprised, but she hadn't expected such a direct appeal. Though she should have done, she supposed. After all, she had for many years been the only landlord. 'Confound you, George!' she said silently. Aloud, she invited her visitor once more to sit down. 'Would you like some coffee?'

'No thank you, ma'am.' Deborah did not move. 'I haven't come to waste your time and I know my place. It's not for me to sit drinking coffee in a lady's room. I only want to know if you'll help us or not.'

Lucy-Anne hesitated. Without knowing it, she thought, she had dreaded something like this. How could she ever induce George to listen to her? He would just be angry. But her friends Mr and Mrs Bird, and certainly Julia and Edward Harper, would think she ought to try. And this woman with the disconcerting stare would despise her if she didn't. You poor thing, the slanting eyes would say. Fine clothes and all the food you want, and you're frightened to speak a few words for the sake of the people whose toil pays for it all.

It was mainly the East India Company that paid for it, but Deborah Craddock wouldn't see it like that. Somehow or other, Lucy-Anne must try to help, even if she didn't succeed.

'It would be better,' she said, 'if I had as many facts as possible and it will be easier if we are both seated and comfortable. I wish to take coffee, even if you don't. So once again, Mrs Craddock, please take a seat, while I pull the bell.'

Unwillingly, Deborah complied. Lucy-Anne ordered the coffee, requesting two cups, and then turned conversationally to her visitor. 'You have a large family, I believe, Mrs Craddock? How many is it now? Five?'

'Five living. We lost three,' said Deborah dispassionately. 'Five's enough. And we want to build up our herd and leave the young ones something worth having when we go – portions for the three girls, anyhow, and the cottage and the herd for our Abel. Joe'll have to go into the army, I 'spect. Abel'll be the fifth generation in the cottage if we're still there. But if that land gets fenced off, we won't be. I don't know what we'll do. We've a right to that grazing, Mrs Whitmead. If five generations don't count as a right, what does?'

Money, Lucy-Anne could have said, not to mention George's inborn belief that his wishes were the only ones that mattered.

179

Deborah was still talking, her manner a fraction warmer now that she had sensed that Lucy-Anne was sympathetic.

'We said to Mr Cottrell that we had a right to that grazing, but he shook his head at us. Then Craddock, he said, you go and see Mrs Whitmead, one woman to another. We saw your husband and Mr Henry ride off round the fields this morning and we reckoned that today I'd have a chance to see you, private-like.'

'What exactly have you been told?' Lucy-Anne asked. The coffee arrived, and she poured for them both. 'Do please take some of this, Mrs Craddock.'

'I may as well, I s'pose.' Deborah let out a sigh, which revealed tiredness beneath the aggression. 'It was Mr Cottrell as did the telling, Mrs Whitmead. He came and told us that some of the grazing was going to be fenced and tried to show us on a map, only Craddock said to him, "You take us round and show us properly". So he did. And it's three quarters of our cows' pasture, that's what it is.'

'And he offered you no alternative? No . . . er . . . deal?'

'Oh, yes!' Deborah gulped coffee as if hoping it would confer strength. New anger surged into her voice. 'We were offered a deal all right. Pay rent for the land and Mr Whitmead won't fence it. We can't afford to rent it. It'll take the best part of our earnings. We've five to clothe and feed and we've to pay rent for the cottage and buy fodder and pay the old grazing rights fee . . . well, we can't do it and that's a fact.'

'Is there nowhere else for you to keep your cows?'

'No, there *ain't*. There used to be plenty of common land but it's fences everywhere these days. If we lose our grazing, we lose our livelihood and that's the end of it. Before Mr Whitmead came home . . . well, you were always pretty fair with us. Mr Whitmead's maybe not used to how things are in England. So we've come to you.'

'Mrs Craddock,' said Lucy-Anne, 'I have to tell you that I have perhaps less influence with my husband than you believe. But I will speak to him.' She shrank inwardly at the prospect, but she would have to attempt it. 'That is all I can promise. Will you tell me as much as you can please, of what you can and can't afford . . . ?'

George and Henry were out until dinner time and when they came home they were full of the virtues and faults of the horse George had given Henry as a welcome-home present. Lucy-Anne's efforts to break into the conversation were half-hearted to begin with, and were all foiled.

'You'll need to train him over jumps, of course. Miller said to me that you would very likely enjoy it and that there's no horse so completely one's own as the mount you train yourself.'

'I'll have to teach him about opening gates as well; he has no notion. But he has easy paces and a soft mouth; I fancy I'll get on well with him.'

'George, my dear. May I interrupt for a moment? I had a visitor today who asked me to—'

'We'll have the Millers over to dine soon and we'll roast Miller about those gates. Not that he actually mentioned gates – he only said that Caesar was well schooled. We'll have the Kendalls over too, and Ned and Ellen as well. Have you met their girl Emma, my boy? She was there when I paid a call on the Kendalls just after I came home, while you were still at school. Emma's an amazingly pretty little thing . . . must be nearly sixteen by now—'

'It was Mrs Craddock, from the cottages. She was in some anxiety and desired me to ask you—'

'Caesar certainly has sound wind. I hope I can get him ready for hunting next winter.'

'Oh, surely you will. I'll tell Cottrell to have some jumps put up for you. My dear, should you not now leave us to our port?'

It was hopeless. Indeed, it had never been a good idea to talk to George over a meal table. The best hope of persuading him into anything was to catch him alone, when he would not lose face by changing his mind before a third party. She would do better to wait until tomorrow.

She saw nothing of them during the afternoon and early evening, but they appeared for supper and then, after consuming a little more port, joined her in the drawing room.

George was fuddled, but Henry was not. Lucy-Anne had never felt close to her son, whose physical resemblance to his father was off-putting, but he did have certain virtues, one of which was a respect for his elders. Henry never vied with his father, in drinking or anything else. After George had gulped some coffee and wandered, somewhat unsteadily, away to his bed, Henry sat on in the drawing room while Lucy-Anne played the harpsichord.

As though the act of playing had released her mind, she found herself coming to a decision. With a sudden flourish of her own, she finished a piece and twisted round on her stool.

'Henry!'

'Yes, Mother?'

'You are spending some time nowadays with your father and Cottrell, learning about the estate, are you not?'

'Yes, that is so. Now that I have left school, Father thought it advisable that I should begin to learn what he could teach me.'

He won't have to teach you to be wordy, thought Lucy-Anne with a flash of exasperation. You were born knowing that. It must be in the blood.

Smiling, she said: 'Something is happening on the estate which worries me and I wish to interest you in it. In fact, I should like you to ask your father to reconsider a certain decision. Good management is more than just getting the most out of the land, you know, Henry. One also has a responsibility towards the people who work on it. Mrs Craddock, the wife of one of the cottagers, came to see me today . . .'

Lucy-Anne lay awake, thinking about her husband and her son and quietly cursing both of them.

She should have taken Henry in hand years ago – taught him her own ways of estate management, made sure that he saw more of people like the Birds and the Harpers. As it was, he had met the Birds only occasionally and scarcely knew the Harpers at all.

181

Since Stephen left Chestnuts she had visited it rarely, and usually when Henry was at school, and she had not taken him to Bath since he was a small boy. It made her uneasy to see him under the same roof with Hugo.

This was not because she feared that any resemblance between them might arouse someone's suspicion, for they took after their respective fathers so thoroughly that no such resemblance existed. Nor did they have any mental rapport; in fact they had little in common and if anything seemed to dislike each other. The trouble lay in the fact that it was hard, so very hard, that she could be openly Henry's mother but must not acknowledge Hugo. She preferred to keep them apart.

And now Henry, who had not had the advantage during his formative years of imbibing the humanitarian principles of either the Birds or the Harpers, had listened to her politely while she described Deborah Craddock's visit, and smiled at her, not as though he understood her, but as though he understood something that was beyond her, a mere female. He had promised to tell his father what she had just told him, but the promise was made in such a kindly tone that Lucy-Anne feared the worst and had been hard put to it not to box his ears.

'The welfare of the tenants matters, Henry,' she said, trying to drive the point home. 'Cottrell's predecessor, Stephen Clarke' – it was odd, but even though her feeling for Stephen was gone there were times when she couldn't resist saying his name – 'believed in treating the tenants with consideration. Mr Cottrell is less inclined to stand up for them.'

'Oh, come, Mother! His first duty is to his employer, and that means Father.'

'Precisely. So let us try to influence your father. Talk to him,' said Lucy-Anne. 'Remember that Chestnuts will be yours one day and that means the tenants as well as the land. I'm going to bed now.'

As she left the drawing room, Henry bowed and held the door open for her. He might respect his elders, Lucy-Anne thought angrily, but if the elders were women the respect was only superficial, a matter of inclining from the middle and turning door handles. She had been running this estate for years and years but Henry obviously didn't think that she knew what she was doing. He was going to mature into a man as pompous and opinionated as George himself. He didn't have any signs of a paunch yet but it would come, no doubt.

But he was her only hope. She could not talk to George. She'd failed to make herself heard at dinner because at heart, she'd known it.

'Well, really! This is the outside of enough. And what, may I ask, is your own opinion, sir?' said George to his son, addressing him across the width of the study.

'Surely you need not ask that, sir,' said Henry. Although it was early in the day, George observed with satisfaction that the boy was properly dressed; there was nothing slack or ill-behaved about this heir he had sired. A pity there was only the one, but if the quantity was small the quality was admirable. A good, respectful manner, too. It had been worth the fees at Eton. It was true that a classical education didn't give a boy much knowledge of commerce or accounts, but Latin grammar undoubtedly exercised the mind. Henry was picking up estate management very fast. Still, he mustn't be allowed to get above himself.

'And what might that mean? Surely I need not ask your opinion, you say. You have presented yourself, this morning, as the mouthpiece of your mother, who appears to be setting her judgement up against mine as regards the way to keep Chestnuts profitable. How do I know which opinion you favour?'

'I gave my mother my word that I would tell you what she had said, sir. To have refused would have been discourteous to her. But, naturally, your decision must be the right one. We have all benefited, all these years, from the income you have earned, Father, through your skill at trading. My mother is a good woman and charitable, as a woman should be, but she cannot be expected to understand business.'

'And Chestnuts is not a charitable institution.' George was mollified. 'I follow your drift.'

'I have seen the Craddocks,' said Henry. He produced a small gold snuffbox and held it out to George. 'Snuff was in fashion among the seniors at school. I find this particular blend excellent.'

'Thank you, my boy. Yes, very aromatic. You must give me your supplier's name. You have called on the Craddocks, you say?'

'Yesterday, sir.' Henry helped himself to snuff. 'They seem adequately fed and clad; I would say that their situation has improved since I was a boy. I feel sure that they have savings hidden away. They will pretend that to pay a full rent for their grazing land is a shocking hardship, but it may be more a matter of won't than can't. I didn't take to Deborah Craddock; she hasn't a proper deference. I would say that she is the sort who will take advantage, given the opportunity. It is of course for you to say whether you are willing to leave some of the land as pasture, with or without rent, and whether, indeed, you wish the Craddocks to keep their tenancy of the cottage. They have behaved very ill, in going to my mother behind your back.'

'They have indeed, my boy. Upon my word, you're quite right.'

Yes, he could congratulate himself on his son. The lad would do. But with Lucy-Anne he was furious. Why, oh why, must he be saddled with a wife who would not learn to keep out of masculine affairs? Why must she uphold the so-called rights of a lot of unwashed cottagers against the rights of her own husband? She was trying to dominate him. No Indian lady would behave so.

'I will see you again presently,' he said to Henry, and made for the stairs, and Lucy-Anne's bedchamber.

His unprepossessing wife was still asleep, her forehead resting on a podgy wrist, greying hair straggling over the pillow and yesterday's face-paint smeared on the linen. Sita had always cleaned her face of cosmetics before retiring for the night. (Where are you at this moment, Sita? What are you doing? Who has the lovely privilege at this moment of seeing you, talking to you, being in your presence?)

'Lucy-Anne!' he thundered, jerking back the bedcurtains roughly so that the rings rattled. 'Wake up!'

She stirred and sat up. Her mouth opened, a spectacle which always disgusted him. 'What time is it?'

'Past nine of the clock, madam! Sit up and attend to me. How *dare* you try to enlist my son on your side in a stupid, sentimental scheme to help some able-bodied cottagers who can very well help themselves? Will you never learn not to attempt to undermine my authority? What have you to say for yourself?'

'Wh . . . what?'

'Have you lost your hearing as well as your common-sense? Need I say it all over again?'

Thrusting sleep away, Lucy-Anne tried to answer. 'Mrs Craddock asked me to put their case to you. I thought you might listen to Henry more willingly than to me, that's all. Evidently, Henry didn't make a very persuasive case!'

'Henry has more wisdom than you have, madam. He obeys me as a son. He told me what you had said, but naturally, he accepts my decision. A pity you cannot do the same.'

Lucy-Anne was aware that first thing in the morning she was an even more depressing sight than usual, and was therefore at an added disadvantage. But she made an effort, propping her pillow behind her and running her fingers through her hair as a makeshift comb. 'George, please listen. I don't at all want to undermine your authority, but I am anxious about the Craddocks. They've been here for four – nearly five – generations and they have always grazed their animals on that common land. The right is part of the tenancy agreement.'

'Times have changed, as you would know, madam, if you had really attended to the estate in my absence.'

'They can't afford extra rent. Mrs Craddock came to see me—'

'So I hear. Women getting together and trying to interfere with the business of the men—'

'No, George. A worried woman asking another woman for help and advice, that's all.'

'Stuff and nonsense. Henry has given me a bad report of Deborah Craddock. She is clearly not to be relied on. I have decided to get rid of the Craddocks altogether. My decision is final and in future, madam, I trust you will mind your own business. I fear you have been influenced by others while I was in India . . .'

His voice died away. The very word 'India' had called up such memories that for a moment he only wanted to contemplate them. He missed it so much. He kept on dreaming about it – the hot blue skies and the household that unquestioningly obeyed him, as if he were a prince.

Nothing in England appealed to his senses or his emotions as India had. His eyes hungered for fretted arches and stone shaped into the likeness of filigree, for sensually carved pagodas and the scent of jasmine and sandalwood and dust and ordure mingled, for the disturbing rhythms of eastern music.

He had his reminders, of course. He had the folly, with its echo of Mughal architecture. He had had two attacks of fever since returning home and almost welcomed them because they had been so much a part

184

of life in Madras and Calcutta. He had a scheme to alter his town house so that it would remind him of the east. He had already placed an order for a filigree lattice screen – wood, not stone, but he could have it gilded – to replace the existing balustrade where the second-floor landing overlooked the stairwell. It could be tall, right up to the ceiling, and it would give the upper part of the house an air of mystery. He saw it in his mind's eye, and behind it a lissom female figure – decidedly not Lucy-Anne – moved, with a breath of fragrance and a rustle of silk.

But Sita was gone. Her part of the fantasy must remain for ever locked within his mind.

He came back abruptly to his wife's bedchamber and the unattractive spectacle of his partner in life, and could have killed her for not being Sita.

He knew instinctively what would hurt her, and attacked accordingly. 'I fear that I always did have the impression that your friends the Harpers had dangerously radical tendencies. No doubt you take your attitudes from them. I must reconsider whether or not I should permit you to visit Bath this summer.'

Oh no, thought Lucy-Anne. Oh, no. He can't do this. Not Bath; he mustn't stop me from going to Bath.

She had learned, long ago, to lie with conviction, in word and in deed. No one had ever discovered her affair with Stephen; no one knew who Hugo's mother was. She lied now, smoothly.

'The Harpers? Oh, you mean Edward. But he rarely talks to me about serious matters. I *have* been influenced, as you say, but mainly by Mr and Mrs Bird.' George had known the Birds for ever. It was most unlikely that he would now begin claiming that they were a bad influence. 'They are most disturbed by this present tendency towards enclosing the land,' said Lucy-Anne craftily, 'and its effect on the poorer tenants. They talk of it often.'

'Indeed!'

'I go to Bath,' said Lucy-Anne, following up her advantage, 'only for the spa waters. The fact is that I would ail a great deal more than I do if I had no access to them. I trust, George, that you don't want me to ail – or to die early?'

'I . . . what . . . harrumph. No, of course not!'

He was thoroughly disconcerted. George, in fact, had come shockingly face to face with the fact that he would not mind at all if Lucy-Anne died. A moment ago he had actually wished she would. Now, recognising this as shameful, he harrumphed again and turned pink and hurried into earnest denials.

'Then please allow me to go to Bath as usual.' Lucy-Anne saw that, although he wanted to give in, he was going to find it difficult, and called up further reserves of cunning to help him. Change the subject, that was the thing. Abandon the Craddocks, who were beyond redemption, let George evict them. And let the subject of Bath drop now, and assume that when in due course she prepared to set out, George would pretend the argument hadn't happened, and not prevent her.

She sought frantically for something with which to divert him, and found it.

'I'm glad you came to see me this morning,' she said. 'If I ring for chocolate, will you take a cup with me? There is something I wanted to ask you about, of great interest to us both. Henry is young, of course, but is it ever too soon to think of the future? You have seen the Kendalls' grand-daughter Emma and I believe you think her pleasing? She's been strictly reared and I think she is a biddable girl without romantic notions. Also, of course, her mother was a Miller – both sides of her family are well-known to us. Suppose we were to sound her parents on the possibility of a betrothal between Emma and Henry . . .?'

George was willing to entertain the idea and so, when approached, was Henry. 'Certainly, sir. If you think it a good idea, I shall be happy to comply. I know you would not suggest any but an appropriate match for me.'

The younger Kendalls lived on the other side of Farnham, not too far away. Lucy-Anne, however, sent an invitation for them to call on her and bring Emma. She did not suggest calling on them. It might be as well, she thought, to give colour to her claim that she ailed a good deal. She was suffering from fatigue, she told Henry. She had never been quite the same since that recurrent fever she had had years ago. If it hadn't been for the wonderful Bath waters, and the care her good friends the Harpers had taken of her, she might well not have recovered at all.

There was a curious pleasure to be had, on occasion, from making little secret allusions whose inner meaning was known only to her. She found the same pleasure in her occasional mention of Stephen Clarke.

She was on the sofa, therefore, when Ned and Ellen Kendall and their daughter Emma came to call, and stayed there throughout the interview.

It went very well. Henry and Emma seemed to like each other. By the end of the visit it was settled that, in due course, the Kendall and Whitmead families should be united.

Lucy-Anne expressed pleasure and relief and then staged a carefully gradual return to strength, just in time for her projected journey to Bath.

By that time the notion that she actually needed regular visits to the place had taken firm root in the minds both of George and of Henry. There would, she thought as she set out, be no more difficulty about Bath.

Chapter Seventeen

Dancing on Thin Ice

Emma Whitmead, born Kendall, had been four years married when she realised that her father-in-law George Whitmead was not merely a little eccentric but quite definitely, if intermittently, mad.

The day when she made this discovery had begun so well, too. The July dawn had the soft mistiness that promised hot weather later, and this was excellent because that evening Chestnuts was to hold a dance, which was a rare pleasure and would, for once, put the splendid new wing to use.

Nabob – that was the word used in England to label the men who had come home from India laden with riches. George Whitmead was a nabob and, since a wealthy man must show his money off somehow, he had spent some of his on what he called his Indian wing.

It was built on to the drawing room, which now received its daylight only through its front windows. The drawing room remained conventional, but at the door to the Indian wing convention gave way to fantasy.

'My father planned it to match the folly,' Emma's husband Henry had told her, but even Emma, who knew little of English architecture, let alone Mughal, could see that the extra wing did not merely repeat the theme of the folly but vastly expanded on it.

Built of white stone, it contained a ballroom, which used the whole height of the wing, right up to the roof, and the roof itself was extraordinary, since part of it was a dome. The ballroom had three doors, opening into the drawing room, into a conservatory at the side, and on to a terrace overlooking the garden. All three were double doors, immense, faced with bronze and set in extravagantly scalloped arches, and the aperture between the tops of the doors and the arch above was filled with gilded wrought iron like metallic lace.

Round each door the stone had been left bare of plaster for a couple of feet and decorated with flower patterns made of inlaid malachite and rose quartz. 'This cost a fortune,' Henry said proudly, showing it to her when the new wing was completed, near the end of their rather lengthy betrothal. 'The malachite had to be imported. My father also had great difficulty in finding suitable foundries to make the wrought iron but for this purpose he was determined. In our town house, we have a lattice screen made of oak, but Father didn't consider such a material suitable for this wing. He had a hard task too to find artists to do the wall paintings. But as you see, he did at last succeed.'

'Yes, indeed,' said Emma, and also thought, wistfully, that the polished wooden floor cried out for someone to dance on it.

187

But although the wing had been completed six years ago now, she had seen the dance floor used only once, by the guests at her wedding. Otherwise the splendid room had remained silent, except that it was regularly cleaned and George Whitmead often went there to wander around it by himself, from which he seemed to derive pleasure.

Social life at Chestnuts, as Emma soon discovered, was very quiet, at least for the women. George and Henry held all-male gatherings at times, but she and Lucy-Anne were not permitted to join these. For them there were only unexciting dinners at a few selected households, mainly those of her relatives, a category which embraced the Kendalls, the Millers and the Birds as well. Occasionally, return dinners were given at Chestnuts.

Sometimes there was dancing, but only for a handful of couples, and at Chestnuts it took place in the drawing room.

And even that was a social whirl compared to the routine at the town house. Most people went to town to enjoy the season, but when the household visited Hanover Square Lucy-Anne and Emma lived obscurely, going out only to stroll or shop and entertaining not at all, although, once more, George and Henry held parties of their own.

In the town house, Emma and her mother-in-law were banished on these occasions to a second-floor sitting room and could glimpse the guests only from above, through the gilded lattice screen which George had had installed above the stairwell. Lucy-Anne sometimes complained to Emma that she never set foot on that landing without feeling as though she were an animal in an elaborate menagerie.

But a few years after Emma's mother had married, her brother Harry had married too, a Miss Catherine Stonely from Guildford, and in this autumn of 1774 their eldest daughter Elizabeth had turned eighteen and was to be launched into society. Her parents wished her to obtain a little practice before going to London. They had held a big dance at their own house and for once, since Elizabeth was Emma's first cousin, George and Henry had agreed that the invitation ought to be accepted. And now the Millers and the Kendalls had somehow prevailed upon George to give a ball himself.

'Chestnuts is the ideal place. That ballroom of yours will show Lizzie off to the greatest advantage,' Harry Miller said to Henry, and Walter Kendall, talking to George, was even more outspoken.

'What the devil did you build a great big ballroom like that for, except to use it? Going to turn it into a museum? And don't give me any of that nonsense about preferring your wife and daughter-in-law to live quietly. Do you think your guests will run mad and rape their partners in the middle of a minuet? This girl Elizabeth is Emma's cousin, and Emma is my grand-daughter; it's a family affair!'

'I have never cared much for Walter Kendall,' Lucy-Anne said to Emma afterwards, 'but there are times when I admit that he's exhilaratingly reasonable.'

George, under pressure from several directions at once, had given in. The ballroom was to be decorated and an orchestra hired. The guests, of course, would not be limited to Kendall and Miller connections but would come from half the county, and Miss Elizabeth Miller would be the guest of honour and would open the dancing with Henry. Emma was happy today, because the sun was going to shine and there was jollity in prospect, and also for private reasons of her own. She sipped slowly at the early morning dish of tea which she found, just now, more palatable than hot chocolate, called Anna, her maid, and took her time over getting dressed. Then she went to call on Lucy-Anne.

She found her mother-in-law sitting up in bed, reading a letter, while her own maid, Letty, with one knee on the side of the bed, tended the piled-up hairstyle which had been tied into a cap overnight but had still been disturbed by the pressure of the pillow. Lucy-Anne laid the letter aside as Emma came in.

'Good morning, my dear. I've just had delightful news from Julia Harper. Her nephew Hugo is to be married. Leave my hair now, Letty. You'll have to do it fresh for this evening anyway and a good thing too. It itches. It wants a thorough combing, and a wash wouldn't be a bad idea.'

'But ma'am, that can be dangerous.' Letty was quite young and believed in all the latest fads and fashions. 'You could take cold.'

'I've never come to harm yet from washing my hair and I'm nearly fifty years old. So go along now and tell the kitchen that Mrs Emma and I will have our breakfast here. You're agreeable, Emma?'

'Oh yes. Please,' said Emma eagerly. 'I want some private talk with you, if I may.'

Letty withdrew, though still looking fussed, and Lucy-Anne patted the coverlet in an invitation to Emma to perch on the bed. Emma, who didn't mind Lucy-Anne's gap teeth at all, complied. 'How are you this morning?' Lucy-Anne asked.. 'Looking forward to the ball? You're a trifle pale – did you sleep badly? Everything will be faultlessly organised, you know. Ames will remember anything we've forgotten.'

'Oh, I know. I slept very well; it isn't that. It's good news about Hugo, isn't it? I know you're fond of him, Mother-in-law. Well,' said Emma, 'I may have some good news, too.'

'Emma!'

'I'll be very glad of my breakfast,' said Emma gravely. 'I'm prodigiously hungry.' They gazed at each other and then Emma burst out laughing, which changed her face completely. Her blue eyes danced and her straight, Grecian nose wrinkled absurdly, while her classically chiselled mouth softened, revealing small, sparkling teeth.

Lucy-Anne studied her appreciatively. 'You look charming when you laugh. Life in this family isn't often hilarious and I sometimes think I did you no favours in bringing you here. Is your news what I think – what I hope? At last?'

Emma nodded. 'I think so. I feel sick when I wake up, but very soon I become extremely hungry, and it's been over eight weeks now since I . . . well . . .'

'Oh, my dear. After all this time. Henry will be so pleased.'

'I'd given up hope,' said Emma. 'I'd just given up hope. I'm so thankful.'

She began to laugh again, but in the midst of it caught her breath and burst into tears instead.

'It's been so long,' she said as Lucy-Anne pulled her into her arms. 'It's been so long . . .'

189

'Four years,' said Lucy-Anne as, with Emma soothed and comforted, they consumed coffee and rolls together. 'It's four years and two months since your wedding day. You and Henry were married in May 1770. You were just twenty and Henry was getting on for twenty-two. You'd been betrothed for four years but your parents thought the two of you should grow up a little before you went to the altar and I agreed. I was too young myself when I was married. I always had your interests in mind. But even so, I have wondered, since you came here, if this was quite the right family for you. You have a calm, serious face but at heart you are merry and gentle. I think you might have liked – how shall I put it? – warmer air to breathe.'

'It would have been all right,' said Emma, 'if only I could have had a child sooner. But none of you have ever reproached me, or not in words; I can't complain of that.'

'I've been very sorry for you,' Lucy-Anne said. 'I hadn't the slightest wish to reproach you, believe me.'

'I know. And Henry hasn't said anything, either. Only, he . . . I mean he . . .'

'Withdrew himself from you. I know that, too.'

'Not altogether. Well, obviously. But he did become, well, a trifle distant,' said Emma.

She said no more. She could not bear to say much about the chilly space which had opened between them, the awareness that now when Henry made love to her it was because his body needed it, not his heart or mind. 'I have brought you up not to have romantic ideas,' her mother had once said to her. But romantic ideas grew by themselves, it seemed. She had longed for romance between herself and her husband, and she had been forlorn, often, for the want of it.

That careful upbringing had meant that she was sheltered from everything her mother considered crude. But since her marriage she had been less protected and once, when Ames was chivvying the footmen over getting the dining room ready for one of the all-male parties, she had heard him tell them to put clean pisspots in the sideboard and look sharp about it.

For the last three years she had been, to Henry, little more than a human pisspot.

But not now. Oh no, not now. She would tell him later today. And then he would look at her again as though she were a real person, not a mere receptacle but Emma, his wife and his love.

'All I pray,' she said, 'is that all goes well.'

'You must take care of yourself,' Lucy-Anne agreed. She tapped the letter from Julia. 'This is an invitation to go to Bath for Hugo's wedding. I think we will. I have been feeling tired sometimes of late.' They exchanged smiles. Emma knew quite well why her mother-in-law had occasional, inexplicable attacks of fatigue. 'Meanwhile,' said Lucy-Anne, 'let the servants do the hard work today and content yourself with arranging flowers. Which room are we going to use for supper, by the way? Have you decided?'

'I was waiting to see if it would be fine. Since it is, and people can wander to and fro in the garden, I thought we could set supper in the folly,' Emma said.

For four years Emma had waited to say to Henry the words, 'You are to be a father,' and for four years, because the words were not forthcoming, she had had to live with his unspoken disappointment. Now, at last, the longed-for words had been uttered. She had seen his light-brown eyes light up with pleasure and felt herself, at last, wrapped in the warmth of his approval.

For four years, she thought, she had been like a kitten shut out on a cold day and shivering on a doorstep; now she had been let into the house and invited to the fireside.

The ball was splendidly under way. Henry had partnered her in a gavotte and was now escorting her across the garden to supper in the folly, and under her hand, his arm was solid and companionable. She had originally been drawn to that solidity. Stocky Henry, with his plain but very masculine features, had seemed to her reassuring. Perhaps the comfortable early days of marriage were going to return.

For he had not only danced with her this evening; he had also complimented her, first on her dress of pale blue brocade and white Indian muslin, and then on the arrangements she had made for the ball.

She was pleased with both compliments, but especially with the second. It was she who had decreed the garlands of fresh flowers with which the ballroom was so elegantly festooned; she who had chosen the orchestra and ordered the gilt printing on the invitation cards. Lucy-Anne had admired her efforts, and so had her parents and her younger brother Frederick, who were all now in the ballroom. But it was Henry's recognition that she craved.

As they crossed the garden the soft July evening was just turning to dusk. In the last of the sunshine the shadows of the chestnuts in the avenue stretched to meet them, and the air was full of sweetness from the flowers in the parterre beds.

As she and Henry reached the end of the avenue she saw a footman lighting the lanterns she had had strung around the door of the folly, and observed others beside themselves now strolling through the garden in the direction of the folly, and supper.

'The lanterns were an inspiration,' Henry said. 'I had no idea that you had so many hidden talents, my love. Perhaps we should hold balls oftener.'

'I should like that,' Emma said shyly.

'Although of course, with the new responsibilities that we are soon to enjoy...'

'Oh yes, naturally,' said Emma, and prevented herself from sighing. George Whitmead's views being what they were it wasn't likely that balls would ever form a regular feature of life at Chestnuts.

But he seemed to be having a good time at this one. 'I saw your father dancing with Lizzie in the gavotte,' she said. 'My cousin is very beautiful, is she not?'

'In a toplofty, high-coloured sort of way,' Henry agreed. 'But I would choose you before her, my love, any day.'

An imp inside Emma's brain enquired, 'Even if you were sure she would fall pregnant in four days instead of four years?' but she quelled it. Nothing must spoil this lovely evening, not as much as an unspoken thought. As they strolled into the folly, Henry remarked: 'The Millers have been fortunate in their family. There's Elizabeth, then the three boys, and another little girl. Horatia, I believe her name is.'

'Yes, it is. I saw her last time we visited. She's about five,' Emma said. 'I think she'll look very like Elizabeth when she's older.'

'I hope we shall one day have as fine a family. Ah, how well arranged everything looks.'

The interior of the folly was candlelit and busy. In the centre of the floor four tables, draped in white damask and arranged in a square, held the food which the Chestnuts' cook, Mrs Drayton, who had succeeded Mrs Cobham, had been working on for days. In the space at the centre of the square four maidservants were helpfully dispensing it.

More small tables and chairs were dotted about and Lucy-Anne was seated at one of them in company with Mr Bird. Emma's mother-in-law, dressed for a ball, could not be called a beautiful sight, but she was impressive. Her dress of purple over a brick-red underskirt was all of stiff and rustling silk, and if her face was shiny with sweat the powdered hair above it had been freshly piled up into a complicated edifice eighteen inches high, with a ruby ornament glittering in it which drew the eye to itself.

Emma and Henry went to join her. 'I hope you are both enjoying yourselves,' said Lucy-Anne. 'It's my son and his wife,' she added to Mr Bird, who was elderly now and very shortsighted. He had failed a good deal after the death of his own wife. He rose and bowed. 'You look very well tonight, Emma,' Lucy-Anne observed. 'Your hair is best unpowdered – pale gold hair like yours is very rare. I must say that using the folly in this way was an inspiration.' She flicked a painted silk fan open, fanned herself, and then snapped the fan shut in order to indicate the supper room with it. 'I've known it all these years – summer and winter – but never before like this.'

Her mother-in-law sounded oddly pensive, Emma thought, as though she were remembering the folly in some particular way, but she did not enlarge. 'I felt,' Emma said, 'that it would be in keeping with the ballroom, since both are in the Indian style.'

'And so they are,' Henry said heartily. 'Lord, what a spread. Mrs Drayton is a find, I must admit, although hardly an inexpensive one. Mrs Cobham would never have managed anything so elaborate. I trust, however, that there will be enough for so many guests?'

'Quite enough,' Emma assured him. 'I have used the upper level as a store-room and more dishes are waiting there. I have been all ideas!'

'Come and recruit your strength,' said Henry jovially.

They left Lucy-Anne with Mr Bird. Over supper they shared a table with Emma's uncle, Harry Miller, and with Walter Kendall and one of George's friends, a Guildford dignitary called Councillor John Russell. The conversation became masculine and Emma, tired not only from dancing but also from organising, supervising and being a hostess, was glad to sit still, enjoy the food and let her mind drift.

Bits of the conversation caught her attention now and then. The name of Robert Clive came up. She knew him as someone with whom George had had much to do in India, and as the brother-in-law of the present Astronomer Royal, Nevil Maskelyne. Lucy-Anne sometimes corresponded with Maskelyne. Clive had been home in England for some time now and had been in serious trouble over the source of his fortune, much to George's satisfaction.

Her father-in-law, Emma knew, had once regarded Clive as a friend, but now detested him because he had put a stop to George's own methods of amassing money. George had fairly spluttered with delight on hearing that Clive's right to an annual income of £27,000 from the Nawab of Bengal had been challenged in Parliament. He had then sulked for a week after hearing that Parliament had decided in Clive's favour.

Now it seemed that Clive, although vindicated, was in poor health, with persistent abdominal trouble.

'. . . he'd be a power in the government by now but for the way he ails,' John Russell said. Russell was well into middle age, but healthy. 'Though he's achieved enough, lord knows. Amazing, that a man who keeps on going sick should have done what he's done. He seems to have led armies and pacified provinces with a permanently upset stomach.'

'Illness plagues him more in England than in India, I fancy,' Harry Miller drawled. In his forties he had become very like his mother, with much of her air of superiority. He offered snuff to the other men. 'The climate of England doesn't suit him, I hear.'

'And that includes the political climate,' Walter Kendall said. 'There was a time when no one expected a man to do other than make the best fortune he could by whatever means came to hand, short of putting on a mask and holding up stage-coaches. We didn't hear nonsense about corruption charges then. Our third King George is too pure-minded to understand the real world. Farming's prospering, though,' he added.

The conversation drifted on to matters of agriculture and then to trade, which Emma found soporific. She finished eating and then caught herself dozing where she sat. She jerked herself awake. A hostess must not fall asleep in the middle of a party. In a moment she must return to the house and preside over the ballroom. She was about to get to her feet when George Whitmead blundered into the supper room, his steps so weaving and unsteady that at half-a-dozen tables conversation stopped and heads turned.

'Good Gad, he's drunk!' said Walter Kendall. 'Well, I'm damned. He likes his bumper, but it's not like him to get pissed in company when the ladies are there.'

'He can't be drunk,' said Emma. 'It's not possible. It's not half an hour since I left him in the ballroom, dancing with Elizabeth.'

'What? He was dancing with my girl, in that state?' demanded Harry.

'No, *no*. He was perfectly sober and perfectly decorous. Excuse me!' said Emma, and made haste to George's side.

Lucy-Anne was already there, steering her husband towards a chair.

'I think he has a touch of fever,' she said to Emma. 'He hasn't had it for years and I thought perhaps it had burned itself out, but he had frequent attacks when he first came home from India. George, my dear . . .'

'I'm not feverish,' said George, in a perfectly lucid voice. He let himself be guided into a seat. Lucy-Anne put the back of her hand on his forehead and said in a perplexed voice, 'It's hard to tell, on such a warm evening. But his skin is certainly hot.'

'Damme, don't talk about me as if I wasn't here,' said George testily. 'What are you all staring for? Not come out all over smallpox pustules, have I? I'm not ill and I'm not drunk either. Got a bit of a headache with the heat, that's all. No European ever quite gets used to these Indian nights. Stifling climate, felt it even as a young man.' He stared about him, aggressively. 'Funny arrangement of tables this evening. Where's Mohammed Ali?'

'Mohammed . . . who?' asked Emma in bewilderment.

'His mother had a demented uncle, I remember her telling us about it,' said Walter Kendall in an undertone. 'Fluffed her feathers like a cock at a fight, she did, all over some talk of the way they treat lunatics in Bedlam. Told you about that, Henry, haven't I? Hope you're not going Bedlam-way, George, old fellow.'

'Of course he isn't,' said Henry angrily. 'It's just a touch of the malarial fever. He's delirious!'

'I am not delirious,' George barked. 'Don't be impertinent, sir. I said, where is Mohammed Ali? This is his banquet, why isn't he here? I was looking for him – ought to pay my respects to my illustrious host.'

Lucy-Anne caught Henry's eye. 'Come, sir, I think we should get you to bed,' Henry said and put a hand under his father's elbow. Harry Miller went to George's other side. George brushed them off and rose to his feet unaided.

'I can stand up on my own, if that's what you want. What's the devil *is* the matter with you all?' He glared round at them. 'What's gone wrong with this evening? Where are the dancing girls? There are always dancing girls at these affairs; I've been looking forward to them. Not that there was ever a girl to compare with Sita. Gad, if you'd ever seen Sita . . .'

'Please come this way, sir,' said Henry.

They steered him out of the folly, ignoring the interested eyes of the other guests. He went with them, grumblingly but without actual resistance. Out of doors it was cooler. The stars were coming out and somewhere a nightingale had begun to sing. In the distance, light streamed from the open ballroom door and the strains of the orchestra floated across the garden. As they emerged from the chestnut avenue George stopped and rubbed his forehead. 'Where in hell's name am I?'

'At home, sir, at Chestnuts,' Henry said calmly. 'It's a July evening and we're giving a ball for Elizabeth Miller.'

'It was so hot. I think it overcame me for a moment. I fancy I've had a little fever after all. I've been dreaming. I thought I was in India.'

'Yes, so it seemed,' Henry said. 'And if you have been feverish you should really take a little rest, sir. May I see you to your room and call Barker for you?'

'I feel a bit trembly. If you'll give me your arm, my boy . . . till we find Barker.'

'Of course, sir,' said Henry.

'There,' said Lucy-Anne. 'There's nothing more to worry about. Let us all return to our suppers or to the ballroom.'

Bemusedly, murmuring among themselves, the little group dispersed. A little later, when Lucy-Anne and Emma were briefly alone together on the terrace, Emma said, 'I don't understand. Mr Whitmead was certainly not drunk and I don't think—'

'You don't think he was feverish, either.' Lucy-Anne fanned herself irritably. 'Quite. I pretended that he was, for the sake of appearances, but when he's feverish he sweats and shivers and his eyes are dull. Nothing like that was happening tonight. There was no fever. As far as I know this has never occurred before in front of anyone except me. But I'm sorry to say, Emma, that this is not the first time he has supposed himself to be still in India.'

'I will not have it said that my father is mad.' Henry Whitmead sat with his chin raised and his square body in a resolute posture. 'Dr Graham is talking nonsense. My father caught a tropical illness in India and it still recurs from time to time. No doubt the excitement of the ball brought it on.' He glared around the drawing room, which had been tidied after yesterday's revels but still had a faintly disrupted air. 'We have so few such occasions in this house,' Henry said. 'It is not at all surprising.'

'All Dr Graham said,' Lucy-Anne responded, 'was that your father seemed a little confused in his manner. It was not necessary to tell him, as you did, that he was talking stuff and nonsense. He was extremely offended.' She shook her fan open and agitated it. The weather was still very hot.

'He said confused; he meant mad. That was perfectly clear,' said Henry coldly. 'I say that my father had a short attack of delirium yesterday and is now recovered. Emma, you have just taken some tea to him. How did he seem to you?'

'A little tired but otherwise quite as usual,' Emma said.

'There you are,' said Henry to his mother. 'Confused, indeed! It is the fashion now to say that almost any symptom is a sign of confusion, as the doctors call it. It's been so ever since the king had a bad cold nearly ten years ago and some foolish gossip-mongers put it about that he had had an attack of melancholy. The word confused was used then. Madness was what was meant, and it was rubbish, just as Dr Graham's remarks were rubbish.'

Lucy-Anne sighed. 'Very well, dear. Your father has had a return of his malaria. But the point is that he does seem pulled down by it. After all, he doesn't usually spend the day in bed. Now, I have a suggestion. Julia Harper has written to invite us all to her nephew Hugo's wedding. I think we should accept, including your father. The Harpers can accommodate us all, they say. I have, as you know, always found the waters most invigorating. If I did not take them at least once a year I should spend my days lying on a sofa. I think that Emma, at the moment, might also benefit from them, and so might George. They may be just what is wanted to set him up again. There's no harm in trying.'

It was such an extremely reasonable suggestion that Henry seemed almost taken aback.

'Well . . . yes, I suppose it's good sense. I was going to send Cottrell soon to look at that place, Broom Cottage. The present tenants have been late with their rent for the third time. Really, some tenants are more trouble than they're worth. I've never regretted that we got rid of the Craddocks, though I know you disapproved, Mother. I can pay a call on Broom Cottage myself while we're in the West Country. I don't even mind,' he added large-mindedly, 'taking a sip or two of the waters myself to encourage my father into it, if they might do him good, though I've heard they taste appalling. Very well. That's settled. And now,' said Henry, getting up, 'I think I'll take a ride round the fields.'

When he had left the room, Emma turned enquiringly to Lucy-Anne. 'Mother-in-law, what do you think is really the matter with Mr Whitmead?'

'I don't know.' Gently, Lucy-Anne closed her fan and laid it on her lap. 'I know very little of these things, Emma. He's not a young man and heat, excitement, perhaps just a touch of some old tropical malaise – all that might account for a great deal. Dr Graham has offered no better suggestion. A regular life, he said, and a lowering diet. Well, George can have all that in Bath, and try the waters too. It's the best I can think of.'

'Will he agree to go?'

'I hope so. He's quite used to us going, after all, and it is an invitation to a wedding.' Lucy-Anne smiled her eldritch smile. 'If it came as a new idea, he would object. Ladies shouldn't go in for travelling, he'd say. But I long ago convinced him that the waters were essential for my health and that's why you and I are allowed to make the journey now and then. Provided, of course, that we avoid making a public show of ourselves at balls and assemblies.'

'Why are they forbidden to us?' Emma asked. 'The Harpers would escort us if we asked them, after all.'

'My husband,' said Lucy-Anne dryly, 'is a strange man.'

'How strange?' asked Emma directly.

Their eyes met.

'I don't know,' Lucy-Anne said. 'I admit to being worried but I hope I am merely being foolish.'

'Henry's worried too, isn't he? Or he wouldn't have been so angry with Dr Graham just for saying that Mr Whitmead was confused.'

'You are too sharp for comfort sometimes, Emma. Yes, Henry is anxious, very much so. It's because of his grandmother – George's mother, I mean,' said Lucy-Anne. 'She was sound enough in mind herself, but she had a mad uncle. Henry knows about it because Walter Kendall told him. I wish he hadn't. I understand Henry perfectly well. He fears that the taint may have come down to him.'

'Oh, no!' Instinctively, Emma put protective hands over her stomach.

'Don't do that,' said Lucy-Anne. 'That kind of fear is no earthly use, believe me. In the course of my life I've learned that there are a lot of things one would like to change and can't. Mad relatives are among them.'

Chapter Eighteen

The Star-Crossed Cure

Emma liked Bath. Even though, because of George Whitmead's eccentricities, she could only partake of a few of its social pleasures, she could still admire the pale stone of the buildings and could still enjoy the shops and the orchestra playing in the Pump Room. She liked her mother-in-law's friends the Harpers, too, and their family.

'Time goes so fast,' Lucy-Anne said, as the carriage rolled up the hill towards the vicarage. 'I half-expect, every time, to find the place full of small children, but the children one encounters at the Harpers' now are grandchildren. And even they're growing up. Dotty, who used to live at Broom Cottage, died twenty-five years ago, but I can remember her as though it were yesterday and she was alive when the nephew, Hugo, was born. And now Hugo is a grown man and a parson like his uncle.'

The carriage turned in at the gates and the Harpers came down the front steps to meet it, followed by the maids Letty and Anna, and George's man, Barker, who had travelled ahead. Lucy-Anne pulled down the window and put her head out, to the considerable danger of her piled-up hair. 'Julia! What a joy to see you! How is Hugo?'

'Harassing the workmen at his house. He's taken on a living just outside the town!' As the carriage halted Julia's large form blocked the light from the window. 'But his vicarage is in a terrible condition and he says it isn't fit for his bride, so he's having it painted and a new roof put on. Such a to-do! He drives the workmen as if they were slaves! Nothing's too good for his Mary, he says.'

Henry, who had accompanied them on horseback, dismounted, handed his horse to Edward, and came to help the ladies down. George followed them. 'What's Mary like?' Lucy-Anne wanted to know, shaking out her skirts, while Letty came hurrying to rearrange her mistress's shawl. 'Is she pretty? Will she make Hugo happy?'

'She's a darling and I'm sure you'll like her. Don't fuss over Hugo so much,' said Julia, laughing. 'He can decide these things for himself now, you know.'

There was a trace of warning in her tone. It was not the first time Emma had heard her use that tone to Lucy-Anne when speaking of Hugo, and it always puzzled her. But she had no time to do much puzzling now. Julia had taken her arm. 'Emma! How are you? Lucy-Anne has told me your news. How did you find the journey?'

'Oh, it was very comfortable. I am a little tired now, nothing more.'

'Come indoors and put your feet up.'

'You're very kind. I always feel I'll be well looked after when I come to Bath.'

'Julia and Edward are good at looking after people,' said Lucy-Anne.

'We do our best. The world's full of people who need looking after,' Julia said. 'Even you do, on occasion.'

Once more, there was an unexplained note in her voice. As the men took the horses away and the ladies went inside to the Harpers' familiar, shabby parlour, where the cushions were plump but all their covers were worn and most of the chairs sagged a little, Emma puzzled over it again. Every time she came here with her mother-in-law there was an exchange like that between Lucy-Anne and Julia. It was as if they shared some private memory, of a time when Lucy-Anne had been somehow lost or in trouble and Julia had rescued her. And always Julia seemed to be slightly in the ascendant and Lucy-Anne, who was usually so commanding, seemed to grow very slightly smaller.

It was a mystery and she had a suspicion that she would never know the answer to it.

'Is George all right? What is he talking about? I could swear I heard the word India!' said Lucy-Anne out of the corner of her mouth as the marriage party made its way across the sunlit grass from the church to the vicarage and the wedding breakfast.

'He's telling Mr and Mrs Logan about Calcutta,' said Emma. 'But he doesn't think this is India, or anything like that. It's quite all right. Look, Henry's with them too and he isn't at all upset.'

'George has been perfectly normal since he woke up the morning after the ball,' Lucy-Anne said. 'But, all the same, whenever I hear him say "India", I feel uneasy.'

'I'm sure there's no need. I think the waters really have improved his health. What a beautiful day it is. And isn't Mary Logan a lovely bride?'

'Mary Harper, now,' Lucy-Anne said. Her eyes rested on the newly wed couple walking arm in arm ahead of them. They were of a height, the top of Hugo's best wig exactly level with Mary's crown of flowers. The bride's hair had been dressed in a very simple style, to go with an equally simple gown, but the effect, if unfashionable, was endearing, and so was her obvious happiness. Like Emma, she was fair, although she was a honey- rather than an ash-blonde, and her curls bounced in time with her buoyant walk.

'I like her very much, don't you?' said Emma. 'I'm sure they'll be happy.'

'I hope so,' said Lucy-Anne. 'I do hope so.'

She sounded so intense that Emma glanced at her enquiringly. Lucy-Anne smiled. 'I want all young couples to be happy,' she said. 'It's so easy, so very easy, not to be.'

Emma, remembering the recent state of her own marriage and well aware that for Lucy-Anne life with George could hardly have been smooth, decided not to answer.

Inside the vicarage all the doors stood open to the warm August air and in the largest room, where the table was set for a festive meal, the bride and groom and their respective parents and guardians were receiving guests, with laughter and kisses and much joyful clasping of hands, and a happy absence of formality.

Emma was amused to see a sternly corseted lady – a distant Harper connection, she thought – hold out fastidious fingertips to Mr Logan and have her entire hand swallowed warmly by both of his, and to observe Mrs Logan, unimpressed by George Whitmead's air of consequence, giving him an unceremonious hug. Edward Harper was still in the vestments in which he had married the young pair and Julia was majestically hooped and brocaded, but the Logans, like their daughter, were dressed with simplicity and somehow or other it was they who set the tone of the occasion. In their presence, stiffness and affectation simply melted away.

'They're Quakers, of a sort,' Julia had told Lucy-Anne and Emma. 'They're not strict and they don't mind Mary marrying an Anglican vicar; indeed they would not have tried to prevent her even if they did mind. They believe in friendly persuasion – Mary often uses the term. If that doesn't work, they just say, "God go with you." I suppose they'd intervene if they actually saw someone about to commit a murder, but it would need to be that serious! They certainly wouldn't stop a young couple in love from marrying. As a matter of fact we and they get on together very well. We are all interested in charitable work, and Edward has worked with Mary's father on trying to found refuges for young girls who have got into trouble and been rejected by their families. It didn't work out too well because the other people involved wanted the places to be much too harsh. Edward and Mr Logan said that the women should be protected and helped to begin new lives, not imprisoned and turned into slaves, sewing and laundering to make profits for those in charge of them. My husband and Mr Logan withdrew from the venture in the end. But they became good friends with each other and that led to the meeting between Hugo and Mary. They were pleased, though, that Edward performed the wedding here at our own little St Oswald's. They didn't want St Peter and St Paul's Abbey. And they don't go in for elaborate fashions.'

Emma, feeling that it would be somehow polite to Mary, had had her own hair dressed with simplicity today. But Lucy-Anne had not. 'I make people look at my toilette so that they won't look at my ugly face,' she had said. Now, in royal blue and old gold satin, with three horizontal sausages of hair over each ear and a powdered pyramid on top, adorned with ostrich feathers, it was clear that in this respect she had taken no chances.

The guests were numerous, but the mild formalities were swiftly over. The last stragglers arrived from the church to exchange kisses and handshakes, and then the receiving line dissolved. The bride was at once surrounded by a bevy of friends and Lucy-Anne made straight for Hugo, George wandering after her. Henry, taking Emma's arm and strolling with her on George's heels, remarked that it was a queer thing, damme, but since they'd arrived he noticed that Mother positively doted on the Harpers' nephew. 'Have you noticed it too?'

'Yes, I have. I think perhaps she is sorry that she did not have more children,' Emma said. 'And perhaps she is sorry too for Hugo, since he

199

is said to be a love-child. That was why the Harpers adopted him, I think.'

'It still seems odd,' Henry said, quite grumpily.

The Harpers, however, had noticed it as well and were bearing down on Lucy-Anne with a distraction. 'Your pardon, Hugo, but do allow us to intrude. My love,' said Julia to her friend, 'there are some people I want you to meet. Do come and let me introduce them to you before the meal is served. Their names are William and Caroline Herschel – brother and sister, not a married couple. William's an astronomer, not quite a professional, but nearly.'

'An astronomer?' George let out a harrumph, albeit a goodhumoured one. 'So now you'll talk stargazing all the rest of the day. Extraordinary how you women take to it. Clive's wife is just the same. Stars and music, that's Margaret Clive. I'd better go and find the punch bowl. Take it there is punch, hey, Harper?'

'Certainly. All tastes have been considered,' Edward Harper assured him. 'We have ale, punch, wine, lemonade, tea and coffee.'

'Herschel combines stars with music, too,' said Julia. 'His first profession is that of musician. We've told him that you'd love to meet him and Caroline. Come now, while they're not caught up with anyone else.'

George harrumphed away in the direction of the punch, taking Henry with him, while Emma and Lucy-Anne went with Julia towards a couple who were standing in a bay window and looking out on the untidy vicarage garden.

Ten minutes later Emma knew that her life hitherto had been lived in slow motion and in shadows. She had begun to imagine that the world of Mrs Henry Whitmead – in which she peered through a screen at business guests in London, thought it a great matter when at Chestnuts a fine ballroom was used twice in four years, and worried endlessly because she was slow in getting with child – was actually, genuinely a world, and that she might live wholly within it.

Now she learned otherwise.

The Herschel brother and sister were different in age, since William must be well into his thirties while Caroline was no more than twenty-four. They came from Hanover and they were very alike, with their fair skins and high foreheads, and elegantly arched nostrils which could have made them look haughty, except for the mobility of their mouths and the frankness in their eyes. They had the same kind of eyes, too, grey-blue with dark, well-opened pupils and a darker rim around the iris. Caroline, poor soul, had had smallpox at some time and had marks on her forehead and a drooping eyelid, but her expression was still sweet and, although her English was not as good as her brother's, her voice was very pretty.

But they were more than simply agreeable. They had lived. Nor merely existed, but lived, and they were charmingly, blandly, amusing about it.

'... Lucy-Anne, these are the Herschels. Caro, William, I'd like you to meet my friend Mrs Lucy-Anne Whitmead and her daughter-in-law Emma ...'

200

'I am quite delighted to meet you, Mrs Whitmead and – er – well, you are both Mrs Whitmead, I take it?'

'And I also am delighted,' said Caroline. 'Mrs Harper has of Mrs Lucy-Anne Whitmead spoken. You too make a study of astronomy?'

'I have an amateur's interest,' said Lucy-Anne, 'which is to say that I have a little telescope and look at the sky on fine nights. I have interested Emma in it to some extent. But I believe you are almost a professional, sir? And your sister too?'

'My sister Caroline is a singer, Mrs Whitmead, but she helps me in the study of the stars. I do not quite earn my living by astronomy, but I work at it most systematically, and I have lately begun manufacturing telescopes of various sizes, by which I have augmented my earnings. I know that Mr Harper has an ambition to make some great discovery concerning the stars and I share the same dream, though I fear it may remain a dream. It is hardly likely that a musician turned astronomer in near middle-age will shake the world with his discoveries.'

'Mrs Harper told me that you are also a musician.'

'Yes, indeed. I was once,' said William Herschel, his wide lips quirking with amusement and his eyes bright, 'an oboe player in the Hanoverian Foot Guards. I learned English when I was in Dover with them ten years ago when a French invasion was feared in England and Hanoverian troops were brought over. I returned to the Continent with the army but I left them after, alas, their defeat at the hands of the French two years later.'

'Left the army?' asked Emma. 'Can one just do that?'

'Normally, no,' said William. 'But I had never actually signed on. I joined, in a rather unofficial fashion, when I was fourteen and I was still only sixteen at the time of that defeat. Father was in the same regiment and he said it would be safer for me to go home—'

'Father did so worry. For us all he worried,' Caroline said. 'All the family – what is the phrase? – yes, followed the drum in those days. In such wet fields we slept! I was very ill once, with rheumatism and asthma, and after that, always, for our safety, Father worried.'

'He was certainly concerned for mine,' said William. 'He said it was quite within the law for me to go home. But when I tried I was turned back for lack of a passport and so I went back to the regiment. Only when I got there no one wanted me. All was in confusion, in the midst of a mixture of a retreat and a surrender, and no one cared what happened to the musicians. I tried to report to this officer and that and they all said go away, we haven't time to worry about an oboe-player now. And so there I was, wandering about on this battlefield with my oboe, tripping over bodies now and then, and the tents where I had slept and eaten before all vanished, and I wondered what to do. I had given my weapons away when I left the field the first time. I was so much afraid of meeting a drunken Frenchman and having only an oboe to hit him with . . .'

Emma began to laugh and they all joined in. 'But it was a desperate situation,' said Herschel, pulling a solemn face. 'What was I to do? In the end, once more I took my leave and this time I got away. I came to England and made my career here as a musician and a year ago I asked my sister to join me.'

'The family had a settled home in Hanover by then,' said Caroline, taking care with her English. 'But Father had died and I was not happy. My mother and my elder brother thought a daughter at home should be only a domestic servant.'

'She was not allowed to sing,' William added, 'although she longed to have her voice trained. But then I paid a visit home and rescued her. Here in Bath she keeps house for me, but I have seen that she has singing lessons and lately she has begun to perform at concerts. You must come to hear her.'

'Did you learn English all in one year?' Emma asked Caroline, impressed.

'Yes, but as you must realise, I am not yet easy with it,' Caroline said.

'But this is all amazing,' said Emma, trying to imagine going to a foreign land and learning a new language and taking up a profession all in the space of twelve months. Sleeping in fields and wandering about on battlefields with an oboe sounded even more incredible. The Herschels did not look extraordinary, but their experience of life was a thousand times greater than her own. She gazed at them, marvelling.

'Caroline is to sing at a concert in Bath next week,' William Herschel said. 'I will be conducting. Afterwards, we will have a few friends to supper at our home – it is in New King Street – and if it is a clear night we will all look through my latest telescope. We would be so happy to welcome you to that supper. It would be a delight. Mrs Emma, you could almost be of German birth – such fairness as yours is so rare in England. My dear Mrs Whitmeads, I have already invited the Harpers but please say you will both come too, and bring your husbands.'

Since the bridegroom was a vicar and the bride a girl of Quaker origin, the wedding day wasn't likely to culminate in anything rumbustious. Emma's own marriage celebrations had included an embarrassingly boisterous bedding, and she was agreeably surprised by Hugo and Mary's decorous nuptials. When the wedding breakfast was over and everyone had wished the young pair well, Hugo Harper put his Mary into a hired chaise, drawn by grey horses and decorated with white ribbons, which had been waiting for an hour, and took her away to his own vicarage.

Everyone gathered at the gate to wave them goodbye and Mary shyly blew kisses back to them as she was driven off. With that, the excitement was over. Those guests who lived nearby, including the Herschels, took their leave.

'But you will not forget my sister's concert next week,' William Herschel said earnestly to the Whitmeads.

George and Henry had heard about it by this time. 'We can go if you wish it,' Henry said to Emma. 'It won't be too much for you? You get tired early, these days.'

'I can rest in the afternoon. I should like to go.'

George, who seemed to be feeling the heat, said a little irritably that, although the Herschels seemed a most respectable brother and sister, he personally would not care to see any lady of his family singing in public or mixing with women who did.

'She only sings classical material,' said Edward mildly. 'I have no hesitation in joining the party, and I'm a vicar!'

'Classical music can be a damned bore,' George told him. 'But it'll be no worse, I daresay, than having to sit through one of Margaret Clive's musical evenings. Very well, since you vouch for the occasion, we will attend.'

'There,' said Julia, as they all drifted into the parlour and sat down. 'We have a pleasant outing to look forward to. Though for the moment I must say I'm glad to take the weight off my feet at home. What did you think of the Herschels, Emma?'

In imagination, Emma could still see William Herschel's eyes, smiling into hers, full of admiration and an uncomplicated friendliness which she had never seen in Henry's. Henry had desired her and married her and then been disappointed because, until now, he hadn't had the expected return on his investment. She could never remember seeing friendship in her husband's face.

She would see William Herschel again next week. And the thought of it, incredibly, made her want to lift her skirt hem and pirouette around the drawing room and then burst into song. She had never felt like this with Henry even at the beginning, when he first came courting her.

In a carefully colourless voice she said, 'I thought them very pleasant. Do you agree, Mother-in-law?'

'Indeed, yes,' said Lucy-Anne.

On the morning before the concert they visited Milsom Street, where the shops could stand comparison with anything in London, so that Emma could buy trimmings for a new gown she was planning for after her baby was born. She also bought a pair of shoes which she said she would wear that evening, and Lucy-Anne bought a new fan, made of parchment, with Japanese scenes painted on it.

Julia, who had come with them, said that they were sadly extravagant, but a moment later plunged into a draper's and emerged with a parcel which she thrust into Emma's arms.

'Plain white cotton material and a length of white linen. You'll want so many things for the baby. Are you going to put the Whitmead device on the baby's bedlinen? You know, that pretty little picture of a bridge over a river, which is embroidered on most of the sheets in your house. I've helped Lucy-Anne put it on new sheets on occasion.'

'Well, I hadn't thought . . . yes, why not?' said Emma, whose mind had for nearly a week been almost entirely engaged with the coming concert. She came back to reality with a start. She would soon have to go back to Chestnuts or to London and there would be no Herschels there. Would it be possible to make friends with them sufficiently to ask them to stay? Or would it be possible, rather, to get Henry to make friends with them sufficiently? Would there be any harm in it? Very few, if any, of the people they knew were friends of hers in any real sense. Most of the company they kept were relatives, or were people chosen by Henry and his father. All she wanted was just to have people near her who liked *her*. There surely wasn't anything wrong in that.

203

Did Caroline embroider? She visualised herself and Caroline Herschel putting bridge-and-river pictures on sheets, seated in the drawing room at Chestnuts, while William played music for them and talked about astronomy.

'If you do want to embroider your baby's things,' Julia was saying, 'there's a haberdashers just along here where we could get just the silks.'

'Yes, of course,' said Emma. 'Let's get them now.'

'Are you well?' Julia was looking at her anxiously. Lucy-Anne, hearing the worry in her friend's voice, turned from peering at the rolls of brocade in a shop window and said: 'Emma?'

'Yes, I'm quite well. Why, don't I seem so?'

'You seem a little distrait. I think,' said Julia, 'that we should go home now and that you should rest. It really is very warm. We can get the embroidery silks some other time.'

'If you think it best,' said Emma obediently.

The concert pleased all of them except George. William Herschel, exuding an unexpected air of authority, conducted the orchestra in excerpts from Handel's *Messiah*, in anthems by Maurice Greene and, by way of contrast, in some lively songs by Thomas Arne and Charles Dibdin. Caroline's part in the concert involved only the *Messiah* and an Arne setting of words by Shakespeare.

Emma, Lucy-Anne and the Harpers applauded heartily and even Henry, who was not much of a music-lover, murmured some approving comments to Emma. Only George, whose ear for music was poor and more attuned to eastern rhythms anyway, fidgeted.

When, after a pause to take coffee and let the Herschels reach home ahead of them, they hired the sedan chairs which were the easiest method of getting about in the hilly streets of Bath, and repaired to New King Street for supper, he seemed grumpy, and as he descended from his chair in the narrow street in front of number 7, he showed signs of wanting to cavil.

'Upon my word, these Herschels live in an uncommonly plain fashion. What sort of place is this?'

'A very unpretentious house.' Julia did not have to live with George and could afford, gently, to laugh at him. Lucy-Anne had noticed it before, with envy. 'William and Caroline live modestly on an upper floor,' said Julia. 'Their landlord has the ground floor.'

'They are not even owner-occupiers?' Henry asked.

'No, and they're very untidy. Their rooms are as bad as our garden. But Caroline keeps a good table,' Julia assured him.

'*We're* not owner-occupiers,' said Edward amiably, over his shoulder, as he paid off the chairmen. 'My parsonage is church property.'

'Come, now, Mr Whitmead.' Julia invited George to give her his arm. 'You sometimes dine with your Upwood tenants in their farmhouse. So why not take supper at the Herschels? The company is admirable. My goodness, where would you find a more accomplished pair?'

With an inclination of her head, she encouraged the party towards the front door. George harrumphed, but complied. Edward, striding past them to get there first, plied the knocker and a very young maid let them in.

Inside, they followed her up a narrow wooden staircase to a cramped first-floor landing where the Herschels greeted them, beaming. They stood back against the wall to let their guests off the stairs. It was certainly a far remove from the gracious spaces of Chestnuts or even the Hanover Square house, which, although not so large as Chestnuts, was nevertheless much bigger than this and had landings the size of small rooms. But the Herschels clearly saw nothing out of the way about it.

'Welcome, welcome,' William said. 'This is all our territory from now on. We keep the poor Bulmans well in their place. They live downstairs and we enjoy the best of the house. Come along in. We have wine and coffee waiting, and then, if you like, I can show you round while Caroline and the girl put the finishing touches to supper. Make yourselves at home.'

It had taken just a few minutes for Emma to recognise that the Herschels represented something new and exhilarating in her life. It took only five more for her to know that, whatever her strange feelings about her host and hostess – especially her host – might mean, she was utterly in love with their congested, chaotic, badly cared for and completely hospitable home.

Her life had been passed hitherto in very well-run houses. Her parents believed in a place for everything and everything in its place. In Emma's family home, books, while being read, were placed neatly on a table beside the usual chair of whoever was reading them, closed, with a bookmark to keep the place, and were never left carelessly about but were returned to their bookcases as soon as they were finished; ornaments were few, were carefully dusted and positioned with the utmost precision; wilting flowers were whisked instantly from their vases; clothes were put away as soon as they were taken off.

In the Whitmead household, whether at Chestnuts or in London, the regime was not quite so severe but it was of the same order. One might perhaps leave a book lying open on a table, or a shawl tossed over a chairback, and there would be no censure but somehow or other the item would always be quietly tidied away before long. Dust was removed as fast as it appeared and all the furniture was ardently polished with a mixture of beeswax, turpentine and linseed oil and Ames had been known to reduce housemaids to tears for leaving a solitary fingermark on the glossy veneer of a table or sideboard.

The Herschel household, to put it mildly, was different. Here, flowers were free to wilt as they would, while ornaments stood everywhere and shared their shelves or window ledges with a casual drift of books, quills, inkpots, rulers, letters, gloves, and the assorted impedimenta of music and astronomy. The top of a handsome piano had been used as an extra table, on which stood three globes, a couple of small telescopes, and a pile of maps and charts, so badly stacked that they looked ready to cascade to the floor if anyone sneezed too close to them.

Dusting and polishing presumably took place sometimes, but in an endearingly haphazard fashion. The sideboard in the dining parlour gleamed pleasantly and someone had recently wiped most of the brass candlesticks, but one pair had been overlooked and left tarnished, and dust lay undisturbed on the clawed feet of chairs and table and on the top of the cello, which had been stood on its nose in a corner.

'I don't play much any more,' Herschel said cheerfully. 'I only conduct nowadays, and otherwise concentrate on my star-watching and telescope-making. Caroline unearths the piano now and then and gives me a private concert on it.'

'It is all delightful,' said Emma, so warmly that Henry glanced at her in surprise. 'It is so informal,' she explained. 'So . . . so full of the life that is lived here and the interests that are pursued.'

'You mean we're careless folk,' said William Herschel, acutely, but with amusement. 'But life is brief and there is much to do. Sometimes there is no time for little domestic things when there are the wonders of the heavens to explore and the depths of an oratorio to search out and make an orchestra express. But come to supper. You will not find that careless, I promise.'

Lucy-Anne and Emma hoped earnestly that this would turn out to be true. They knew – better than the Harpers did – how thoroughly their respective husbands could spoil an occasion if they disapproved of the surroundings, the company, or the food. George could pack the sound *harrumph* with a whole vocabulary of meaning and then Henry, so apt to take on his father's opinions, would become restless and make edged remarks and suggest leaving early. Lucy-Anne, who had taken a liking to the Herschels and wanted to cultivate William, and Emma, who had taken rather more than just a liking, went into the dining room with secretly crossed fingers.

The supper, however, was excellent. It was nearer to a dinner, with not only soup and bread and cold sliced beef but ducklings cooked with horseradish and accompanied by asparagus in cream and some sweet potato rissoles, followed by buttered oranges and apple tart.

Caroline, still in the black gown in which she had sung, presided in dignified fashion and urged large helpings on them all, while William, an excellent host, kept the conversation going, skilfully aided by the Harpers, who encouraged him to describe how he had supported himself when first he came to England.

'It was an alarming time,' Herschel said. 'And I was only a boy. But I knew more about music than just how to play an instrument or two. My father taught me how to read and write it. It is a language to itself and, boy or not, it was a language I knew. So I walked into a music shop in London and asked for work copying music. They gave me an opera to copy. I pleased them. And so I was given my first job. But later on I wished to play again, and I became an organist. I lived in Halifax then. But presently I joined a band of musicians and came with them to Bath. We would play in the Pump Room, and at balls, and I took some pupils, too. That was how I first came to Bath. What a lovely town it is. Such buildings! If I were not a musician and an astronomer, perhaps I would become an architect.'

'Oh no. Music and astronomy and telescope-making are quite enough,' said Caroline.

'We can see! This house,' said Edward Harper, 'has always reminded me of those seaside cliffs where the layers of the different kinds of rock are visible, one on top of the another. In your house, Herschel, one can see your successive interests preserved in layers just like the rock strata.'

'And a layer of architects' drawings and samples of stone on top of the rest would be unbearable,' said Caroline. 'Our maid would give up altogether.'

'But how did it come about that you turned into an astronomer?' Henry enquired. 'What drew you from music to the contemplation of the heavens?'

'In India,' George pronounced, 'it is not unusual for princes to concern themselves with astronomical observations. It is a proper study for a gentleman and I suppose harmless for a lady, although perhaps not for the lower orders.'

There was a faint tinge in his voice which suggested that he wasn't sure whether an ex-oboe-player who had once scratched a living by copying music qualified as a gentleman or not, especially when he lived in rented accommodation where the dusting was erratic.

'But, Mr Whitmead,' said Julia, 'why must astronomy be limited to gentlemen and ladies? To gaze upon the wonders of the skies, and marvel at the immensity of the Creator's works – what could be more innocent and more likely to elevate the tone of anyone's mind?'

'It can also distract the mind from its proper tasks,' said George, 'and encourage thoughts beyond one's station. It is scarcely fitting, for instance, for a servant to aspire to knowledge that the employer does not possess. Indeed, on occasion, I wonder if the same does not apply to wives in relation to husbands. Should a woman reach for knowledge not shared by her spouse? An indulgent man may permit it, but should a woman do it?'

'The husband in that case had better study astronomy himself,' said Edward astringently. 'He should enlarge his own mind, not expect other people to limit theirs.'

'But there are so many branches of knowledge.' Beside her, Emma had felt Lucy-Anne stiffen. Her mother-in-law was, she knew, always haunted by the fear that George would attack the things she cared for. She defended her visits to Bath by wilting periodically on sofas, but her telescope and her correspondence with the Royal Society would be harder to protect. 'Even embroidery is a kind of knowledge,' Emma said gently. 'Certainly it is a skill. But few men practise it. Must women therefore give it up?'

Herschel burst out laughing. 'That is a clever answer, Mrs Whitmead. Indeed it is! But let me answer the younger Mr Whitmead's original question. I was first drawn to the study of the stars by reading the works of the astronomer James Ferguson, a member of the Royal Society. There had come a time in my life when music seemed not enough. I desired a new field of study, and Ferguson's book, *Astronomy Explained Upon Sir Isaac Newton's Principles—*'

'I have read it,' said Lucy-Anne quietly. She did not look at George. 'It was most interesting.'

'Indeed, yes, Mrs Whitmead. In especial I was intrigued by his mention of the patches of luminous cloud that here and there appear in the night skies. There is one in the Sword of Orion. They seem to contain stars, but they are a puzzle. I have been trying to build bigger and better telescopes with a view, mainly, to seeing them more clearly.' He glanced at George with rueful amusement. 'I am afraid, Mr Whitmead, that you would not approve of James Ferguson.'

'Wouldn't I?' said George, sounding, for some reason, a little bemused.

'Why would that be?' Emma asked.

Herschel smiled at her. 'Ferguson began life as an unlettered shepherd boy, lying out in the fields at night with the sheep and gazing at the stars. He was so fascinated that in the end, somehow, he learned to read, began to study the stars, and later became a teacher and the author of books on the subject. He began life as one of the lower orders, in fact. But he saw no necessity for remaining so.'

'But what if every shepherd boy did the same?' said Henry. 'Who would look after the sheep?'

'They wouldn't all do the same,' said Edward Harper. 'They wouldn't all want to.'

'And perhaps could not, anyway, even if they wished,' Emma agreed. 'Surely Mr Ferguson had unusual talents?'

'Yes, you are again very right,' said Herschel. 'The sheep are in no danger; Ferguson was an exception among shepherds. Well.' He looked at the table, where there were more empty dishes now than full ones. 'Supper seems to be over. Would you like to look through a telescope – a bigger one, perhaps, than you have seen before? I have made a ten-foot reflector model. We could look at one of the cloudy patches to which his book refers. Orion is only visible in winter but there are others.'

Henry had been observing Emma's air of animation with a slight frown on his brow. 'I think not,' he said, before Emma could answer. 'My wife is in a delicate state of health and I think we should return home after supper so that she can rest. You have had a long day, my dear, and you have been talking with such liveliness that you must be weary.'

'Oh, Henry, not just one peep? I should like it so.'

'You will take cold and that will certainly not do.'

'But, Henry—'

'No, no, you must listen to your husband. We must cherish you, my dear,' said George, clumsily gallant. 'I hope for a grandson by next spring,' he added.

Emma was not accustomed to feeling angry. It was not an emotion in which she had been encouraged as a child. The resentment which now surged up in her was not only unexpected but so violent that it shocked her. She wanted to strike her father-in-law and scream at her husband to let her, for the love of God, just decide for herself whether she would look through William Herschel's damned telescope.

'*We must cherish you.*' Keep her a prisoner, that's what her father-in-law meant, preferably on an upper floor, peering down at life through a latticed screen and prevented, of course, from talking too much to anyone. How much harm could she come to by glancing briefly through a telescope?

But to argue any more would bring about a set-down, and in front of company, too, and therefore she bent her head in acquiescence. Her body, however, throbbed with rage. It was as though her whole personality were suddenly changing, without warning, and in a manner beyond her power to control.

'You are disappointed, Mrs Emma,' said Herschel kindly. 'But perhaps some other time?'

'Yes, indeed,' she said, managing to sound bright and to raise her eyes again and smile. 'Another time.' Her fury went on throbbing, demanding an outlet.

Turning to George, she infused her voice with a deceptive sweetness. 'I do hope,' she said, 'that you will not be too disappointed, or blame me, if I present you with a grand-daughter instead of a grandson. It is not in my power to choose, you know.'

George turned crimson with indignation and surprise. Henry looked disapproving. 'Well, really, Emma. Has anyone ever suggested such a thing? I think you must be exceedingly tired. It's time we went home.'

'And, indeed, a girl-child should be as welcome as any boy,' said Herschel quietly. 'My sister Caroline there was sadly undervalued by my mother and the brother from whom I rescued her. She is as it happens the worthiest possible assistant for my work.'

Emma looked at him again and found in his face a remarkable degree of understanding. Their eyes clung and held, pupils widening. Once more, she knew that here was a man to whom she was not only a desirable woman but also an equal and perhaps a friend. A man whom she in turn . . .

Had desired from the moment she first saw him. This was why she had wanted to dance and sing at the prospect of seeing him again. It would have seemed, now, the most natural thing in the world to get up and go to him, to stroll out of the room with him, to share with him the wonders of the night sky and then, letting the pleasures of the mind melt and blend into those of the body, to withdraw with him to bed.

And, of course, it was all quite out of the question. Henry Whitmead's wife, carrying his child, could not run after a William Herschel. She must not cultivate the Herschels, must not, ever, invite them to Chestnuts. Henry was watching her. George was watching her. She must seize hold of this magical moment, wring its neck and bury it deep. She would be well advised to say afterwards that she wished to leave Bath as soon as possible, and better advised still never to return.

'You are very kind,' she said courteously to Herschel, and then turned to Henry. 'I am so sorry. I did not mean to speak so forcefully.' She wondered in alarm whether Henry, or anyone else, had sensed that secret lightning flash between herself and William. 'I think,' she said to her husband, in a slightly fading tone of voice, 'that you are right and I am somewhat overtired. We have had a delightful evening. Miss

Herschel's voice was a pleasure to hear and we could not have had a more delicious supper.'

Henry rose to his feet. 'Of course. I will procure a chair for you. Perhaps the maid will fetch your wrap.'

Lucy-Anne and the Harpers were also on their feet, making social farewells. George, however, had not moved.

'Why a chair?' he said grumblingly. 'What's wrong with a rickshaw? Where's Ahmed? I always have Ahmed with me; he'll find us some rickshaws.'

Lucy-Anne whitened. 'George, please!' She flicked her fan open and began agitatedly to fan herself.

George, ignoring her, twisted round in his chair, looked at the door, and raised his voice to a bellow. '*Ahmed!*'

As they all stood there, horrified, it crossed Emma's mind that this, at least, was a distraction. This evening was likely enough to stick in the minds of those present, but not on account of Emma Whitmead and William Herschel.

'That was dreadful. Dreadful!' said Julia, when Edward had finished the prayers with which he always closed the day and had come to bed. 'It was clever of you to say that Ahmed was already out finding rickshaws. And yet George was perfectly normal again once we were downstairs and out of doors. I don't understand it.'

'Nor do I, quite, but madness can be intermittent, I believe. The king is said to have had an attack of it once, but recovered.'

'Madness! Lucy-Anne has mentioned to me that she is concerned about her husband's health, but can she really have meant that? I know about the king, of course, but – George?'

'I think so. Don't you?'

'It did look like it. The others were certainly frightened. There was Lucy-Anne flapping that fan about, and Henry talking nonsense about his father being apt to attacks of fever—'

'Fever, my foot!' said Edward.

'Quite. Emma just seemed bewildered. But what a terrible thing. If George's mind is seriously afflicted, what will become of him?'

'Nearly everyone,' said Edward, 'when they hear of a sudden death, exclaims over what a sad thing it is. But there are worse things than sudden death, are there not?'

George remained himself until the following November, when Bath resounded with the news that the famous, controversial Robert Clive, who was staying in the town for his health after serious attacks of abdominal pain and consequent morbid depression, had abruptly left a card-game, gone to the water closet and there slashed his own throat with a knife.

The news reached Chestnuts from two sources simultaneously, one a newspaper report and the other a letter from the Harpers. George, having studied both, observed obscurely, 'Hah! Now the elephants will be all mine!' and for days thereafter seemed to imagine himself a ruler in India and kept on asking for somebody called Sita.

Chapter Nineteen
The Folly

Having come to the bleak but wise conclusion that she ought to leave Bath as soon as possible and never return, Emma took her own advice. Since her husband and her father-in-law had never cared much for what they called 'these jaunts to Bath', she had only to remark that she was missing Chestnuts and found the soft West Country air of Bath too enervating, and they were on their way. Lucy-Anne raised no objection. 'I fear that Bath hasn't after all benefited my husband as I hoped,' she said to Julia. 'Well – you see now what manner of ailment is plaguing him. I think it would be best if we went home.'

I will forget, Emma told herself, as she settled back into life at Chestnuts – an uneasy life, for it was plain now how precariously George's sanity was balanced. I only saw William Herschel on four occasions, she told herself – at the wedding breakfast, when he conducted the concert, at the supper in his home, and when he came to say goodbye. I hardly know him. *I will forget.*

Perhaps she might have done, if Herschel himself had forgotten. But he had not. It would have been easier to put him out of her mind if she could have said to herself: 'I imagined it. Henry and Mr Whitmead made me unhappy that evening, watching me and disapproving of me. William Herschel was kind and amusing and, like a silly schoolgirl, I imagined that I had attracted him.'

But she hadn't imagined it. They left for home the day after that extraordinary evening, but the Herschels called to enquire after George's health – or so William said – and arrived in time to see them set off. William made a special point of saying farewell to her, bowing over her hand and looking into her eyes in a way that she could not mistake.

He did more. While bidding farewell to Lucy-Anne he arranged to correspond with her on the subject of astronomy, and he kept his word. His letters came regularly, describing his latest observations; his method of sweeping the sky in broad swathes ('as though I were harvesting the stars'); Caroline's patience in being kept up at night to take notes and make hot drinks; his latest essays in telescope-building.

Every letter asked for news of Lucy-Anne's family. Sandwiched between regrets about a week of unbroken cloud, and details of an experiment with the proportions of tin and copper used to make the metal mirrors required for reflector telescopes, was an enquiry after George's health. A letter enthusiastically describing how he had worked through until dawn on a brilliant, frosty night ended by asking if Mr Henry Whitmead were well.

In a similar, casual fashion he was delighted to learn that Mr Henry and Mrs Emma had been blessed with the safe arrival of their daughter Anne ... their second daughter Phoebe ... he hoped the little ones were thriving ...

And in every letter, without fail, slipped in as if absent-mindedly, he asked to be remembered to Emma. And when the Harpers came to stay, or when Lucy-Anne returned from the visits which she continued to make to them, although Emma now said she didn't want to go, they or she would bring William Herschel's respects.

To deny herself the pleasure of visiting Bath was painful, although it met with Henry's approval. But deny herself she must. To see Herschel again could lead nowhere except into temptation and a dreadful choice between anguish and risk.

Not quite seven years after her meeting with William Herschel she was so far from forgetting him that she saw him often in the dreams which were her only escape from a waking life which had grown steadily harder to bear. Henry might be pleased with her for wanting to stay at home, but he was difficult to please otherwise, and growing worse. And there were other things ...

'It's Bedlam in here today, isn't it, ma'am?' Nanny Howell said in her hearty fashion, through the howls of six-year-old Anne, who resented being told that she couldn't have any sweetmeats until she had eaten her dinner, and of two-year-old Phoebe, who was apparently just howling for fun. 'But Miss Anne mustn't think she can get whatever she wants just by screaming for it. You leave them to me; they're too much for you just now. You ought to take care of yourself. Don't want any more upsets like last year, now.'

With a hand to her aching head, Emma said: 'No. But I'd have more chance of avoiding upsets, as you put it, if the children weren't so noisy. It irritates their father and as for their grandfather – well, you know that he has delicate health. This last attack of ... of malarial fever ... has been very prolonged and I'm sure all this disturbance doesn't help. Oh, hush, Phoebe, there's a good girl.'

She picked her younger daughter up. Phoebe's yells subsided, but Anne, feeling left out, redoubled hers. Nanny Howell, clicking her tongue, took Phoebe out of Emma's arms, whereupon the earsplitting duet resumed.

'You leave 'em to me, Mrs Whitmead, ma'am. They'll soon tire and then the noise'll stop.'

'Nanny,' said Emma, feeling as though she were hammering in vain at a locked door three feet thick, 'I would like it to stop *now*. Please do something about it.'

She left the nursery, brushing her fingertips once more across her throbbing forehead and feeling her current pregnancy like a burden fastened to her abdomen. She would like to replace Nanny Howell, but the woman was at least clean and, more than that, she seemed prepared to stay despite the ... well, the peculiarities of the Chestnuts household. Her three predecessors had all packed up and left inside a few months.

Perhaps when this pregnancy was over she would feel equal to re-organising the nursery. She certainly couldn't face it now.

She was seven months gone, having carried this child for longer than either of the two failures in between Anne and Phoebe, and longer too than last summer's disaster (euphemistically described by Nanny Howell as an 'upset') when she had miscarried the son Henry so much wanted.

She dreaded her confinements. If only . . . if only she could produce a healthy son this time, perhaps Henry would let her have a rest. If she produced another daughter . . .

If this one were a daughter, Emma thought, she would probably do what she had felt very much like doing after the prolonged and excruciating births of Anne and Phoebe, and all three of the wretched miscarriages – which was to stop fighting, and just die.

The din in the nursery faded mercifully behind her as she made her way towards the stairs. But as she passed the landing window, which overlooked the garden, she saw that she had exchanged one problem for another. Walking disconsolately towards the house from the direction of the folly, carrying a laden tray, and every now and then glancing uneasily over his shoulder, was Thomas, the senior footman.

'Oh, no,' said Emma, aloud.

She went downstairs as quickly as her bulk would allow, and met him at the back entrance. 'Thomas? Is that Mr George Whitmead's tray?'

'Yes, madam.'

'And he wouldn't let you give it to him?'

'No, madam.'

'I'm sorry. This is very difficult for you, Thomas. It's really no wonder that Mr Barker gave in his notice.'

Timothy Barker had done rather more than merely resign from his post as George's manservant. He had declared roundly and loudly, to an enthralled circle of fellow-servants in the kitchen, that serving an old India hand was one thing; but serving an old India lunatic was quite another.

Henry had overheard him and Mr Barker did not work out his notice but was ordered off the premises the same day. Lucy-Anne had provided him with a reference, slipping it to him secretly at the last minute.

'It was the same as last time, madam,' Thomas was saying. 'He wouldn't even let me leave the tray. He said he'd throw it at me if I tried to go away without it; that it wasn't his meal at all; that Ahmed or Sita always served his dinner and where had they gone, why hadn't he seen them for so long?'

He turned slightly pink as he spoke. Any mention of Sita always embarrassed the Methodist and respectable Thomas. No one knew who Sita had been, but it wasn't very likely that she was the sort of woman respectable Methodist families invited to dinner.

'What do I do now, madam?' Thomas asked. 'It's the third day running he hasn't eaten his main meal. All he's had each day is a bite of breakfast and supper and only that because I suppose he's hungry. He sends the younger footmen away, just as he does me. He might let one of

213

the maids leave the tray. I could go with the girl, but—'

'But you can't stop him from saying things. No, I know. Anyway, Ames and Mrs Drayton won't allow the maids to wait on him and quite rightly,' Emma agreed.

That George Whitmead was in the habit of asking the maidservants to dance for him had been known, but not taken too seriously at Chestnuts, until the advent of a parlourmaid called Carrie. Unlike her colleagues, Carrie did not respond to Mr Whitmead senior's strange request by blushing and hurrying away, but agreed to them. And had been discovered, clad only in a diaphanous muslin affair which George had found for her among his Indian souvenirs, dancing sensuously while George, himself dressed in his Indian suit, sat cross-legged on the floor on a cushion and clapped a rhythm for her.

Carrie too had been dismissed without a reference – completely without one in her case. But the turnover in servants at Chestnuts was becoming much too rapid. It could well be Thomas next, or Ames or Mrs Drayton. In the last year or so they had all shown signs of stress.

'I'll take the tray to him,' Emma said. 'He recognises me, you know, however – er – feverish he is, especially if I go in alone. But as it's heavy, please carry the tray for me as far as the door of the folly.'

'If you're sure, madam.'

'Oh yes,' said Emma, cheerfully.

The cheerfulness was a pretence. It would have been easier to keep her spirits genuinely up if she could have exchanged a conspiratorial smile with Thomas over Carrie's antics, or over having to say *feverish* or *delirious* because Henry became so angry if he heard anyone state that his father was out of his mind.

But Thomas had no sense of humour; he could not help her see the ridiculous side of it all. He turned round, his face blankly respectful, and accompanied her back to the folly.

When the weather was warm enough, as now, in this pleasant April, George used the folly as his private Indian palace, repairing to it whenever he had a 'feverish turn'. When it wasn't warm enough he stayed in his room, which had a view of the folly, and stared at it out of the window.

During the attacks, Lucy-Anne and Henry both kept away from him, Lucy-Anne because he revolted her and Henry because he seemed to be afraid. But he encouraged Emma to visit his father at these times, because George generally seemed to recognise her. Occasionally he even came back to the real, English world while she was there.

'You help him,' Henry said, and because she was anxious to please Henry, she made a point of going to see her father-in-law when he was ill, and did not tell either her husband or Lucy-Anne what a strain she found it.

But the strain was great. She couldn't blame the servants for disliking it. The jabs of pain over her left eye increased as she neared the folly, and she suppressed a sigh as she reached the door, took the tray from Thomas and went in.

George had furnished the folly himself. On his orders, the floor was swept every day – the groom usually did it – and on the clean wooden floorboards stood a divan, made to his instructions. It was upholstered in blue silk with gold embroidery and strewn with big matching cushions. More cushions, in a rainbow of bright colours, littered the floor and there was a low wooden table in front of the divan.

The upper room was similarly clean, and contained a bed with an embroidered coverlet from India, a washstand with a set of Benares brass ewers and a basin, all inlaid with an intricate pattern in red and blue enamel, a cupboard for clothes and a chest in which George kept various other things he had brought back from India. The furnishings of the folly created a curiously exotic atmosphere, even in George's absence. In his presence, the atmosphere was not just exotic, but disquieting.

The first thing to greet Emma as she entered was the smell of tobacco. Her father-in-law was smoking a pipe. For a portly elderly man he was surprisingly supple and he had curled himself up on the divan, his feet drawn up beside him. He was wearing his Indian dress – his button-through coat of gold brocade, his gold turban and green silk pantaloons. His eyes were half-closed, but as Emma set the tray down on the low table they flickered open.

'Your dinner, Father-in-law,' said Emma in a brisk voice.

'Take off the dish-covers. Let me see.' George raised his chin. It was the haughty gesture and lofty tone of a prince, but to Emma he looked not so much princely as lonely and absurd. She lifted the dish-covers obediently.

'Here are potato rissoles, Father-in-law, and gammon steaks on toast, and fresh warm rolls. There is a dish of burnt cream to follow with a couple of fruit dumplings. And there is a pot of coffee and a decanter of wine and some port as well. All good English fare,' said Emma clearly.

'I would prefer some curried meat. Why do you not bring me curried meat?'

'You don't like the way Mrs Drayton cooks curry,' said Emma patiently.

'Mrs Drayton? Who is Mrs Drayton? Ahmed cooks my food, or sometimes Sita or her maidservant. Where is Sita? Why does she not come to me?'

'Please try the gammon steaks, Father-in-law. They are truly excellent. Do you know who I am?' Emma asked.

'Yes, yes, you are Emma, my son's wife.' He used a sing-song intonation which Emma supposed was the way Indian people spoke. 'You are soon to give us an heir. I never let Sita have a child,' he said in a reminiscent voice. 'You need not stand all the time. Sit there.'

He pointed to a cushion and Emma sank on to it, glad enough to do so. Her head felt as though a woodpecker were trying to drill a hole in it. George put his pipe aside and began to eat, hesitantly, nibbling at this and that, but at least taking some dinner. Yesterday, and the day before, he had refused the meal altogether. He had had previous fits of refusing food unless it were brought by herself or a maidservant, but he had never before kept it up like this. It was a worrying development. Was he getting worse?

'The food is good,' he pronounced suddenly. 'Did Sita prepare it?'

'No, Father-in-law. You're in England now. Sita is . . . is still in India.'

George put the dish he was holding back on the table, roughly, with a clatter. 'Sita should have come with me. Why did I not bring Sita with me? I want Sita.'

No one had ever asked him about Sita. 'I can guess, but I'd rather not know for sure,' Lucy-Anne had said. Emma hesitated, wondering whether, if he were really getting worse, such questioning would be helpful or harmful. On impulse, she risked it.

'Who was Sita? Will you tell me about her?'

'She was beautiful.' He wasn't looking at her as he spoke, but gazing blankly straight ahead of him. 'She was so very beautiful. She said she loved me. But she has gone away. No, that isn't right.' He frowned in a puzzled fashion. 'I *told* her to go. But she shouldn't have done it, she shouldn't have left me, she must have known I didn't mean it. Where is she? *Where is she?*'

In sudden anger, he leant forward and swept the tray and all its contents off the table. Emma came to her feet in alarm.

'Father-in-law! Mr Whitmead! Oh, please, please . . .'

He had shouted and thrown things at other people, and even struck Timothy Barker once, but he had never behaved violently in her presence. His malady must have worsened very substantially, without anyone being aware of it. Terrified, Emma realised that she was alone in the folly with a madman and that she had not the least idea what he might do next. He was between her and the door.

'I want *Sita*,' said George again, but this time pitifully. 'I miss her.'

He was crying. Tears rolled down his face and splashed on to the gold brocade. Emma found tears of pity in her own eyes. 'Father-in-law, please don't,' she pleaded.

But pity couldn't, and shouldn't, overcome self-preservation. She began to edge warily round the mess on the floor, trying to reach the door without going too near him. But he slid off the divan and came to stand in her way. She stopped, trembling.

'Who are you? You're not Sita. I only want Sita.' Turning scarlet, he bellowed it into her face. '*I want Sita. You're not Sita. Go away. Go away, I say! Go away or I'll kill you! Go, go!*'

She couldn't go away without walking around him. She made to do so, but he clutched at her dress and pulled her back, staring once more into her face. 'Sita?' he said. 'My head gets muddled at times. Are you Emma or Sita? I don't know. Sita?'

He was holding her with one hand and fumbling at his coat buttons with the other. Emma screamed. She wrenched herself free, tearing her dress, and fled, treading in burnt cream and squashed dumplings, grinding broken glass and crockery underfoot. She was afraid that he would follow her, but he only called 'Sita!' in a voice which made her own tears overflow, and as she stumbled through the door, she heard him break into a harsh and desolate sobbing.

'There's no harm done that I can see,' said Dr Graham. 'You have had a fright, my dear, but I see no sign that your unborn child is in danger. You should rest now and try not to think about it. I feel sure that—'

'And I feel sure that I want to go away from here! I want to go *away*!'

It could not be said that Emma broke down in tears, for she had not stopped crying since she blundered back into the house, dress torn and face blanched, in frantic search of Lucy-Anne. Unable to calm her, Lucy-Anne had told Anna and Letty to put her to bed, and meanwhile had herself despatched the groom for the physician.

But the tears could and did gain a new momentum. Even Dr Graham, brisk, reassuring, and as normal as apple tart, was no comfort. She had done her very best to be all the things expected of her, to be biddable and fertile and faithful, to relieve her mother-in-law of the task of keeping the household smooth, to accept as natural the unspoken blame because there was no male child, to make no inconvenient demands on Henry for love or friendship. Now her own needs had erupted and her tears were of rage as well as fear.

'If I have to stay here, I'll die in childbed and the baby will die too! I want to go away, right away. Even in London, I'll keep being reminded of . . . of him. I can't bear to be anywhere that reminds me of him. He's pitiful; I'm sorry for him, but he's horrible too, *horrible* and I want to *go away*!'

'Hush.' Lucy-Anne, seated beside the bed, leant forward reassuringly. 'You're safe now.'

'I don't feel safe!'

'Now that,' said Henry, standing beside the doctor, 'is nonsense. You cannot think that I would allow any harm to come to you. You need never go near my father again.'

'Yes, but I know he's there!'

'Mr Whitmead,' said the doctor, taking Henry's elbow, 'if I might have a private word? Mrs Whitmead, perhaps you would remain with the patient.'

In George's empty room, two doors along, Dr Graham fixed Henry with a steady gaze. 'Your wife is not miscarrying at the moment, Mr Whitmead. But she has had a very serious shock, and with her history . . . well, frankly, I find it regrettable that Mrs Whitmead, while in a delicate condition, should have been allowed to go alone to visit your father while he is in his present mental state.'

'Are you implying that my father is demented?' asked Henry coldly. 'You know as well as I do that he suffers from time to time from an extreme form of malaria. He was feverish, not mad.'

'Possibly.' It was no use alienating Henry, who was quite capable of ordering him to leave and then sending for some more obsequious physician. Graham could think of two straight off. One was permanently covered in snuff-stains and the other so fastidious that he would scarcely come within arm's length of his patients; both had qualified over thirty years ago and neither had adopted a new idea since. Both were highly gifted sycophants, too. They would say what Henry, the patient's husband and the virtual master of the house, wanted to hear, whether it was in Emma's best interests or not.

'The exact cause of your father's behaviour is not really the point at

217

the moment,' he said quietly. 'What is the point is that Mr George Whitmead's actions have upset your good lady to an intense degree. As I said, I can see no sign of mischief as yet, but unless she can be calmed and reassured that situation could change.'

'She seems unable to stop crying,' Henry said. 'I thought you could recommend a sedative draught.'

'I can, but for the child's sake it can only be a very mild one and in my opinion could be only a temporary solution anyway. The problem goes deeper. She says she wants to leave this house and I fancy she wishes to have the child somewhere else. I think she should be allowed to do so. The atmosphere here is bad for her.'

'What do you mean, atmosphere?' Henry demanded. 'She has every comfort here. She has gardens, numerous beautiful rooms, the company of my mother – they are attached to each other – and servants to obey her least wish. She has healthy country air and excellent food. What more can she need?'

Graham wondered how to explain that after what had happened Emma could sense George's decaying mind as though there were a decomposing corpse in the folly, diffusing its stench through all the Whitmead domains. He studied Henry and decided not to try. He adopted a man-to-man tone instead.

'Women are over-sensitive when they are with child,' he said. 'We men can scarcely understand it, but so it is. Their feelings may not seem reasonable to us, but we must respect them, because those feelings can actually endanger the health of mother and baby. You must remember, Mr Whitmead, that your unborn son may be in jeopardy as well as your wife.'

Henry grunted. 'Well, naturally, I would wish to do everything possible to protect them both. But how can my wife go away from here? Is it safe for her to travel? My father – whose wisdom I respect more than you do – has always felt that ladies are best and safest in their own homes, and I think he is right. My mother goes nowhere except to our London house and to some friends in Bath, and the latter purely to take the waters. I hardly think that in her present delicate state my wife should attempt to ride in a carriage.'

'I doubt if it would be more risky than compelling her to stay here,' said Graham. 'She clearly doesn't want to go to your town house either, but has she no relatives within a reasonable distance?'

'She has no living grandparents now,' said Henry, 'and her parents are in Harrogate. They take spa waters too, and Harrogate's a spa. They also go there, I understand, to drive about and admire a great deal of barren countryside, as is the modern fashion. The whole world has gone travel-mad, it seems to me, and why empty hillsides should suddenly be thought so beautiful that people will journey hundreds of miles, cluttering the roads with their carriages, to stare at them, passes my comprehension, but so it is. There is a future in coach-building,' he added thoughtfully. 'I am thinking of investing in it. But I cannot approve of my own family continually traipsing about, and now we see the evil of it. People are not there when they're wanted. My wife's parents are out of reach and her other relatives are little better. Her brother Frederick and her uncle Harry Miller and their families are all racketing about in town and all her other connections live at considerable distances. So what is to be done?'

'Mrs Whitmead herself may have a preference,' said Graham. 'Perhaps we should ask her?'

When they returned to her bedchamber, Emma was sitting up. Lucy-Anne was coaxing her to staunch her tears. 'You'll weep yourself away into a pool of water if you're not careful,' Lucy-Anne was saying. 'There'll be a little puddle on the floor and we'll all be standing round it saying oh dear, that's all that's left of Emma.'

Emma managed a shaky smile. 'That's better,' said Henry. 'Now, Emma. Dr Graham thinks it might be advisable for you to go away, perhaps until after your confinement. I must say I can't myself see the need, but . . .'

'You don't understand.' Emma's smile faded.

'I certainly don't understand why you should still be afraid of my father when I have promised that you need never even set eyes on him again. I daresay his fevered ramblings appeared alarming but—'

'He wasn't rambling,' Emma said tremulously. 'He's mad, I tell you. *Mad.*'

'Don't say that. I forbid you to say that.' Henry jerked back angrily. Lucy-Anne put a restraining hand on his arm.

'Please, Mr Whitmead!' said Dr Graham.

'It's all right.' Emma put out a hand to Henry and, hesitantly, he took it. She was sorry for her husband. She rarely looked closely into his eyes, for during the day his sense of dignity always kept him somewhat aloof and when they lay side by side at night there was only candlelight, or darkness. But now she could see them clearly, and in them she had recognised not only worry but a dreadful, shrinking fear. Lucy-Anne had told her that Henry was afraid to believe that his father was insane, and now she saw that it was true. He was more than afraid; he was terrified.

'I may not understand,' said Henry, 'but what I was going to say was that Dr Graham tells me that I cannot hope to make sense of all this, and advises me simply to let you have your way. Therefore, I am willing to make whatever arrangements you wish, provided the doctor agrees that they are safe. But where do you want to go?'

Poor Henry. Steadied now, Emma gazed at him sadly. If only he could have loved her as she needed, he could have bounded her entire horizon. She had tried very hard to fill her world with him, even so. But without his help she couldn't do it. So she had built a folly in her mind just as beautiful and useless as the folly George had built in his garden, and just as full of madness. Her answer rose up in her and came out without waiting for her permission.

'I'd like to go to Bath,' she said.

'But it's at least a hundred miles!' Henry protested to the doctor, having dragged him outside for another private consultation. 'Twenty hours in a carriage all told, when she is seven months gone! If that isn't dangerous, I don't know what is.'

'A good modern carriage on a good modern road won't be particularly hazardous,' said Graham. 'I might not encourage it normally, but her dislike of this house I think justifies it. Travel in slow stages. She could pause for a day or two between journeys. The mere fact that she is travelling away from here, and towards a place to which she wants to go, should help her. She is frightened, not ill. By the way, why is it that uproar breaks out in your nursery so often?'

'What?' Distractedly, Henry had not noticed the wails and shrieks that had started up somewhere just above them. 'Oh, the children. Anne and Phoebe have loud voices for their age. My wife seems unable to insist that their nurse should control them properly. She is not good at managing servants. Maids leave frequently and this is the fourth nursemaid my daughters have had.'

'Well, I am no advocate of being too harsh with children but that noise is intolerable and I hear it whenever I visit this house.' Once more, however, Dr Graham decided to tread carefully. It was no use telling Henry that his father was the reason why the servants were restless and the previous nurses hadn't stayed. 'Your wife is not very robust and household cares can weigh heavily,' he said. 'I suspect that Mrs Whitmead is exhausted as well as frightened. For God's sake, get her away to Bath. She can stay with the Harpers, can't she? I know of them from talking to your mother. A quiet clergyman's household and a hostess who has herself been the mother of a large brood – I can think of no better place for her confinement.'

Chapter Twenty

The Shattered Mould

On the way to Bath, none of the ruts in the road upset Emma in the least and she considered the two careful pauses they made at hostelries on the way, resting for a complete day each time, to be mere tiresome delays.

For with every rumble of the carriage wheels and every creak of the horses' harness, she was leaving Chestnuts further behind, along with her pathetic and frightening father-in-law. She was leaving Henry behind, too. Henry had said he was too busy with some new investments he had in mind to accompany her, and she wasn't sorry. Instead, she had Lucy-Anne, with the maids Anna and Letty, Flaxman the second footman, and two hired postilions to look after them. No screaming children, no disapproving Henry, no demented George.

Just a springtime world of light green leaves, of bluebells in the woods and Queen Anne's Lace along the roadsides, and blackbirds whistling – and somewhere ahead of her was William Herschel.

She did not feel guilty about her longing for him, for she had no immoral intentions. With a baby due in two months she was free of desire. But she did with all her heart want to see his face again, and to look once more into those friendly grey-blue eyes, which were kind, and understanding, and didn't criticise.

Her euphoria dimmed a little at the parsonage, however, because although the house and the pleasantly unkempt garden were just as she remembered them, the Harpers were not. They welcomed their visitors with pleasure, but Edward had a furrowed brow and Julia had lost weight. Her clothes had obviously been taken in, and her eyes were shadowed and much too luminous. When her guests asked how she was she assured them that she was in the best of health, in a voice which was too bright.

'I haven't seen her for nearly a year,' Lucy-Anne said, coming into Emma's room when they had been shown upstairs. 'I think she's ill.'

'Oh, I do hope not!' said Emma worriedly.

'She looks just as George's mother did before ... well, I hope I'm wrong, that's all,' said Lucy-Anne dejectedly.

But at supper Julia seemed better, and there was no need for Emma to bring up the subject that was foremost in her mind, for Julia, apparently full of vivacity, could hardly stop talking about William Herschel.

'He's discovered a new planet. He had a seven-foot telescope in his back garden and he'd been making systematic sweeps of the sky – you know his methods. Caroline swears he only sleeps when the skies are cloudy or the moon too bright. You knew nothing of his discovery, Lucy-Anne? When did you last hear from him?'

'A month ago,' said Lucy-Anne. 'And he did say something about an observation he had made on the thirteenth of March. He thought it was a comet and he was going to London to consult the Astronomer Royal.'

'He's in London now,' said Julia, to Emma's disappointment, but then put everything right again by adding: 'We expect him home soon, though. Caroline came to see us yesterday and told us. The Astronomer Royal, Nevil Maskelyne, has enquired into this apparent new comet, and it isn't a comet at all. It's been seen before and mistaken for a star, but Maskelyne looked at other records, calculated its orbit, and there's no doubt about it. It's a planet and it's probably going to be called Uranus.'

'And Herschel has had an audience with the king and, since apparently he talked about his interest in building bigger and better telescopes, he's to be given a grant to build the biggest reflector ever,' Edward said.

'It's a most exciting project. It is hoped that the new telescope will be able to probe deeper into the heavens than any telescope before,' Julia told them. 'What a wonderful century this is to live in. It is all new discoveries all the time.'

'If only,' said Edward, his voice suddenly grave, 'some of these discoveries could show us how to conquer poverty – and disease.'

Julia looked down at her plate. There was a momentary, awkward silence.

'When is Mr Herschel returning?' Emma asked, making it sound like a tactful change of subject.

'Oh, in three days' time, so Caroline says,' said Julia. 'We'll have them all to dine as soon as he comes.'

'All?' asked Lucy-Anne.

'Yes, his younger brother Alex is living with them now, and Caroline says that William is bringing a friend from London to stay – another astronomer, also called William. Will Watson, his name is. She'll have quite a houseful,' said Julia.

Julia tapped on Lucy-Anne's door at bedtime and Lucy-Anne, sending Letty away, offered her friend a chair.

'Are you quite comfortable? Your usual room has developed a damp patch on the wall. We expect the builder daily, but you know what builders are,' Julia said.

'Come and talk to me.' Lucy-Anne was sitting before her dressing table. She moved her candle to give her a better view of Julia's face. The vivacity which had animated it briefly earlier on had vanished. 'You seem . . . are you thinner?'

Once, Julia had been the one in authority, the magisterial one, and Lucy-Anne the supplicant. Now, subtly, their positions were reversed. Lucy-Anne was strong, and Julia in need.

'You can see it, then?' Julia asked, and Lucy-Anne nodded. 'I try to remember,' said Julia, 'that all is according to the will of God, but it can be hard. I have consulted physicians, of course, but no one seems able to help. I felt that I should . . . warn you.'

'What is it? What's wrong?' Lucy-Anne asked.

'I bleed all the time. Not much; but I'm over seventy, my love, far past the age when I should bleed at all. It's a bad sign.'

'Oh, Julia!' said Lucy-Anne, distressed.

'I'm sorry for Edward,' Julia said. 'He'll be desolate when . . . the time comes. Sometimes he asks me how I am. His eyes plead with me to say I'm better, that it's stopped, but it hasn't and it won't. I didn't come here to cry on your shoulder, though. Crying won't help. There's something else.'

'What is it?'

'You know how I dislike deception?' said Julia.

'Yes. Although you do it rather well when you have to.'

Julia smiled a little. 'Over Hugo? It's Hugo who's on my mind. All these years we have carefully kept to what we decided. Hugo knows his father's identity, but not his mother's. He's been told that we don't know it, that his father wouldn't tell us. I've hated lying to him – you don't know how much. Lucy-Anne, would you agree to leave a letter to be given to him after your death?'

There was a long silence.

'If you only knew,' said Lucy-Anne at last, 'how much I have wanted to acknowledge him.'

'I do know. Sometimes – to those aware of the truth – it's visible. Lucy-Anne, truth has a way of getting out in the end. It's an egg that's apt, eventually, to hatch. So, I ask you again, will you leave a letter for him?'

Lucy-Anne thought about it and then slowly shook her head. 'Truth may or may not hatch eventually but I see no need to help it do so. I'm sorry, Julia. But long ago I accepted that it was best for Hugo never to know. No letter, Julia, if you please. Let us keep the secret.'

Perhaps, Emma thought as she settled to sleep the night after the Herschels had come to the parsonage to dine, perhaps this is the best kind of love. It can never be consummated; it can never even be spoken. But for that very reason it can never be spoilt. We cannot come close enough either to hurt one another or to offend the world.

We sat opposite each other at table tonight and smiled at each other and exchanged conversation. He asked after my health and told me my looks were blooming; and then he talked of stars and planets and curious glowing nebulae in the sky, and how he first saw Uranus and could not identify this strange greenish dot which looked like a star but shone where no star should have been. I could have listened to him for ever and ever.

I want to stay in Bath and be near him always. I know I can't, but I want to. I'd be satisfied just to be in the same room with him sometimes and hear him talk . . . of stars and planets and curious glowing nebulae.

The Herschels had moved house – out of Bath for a short time and then back again to New King Street, number 19 this time, where they had the use of the whole house including the basement and the little garden where the seven-foot reflector telescope was set up.

At dead of night some ladies might have been alarmed to discover a man cowled in black, like the ghost of a medieval monk, peering through the telescope, but Caroline, being used to her brother's method of blinkering out irrelevant light, merely tapped his shoulder, handed him a bowl of steaming soup, and said prosaically: 'The nights are still cold. Also, you must conserve your strength if we are to start work on your giant telescope tomorrow. That is, if you really mean to construct it yourself. I am sure that with the royal grant you could find a foundry if you tried.'

'Alex and Will keep telling me that, although I sometimes think they are just a pair of idle fellows. I note that they are snug in bed now, on a fine viewing night like this,' said Herschel good-naturedly. He accepted the soup and took a long gulp. 'But I did look for a foundry, Caro, and all the foremen say that a three-foot-diameter copper and tin mirror is too big, that it will crack. Such a fuss they make over the proportion of the tin. It's not like bronze, they say, where the tin is only one part in ten. I want the tin to be between a quarter and a third and it's too brittle, they tell me. They won't handle it. Faint hearts! What good warming soup this is! My thanks. So I shall cast the mirror myself and prove that it can be done. Such a big telescope has never before been made. Upon my word, I'm not willing to let a foundry foreman have the credit, anyway. I know I shall succeed. Tonight, my Caro, I feel I could do anything.'

'Why tonight, in particular?'

'It is hard to say. Perhaps that our dinner with the Harpers was such a pleasure. I am delighted, by the way, that you have asked them back in return. There is nothing like the company of friends to inspire one.'

'Or the company of an attractive woman,' said Caroline, with a sigh. Her brother was surprised enough to push back his hood and peer at her in the starlight.

'Caroline? What do you mean?'

'You like Emma Whitmead, don't you?' said Caroline after a pause.

'Indeed, I do. A very charming young woman, and beautiful in her pregnancy, but I think not very happy.'

'And that has awakened your sympathy. You are a kind man, William. You came to rescue me when I was not happy, did you not? But I am your sister and you had a right to interfere. With Emma Whitmead, that is not so.'

'I know. My dearest Caro . . . please not to worry. I will not make love to her, not even whisper of it. But if she likes to sit and hear me talk away about stars and nebulae and shining green dots that turn into planets – if that can bring any peace to her, well, why not? Her mother-in-law says she has come to Bath to take the medicinal waters and rest – from what, one wonders? – until the child is born. Then she will go away. There is nothing to fear.'

'I sometimes think that you ought to marry, William. It would feel strange, having another woman here, but I think it would be right for you. You and Alex are as bad as each other! He is in his thirties and you are in your forties and neither of you is married, though neither of you is scarred with smallpox as I am. William, wouldn't you like children? A son to train in astronomy and music?'

'All in good time. Meanwhile, I promise you, I will do Emma Whitmead no harm.'

In the private world of unspoken love, Emma found, the gaps between the meetings with one's love were almost as joyful as the meetings themselves, because they were so full of shining anticipation.

A week of purest happiness elapsed between the dinner at the Harpers and the return dinner given by Caroline. With Lucy-Anne, Emma drove each day into the town, where they stabled the horse and hired sedan chairs in which they were carried to Milsom Street to shop and to the Pump Room to drink the waters and listen to the orchestra – although Herschel was not, these days, playing in it or conducting it – before returning home.

Julia sometimes came with them, although not always, for there were days when she said she felt too tired. But later in the day one or other of her married children often called, accompanied by their own families. Once Hugo came with his wife and their small son, Richard, now aged nearly six. Two subsequent babies had died, but Richard was strong and lively. Both Lucy-Anne and Emma enjoyed playing with him.

And for Emma all enjoyments were now enhanced, as a counterpoint might enhance a melody, by the thought of William Herschel.

In all her unexceptionable, ladylike doings William Herschel was invisibly with her. When Flaxman handed her into a sedan chair, it was Herschel's hand she felt under her arm; when in Milsom Street she admired the straw hats and taffeta bonnets which were the newest fashion, she wondered which William would think the most becoming.

She drank the oddly flavoured waters with gladness because they were part of the price she must pay for being in the same town as Herschel. When she listened to music she spoke to him in her mind, asking him which pieces he would prefer. Her heavy body sat quietly on a chair to listen, but her spirit danced with him in a ballroom roofed with stars.

And every day, on waking, she said to herself, in seven days' time . . . six days' . . . five . . . I shall see him again.

When it came, the dinner at New King Street started rather badly. It was served late, because the Herschel brothers and Will Watson were tardy in coming to the table, and when they did arrive they were all curiously dishevelled. They had evidently tried to make themselves presentable, but Alex Herschel's neckcloth was grimy, the scholarly and dignified Watson's wig was slightly askew and all three had highly questionable fingernails.

Moreover, when they entered the room, the faint, familiar but very earthy smell which pervaded the whole house, and upon which the guests had carefully not remarked, suddenly increased.

The guests could not comment, but Caroline, whose English was now fluent if sometimes idiosyncratic, exclaimed: 'Oh, really. It is too bad of the three of you. Is it not enough that Becky and I must cook in the basement alongside your project? Becky has threatened to give notice except that I have promised her it isn't for long. And now! Anyone would think you had brought a horse into the dining room.'

'It is so noticeable?' enquired William. 'But it is a clean, honest smell. There are worse things.'

'Over dinner,' said Caroline, but with typical Herschel good nature, 'I think not many things are much worse. Well, no doubt we shall get used to it. Only I think you should tell our guests why it is you smell of stables.'

'Oh, we can do better than that,' Alex assured them. 'Can we not, William? After dinner, we can show you.'

'A marvel is going to emerge from our basement,' Watson agreed. 'Provided the mirror doesn't crack.'

After dinner, therefore, they all descended the stairs. The big basement kitchen ought to have smelt agreeably of baking and roasting, but the maid, Becky, was washing up resignedly amid a powerful farmyard reek. William Herschel flung open the door to a rear scullery and the reek intensified. The party followed him through into a small flag-stoned room. On the left, a second door led into the garden, and to the right, fitted into the wall, was a furnace, at this moment cold and empty. At the far end of the room was a workbench littered with metalworking tools. And in the middle of the floor was a large pile of something pale brown and smelly.

'Are you starting up as a mushroom grower?' Edward Harper enquired, while the ladies, one and all, lifted their skirts fastidiously clear of the floor. 'Why in the world have you got a scullery full of horsedung?'

'And such a lot of it,' said Lucy-Anne, holding her nose. She and Emma and the Harpers, however, advanced for a closer look. The dung had been roughly shaped into a square, several feet across, and a circular depression had been made in it. Spades lay beside it, and a wooden disc, matching the size and shape of the depression, was propped against the wall.

'I am making a mould with it, to cast a telescope mirror in what is called speculum metal,' said William Herschel cheerfully. 'Dung is an excellent material for the purpose. We've been working it like clay to get it malleable and that is why we're all so grimy.

'But is all this needed for one mirror?' Julia asked.

'It is indeed,' Watson told her. 'The mirror will be three feet across and it will gather three times as much light as the eighteen-inch mirror in William's largest telescope so far.'

'But is it going to be cast *here*?' asked Lucy-Anne.

'No foundry would take it on,' Alex said. 'They all insisted it was too big.'

'And so,' said William, picking up a spade and patting the heap into tidier order, 'I – with assistance from Alex and Will – must see to it myself.'

Caroline rolled her eyes. 'I am *sure* that if you offered more money you would find someone willing to cast the mirror.' She turned to her guests. 'It is for the telescope the king himself wishes made. It will be thirty feet long, a monster among telescopes! William has dug up half the garden to make foundations for it. The mirror *needs* a foundry and there is ample money. The royal grant is four thousand pounds. But he *wants* to make it himself. I went with him to one foundry and even as he talked to the manager he was backing towards the door. The first words he said were, "I know you will not be able to undertake this task!" And so of course they did not. At times I am in despair. So often my home has reeked of dung, for William *always* uses it for moulds, but never before has there been so much of it. This is beyond everything!'

'Stop sounding as if I were a monster of parsimony,' said Herschel. They were arguing, yet their good humour remained completely unimpaired. If only, Emma thought, listening, and unaware that Lucy-Anne had once felt exactly the same thing about Mr and Mrs Bird, if only her parents, her husband, her father-in-law, had ever taken life in this warm and casual way! 'What does a little stable stink matter?' Herschel was saying, apparently much amused. 'Yes, it is true. I do wish to make this telescope myself, for the satisfaction of it, the triumph. I shall set it up in the garden and use it, knowing that I designed and built it, every bit.'

'But, is dung *really* the best material for the mould?' Emma ventured, puzzled.

'It is amazingly cheap and quite efficient,' Herschel said. 'It takes a shape and dries as hard as brick. Old farmhouses I have seen, their walls covered with a plaster made of cowdung that has lasted centuries. You must all come on the day we cast the mirror. You must see Alex and Will and myself pour the molten metal into the mould and later see us break it out. We will have a special dinner that day, eh, Caroline?'

Caroline rolled her eyes again but laughed. 'Yes, William, of course!'

Very occasionally Henry Whitmead admitted to himself that, much as he loved and respected his father, it was a moot point whether George was more of a problem when suffering from malarial delusions or when he was in his right mind.

When fevered he stayed in his room or in the folly pretending to be an Indian prince, but one only had to humour the pretence when actually in his presence. When he was well, however, he made demands and imposed his will on the entire household and you couldn't escape simply by walking away and closing the door after you.

'The reason why my mother and Emma have gone to Bath is because Emma needs a change of scene and—'

'It is quite ineligible for your wife to undertake such a journey in her present condition. You were most unwise to allow it, Henry, and if I had not been unwell at the time I must have said so plainly, and forbidden the undertaking.'

For once, Henry let himself be irritated with his father. 'I would ask you to remember, sir, that Emma is *my* wife.'

'And your mother is mine. I could have forbidden her to make the journey and then Emma would have had no one to escort her. How could she have gone then? Answer me that? Hah!'

Henry tried, not very successfully, to check his annoyance. His father couldn't help being ill; one could only feel sorry for him. But to mistake Emma for Sita – whoever Sita was, not that one couldn't guess! – and to grab at her as though . . . well, as though she were the kind of woman this Sita *undoubtedly* was or had been . . . well, it was shocking and not the kind of thing one expected in one's own family.

There was still an edge to his voice as he said: 'I should have had to leave my business concerns and escort Emma myself. I am very glad my mother was able to do so instead.'

'And even so I would have deplored it,' retorted his father. 'But as things are I am of the opinion that we should proceed at once to Bath and fetch the women back. You don't understand, my boy. This habit of visiting the place grew up when I was not here to watch over your mother and I tell you there is something pernicious about it.'

'What do you mean, sir?'

'Do you know, I'm not sure myself.' George's eyes, so lately full of visions, were now as shrewd as when he was in India, out-haggling men who had been born to it. 'I sense something amiss, that's all. Your mother always says she goes there to take the waters and see the Harpers and discuss astronomy with them – she's got some pet astronomer or other down there. But I tell you there's something else, something I don't know about. Something that's wrong.'

'I haven't the least idea what you're talking about.'

'Nor have I,' said George, with unusual brevity. 'But I tell you we must go to Bath and fetch them back, at once.'

They travelled post for the sake of speed, reaching the Harpers' parsonage on the afternoon of the second day. George was uneasy and impatient all the way and Henry, infected by his father's mood, applied the door knocker with a certain amount of energy. The door was opened by Julia herself, her face startled.

'Good gracious, Mr Whitmead!' Her gaze travelled past Henry to the chaise in the drive. 'Both Mr Whitmeads, in fact. We weren't expecting you, were we? Is something wrong?'

'No, not exactly.' Henry had noticed that Julia was not only startled but wan. From being a big woman she had become a thin one, and the hand holding the door open was like a claw. He had the grace to feel uncomfortable. 'We are sorry to disturb you unexpectedly, but my father decided at short notice that he wished my mother and Emma to come home. Are they in the house now?'

'No,' Julia said. 'I'm the only one here. The maid has an afternoon off and the cook's out marketing. Edward's over in the church and Lucy-Anne and Emma have gone to see the Herschels in Bath. I should have gone with them but I wasn't feeling well. Look, please come in. It's tiring for me to stand for long, as a matter of fact.'

George had climbed out of the chaise and was mounting the steps towards Henry. 'They're in Bath, at the Herschels,' said Henry over his shoulder.

'It's something to do with casting a giant mirror,' Julia said. 'Mr

Herschel invited us all to be present, but Edward was busy and, as I said, I didn't feel like going. But please, I'm sure you'd like some tea and—'

George swept his hat off. 'We are sorry to have discommoded you, Mrs Harper. I cannot recall the Herschels' direction, but if you will instruct us, we will go there immediately.'

'They've moved. They're back in New King Street now but at number 19. But surely, after your journey—'

'We're going straight there,' said George. 'Once again, Mrs Harper, our heartfelt apologies for disturbing you. Please forgive us. Come, my boy.'

'Mrs Harper looks ill,' Henry said as they drove away. Julia was still at the door, leaning on the doorpost in a tired fashion and gazing after them in puzzlement.

'She does indeed, and she should not be troubled with guests at such a time. I am most surprised at Edward for allowing it. Now we must find New King Street. Can you remember where it is?'

'No. We'll have to ask the way.'

The horses were tired and the afternoon warm, and the postilion, who on beholding the parsonage had entertained hopes of a rest in a comfortable kitchen and possibly a tankard of beer, was not best pleased at being ordered to drive on into Bath. Also, they were misdirected twice before they eventually clattered into the narrow road which was New King Street and pulled up in front of the tall, narrow house which was number 19. By then they were all in bad tempers. Henry and George descended from the chaise together and Henry's knock on the Herschels' door was almost an onslaught.

There was no reply.

'There's smoke coming from the chimney,' George said irritably. 'Try again.'

Henry hammered the knocker again and this time was rewarded by the sound of a door opening somewhere down below and someone shouting, 'Becky, see to the door!' Footsteps hurried upwards and the door was jerked sharply open by an annoyed maidservant, presumably Becky, who stared at them disapprovingly. A gust of warm air blew out around her and a curious smell, as though somewhere in the house someone was shoeing a horse.

'Mr George Whitmead and Mr Henry Whitmead,' said Henry briefly. 'I believe that this is the residence of Mr William Herschel, and that the two Mrs Whitmeads may be here.'

'Aye, that be right. They'm here.'

'Then will you kindly announce us to Mr Herschel and to the ladies?'

'Mr Herschel's busy.' Becky, a solidly built girl, stood firmly in their way. 'He said no callers today except them he and Miss Caroline have invited.'

'We are by no means paying a casual call,' George informed her. 'We are the husbands of the two Mrs Whitmeads. Are they also busy, or may we see our wives?'

'Oh. Oh, well, I s'pose you can come in, then. But what about that chaise? Can't leave that in this narrow street, it's blocking it.'

They dismissed the chaise and its grumpily relieved postilion to an inn, after which Becky consented to show them into the house, although not into the parlour or drawing room as they expected. Instead, to their surprise, she led them straight down a steep wooden staircase into the basement and through a kitchen towards what looked like a scullery door. It stood open, and beyond it they could see a cluster of people, a garden door, also open, and a flickering glow. The smithying smell was overwhelming.

'Mr George and Mr Henry Whitmead,' Becky announced, pausing in the doorway.

William Herschel, perspiring and grimy, his shirtsleeves rolled up and a leather apron round his waist, glanced round from stoking the furnace and said: 'Good day, but please excuse me if I can't attend to visitors just now. I shall be only a short time and you may watch if you wish. Caroline, Watson and I will require the tongs, and the wet cloths for our hands. We are almost ready.'

George and Henry, edging gingerly past Becky into the scullery, found Lucy-Anne, Emma and Caroline there along with William Herschel and two men whom they did not know. The three women all wore unfashionably simple clothes without hoops, although it was easy to guess that this was by request, because the room was congested and the work being carried out in it highly combustible. Heat wafted from the furnace, and the middle of the flag-stoned floor was occupied by what, astonishingly, looked like a quantity of dried manure confined in a square of planks. An iron funnel jutted upwards from one side of it.

Caroline Herschel, handing tongs and wet cloths to her brother, hurriedly greeted the newcomers and introduced them to the two other men, who turned out to be Herschel's younger brother Alex and a man called Watson.

'But what is going on?' George demanded. 'Upon my word, Lucy-Anne, I am most surprised to find you here. We are in a sort of workshop, it appears.'

'Mr Herschel is casting a mirror for a reflecting telescope,' said Lucy-Anne. 'It will be the biggest such mirror ever made.'

'What the devil is *that*?' said George, pointing to the manure.

'That's the mould,' said Watson. 'It will cast the molten alloy into the shape required for the mirror, and then Mr Herschel will finish it with emery grains to make the curvature precise.'

'It is all so exciting. It is a privilege to watch,' said Emma, smiling nervously. She had paled at the sight of George, and edged herself away from him.

'You should not be here, standing about,' said Henry in an angry undertone. 'Look at you; you are rubbing your back. I suppose it aches. We have come to fetch you and my mother home and—'

'Oh, please, we must just see this. It will be only a few minutes. Mr Herschel is going to achieve something that has never been done before and that no foundry was willing to attempt. Is that not wonderful, Henry?'

'Stand back, all of you except Watson,' said William Herschel. 'The moment has come.'

Emma had been watching Herschel with an intensity, an attention to detail, which she had never given to any person or subject in all her life before. This, it seemed, was something that love did to you. She wanted to study him, to imprint on her mind every movement of his body and every expression of his face, to remember every nuance of his voice. She could never take his body into hers, but instead she would absorb the memory of him, so that when she was parted from him, as she knew must happen soon, she could take with her a knowledge of him so thorough that it would keep her company in his stead.

She had never been less pleased to see her husband. It was not only that she did not want to be distracted from watching Herschel as he embarked on the final stages of this enterprise which meant so much to him, and therefore to her. She was discomforted, now, to see them together. They belonged to different sides of her life and of herself, and to see them in the same room was like seeing dream become mixed with reality. She wasn't sure which was which, either.

But she was even less happy to see George. He appeared, today, to be quite normal and they were surrounded by people, but the memory of those dreadful moments in the folly was still too vivid. She drew back from him still further, putting Caroline between them.

But the task in hand was now claiming everyone's attention. Watson had gone to Herschel's side, and both were putting cloths round their hands. Herschel opened the furnace and together, each gripping a pair of tongs, they lifted out the vessel of molten alloy.

'Quite still, everyone, and quite quiet, please,' said Caroline, with unexpected authority.

The crucible containing the metal had a lip. Carefully, the muscles standing out in knots on their forearms, Herschel and Watson moved it towards the funnel.

'Steady now. These flagstones aren't quite even.'

'My God, it's heavy.'

'We're there. Tilt,' said Herschel.

They tipped the crucible. The incandescent liquid flowed smoothly over the lip and into the funnel, sizzling as it entered the horsedung mould.

'Beautiful,' said Herschel with relief as the weight left their tensed arms, and they moved the empty crucible away to put it down on the brick hearth in front of the furnace. 'And not even difficult after all. Now, my good friends, the metal must be left to cool. Becky, we should all like some tea. Would you—'

'The mould!' said Caroline in alarm, and pointed, just as Emma screamed.

Something was happening to the horsedung mass. It was bulging and throbbing as though something inside it were alive and trying to escape. A glowing fissure appeared.

For a few seconds they all stood paralysed. Then Herschel shouted, '*Out!*' and with arms wide drove them all headlong through the doors. Lucy-Anne and Becky fled into the kitchen while the rest jostled their way into the garden, just in time, as the planks flew apart and the mould exploded and the molten alloy poured out in a surge of terrifying heat.

The air rippled and, in a deafening cannonade, the flagstones cracked and flew, ricocheting from the ceiling and descending like a red-hot, outsize hailstorm. A chunk of flagstone hurtled through the door to the kitchen and Lucy-Anne and Becky fled shrieking on into the basement hallway and up the stairs. Out in the garden, Emma sobbed with fright while Caroline beat out smouldering sparks on both their dresses, and Henry angrily accused Herschel of arrant carelessness and setting the lives of all of them at risk.

Herschel, scarcely listening, had sunk down, head in hands, on a pile of the bricks destined for the telescope's foundations. Accompanied by billows of smoke, the blazing tide rolled into the garden as if in pursuit of its victims. Fire ran up the doorposts, grass burst into flame. Inside the room the planks and the wooden worktable were burning.

Watson and Alex seized a rain barrel, fortunately full, and tipped half of it over the deadly stream. Through the ensuing clouds of steam they could be seen hurling the rest through the scullery door. Shouts from the adjoining gardens announced that help was on its way. Buckets of water were handed over the fences from both sides and Becky and Lucy-Anne appeared in the garden of number 17, having rushed out of the front door and alerted the neighbours.

'It is like a war.' George stared at Watson and Alex as they rushed to and fro with buckets and a long-legged neighbour clambered over the fence to join in. 'It reminds me of when the French besieged Fort St George.' He wiped his sweating forehead and looked up, frowning, into the blue sky.

'Oh, no!' Emma had heard. As Caroline helped her to sit down on the bricks beside Herschel, Emma's eyes turned fearfully to her father-in-law. 'Not India,' she whispered. 'Not now.'

'Are you hurt?' Henry broke off his diatribe to enquire. 'Have you come to any harm?'

'No, no, I think not. Caro was so quick, so deft. Is everyone else all right? Oh, Wi ... Mr Herschel, I'm so sorry. This must be such a disappointment.'

'I'm sorry too, for putting everyone in danger,' Herschel said dejectedly. 'It seems this task is beyond me to do with my own hands. I shall have to hire foundrymen, employ them myself and get the mirror cast that way. It has to be done somehow. I suppose I may call myself lucky that the house has not gone up in flames. Watson and Alex seem to be putting the fire out.'

'We've acquired a speculum-metal doormat for the garden door,' said Caroline, trying to make a joke of it.

'I can hardly understand anything that is happening.' George also sat down on the pile of bricks. His face was very red. 'Henry, why are you here?' he asked confusedly. 'I did not know you had come out to India. You never wrote to say that you were coming. And why is Sita here? Sita, why are you not at home?'

He put a hand on Emma's arm. Emma looked at it, as revolted as though a huge spider had alighted there, and with a cry of disgust jerked away and scrambled to her feet. As she did so, his vague gaze took in her outline. 'Sita? But I said we should not have any children. Sita, how could you—?'

'I'm not Sita!' Once more, as when she insisted that she could not remain at Chestnuts, the normally biddable Emma lost her temper. 'I'm not Sita and this isn't India! I'm Emma, your son's wife and this is England! It's Bath, *Bath*, and this is number nineteen New King Street!' William Herschel looked up in concern and she longed to throw herself into his arms but remembered in time that her husband was present. 'Henry, do something!'

'Emma, what on earth is the matter? Father is a little upset – hardly a matter for surprise. I expect his fever is coming on again—'

'It isn't fever; he's mad!'

'How dare you say that? Emma, I'm surprised at you. I suppose I must make allowances because of the frightening experience to which you have just been subjected—'

'Oh, stop using long phrases and talking like a sermon! Your father's mad. He thinks he's in India and he thinks I'm a ... he thinks I'm a strumpet called Sita and—'

'I am most certainly not mad.' It seemed that this time George's mind had flickered only briefly. He had returned to reality. 'Of course I do not think I am in India and of course I don't imagine you are Sita. What is the matter with you, girl?'

It was unbearable. Why had they had to come here, Henry and her father-in-law, intruding? Why couldn't she just have had this special afternoon with William Herschel, to share without distraction his hope and his failure, to give him the encouragement for his future work which was the only gift she could ever offer him, to concentrate on him in peace? Lucy-Anne was calling her name worriedly from the next-door garden, but couldn't climb the fence to reach her. Henry was shaking his head at her gravely. And her father-in-law was unable apparently to make up his mind whether he was mad or sane. Bursting into noisy tears, Emma cast herself into the only safe embrace in sight, which was that of Caroline.

'Emma, really!' Henry was scandalised. 'I am amazed at you. Such passions will be good neither for you nor for the child—'

'She's upset. Why can you not be kind to her?' demanded Caroline, over Emma's shaking shoulders. 'Oh, mein Gott, I think she is fainting – I cannot hold her – somebody, quickly!'

It was William who got there first, William who steadied Emma gently to the ground. She came round to find his arm under her shoulders and his face looking down into hers. But he withdrew even as she woke, resigning her to Henry, who knelt beside her in a mixture of anger and alarm. He scarcely seemed aware of Herschel.

But Lucy-Anne, watching from the other side of the fence, was very much aware of Herschel, and the tenderness and wonder with which he and Emma had for a moment looked at each other, and then, turning her eyes to George, she saw that her husband too had noticed it. There was no madness in his face now, but a frowning wrath. Oh God, Lucy-Anne thought, oh, God, no. Don't let it be true. Don't let Emma love

William Herschel as I once loved Stephen Clarke. Don't let history repeat itself.

Over the fence, she said in a clear and decisive voice, 'Henry, we must take Emma back to the parsonage at once.'

'The child is certainly premature, by about three weeks, I fancy,' said the physician. 'But she is a healthy baby and the birth itself was very easy. It is probably true that the mother's frightening experience brought her to bed early, but it is not responsible for the childbed fever from which she is suffering.'

Dr Marley was the Harpers' doctor and was distantly related to Edward, whom he somewhat resembled. Serious, knowledgeable and kind, he stood in the vicarage parlour and tried to convince his worried hearers that what he was saying was true.

George was not impressed. 'I still maintain,' he said obstinately, 'that if she had stayed quietly at home as she should, this would not have happened. None of it would. If she loses her life . . .' His face crimsoned. He turned to Lucy-Anne. 'This is what comes of all this junketing. I have never approved, but you would not heed me. In future you shall heed me. Whether Emma recovers or not, these journeys to Bath are at an end. Do you hear me?'

'George, please!' Lucy-Anne shot an embarrassed glance at Edward. 'The Harpers are our friends, our hosts. Please don't . . .'

George ignored this. 'You will sever all connection with Bath. I insist on it. I shall put that cottage – what's its name? Broom Cottage? – up for sale and then you'll have no excuse of any kind to come gallivanting to anywhere near this part of the country again. Henry, you'll see to it.'

'Yes, Father, in due course.' Henry was moving restlessly about the room, his eyes constantly turning to the open door through which he could see the stairs which led to his wife's sickroom. His eyes were pink-rimmed with sleeplessness and worry. Lucy-Anne was sorry for him. If he had not made Emma very happy, it was not intentional. Henry meant well. It was just that, like his father, he did not have much understanding of a woman's needs.

He turned sharply to the doctor. 'How seriously ill is Mrs Whitmead? Is she really in danger?'

'As yet,' said Marley gently, 'I cannot be sure. But she is young, although not, I think, particularly strong. She is also apparently rather upset because the child is a girl. She fears this will displease you. You can help, perhaps, by reassuring her.'

'Dr Marley!' Julia's voice called urgently from the top of the stairs. 'Dr Marley!'

'Excuse me,' said Marley and was out of the room instantly, and racing up the stairs. Those left in the parlour looked anxiously at each other.

'If there is a crisis, I should be present,' said Henry. 'Emma is my wife. I shall go upstairs to her.'

'It would be best to wait a moment. Marley will call you if necessary,' Edward said. 'There may not be a crisis. The doctor and Julia may be dealing with something quite commonplace.'

'I did want a son,' said Henry. 'But I didn't want to harm Emma. I'd rather never have a son than that.' He sat down in an armchair and put his face in his hands.

Dr Marley reappeared. His face was grave. 'Mrs Whitmead senior, Mr Henry Whitmead, I think you should come. The patient is asking for both of you.'

Emma was glad to see them but could not make their faces out very clearly. It was as though the discomfort of her burning, aching body had formed a wall of glass, flawed and distorted, between herself and them.

Lucy-Anne was holding her hand. 'You'll soon be well again. These things happen, but they pass. The baby is beautiful and she is going to thrive.'

'You must get well quickly. You have the best of care here.' To Emma's fever-sharpened ears, Henry's voice boomed like thunder. But, oddly enough, it was comforting to have him there. At this moment she did not want William Herschel. She would not like him to see her like this. With Henry, she did not mind. Poor dear Henry – he'd never have wished to injure her. He had always believed he was cherishing her. Which one of them did she really love?

She didn't know and couldn't think about it now. It was all too difficult, like everything else, like moving or speaking or even thinking about getting better. She felt so very ill and she was so tired.

She didn't want to leave Henry, or Lucy-Anne, and still less did she want to leave her new baby and those other two little daughters now so far away with their nurse at Chestnuts. But the choice was not hers.

Was she really dying? Was life itself, the bright sphere which enclosed everything, all feeling, all awareness, about to vanish into nothing like a pricked bubble? For a moment she was terrified. She tried to cry out but could only whimper and stare with distended eyes at the faces above her. Her mother-in-law's hand still held hers and she tried to tighten her grip on it.

But her fingers wouldn't obey her and after all perhaps it didn't matter. She was drifting into sleep and even the ability to feel afraid was growing numb . . .

'Is it settled?' Lucy-Anne turned as Julia came towards her. She had not been able to bear the dimness of the house, where all the curtains were closed. She had gone out into the garden and was sitting on a bench which the Harpers kept under one of their unpruned apple trees. Out of doors the summer world was still normal. No one could draw curtains round a garden.

Julia sat down beside her. 'It's settled. Henry has decided to have Emma buried here, and Edward will perform the service. George is being difficult. He says the Herschels are not on any account to attend. I don't understand that, for I'm sure they'll want to come.'

'George has always felt that . . . that Emma and I would do better not to make acquaintances of our own, and he has never really approved of our interest in astronomy,' Lucy-Anne said. She did not want to speak of the thing she had sensed between Herschel and Emma. George had certainly sensed it. Mad or not, he could be very acute. Perhaps he did indeed possess a little of the second sight which was supposed to run in the family.

'Naturally, if he doesn't wish it, we will see that William and Caroline don't attend,' Julia said. 'But it is a pity.'

'I feel I must apologise for George,' Lucy-Anne remarked. 'He has been somewhat discourteous. You were not there when he said that we were to sever all connection with Bath, but Edward was, and I suppose he has told you. I can only say that George's mind is, well, not . . .'

'It's all right. In fact,' said Julia, 'I wanted to talk to you about that. In this respect, I think George may be quite right. You should sever your link with us; it would be wise.'

'I don't understand.' Bewildered, Lucy-Anne looked into her friend's face. Julia looked sadly back at her.

'What do you see in my face, my love? You need not pretend. My mirror tells me the truth every day.'

'I was only thinking that black didn't suit you.'

'I'd look equally dreadful in anything. I'm gaunt and yellow, with all the signs of mortal disease and I don't want you to watch the final stages. When Emma is buried and you leave here, don't come back. Edward will write to you when it's all over.'

'How can you talk of it like that, so calmly?' Lucy-Anne cried out. 'How *can* you?'

'I don't really know. I suppose I hope for a life to come, in the hereafter, but mostly I think I've just grown used to the idea,' Julia said. 'Listen, my dear. Please listen, because it's important. It would be best for you, when you leave Bath, to stay away for good, not just because I don't want you to visit me and be harrowed, but because I think it may be better for you to keep right away from Hugo. It would be wise. Surely you see that?'

'But he's my son. Oh, I know that I need not worry about him. He had a happy childhood with you; he didn't end up on the parish, being sent out to help sweep chimneys and maybe to suffocate to death in one. And now he's a vicar, respected, with a growing family, and we've managed to keep the secret of his parentage hidden. I understand all that. But never to see him, not even to hear news of him . . . how *will* I get news of him?' Lucy-Anne cried, 'if you're . . . not here . . . it won't do for Edward to write to me. George would wonder why. Even astronomy can't be the excuse any more; George says I am to give that up, too.' Her voice was bitter.

'Do as he says,' said Julia. 'You may as well. You can't fight him and win, and if he's pleased you'll be happier.'

'I doubt it. His . . . his affliction . . .'

'Perhaps if he's humoured, it may preserve his mental health.'

'He also,' said Lucy-Anne, 'intends to sell Broom Cottage. Great-aunt Henrietta left it to me, but the law makes it his and he regards it as such. At my wedding, great-aunt Henrietta wished me power and freedom. She must have been as mad as George, in a different way.'

'She was single, was she not? You've told me about her and you never said she was ever married. It may be possible for a single woman to have a measure of power and freedom,' Julia said. 'In marriage, one looks instead for security. And it's your security I want to protect. What I'm trying to say is that it would be far better for you not to have news of Hugo. Let him go. When he's here you look at him too much, you know, and you ask after him too often. I sometimes worry in case you arouse suspicion even now. George can still be very shrewd.'

'I know,' said Lucy-Anne grimly.

'Think about it,' said Julia.

They were sitting together in silence, two sad ladies in black dresses, when Edward came out of the house in search of them.

'The funeral will be tomorrow, at three,' he said. 'But I have also come to raise a happier subject. I have two ceremonies to perform, not just one, and the second one is a baptism. I have arranged with Henry that his new daughter will be christened this afternoon. The only thing is, he doesn't seem able to think of a name. He suggests that you should decide, Lucy-Anne. Have you any ideas? He says he doesn't want to call her Emma.'

'She's going to be like Emma, I think,' said Lucy-Anne. 'She's very fair of skin, anyway, and the down on her head is so pale one can scarcely see it. One can't tell so soon what colour her eyes will be but I imagine they'll be blue, like her mother's. Emma had lovely eyes, like light blue sapphires. Sophia sounds a little like *sapphire*. Why not call her that?'

PART IV
The Grandmother
1781–1801

The vacant mind is ever on the watch for relief, and ready to plunge into error to escape from the languor of idleness . . .

The Mysteries of Udolpho, Mrs Ann Radcliffe, 1764–1823

Chapter Twenty-one

The Broken Casket

Great-aunt Henrietta had been gone for nearly forty years when George Whitmead died, but in a sense she killed him.

Lucy-Anne did not try to dissuade George from selling Broom Cottage. She knew she would not succeed and Broom, in any case, could serve no further purpose. It was not even a memento of Henrietta, for what was the use of a memento at which one couldn't look? To this day, she dared not go there as Mrs Whitmead, for fear that someone in Chugg's Fiddle might recognise her as Mrs Roberts.

All it had been, for a long time, was a vague reminder of Hugo and the Harpers and she knew that Julia was right in urging her now to sever her links with them. She let Broom go without protest.

Henry, as his father bade him, took charge of the sale. Lucy-Anne's only comment to him was a mild remark that there was some good furniture in Broom. 'Especially a bureau and some dining chairs which came originally from great-uncle Matthew. It might be worth keeping those. If not, make sure you sell them for what they're worth.'

Henry decided to keep them and, since his parents were by then back at Chestnuts with the baby Sophia, he had the bureau and chairs despatched to Surrey.

George, who since Emma's death had remained mentally more or less in England, except for a few small, brief lapses, went interestedly out to see the cart unloaded. He patted the heavy horses which drew it, berated the carter's men for handling the pieces too roughly, and supervised busily as they piled everything in the entrance hall.

The men were beginning to look harassed. Lucy-Anne came tactfully to their aid and sent them to the kitchen for some beer. Then she called two footmen and told them to put the chairs in the morning room for the time being. 'But I think, George, that they should bring the bureau and its drawers into the drawing room. I see the drawers have been taken out and packed separately. I shall assemble the bureau with my own hands.'

The sight of the once-familiar furniture had brought back memories, reminding her of so much which she could never again share with anyone. She had seen Julia for the last time and was painfully aware of it. George came fussily to help her and she wished he wouldn't, but she could hardly prevent him. Averting her head so that he shouldn't see her misty eyes, she agreed with his remark that it was a very fine bureau indeed, damme.

241

She was pushing a drawer into position, seeing it only dimly, and wondering why it wouldn't slide smoothly, when George reached into its cavity and said, 'Here's the obstruction. Upon my word, how long must this have been there?' and drew out a rolled-up piece of paper which had been caught at the back.

He opened it out and spread it on top of the bureau and they read it together.

It was new to George, but Lucy-Anne had seen it before, long ago, in the garden of Chestnuts, when she walked there with great-uncle Matthew, just after Henrietta's death. The words stared up at her, like an accusation.

'My dear Matthew, I am leaving this letter under a casket containing £500 in sovereigns. When I am gone, I wish the casket and the money to be given to our great-niece Lucy-Anne ... try to persuade her to keep it for herself and not reveal it to her husband. He'll claim it if she does ... your sister, Henrietta Whitmead.'

'What the ... ?' said George.

Just like that, Lucy-Anne thought. Just when you least expect it, the past rises up against you. Great-uncle Matthew must have gone home and put the letter back where, probably, he had found it. And then he had himself died and the letter had lain here all this time, a seed of trouble, waiting its chance to grow.

George was staring at her, pale brown eyes hard with affronted suspicion. Instinct said: lie, say you never received the money, accuse your great-uncle of stealing it, say Henrietta must have changed her mind, say anything but don't admit you ever had it.

But it was too late. Her guilt was written on her face and George, with that weird acuteness which seemed to have grown along with his illness, had seen it.

'You knew about this? You received the money? How? When?'

'Great-uncle Matthew – your grandfather – gave it to me here, when he came to tell us that Great-aunt Henrietta was dead.'

'*Five hundred sovereigns?*'

'Yes,' said Lucy-Anne in a low voice.

'And what did you do with it?'

'I kept it for a long time in my desk in the parlour. The casket's still there.'

'Bring it here!'

It was as though she were back in the early days of her marriage when she was afraid of George and his strange, sulky temper. She still feared him, but differently. Now, it was an outbreak of madness that she dreaded. She would do well to be very calm, to speak in an ordinary tone of voice, to try to keep the drama at bay and concentrate instead on the mundane.

Quietly, she went to the parlour to fetch the silver casket, and just as quietly returned, carrying it.

'This is it.'

'Open it! Ah. No sign of any sovereigns now, I see. Well, madam, what did you do with them, these five hundred sovereigns which you did not want me to know about? Come. You must have put them to some use.'

This time she *must* lie, and do it successfully. 'I just . . . spent it. Over a period of time.'

'On what, pray?'

'Dresses . . . lace, jewels . . . and books and telescopes,' Lucy-Anne added, inspired.

'Just frittered the money away, eh? Five hundred sovereigns, just frittered away!'

'Yes.'

'And you never saw fit to tell me! You never saw fit . . . why? May I know the answer, madam? Why was I not told?'

'Because Great-uncle Matthew – *your grandfather* – said I was not to, and that was what Great-aunt Henrietta wished.'

'I am appalled. It is disgraceful. No woman should keep such a secret from her husband. That my own relatives should tell you to deceive me and that you should agree with them . . . I can hardly believe it. It opens the door to all manner of abuses.' His eyes were bulging with fury. 'I suppose I may think myself fortunate that you spent the money in ways so harmless, though I would have spent it for you more wisely, or invested it. Upon my word, all these years I never thought you were deceitful. It seems I was mistaken, madam, sorely mistaken.'

'Please, George. I was very young and I only wished to humour two old people. It didn't seem so very important—'

'Didn't seem important? You hide a legacy from your husband – your guardian – and you think it not important?' George snatched up the casket and threw it down on the drawing-room floor. 'Fetch me that poker from the hearth!'

'But, George, that casket is probably quite valuable. And it's so beautifully chased—'

'*Fetch me that poker!*'

It was best to humour him. Lucy-Anne fetched the poker and watched while George, scarlet of face and grunting with effort, pounded the casket into a glittering lump of wreckage and then bellowed for a footman. When Thomas came, George barked, 'Take that away and throw it out with the rubbish!' and Thomas, his expression correctly blank, did as he was told. Lucy-Anne waited, hands folded, until it was done and Thomas had gone.

Then she looked at George. She had no idea what would happen next. Would he harangue her again and then, for the next week, or month, or year, behave as though she were a stranger to him? Or would he think of some other means of revenge? He couldn't forbid her to go on with her astronomy because he had already done so. Her telescope and her books had been sold a week ago.

And she hadn't cared. The fact was that she didn't seem to care very much about anything now. Emma was dead and Julia was dying – against that Broom Cottage, the casket, the astronomy had all lost their significance.

George stood there gazing at her. Nothing happened. Then he turned his back and walked out of the room. Presently Ames came to say that he had seen Mr Whitmead going towards the folly; was the master going to take his dinner out there?

'I don't know, but very likely,' Lucy-Anne said. 'Ask Thomas to go and find out.'

'And there's the new dining chairs, madam. They're taking up space in the morning room. Where ought they to go finally? And do you require any assistance with that bureau?'

'Oh, put the chairs in the dining room. There's an old set in there that can be distributed round the house. I'll see to the bureau,' said Lucy-Anne.

She might as well; the task had to be finished. She had all the drawers back in place, and had fetched a cloth and was rubbing away some fingermarks left by the carters, when Thomas came in, almost at a run, his face white.

'It's the master – Mrs Whitmead. He's in the folly, madam, and . . . and . ... oh, Mrs Whitmead, can you come?'

She went with Thomas to the folly. George was lying on the floor. His face was distorted, one side still mobile, the other frozen, with the corner of the mouth dragged down, and he seemed unable to use the arm or leg on that side. He tried to speak to them with the other half of his mouth but the words made little sense and seemed mostly to be concerned with India.

His death was very much as Henrietta's own must have been – perhaps a little more swift. He lived a few days longer, but was gone before Henry could be recalled from Somerset.

'I suppose one must think that it was merciful. I have heard of people lingering for years, with only half their bodies working,' Henry said when at last, in a post-chaise driven by lathered horses, he arrived at Chestnuts. 'If Father has been spared that, one can only be thankful. But if only I had been here in time to see him. This is hard to bear, my wife and now my father. Did anything cause it, Mother? Did he have a shock; did anything upset him?'

Lucy-Anne had destroyed Henrietta's letter. Letters could be dangerous things, she thought, and thanked God she had refused to leave one for Hugo. But the servants certainly knew that George had been, to put it mildly, upset about something. Thomas had seen the smashed casket and it was in any case a drawback at Chestnuts that the servants' domain and the main living rooms were all on the same level. George's frenzy must have been overheard, and possibly some of the quarrel that preceded it. Gossip might eventually reach Henry and she had better draw its teeth.

'Something did anger him,' she said. 'We found an old note in the bureau – it was a memorandum made by my Great-uncle Matthew. It concerned a little gift of money he gave me long ago. It was not important, but your father chose to feel slighted because he did not know of it. I fear it may have done him harm.'

'Poor Father. If he had a fault, it was that he was too punctilious and somewhat apt to inflate the importance of quite small things,' said Henry.

And that was a good epitaph for George, Lucy-Anne thought, as she looked for the last time on her husband's face. In a moment the coffin would be closed and carried out of the house to the hearse, on its way to Southdene churchyard. Her difficult married life was over. George had made it difficult, because all his days he had made too much fuss over things that didn't matter, rendering her miserable and probably himself too. Henry had summed him up well.

The depth of her grief surprised her. Love, it seemed, was not the point. George, whether in England or in India, in his right mind or out of it, had been part of the pattern of her life and now the pattern had fallen apart. If some of the tears she was shedding were for what might have been rather than for what had been, they were still genuine.

Beside her, Henry was nearly as overcome as she was, but he was trying to help her. 'Come away now, Mother. It's best. Dear me, I'm afraid the world will seem very empty to you now.'

'I ought to be used to that. He was away in India so much. But your father in India was one thing and your father not anywhere at all is something quite different.'

'Indeed,' said Henry gravely. 'But perhaps we see even here the workings of providence, sparing my father a lengthy decline. These last few years, he was not always himself.'

'When he imagined he was in India, you mean?' said Lucy-Anne cautiously. She well understood why Henry had been afraid to admit that his father was intermittently insane and wasn't sure why, even now, she wished he would admit it nevertheless. Was he about to?

But no. 'Yes. Those bouts of fever must have caused him great distress,' said Henry. 'Poor old fellow. I shall do all I can hereafter to live as he would have wished.'

Left to await the return of the funeral party, with Harry Miller's wife Catherine and their younger daughter, the twelve-year-old Horatia, to keep her company, Lucy-Anne did find comfort in the fact that George had at least been spared further deterioration. Afterwards, when she had grown used to his absence, she found that relief had overcome sorrow. Her own life was far more serene without him.

But as time rolled on, the days mounting up into weeks and months and then into years, she sometimes had the dreadful thought that, although George's death might have come as a blessing to George, it could have been better in another way if he had lived on. It would have been hideous, shocking, if he had gone finally mad and had to be kept confined, but at least Henry wouldn't then have been able to talk solemnly of his father's wisdom and use George's peculiarities as an excuse to give way to his own inborn faults. Specifically, to his possessiveness.

As her grand-daughters began to grow up, Lucy-Anne, with increasing anxiety, saw the pattern develop and understood that Henry, in his father's name, was going to be a menace to their happiness.

245

Chapter Twenty-two

The Eavesdropper

For Anne, Phoebe and Sophia it was a deep-seated cause of discontent that their father was strongly opposed to the custom of the London season.

'Your grandfather had strict ideas. He would not have approved of his grand-daughters being paraded about in public like horses for sale. He believed that a quiet home life was best for ladies. Your futures will be arranged, naturally; I hope I am a responsible parent. You may safely leave it all in my hands.'

His hands, however, showed every sign of remaining quite inert, and finally Anne, at the age of eighteen, appealed to her grandmother for help. After patient and repeated representations from Lucy-Anne, Henry did make some half-hearted attempts to do a little social entertaining (as distinct from all-male gatherings with business associates) and allowed Anne to attend a few balls and parties.

It was unlucky that her emergence into adult life coincided with financial problems in his. He had already let Chestnuts out to tenants so as to raise the money for a business venture suggested by Emma's brother Frederick, which involved buying into shipping, and he complained a good deal about the cost of Anne's new dresses, which had to be made with the fashionable high waists, and the modern jewellery she needed to go with them.

He tried, in fact, to get out of the expense on the grounds that there was no one to chaperone Anne. 'My wife had a number of Miller relatives on her mother's side but I have lost touch with them now and Emma's brother, unfortunately, is a widower. I really cannot imagine who—'

'I will chaperone Anne,' said Lucy-Anne firmly.

It meant a sacrifice on the part of both grandmother and grand-daughter. Lucy-Anne at sixty-eight was feeling her age, and the late nights in crowded rooms wearied her, while Anne knew, with embarrassment, that her chaperone was easily the ugliest woman in the room. True, Lucy-Anne had presence. She had learned how to intimidate people at need by staring at them through a lorgnette, and she had also learned how to speak clearly despite her lack of teeth. But she mumbled her food and tended to spit when she spoke, so that most people preferred to stand at arm's length. She had also developed a witchlike nutcracker profile. Anne hated introducing people to her.

But one had to have a chaperone and Lucy-Anne was much better than nothing. With her help Anne was for a while able to enjoy something faintly resembling a normal social life for a young girl, while Phoebe, celebrating her fourteenth birthday and Sophia, passing her twelfth, eagerly discussed the dresses they would have when their turns came, teased Anne about her beaux, and promised to be the bridesmaids at her wedding.

But it was not Anne's wedding they attended in the October of 1794.

Henry had gone to some of the balls with his mother and daughter. Such affairs usually included a card room and much business might be done over a card table, he said. Indeed, he had returned from one such outing very pleased with himself because he had closed a deal to buy a tenement building. 'I believe in diversifying my interests, and rents are profitable, very profitable. Shipping, coachbuilding, property – I shall die a rich man, yet, in spite of the cost of your dresses,' he told his daughters, quite jovially.

But in the course of it all he and Lucy-Anne had come across Elizabeth Ford, Emma's first cousin, who had once been Elizabeth Miller and who had been guest of honour at a ball in Chestnuts long ago. They had renewed their acquaintanceship with her. Her parents were now dead, and accordingly she had taken charge of her unmarried younger sister, Horatia.

Horatia was still single at nearly twenty-five, although she was handsome, because her family had never been wealthy and her portion was small – and, on top of that, she was choosy. Henry had admitted to Lucy-Anne that he might consider remarriage, but he had also said candidly that, although he hoped to become rich, he was at the moment still waiting for his ventures to bear fruit and was therefore still quite straitened for money. He would accordingly be looking for a wife with a dowry. 'If she reminds me a little of Emma, so much the better,' he added.

The last thing he or anyone who knew him expected him to do was fall in love with Horatia.

Yet it happened. Henry Whitmead met her in the January of 1794, a girl with glossy ebony-coloured hair and gracious curves and dark eyes. She was certainly beautiful, but she did not in the least resemble Emma. In spite of that he was at once besotted.

He did make an attempt, for a while, to resist, although neither his daughters nor his mother ever knew it. Horatia had too little dowry, he told himself. Regarded as a business venture, she just wasn't viable.

But he couldn't regard her as a business venture. He desired her frantically, in a way hitherto outside his experience even after forty-six years in the world, and amazingly Horatia the choosy seemed also to desire him.

That Horatia was becoming a little desperate, was regretting the suitors she had rejected in the past, and was now willing to settle for any reasonable prospect, did not occur to him. She appeared to want him; Elizabeth and her husband encouraged the match; Henry's own body fairly drove him into it. By June he had given in and proposed to her, and in mid-October she became the second Mrs Henry Whitmead.

He had managed to keep his courtship hidden from his daughters, even from Anne, but they were still aware of it before they were officially informed, because of their reprehensible habit of eavesdropping.

Henry's daughters missed Chestnuts very little because, shortly after Sophia was born, Henry had decided that he preferred Hanover Square and over the years he had used Chestnuts less and less. Long before the place was finally let the girls had become used to thinking of the town house as home. They especially appreciated the unusual feature on its second-floor landing. This was a lattice screen made of carved and gilded oak, fencing the landing off from the stairwell. Their grandmother didn't share their appreciation and frequently made slighting remarks about feeling as though she were in a cage, but the sisters had discovered that the lattice screen in the town house had one wonderful virtue.

Anyone standing, or better still, crouching, behind it was scarcely visible from below. It provided, therefore, a most satisfactory means of watching – and overhearing – what went on down on the first floor, where the main living rooms were, without being detected.

When anything of interest was happening among the adults, Anne, Phoebe and Sophia virtually did shifts at what they called their vantage point in order to inform themselves.

They knew before Henry's bankers did that their father, who had long had money invested in a coachbuilding works, had decided to buy them outright, and Sophia had listened, bewildered, when the unctuous superintendent of something called the Magdalen Hospital for Fallen Women called on Henry, appealing for a donation, and described the regime to which the inmates were subjected.

'Many, poor souls, are beyond reclaim by reason of being mental defectives or else morally abandoned. Alas, the two often go together. But some have been saved and made fit for decent lives in domestic service through our regimen of simple living, plain food, Bible readings and hard work. We have a laundry which takes work from outside, and some of the girls also learn practical sewing. Thus they can earn their keep and be respectably occupied. The devil finds work for idle hands, Mr Whitmead, and we see that our girls are not idle. But it all costs money to maintain. You have a reputation for philanthropy . . .'

'I do what I can,' Henry said. 'Most of my money is tied up in business but it is an object with me to contribute, nevertheless, to deserving charities. I would be willing to guarantee a regular donation of . . . let me see . . .'

Sophia never heard the amount, however, as she withdrew at this point to ask the others what a Fallen Woman was. No one knew. 'But it's obviously something dreadful,' said Sophia.

'And Father contributes for their welfare while he grudges us a season,' said Phoebe resentfully.

On the June day when Horatia and her sister and brother-in-law came formally to dine, it was obvious that the vantage point should be manned. Something was evidently afoot. Ames, the elderly butler, had been seen collecting all the silver from the sideboard and carrying it off to his pantry to be cleaned, and as soon as their father had left the house in accordance with his normal routine, to visit his coachworks, Mrs Trent, the cook, was heard from afar, throwing a fit of temperament because she didn't need telling to take care with the saddle of mutton, nor yet with the pistachio cream ('I've been doing them for years and never had a complaint yet!').

The best china was being fetched out, too, and Sophia, who liked flowers and had a patch of garden of her own, was ordered to provide flower arrangements for the table.

Anne, of course, dined with the adults, but afterwards was sent upstairs instead of joining Lucy-Anne, Elizabeth and Horatia in the drawing room, and was unable to report any reason why so much fuss should have been made about the dinner, although their father, she said, was behaving oddly, making a great many jokes and for some reason plying Horatia with immense quantities of food.

It was Phoebe, presently, who, after half an hour spent crouched behind the lattice and with her pale brown eyes very wide, announced that she had just overheard Grandmamma congratulate their father and Horatia Miller and wish them happiness, and heard Mr Ford declare that the wedding should be held in a month's time.

'But this is awful!' Anne was outraged. 'You hardly know her, but I've seen her quite often. Horatia's affected and haughty and ... and awful. We don't want her here.'

They were officially informed next day, not by their father but by Lucy-Anne, who sat them down in her private sitting room, looked into two pairs of unsmiling light brown eyes and one anxious pair of an exquisite blue, and did her best to reassure them.

'It's all very natural. Your father has been so lonely since your mother died. We must be glad for him. It will make little difference to you. I shall still be here, just as I have always been, and I hope you will soon grow fond of your stepmother. None of you know her yet – even Anne doesn't know her at all well.'

'I know her quite well enough,' said Anne angrily. 'She's ... she's *haughty*.'

'She pretends to be,' said Lucy-Anne unexpectedly. 'In fact, she's quite shy, and she's as nervous of you as you are of her. Don't make your minds up about her too quickly.'

'We'll try not to.' Sophia was kind-hearted and often impulsive. She was a lovely girl, Lucy-Anne thought, the image of Emma but more spirited, with a sparkle in her blue eyes which Emma had not had. Her grandmother could only hope that life, or Henry, wouldn't extinguish that sparkle.

Anne and Phoebe, cooler and less spontaneous in their natures, did not give the same response. 'We'll see,' said Anne, while Phoebe said nothing, but looked sulky.

Being well brought up, they were polite to Horatia and behaved very correctly at the wedding, but to begin with it seemed as if Anne's estimate of their new stepmother was right. Horatia certainly had a haughty appearance. She was tall and straight-backed with high cheekbones and plenty of colour, and she wore her shining hair in the Grecian style, drawn back to the nape of her neck and held by jewelled bands across the top of her head. She also walked with an air of consequence and she made it plain within a week of returning from the short wedding trip to Harrogate that she considered nearly everything in the house to be in need of improvement if not replacement.

Furniture was moved about or thrown out in favour of new; there must be new velvet curtains at every window; the servants must have smart new uniforms. In some cases, Horatia demanded smart new servants as well. Mrs Trent was dismissed in favour of a woman of Horatia's choosing; Ames, the butler, survived but only just; and Horatia's maid Millicent was so terrifyingly well turned out that Letty, Lucy-Anne's devoted and ageing attendant, remarked witheringly that it was hard to tell sometimes who was the lady and who was the maid. Bess, the hard-working girl who looked after all three of the Whitmead sisters, was simply intimidated by her and was actually seen, on occasion, to curtsy to Millicent.

Horatia also insisted on quantities of expensive dresses for herself. From the vantage point behind the lattice her stepdaughters before long heard their father having his first quarrel with his new wife, on the subject of dressmakers' bills. This they enjoyed, but their pleasure was considerably dampened when Anne was told that she must make do this year with last winter's ballgowns. 'You go only to private parties,' Henry said. 'It can scarcely signify.'

Anne protested and so, to the surprise of them all, did Horatia. Horatia had been making awkward attempts to win the friendship of her stepdaughters who were also, after all, her cousins. Sophia had been prepared from the beginning to respond and by this time Phoebe too had begun to see that Lucy-Anne, after all, might be right. Horatia evidently meant them no harm. She was in fact young for her age and many of her apparently haughty demands had been a mere performance, an attempt to appear sure of herself.

But harm she had done, nevertheless. Lucy-Anne added her protests as well, but in vain. There were no new gowns for Anne. Lucy-Anne, who had always gone in for fine clothes regardless of her own unbeautiful appearance, made Letty and Bess alter some of her gowns for Anne but the result wasn't quite right. The heavy brocades favoured by Lucy-Anne were out of fashion.

Despite the handicap of gowns that were peculiar or a season old, however, Anne did, that winter, acquire an admirer, but although he was an East India Company employee, he was only a clerk in their London Office, and very poorly paid. The following year he received a modest promotion and was emboldened thereby to approach Henry and ask for Anne's hand.

The resultant uproar shook the house. There was no need to listen from a crouched position on the landing, for Henry burst out of his study, pushing Anne's embarrassed admirer in front of him, and had his say at the top of his voice in the middle of the landing. He was audible with ease from attic to cellars.

'Marry Anne? Who do you think you are and whose daughter do you think she is? Anne will marry a man with position, who can keep her in the fashion she's used to and bring her father some advantages at the same time. She certainly won't marry a tuppenny-ha'penny clerk and live in a rented house and sponge off me whenever the rent gets behind. Or did you imagine I'd start you off in one of my tenements, rent free? Get out!'

Later, he said to a white-faced Anne: 'If that's the best you can do for yourself after two seasons of balls and parties, I think the balls and parties had better stop. I've never approved of them anyway. My father always believed that the best place for ladies was safely under the roof of husband or father, protected from the world and from their own inferior judgement, and he was right. We'll go back to what I said in the first place. I'll arrange your future myself.'

Lucy-Anne protested once more, not so much on behalf of the rejected lover ('He really wasn't suitable, Anne dear,') but in an attempt to salvage the balls. Her efforts were however in vain. 'I know you mean well, Mother,' Henry said, 'but you may safely leave the welfare of my daughters to me.'

'I hope so,' said Lucy-Anne grimly.

'Really, Mother. I am conscientious in my duties as a parent, I hope. I want the best for the girls. It will not do,' said Henry, preening himself a little, 'for my son to grow up and find himself saddled with unsuitable brothers-in-law.'

'You haven't got a son yet,' Lucy-Anne pointed out. 'He may be another daughter.'

But in the August of 1795 Horatia repaid her husband for all the new furnishings and expensive clothes by presenting him with his longed-for son. It was a lengthy and alarming business and when it was over and the girls were allowed in to see their new brother and congratulate Horatia, they found her so wan that even Anne, who had kept up the feud with the most determination, was inclined to be sorry for her.

The infant Francis, however, was strong. 'Just as well,' Horatia whispered. 'The doctors say I am never likely to have another.'

Henry, who had been genuinely anguished while Horatia was in danger, was philosophical about the news. One healthy son would do, he said. To Lucy-Anne, he remarked: 'For a woman there are dangers in marriage. I lost my dear Emma when Sophia was born and now Horatia has barely escaped with her life. I have decided that I do not wish to see my girls rush too eagerly to the altar.'

In the vicarage of St Aldred's church, not far from Bath, an uncle of whom the Whitmead girls had never heard put the finishing touches to next Sunday's sermon, laid it aside and pulled a list of addresses out of his desk drawer. He studied them for a moment and then ticked three, those of his local Member of Parliament and of two major shipowners. Then he pulled a fresh sheet of paper towards him, dipped his pen and began to write a letter.

He wrote it, with minor variations, three times, and was signing all three versions when there was a tap at the door and his wife's head came round it. 'Hugo? Are you busy?' She sounded unusually flustered. 'I'm so sorry to interrupt, but it's Jimmy.'

Even when busy he didn't often mind being interrupted by Mary.

She never did it needlessly and her pleasant voice and her smoothly combed and parted hair were always pleasing to him. The only drawback to Mary was that, without in the least intending to, she sometimes made him feel guilty. Her hair was fading now to a yellowish-grey and there were careworn lines on her face because he had never had much money and she had had to work so hard. She had borne him nine children but with great effort and only two of them, Richard and Jimmy, had been strong enough to survive. He could never shake off the belief that if only Mary's life had been easier the confinements would have been easier too, and the babies stronger.

He wished he could have done better for them all, and he might well have done better, except for his habit of espousing causes unpopular with the establishment, and therefore with those who held promotions in their hands.

He would never become a bishop or even an archdeacon; he would never be made vicar of a really prosperous parish. For himself, he didn't want to be, but he had once said to Mary, 'It would have been better for you and the children if I had had more ambition and less Christianity.'

'It most certainly would not,' Mary had said, in the most indignant voice he had ever heard her use. 'And you *have* got ambition. It's for others, not for yourself, and that's as it should be.'

His Mary was nearly a saint. But that didn't let him off his responsibility to look after her and their children and he hadn't done it nearly well enough.

He counted himself blessed that she didn't hold it against him and that at least they had the two boys. Richard, now twenty, was going into the Church like his father, and was likely to be an ornament to it. He had taken to heart his mother's Quaker precepts, such as the value of friendly persuasion and the unwisdom of parting in anger from anyone with whom one had disagreed. Yet he had the capacity for passion, especially on behalf of the poor and the mistreated. Richard might well be of use in the world.

His only flaw was something which seemed to be another aspect of friendly persuasiveness, a dark side of the moon as it were, and it had come as a worrying surprise to both Hugo and Mary because it had never before occurred to either of them that such a virtuous attribute could have a dark side. But there it was. Richard was subtle. He was capable of getting his own way, or coaxing people into doing things they didn't want to do, or getting a quiet revenge on those who had crossed him, by methods which were little short of Machiavellian.

His father had seen him, at a fair, making a collection on behalf of a newly set-up local hospital for the poor, and practically compelling people to give generously by something very close to blackmail. To one wealthy but tight-fisted individual Richard had said sadly: 'I am sorry for your obduracy, friend. One day, you may be ill and in need of medical care and a refuge yourself. Anyone can fall on hard times, you know. But I will never let anyone know you have refused a donation; certainly not anyone connected with the hospital.'

He had spoken softly and Hugo only heard it because he came up behind Richard just at that moment. Knowing his son, he also knew that Richard meant exactly what he said. He never would tell anyone of Mr Forrester's stingy behaviour. But he had made his promise sound like a threat and, from the expression on Forrester's face, the point had got home. Forrester had made a private and quite substantial donation the following week.

Hugo still didn't know whether he approved of Richard's tactics or not.

Ten-year-old Jimmy on the other hand had no subtlety at all. He wasn't much impressed by the theory of friendly persuasion, either, and he didn't wish to enter the Church. Lately, indeed, he had shown a distressing tendency to get into fights, and kept saying he wanted to go to sea, which in Hugo's opinion would be a thoroughly dangerous way of life.

And just now Mary, whose very nature was serenity, was in a rare state of flurry and it was on Jimmy's account. 'What's wrong with him?' Hugo asked.

'He's upset about something and he won't let me help. In fact he's out in the garden and won't come in until you say he can come to you. He's just back from school. Richard was with him – it was Richard who came in on his behalf and asked if they could see you. I tried to go out to Jimmy, and he ran off into the shrubbery. But I could see his new shirt was torn.'

'This can scarcely be just a matter of a torn shirt, even a new one. Don't distress yourself, Mary. Of course he can come to me. And Richard with him, please.'

While he waited for the boys to appear he finished signing his letters. He glanced up as the door opened, and put down his pen.

'Father? We are sorry to intrude,' Richard said. 'We know that you prefer to be private when you are writing your sermon. But this is an emergency.'

'I've finished my sermon. I've been doing some further letters of complaint about overloaded ships. Two more vessels were lost at sea last month, one out of Bristol and one out of Liverpool, and almost certainly not just because they met bad weather. They were too old to be seaworthy and they had too much cargo on board. I actually saw the Bristol vessel sail – she was wallowing so deep in the water I'm amazed she got as far as she did. She went down in a gale, just short of Lundy, and a young man of this parish was a seaman on her and went down with her. I've visited his parents; a most heartrending business. Well, well. Now then, what is this emergency?' He noticed that his younger son was hanging back behind Richard. 'Jimmy, come out from there. You said you wanted to see me, so don't hide away from me. That's right. Oh, *Jimmy*,' said Hugo, taking in the details of young James Harper's appearance, 'you've been fighting again. That's the third time this term. What am I to do with you?'

As Mary had said, Jimmy's new shirt was torn. One sleeve was half off and his collar was ripped. In addition he had an angry purple bruise on his left cheekbone, grazed knuckles and a good deal of mud plastered about his person. His eyes held a mixture of truculence and misery.

'I don't want to fight,' he said protestingly. 'I have to. Today there

254

were three of them and they wouldn't leave me alone. I had to fight to get away from them.'

'I was on my way to the village on foot when I met him coming back from school,' said Richard. 'So I turned back with him and brought him home. Look, Father, it isn't his fault. Those other boys were saying things.'

Hugo's glance flicked sideways, over the newly written letters. The prospectus of Jimmy's school, which had been open only two years, described it as an establishment for the sons of ecclesiastics, merchants, landed gentry of modest means and other such persons of the middle rank who desired for their offspring a sound and broad education including but not restricted to Latin and Greek. It contained the sons of several of the shipowners whom Hugo had lately been harassing. 'What things?' he asked.

'Things about the past,' said Richard. 'He wants to ask you something, Father. I know the answer and I've told him, but he wants to hear it from you.'

With a touch of primness which went oddly with his small tough face and square jaw, Jimmy said, 'It's not very nice.'

'Well, never mind about that. What is it?' Jimmy bit his lip and stared at the floor, unwilling to speak. 'Please, somebody say something!' requested Hugo.

'Those shipowners you've annoyed, Father,' Richard said, 'the trouble's coming from their boys. They've been getting at him over a rumour ... well, it isn't just a rumour; I mean, it's true; you told me yourself—'

'Told you what?'

'That your father was called Stephen Clarke and that he was the brother of Mrs Harper who brought you up, but that she never would tell you who your mother was,' said Richard. 'There's a clique of boys at Jimmy's school saying that his father is ... well—'

'Illegitimate?'

Jimmy looked up. 'Richard says it's true,' he said in a small voice. 'Is it? Really?'

'I believe so, yes. But I was taken into the family of Aunt Julia and her husband and was brought up as their son. I would have told you about it in due course, just as I told Richard when he was a little older than you.'

'I called them liars,' said Jimmy 'And I—'

'Pummelled them? Did you start the pummelling?'

'Well ...'

'It was natural,' said Richard, quietly. 'Why should he think it was anything else but a lie? He's been going for them for taunting him, on and off, all this term, apparently. I didn't know till today,' he added. 'Today I'm afraid he tried to take on three of them at once and it was too many! I found him running away from them down the lane, turning round every now and then to shy stones at them and shout that they were liars. I'd brought him halfway home before I could get out of him what it was all about.'

'Oh, dear,' said Hugo. 'If I'd known the story was going round, I'd have talked to you before, Jimmy. It's no reflection, you know, on either you or me. None of us can be held responsible for the actions of our forebears. I wish you had asked me or Richard about it when it first happened, instead of—'

'I couldn't.' Jimmy's face went crimson and he stamped his foot. 'I couldn't ask a thing like that. It isn't *proper*. Mother would say it wasn't proper.'

Belatedly, Hugo wondered if Mary's very well-meant efforts to imbue her young with her own notions of propriety didn't sometimes go too far. One couldn't expect a ten-year-old to respond with good-natured reasoning to a gang of louts who were insulting his family, nor could one expect him to ask his parents for information when he had been as good as told that certain things must never be mentioned under any circumstances.

'It isn't the sort of thing you could discuss with your mother,' he agreed, 'but you may ask me, or your elder brother, anything at all that you wish to know. *Anything*. Always remember that.'

'Does mother know?' Jimmy demanded, lowering his voice as though Mary might be listening at the keyhole.

'Yes. Between mother and son there are some proper reticences, but man and wife should have no secrets from each other. Now, come over here and let me have a close look at you.'

Jimmy came to him and his father examined the bruise and the grazes with care. 'You must go to your mother and get her to clean you up. When you've done that, come back to me. I intend meanwhile to think how best to put a stop to what you are suffering at school. I don't mean that it shall go on; of that you can be certain.'

As soon as Jimmy had left the room, he turned to Richard. 'Did you ever have to deal with anything like this? Was this rumour current in your boyhood?'

'No, Father.'

'I see. Well, boys must learn how to deal with life, but I think Jimmy is rather too young to deal with this. You matured without such a test, after all. I would like to remove him from that school. Before it opened, you know, your uncle Julian in Sussex offered to have him and let him attend school with his own boys. They go to an excellent establishment, and it wouldn't cost any more than this one. I think I might write to Julian. What do you think?'

'I agree, Father. I'll take Jimmy to Sussex if you like. I'd enjoy visiting my cousins.'

'If only he'd told us before.'

'I know. Father . . . ?'

'Yes, Richard?'

'Have you no idea at all who your mother might have been? Did your Aunt Julia or your Uncle Edward never drop a hint? Surely they knew? I mean, wouldn't they have tried to get it out of your father? I wish they were still alive so that I could ask them.'

'Oh, they knew. Aunt Julia admitted as much to me before she died,' Hugo said. 'She still would not tell me my mother's name, but I rather think I can guess who she was. I worked it out for myself. But there's no proof, and no question whatsoever of, well, trying to find out more. If

256

I'm right, my mother may still be alive, and I doubt if any of her family know about me. If I made any kind of approach, and they found out, I might damage her in their eyes.'

'Who was it? I won't make any approaches either, Father, but I'd like to know.'

'I won't name names,' said Hugo. 'But Aunt Julia had a close friend, a woman who lived in Surrey. My father Stephen Clarke once worked for her husband. For many years, that woman – no, that lady, because she was very much a lady – used to visit Aunt Julia and Uncle Edward regularly in Bath. As a small child, you saw her yourself. She was fond of all us Harper children but I had a sort of bond with her. She was alone a good deal during her marriage because her husband spent most of his time in India. I have a feeling – only a feeling, mark you – that she was the one.'

'But you won't tell me her name?'

'No,' said Hugo. 'But I will tell you this. Family resemblances are very odd things. I look like my father, Stephen Clarke. But you are the very image of the woman I believe was my mother.'

'If only,' mourned Phoebe, 'something would happen.'

'Well, it won't, so stop complaining.' Anne stabbed an angry needle into the embroidery which formed such a large and tedious part of their lives. It was a Whitmead tradition to have the family device, a little picture of a river with a bridge across it, on all household linen, and every new sheet or towel or napkin or even handkerchief had to be adorned. Lucy-Anne had always encouraged the custom, but since Henry had bought the coachbuilding business and adopted the device for the sign outside the works, along with the motto *From One Place to Another*, it had become almost a religious observance.

'You never know.' Sophia, who was curled up in an easy chair with Mrs Radcliffe's *Mysteries of Udolpho*, looked up from it with dancing eyes. 'Emily, in this book, never expected exciting things to happen to her, but then her father dies and she falls into the clutches of a wicked guardian who takes her to a remote castle, and I've just got to where she's found a picture with a veil over it, and she's lifted the veil and fainted with horror at what's beneath, only it doesn't say what it was she saw. One never knows. Now, if only we could all go on a visit to the Italian Alps—'

'Nothing exciting would happen whatsoever,' said Anne. 'Father wouldn't let it. We'd travel with so many armed guards that the most determined bandits would run away at the sight of them, and the only castles we'd visit would be so respectable that the only thing to turn us faint would be sheer boredom.'

'Well, at least,' said Sophia, 'we could look at the scenery! What do we ever see? We only go to the morning room when there are callers and to the drawing room in the evening. Father likes it that way. We spend nearly all our time up here in this sitting room. We scarcely leave the house except for decorous shopping expeditions. Sometimes I look at the mail-coaches going along Oxford Street, and I long – *long* – to be aboard them.'

257

'Yes, I feel like that, sometimes, too.' Phoebe, like Anne was trying unenthusiastically to do some embroidery. 'But it won't come true. If only some eligible man would catch sight of us in the street and take such a liking to one of us that he seeks an introduction!'

'We're not beautiful enough. At least, Phoebe and I aren't. Pale red hair and freckles aren't à la mode,' said Anne sharply, and carefully didn't look towards her youngest sister. Sophia had ash-blonde hair and a clear, pale skin, and her blue eyes had the depth and translucency of gems. Anne could not remember her mother very well and Phoebe could recall her hardly at all, but their father often said that Sophia took after her. She certainly had a beauty that the others did not share. Anne tried not to be envious of her, but often was. So was Phoebe, who was inclined to whine about it.

Phoebe was inclined to whine anyway. She was doing it now. 'I can't see why Horatia doesn't do something. She's got lots of relatives. She could find us husbands. At least she might get Father to let us go about. Anne's twenty-four now and even Sophie's eighteen; are we just going to sit stitching in this sitting room for the rest of our lives?'

'I think she has tried to do something for us,' said Sophia. 'I overheard something once. Father just told her playfully that he knew what was best for us and that all he wanted to do was cherish his family. She didn't argue with him. She's so taken up with Francis.'

'She's also lazy,' Anne said with scorn. She stabbed her embroidery as if hoping that it would bleed. 'She's not as proud as I used to think, but she *is* idle.'

'But she managed to get herself married,' said Phoebe. 'How is it done? How does one attract men? We don't even know what really happens when people get married. Having Francis nearly killed Horatia; it seems that when babies are born they come from inside the mother, somehow. But what is it that makes the baby begin to grow?'

The three of them gazed at each other, drawn together and fascinated by the great mystery. They had talked it over a thousand times but never found any answers. They always had a vague hope that one of them would suddenly find out the truth or at least be inspired to a reasonable-sounding guess, but it never happened.

'I'm sure the man does something to the woman,' Anne said. She resumed her stitching, more calmly, filling in the blue ripples of the river in the corner of a napkin. 'I did once hear Bess and Letty gossiping about a girl they knew. She'd been up to something with a young man, Bess said, and Letty said that it probably wasn't the girl's fault; that you couldn't stop a man once he gets going. But I didn't hear any more.'

'I'm quite certain that . . . you know, every month . . . comes into it,' said Phoebe. 'You mustn't get too near a man at those times or you have a baby. Something like that.'

'Our governess never said so,' said Anne. The memory of her first menstrual course was extremely unpleasant. She had had no idea what was wrong with her and only when she whispered fearfully to their governess that she thought she was mortally ill because she was bleeding and couldn't make it stop, had she learned the truth. She had at least been able to forewarn her sisters. But the governess hadn't mentioned men.

'I hope we don't go right through life and never find out,' Sophia said. 'I've thought of asking Horatia, but . . .'

The others nodded without requiring further explanation. *But*. But although Sophia and Phoebe at least were on fairly friendly terms with Horatia, a barrier still remained. Besides, whatever Horatia knew she had learned with their father, and this thought was intolerably embarrassing. As for asking Lucy-Anne, the idea had not even occurred to them. They loved her, but she was too far away from them in time, too much part of that adult world from which they were debarred.

Sophia laid down her book, putting her head on one side. 'Listen! I can hear voices downstairs. Is that Grandmamma? She sounds annoyed.'

'It's your turn. I went last time,' said Phoebe.

On noiseless, satin-slippered feet, Sophia left the room. Stooping a little, she made for the screen above the stairwell and crouched down behind it.

None of their elders had ever shown any sign of knowing about the intelligence service operating on the second floor. But from its landing it was possible to obtain a very good view of the landing below. The dining room and its adjacent saloon and card room were out of range but one could see the doors to the morning room and to Henry's study, with the marriage portrait of Lucy-Anne and George, which had been fetched from Chestnuts when the house was let, hanging between them (fond though the three girls were of their grandmother they found it hard to reconcile Lucy-Anne now with the girl in that portrait).

Part of the drawing-room door was visible, too. There was also a view down the stairs to the front door, allowing one to see visitors as they came in.

It was therefore possible to hear and see a good deal, partly because both Henry and his mother were apt to be casual about closing doors.

'Father really seems to think that we and the servants all have wooden ears,' Anne had once remarked. At present, Lucy-Anne's irritated voice was coming from the drawing room and from where Sophia crouched her grandmother's remarks were clearly audible.

'. . . yes, Henry, I know that you are putting every possible effort, and every last penny too, into your businesses, but frankly I think it's an excuse . . .'

Henry, who must be standing further away from the drawing-room door, said something, but it came out as a mumble. Whatever it was did not impress Lucy-Anne.

'. . . I know that the *Freeman* went down with a great deal of your money on board, but you were fully insured, and I gather that you've just raised the rents in your London tenements. Your income must be more than adequate . . .'

'You know nothing of business, Mother.' Henry had moved nearer to the door, probably in the hope of escaping from the room. 'I have further investments to consider and Horatia—'

'Is more than capable of spending everything you earn, but you have a duty towards your daughters. There are three young women upstairs depending on you to provide for their future. This absurd nonsense about not going out into society or laying out any money on them in any way—'

'They have adequate pin money and, as long as they don't go out unaccompanied, they are free to visit the shops and buy what they like, as well you know. I take us to concerts occasionally. I am very fond of my girls, and I have always taken the greatest care to see that they lead safe, happy lives, of the kind my father would have approved—'

'Meaning lives without any opportunities to meet possible husbands.'

'I have told you, Mother, I am not anxious for my chicks to leave the nest. I'm relieved on the whole that Anne met no one suitable while she was running round all those parties and balls. As I said to you after Francis was born, for women there are dangers in marriage. I wish to protect my girls.'

'So they are to spend their days as spinsters?'

'There can be worse fates,' said Henry. 'And now I must leave you, Mother. I will see you at dinner. I have work awaiting me in my study.'

The door of the drawing room opened and Henry, crimson-faced, hurried out of it. He made straight for his study and plunged into it like fox going to earth. Sophia began to straighten herself, rubbing a knee which had been pressed against the screen, but then paused again as the doorbell rang. She might as well see who the caller was. There was always the chance that it could be someone interesting.

Peering, she saw Ames answer the door, and heard a voice, a man's voice, apparently asking for Mr Whitmead. The accent sounded slightly common. Whoever it was, he was left in the hall while Ames came upstairs, went to the study and announced that a Mr Craddock had called.

'Craddock?' Henry's voice was clearly audible. 'Do I know him? The name's faintly familiar. Who is he?'

'He declined to say, sir. He said only that he had urgent business with you.'

'What manner of man is he?'

'Polite but not a gentleman, sir.'

'Oh, show him up. Just make sure you and a couple of footmen are within call, and leave my study door ajar. One never knows.'

One certainly didn't. Henry, in fact, had quite sound reasons on occasion for leaving doors open. The *Freeman* which Lucy-Anne had mentioned was a ship in which Henry was a major shareholder. The aggrieved brother of a man who had gone down with her had called at the house, accused Henry of knowing that she was overloaded, and attempted to punch him on the nose. The footmen had removed him. Phoebe, who had been at the vantage point, had fetched the others in time for them to hear most of it. They had been thrilled; and eavesdropping thereafter had been even easier.

Peering through the lattice, Sophia tried to estimate whether this caller was likely to produce any drama. As he followed Ames up the stairs, she could at first tell only that he had a young man's step, and had thick dark hair, vigorously curly in spite of being dragged back and tied. That it was his own unpowdered hair was not a guide to his social position. The hair powder which had once divided patrician from pleb with a line like a boundary fence had gone, except for footmen. Taxes had discouraged its use, and wigs would soon follow it. Father wore his own hair, and if it was no longer a light fox-red, but speckled nowadays with grey, it was because he was over fifty.

In fact, it wasn't as easy as it had been to tell someone's background on sight. Most men these days dressed as though they were for ever about to set out on long journeys, wearing boots and plain riding-coats even in the drawing room. Father obeyed the dictates of fashion but sometimes deplored them all the same. These days, he said, one could scarcely tell a courier from a courtier.

But one could recognise actual poverty. As the newcomer stepped up on to the landing she could see that his clothes, though not ragged, were poor. He had shoes, not boots, and his jacket was patched at the elbows. When he turned to follow Ames into the study another patch came into view, on the seat of his breeches. He had no hat and he was lean to the point of being thin, although he was well knit and the hands which Sophia glimpsed were strong and long-fingered. Ames announced, 'Mr Lemuel Craddock, sir,' and withdrew, and she heard her father say in a somewhat chilly voice, 'And what can I do for you, Mr Craddock? I don't believe I know you, do I?' He did not ask his visitor to be seated.

'You knew my family once on a time, sir. My grandparents were your tenants at Chestnuts until the sixties. But that's by the way.' His accent, though undoubtedly Cockney, was not unpleasant and his voice had a deep, masculine rumble to it. Sophia, entranced, nestled still closer to the screen.

'I'm a tenant of yours now, as a matter of fact,' Mr Craddock was saying, 'though it come as a surprise to me when I heard who'd bought the place I live in. It's a small world, as they say. I live in Wagoner Street, with me ma; me father died a few years back. We got a couple of rooms upstairs and the right to use the laundry room in the basement and the privy out the back. And the rent's just gone up.'

'Oh,' said Henry flatly. 'I see.'

'Do you, sir? That's what I'm wondering. Fact is, I tried to get some of the other tenants to come with me, to form a dep . . . depitation—'

'Deputation?'

'Yes, sir, that's the word. I had some schooling but I couldn't stop on; we needed me to be earning. Yes, when we was told about the rise, we had a meeting. But the rest was scared to come and see you. Only it seemed to me someone ought to, so in the end I come on my own.'

'To say what?' enquired Henry.

'Well, sir, ain't it easy enough to guess?'

'Not at all. Pray explain.'

'Well, since I'm here alone, it's me I'd better talk about, but believe me, things ain't much different, for one reason and another, with the rest of the people in Wagoner Street. Things wasn't so bad in my family before my dad died, but when he was gone and there was only me and ma, that's when we moved to Wagoner Street, 'cause it were cheaper. Even at that, four shillings a week was a lot. I get ten shillin' a week or thereabout as a stablehand and me ma used to pull in maybe another half-crown a week taking in washing, only she's not so well now and can't do so much – and there's others doing the same thing and doing it faster.

'But we could just about make ends meet, till now. Mr Whitmead, sir, we can't manage a rent that's gone up to five shillings and sixpence. If it had just gone up a bit less – maybe by ninepence or a shilling – then we could of got by, but five and six ... it's too much, sir, and that's how all the tenants feel. So I'm here to ask you kindly if you'll think about it and maybe not make the rise so big after all.'

'The reason for the rise, Mr Craddock, is quite simple. The landlord is responsible for repairs to the building and repairs cost money. If I am to keep the roof over your head decently watertight and ensure that the drains are in good order and able to carry away the water from the laundry room – which was intended, by the way, for the private use of the tenants and not as their business premises – then I am obliged to raise the rents. Everything these days is going up—'

'Not my wages, sir. And not my mother's earnings. Like I said, she's not as well as she was and with all this worry—'

'Oh, nonsense, Craddock. You're a strong young man. I feel sure you can take on some extra work to help your mother out, or maybe get yourself a better job and—'

'Do you think I haven't tried, sir? There's more people coming in from the country these days since the land's been enclosed and they're all after jobs.'

'Oh, no doubt, no doubt. I wouldn't be surprised if someone isn't after your post as stablehand at this very moment. What, may I ask, are you doing here at this hour? Why are you not at your work?'

'I asked a morning off, sir, saying I'd make the time up, stopping late to clean tack.'

'So you normally have time to spare in the evenings. You could make better use of that time than bartering it in order to come here and ask for charity. People who want extra work can usually find it. Laziness is a besetting sin among your class of people, I'm afraid. You all think your betters owe you a living. Come to think of it, I do remember your family at Chestnuts in the sixties. Your grandparents were troublemakers. Your grandmother came and pestered my mother, I recall. If washing is too heavy a task for your own mother, perhaps she could find light work in a factory. Factories are springing up everywhere, making use of this new steam power. We live in wonderful times, full of wonderful opportunities. You should seize them!'

'My mother's too unwell to seize any opportunities, as you call them, sir, and lazy is one thing neither she nor I, nor my father before me, have ever been.' Craddock's tone was still polite but anger vibrated just under the surface. 'We're not troublemakers. All we want to do is to live, just live.'

Sophia could hear, but not see. Frustrated, she abandoned her place of concealment for the head of the stairs and even ventured down a couple of steps to get a better view of the study door. She could still only see no more than part of Craddock's back. Her father was speaking again.

'Troublemakers I call you and troublemakers is what you are. I see no point in prolonging this interview. Kindly leave at once, and be grateful that as well as raising your rent I am not also having you evicted as unsuitable tenants. I will refrain from that on this occasion for the sake of your mother, who would otherwise be the victim of your misbehaviour. I will even turn a blind eye to the fact that she is making extra money by using laundry equipment provided by me. You should be grateful for my generosity. May I remind you that it is your business to protect your womenfolk? Working hard and pleasing your betters is as good a way to go about it as any. Good *day*, Mr Craddock.'

Her father must have pulled the bell because Sophia heard it jangle in the lower regions and Ames appeared on the stairs, a footman behind him. But before they reached the landing Craddock walked out of the study. It was the first time Sophia had seen his face clearly. It was handsome in a hollowed, asymmetrical fashion, but full of such an intimidating anger that she hurriedly retreated up the stairs.

Her dress rustled, and he looked up. The scowl gave way to a smile, but not at all a pleasant one. By the look of it he had guessed that she was eavesdropping. He bowed to her, sarcastically, sweeping an imaginary hat off his head, and then turned to descend the stairs, pushing past Ames and the footman on the way. Sophia, scarlet-faced, fled out of sight but paused once more behind the screen at the sound of her father's voice on the landing.

'It's all right, Ames. I wished you to show Mr Craddock out but he has evidently made his own way down. Really, these people. A most questionable type. If he calls again, he is not to be admitted.'

It was a fair walk from the Whitmead house in Hanover Square to Wagoner Street, which was near Charing Cross, but it wasn't far enough to cool Lemuel Craddock's fury. He was still full of it when he turned in at the front door of the tenement which was home. The smell of boiling laundry and the clank of the mangle caused him to turn his steps not upwards to the rooms he shared with his mother, but down into the steamy, echoing, brick-walled cavern below ground level.

He found the fire lit in the big hearth and a copper boiling over it, at which his mother was wearily poking with a long stick. A basket piled with wet white linen lay beside the mangle. Mrs Craddock wiped her sweating forehead and gave him a wan smile.

'You've taken on too much again, I see,' Lemuel said grimly.

'I'm doing it all in one go. Comes cheaper on coal that way, so I keep more money. It's the only lot I'll be able to manage this week, anyhow. I'm sorry, Lem, but even with you putting the coal ready for me, the job's that wearing.'

'I'll do the mangling for you anyhow, since I'm here.'

'I take it,' said Mrs Craddock, wistfully, as he set about winding the massive handle and feeding a sheet to the rollers, 'that you didn't have any luck.'

'Nope. The smug old sod just sat there behind his desk, that someone else shines up for him, and called me lazy for not earning enough to pay his bloody rent.'

'I knew it 'ud be no good,' Mrs Craddock sighed.

'I had to try. How're you feeling today?'

'Oh, not so bad. My cough's a bit better.'

She was lying and he knew it. He also knew that she shouldn't be sweating as much as that, even over a boiling copper. It was late September and chilly, and the draught through the door was cold enough. But it was no use saying so. 'Pity summer's nearly gone,' he said. 'Let's hope we have a mild winter.'

'I wish you hadn't gone there today. I wish you'd never found out where he lived.'

'It wasn't hard. It was on that letter that come round when he bought the place. I kept it. Great blessing, being able to read.'

'I daresay, but no good'll come of you going to the landlord in person and bothering him like that.'

'I'd like to do more than bother him,' said Lemuel, winding steadily. 'I'd like to see a revolution here like they had in France ten years back, and I'd like to see that head of his under the blade of a guillotine.'

'Who in the world,' said Horatia, over dinner, 'was that very aggressive-looking young man I saw coming down the front steps as I came back from my shopping this morning? I've never seen him before.'

'I trust you'll never see him again,' said Henry. 'That was one Lemuel Craddock, whose grandparents were once a disturbing influence at Chestnuts and were justly evicted from their cottage. He's now, by coincidence, living in one of my Wagoner Street houses and today, since he evidently takes after his forebears, he decided to come and be a disturbing influence here. He was objecting to a reasonable and necessary rent rise.'

'I remember the Craddocks,' said Lucy-Anne. 'I never thought they were troublemakers. I always felt that they had a case. I never approved of the way you and your father treated them, Henry. How much is the rent rise?'

'Really, mother, is it quite the thing to talk business over the dinner table? It's gone up from four shillings to five and six a week if you want to know.'

'By more than a *quarter*?'

'It was well overdue. My predecessor was too generous for too long but now, if I am to make sufficient profit after seeing to essential repairs – and I insist, as a good landlord, on having those repairs done – then the rents must provide for it. My predecessor should, of course, have instituted smaller rises more frequently. I shall follow that policy in future. This stuffed mackerel is excellent. We must have it more often.'

'Wagoner Street sounds very rustic,' said Sophia. 'But I suppose it can't be. It's not outside the town, is it, Father?'

'No, no, anything but. It's close to Charing Cross, on the Westminster side of it. A sadly run-down area, although I hope to

264

improve my properties and bring the district up somewhat in time. But this can hardly be of interest to you. Tell me, what have you done with yourselves today?'

'We have all worked on embroidering linen. Sophia spent some time reading a book and also weeded her garden,' said Anne. Sophia kept her eyes on her plate, to hide a mischievous gleam. *Sophia hid behind the lattice screen and listened while you talked to Mr Craddock* would not feature in Anne's account. 'And Phoebe practised the harpsichord,' said Anne, finishing her account of unexceptionable occupations.

'Admirable, admirable,' said Henry.

'Sometimes,' said Anne afterwards, when the three of them were alone again, 'sometimes I could kill Father.' There were tears in her eyes. 'He thinks we ought to be content to spend our days like this for ever. Oh, how can we bear it?'

Chapter Twenty-three

Wagoner Street

'You're quite mad, Sophie,' Anne said disparagingly. 'You know none of us would be allowed to go near Wagoner Street. And since we know that Father would refuse us if we asked, we can't pretend that it's all right to go without asking.'

'I'd just like to see what it's like,' Sophia said. 'Wagoner Street, I mean. I'm curious.'

'Look at that!' said Anne.

The three of them were standing in a cluster by their sitting-room window, gazing down at Hanover Square. A fresh autumn wind was blowing the first leaves about and outside a neighbouring house, which was occupied by a family called Faulkner, a high-perch phaeton had pulled up, a perilous affair drawn by two chestnut horses of evidently fiery temperament. The wind was lifting their manes and making them restless. The young man driving them was basking in the admiration of the two daughters of the house, their mother, their aunt and a couple of housemaids, who had all come out to exclaim.

The young man was, as the Whitmead sisters knew, engaged to the elder daughter. Her mother was now telling her, with laughter but decisive shakings of the head, that she was not to drive in such a dangerous vehicle, and reproving the young fiancé, who had presumably suggested taking his beloved for a spin. Anne pushed the window up a little and the voices floated up from the street below.

'When you're married you can do as you please and I shall have nothing to say about it, although I hope you won't expose Nell to such a risk. Those things overturn at the least rut. But it is beautifully made, I grant you that, and where in the world, Charlie, did you find those horses?'

'I wouldn't be surprised if that phaeton came from Father's works,' Anne said. 'I'd like to see those, just as you'd like to see Wagoner Street, Sophie. From what Father sometimes lets fall, I gather that as well as making stage-coaches he's expanded into light vehicles lately, and those sporting phaetons are all the rage so I'm sure he must be building them. But I don't suppose I ever will see the place and you won't see Wagoner Street.'

'I daresay not,' said Sophia with a sigh. Phoebe gave her a keen look. For all her gentleness, Sophia usually argued a point before she gave in and such ready yielding was odd, not to say suspicious. Anne, however, was still entirely riveted by the scene below.

'It must be wonderful to be married. Imagine being free to go out and about with a man, to drive out for rides in an exciting carriage.'

'Horatia doesn't go for rides in an exciting carriage,' Phoebe said. 'Only in our nice safe ordinary phaeton. Father hasn't even kept a travelling carriage since he gave Chestnuts up.'

'But she can come and go very much as she likes. She goes shopping or visiting and she drives in the Park whenever she chooses and doesn't have to ask permission. Father always wants to know exactly where we're going and half the time he finds excuses to keep us at home. He indulges her. Oh, one of these days . . . !'

'One of these days what?' asked Sophia.

'One of these days I'll run off with the butcher's boy.'

'But, Anne,' said Sophia solemnly, 'you know that Father would never let you do that if you asked him, so how can you justify doing it without asking him?'

'Oh, you . . . !' Anne, somewhere between rage and laughter, whirled away from the window, seized a cushion from a chair and threw it at her youngest sister. Sophia caught it and threw it back. Phoebe intercepted it, snatched up another cushion and, laughing, attacked both her sisters equally. It was a good scrimmage. In the course of it, a pile of fashion plates was swept from a table to the floor and the music rack beside the harpsichord was overturned, scattering the works of Haydn and Mozart in all directions, but a good deal of pent-up energy had been relieved before Bess, who had heard the noise, came to the sitting-room door and warned them that Horatia was coming.

Horatia wouldn't report them to their father, but they still didn't want her to catch them throwing cushions about. When their stepmother walked into the room the music rack was the right way up again and the floor had been cleared. The sisters, slightly flushed, were sitting quietly, earnestly studying the fashion-plates, the cushions behind them only slightly disarranged.

Horatia smiled at them. A real mother or even a conscientious stepmother would have reproved Phoebe for lolling instead of sitting upright, and complained at the way Sophia had curled her feet off the floor, but Horatia never attempted to exert authority over them.

'I am going shopping in Oxford Street,' she said. 'I am going on foot, as the weather is dry, if somewhat blowy. Do any of you want to accompany me?'

Usually, Sophia and Phoebe would have said yes, and Anne would have hesitated. But the restless wind had got into Anne as much as into any of them. 'Yes,' she said, putting down her fashion plate, 'yes, I should, if you please.'

'So would I,' said Phoebe, and waited for Sophia to add her voice to the chorus of acceptance.

But Sophia, who was studying a remarkable illustration of a lady in the extreme of high-waisted and diaphanous costume, with ostrich feathers in her hat, unexpectedly shook her head, uncurled herself from her chair and wandered over to the harpsichord. 'I don't feel like going out. I think I'll practise some music instead.'

The others took some time to get themselves out of the house. Warm cloaks, capable of keeping out the wind, had to be found and, after reaching the front door, Phoebe had to come all the way upstairs again for her reticule. Sophia played steadily until she was sure they had really gone. Then she put her music away and hurried to her room. Bess was there, mending a hem.

'We're going out, Bess. My cloak, please, and you'll want your own cloak, street shoes and reticule.'

'Where are we going, miss?'

'Ah,' said Sophia mysteriously, eyes dancing. 'I'll tell you that when we're on our way.' She opened a drawer and found the box where she kept her pin-money allowance. She rarely spent much and her savings were in a healthy state.

'But are we going on our own, miss? Aren't you asking if it's all right? And shouldn't we take a footman?'

'No, Bess. We're not asking anyone or taking anyone. We're going to have an adventure. The first thing to do,' said Sophia, transferring coins to her reticule, 'is to hire a hackney.'

They had on rare occasions returned from shopping expeditions by hackney, when it came on to rain or the number of packages became too much even for the usual footman to carry. But the footman always found it and negotiated the fare. Never in her life before had Sophia walked up to a hackney stand and hired a vehicle on her own behalf. She had never even seen Horatia do so.

The driver, however, only said, 'Where to, miss?' in a phlegmatic voice, and when Sophia said, 'Wagoner Street,' merely nodded. They climbed in and the solidly built horse between the shafts set off.

'But, miss,' said Bess, once she was certain that the driver couldn't hear, '*why* are we going to Wagoner Street?'

'Just to see it, Bess. My father owns some property there and the other day one of the tenants came to see him. I knew he had bought the property, of course,' Sophia said. 'But, until I caught a glimpse of someone who lived there, it was just a name, Wagoner Street. Now I know it's real and I want to know what it looks like. After all, it's part of the family estate. I think we ought to know more about it. When my grandmother was young, she used to visit the tenants of Chestnuts – that's the place near Guildford; you haven't been there.'

'That would have been in the country, miss.' Bess's small features were anxious. 'That's different.'

'We're only going to walk the length of the street and back.'

'Walk? We're not taking the hackney along it?'

'No, I thought if we walked we could see it better and stop and look if anything interested us. But we can ask the driver to wait. Oh, *Bess*, don't look so serious. We'll be home by midday. It isn't really an adventure at all,' said Sophia. 'But it seems like one to me because I've never yet had even the smallest one.'

She developed slight qualms, however, when she saw how the streets deteriorated after a while. This was a part of London she had never entered before. There was still plenty of traffic, including other

269

hackneys, and as yet they weren't attracting attention, but the streets had become very narrow and dirty, and the buildings to either side seemed cramped.

There were small shops and rickety gateways, narrow alleys leading furtively to heaven knew where, dwellings with small doors and grimy windows concealing heaven knew what. The people on foot were poorly dressed and not all of them were about legitimate business. There were beggars and loungers; urchins with *pickpocket* written all over them; women sitting on doorsteps, gossiping and nursing scrawny infants. A solitary woman, red-faced and so bloated that she filled up one whole doorstep, was nursing not an infant but a bottle. Another woman, her clothes superficially respectable, was walking quietly along, but alone, which no really respectable lady would do.

Sophia caught her eye as they drove by and was startled by the hardness of the woman's features and still more by her expression as she took in the youth and fairness of the young girl in the hackney carriage. It was as though she were assessing Sophia's value in some unimaginable market. The look was so unpleasant that Sophia shrank away from it, back into the shelter of the carriage, and when the driver at length pulled up and descended from his box to say that this was Wagoner Street, what number did she want, it was quite an effort to say: 'Will you wait here? We have a short errand to perform on foot but will only be a little while, and then would like you to drive us home.' Suddenly, she didn't want to be on foot in this district at all, even accompanied by Bess.

She made herself do it, however. There was such a thing as pride, although she nearly gave in again when the driver said doubtfully: 'You sure? Hadn't I better take you to whatever number it is, and wait outside for you?'

'No, thank you. No, I'm quite sure. Do you wish me to pay you the fare as far as we've come?'

'No, miss. You pay all at once, at the end of the journey. You don't look to me like a fare-dodger. I'll just wait here. But mind yourself and don't get into no trouble. Clearing a debt your father didn't know you'd run up, are you?'

'I don't know what you're talking about.'

'There's a moneylender down Wagoner Street,' said the driver. 'I only hope that all you spent it on was bonnets and trimmings.' He saw the real bewilderment in Sophia's face and laughed. 'No, I see that that's all it could be. If you're too long, I'll drive down the street to look for you.'

'Well, really. The cheek of the man!' Bess, now that they were here, was self-possessed. She had been born in a street not unlike this. She still didn't think a Miss Whitmead ought to be at large in such a place but it was too late to worry about that now. It was her business now to be on her mistress's side and hearten her. Sophia, hurrying them both into Wagoner Street, was obviously very nervous.

Sophia had undertaken the adventure because the windy day was exhilarating and made her feel a little wild, and because she was young and inquisitive and tired of restrictions and that glimpse of Mr

Craddock had been intriguing, disturbing, in a fashion quite new to her. She wanted to see for herself the place which had bred him. But even before she got out of the hackney the adventure had begun to lose its charm, and before she had gone ten yards she knew her uneasiness was a warning she ought to have heeded.

Wagoner Street was actually a little wider than some of the streets through which they had driven, and not all that dirty, but its atmosphere was disagreeable. Although she and Bess were dressed in plain cloaks and bonnets, their clothes were still far better than those worn by most people here; and also the instinct which allows a community to sense the presence of strangers, especially nervous strangers, was at work. Children playing hopscotch at the side of the road stopped and stared and a woman shaking a mat in front of her house looked them up and down in a way which said *and what do you think you're doing here?* as plainly as if she had shouted it. A little circle of men squatting in the gutter to play some gambling game with counters looked round and laughed as they passed, and one called something after them.

'Take no notice,' muttered Bess. 'They don't mean any harm, but you mustn't turn your head.'

The trouble was, thought Sophia miserably, that presently they would have to walk back and pass the men again. Well, they could cross the road first – that would help. She began to hurry, continuing along the street although she had by now completely lost interest in her original reason for coming and had ceased to feel the slightest curiosity about which of these dingy buildings with their deep front areas and narrow frontages was owned by her father, or was the home of the Craddocks.

Three men appeared from nowhere and got in the way, sidestepping when she and Bess tried to walk round them, and grinning broadly as their victims, perforce, halted.

'Excuse us, *please!*' said Bess, loudly and huffily. The men, still grinning, appeared to deliberate, and then let them pass. Sophia averted her eyes from them, but knew she had gone scarlet and knew, when she heard their laughter behind her, that her embarrassment had caused it.

The small boy who, a few moments later, stopped them to ask if they knew where something called Smiley's Pieshop was, was a pleasant change because, although grubby, he was respectful.

'I'm sorry,' Bess said to him. 'We don't know where the pieshop is. You'd best ask someone who lives here. There're some men playing a game of some sort back there, I expect they'd know—'

With their attention on the small boy and the question of the pieshop, they didn't hear the swift approaching patter of feet until too late. The second small boy came from behind, seized the reticule that dangled from Sophia's wrist in one hand, slashed it free with a knife held in the other and was gone in seconds, tearing away down the street and veering into a side alley. The polite small boy shot after him. It had happened so quickly that neither Bess nor Sophia did more than run a few steps in pursuit before they realised that it was useless. They stopped, Sophia clutching at her wrist, where the reticule cord had cut into it.

Sophia had tears in her eyes. 'Oh, Bess, *now* what shall we do? All my money's gone! Oh, I wish we'd never come. How will we pay the hackney? Have you got any money?'

'Not enough for a hackney fare home, miss, but when we get there you could go in and fetch some more.'

'There'll be questions asked if I'm seen, if Horatia's back, or my sisters, and then Father'll get to hear of it. But we must go home – the sooner the better. Let's hurry.'

They turned round and came face to face once more with the three men who had accosted them before.

The grins were wider now and the obstruction more deliberate. The trio wasn't even pretending, now, to be in the way by accident. 'Well, well. And where might you two be going? You don't look as if you know. Can we help?' enquired one of them.

'It isn't safe for young things like you to be just wandering about round here. If you're lost, you ought to ask the way,' said another.

'We'd thank you kindly to get out of our road,' said Bess. 'We're no business of yours.'

'Oh, now, that's not very friendly, when we're offering our help,' said the first man. He was the biggest, with bold brown eyes and a mop of greasy hair. The one who had said they ought to ask the way was thin, with a smile that went further up one side of his face than the other, and broken brown teeth. The third, who hadn't spoken at all, but merely stared and sniggered, was the youngest of the three, no more than a youth, with acne.

Sophia's heart was pounding with fright. The driver of the hackney had said he would come in search of them if they took too long, but they hadn't been long, not yet, and they were too far away for him to hear if they shouted for him. Nor was anyone else in this horrible street likely to come to their aid. It was no use, either, demanding respect for her status as a lady. She knew without being told that she had left her claim to that kind of respect behind her when she got out of the hackney carriage.

Afterwards she wondered how it was that she did, in fact, do the right thing. It was as though she possessed, without knowing it, instincts of self-preservation handed down from distant ancestors who had not lived her privileged life.

'We're trying to find a Mrs Craddock, who lives in this street,' she said. 'Can you direct us?'

It produced a marked change in the atmosphere. The spotty young fellow started to say, 'Never heard of her,' but the one with the greasy hair cut him short, speaking in a different tone, *to* Sophia this time rather than *at* her.

'That'll be Lemuel Craddock's ma. Yes, I know her.' He sounded slightly surprised that Sophia knew her too.

'Well, can you tell us where she lives?' said Sophia, following up her advantage. 'I know it's in this street but I don't know the house.'

'It ain't a house, it's a couple of rooms. That's the place, over there.'

Greasy hair pointed to a tenement on the other side of the road. 'She's on the second floor – number six.'

'Thank you. I'm much obliged. Come along, Bess,' said Sophia briskly, and without hesitation set off across the road. Neither of them looked back until they reached the door of the building, but when they did the three men were still standing there, staring after them.

'Nothing for it. We go in,' said Sophia.

The door, scarred and hanging on its hinges, was half-open and led into a bare entrance lobby. On the wall someone had scrawled a drawing which Sophia did not understand but vaguely felt was 'nasty', and the building was filled with a curious combination of smells: a steaminess like washday, mixed with dirt and boiling cabbage. To the left a stone staircase led steeply both up and down, and straight ahead was a passage with a door off it to the right and another at the far end. The doors had numbers painted on them.

'Second floor,' said Sophia. 'Up we go.'

'But we're not really going to call on Mrs Craddock, are we?' said Bess, aghast. 'We've no reason to and the hackney's still waiting at the top of the street.'

'We've every reason to,' said Sophia, leading the way briskly upwards. 'We've got to give those three time to go away and we'd do better to wait with a respectable woman than to hang about in this hallway. I'm the landlord's daughter, for goodness sake. If only Mrs Craddock's in, I'm sure she'll let us wait until we see from the window that the hackney's coming down the street.'

'That man said number six, didn't he, miss?' said Bess as they reached the first floor. 'Suppose it's at the back? Number four is, so maybe all the even numbers are.'

'Oh, don't be so depressing, Bess. There are landing windows looking out to the front. You can watch from her landing.'

Bess was right. Number six was to the rear of the building. They looked out of the landing window first but there was no sign of the hackney. The three men, however, were still loitering opposite. Sophia drew back quickly. 'There's no help for it. Knock, will you, Bess?'

They were both afraid there wouldn't be an answer, but after a moment they heard an outbreak of coughing behind the door and then it was opened by a thin woman who was wiping her mouth on the corner of a stained old apron. She tried to say something, but only coughed again.

'Mrs Craddock?' Sophia asked, when the spasm had subsided.

'That's me. Excuse me. I'm a trifle hoarse.'

'I'm Miss Whitmead, the daughter of Mr Henry Whitmead, your landlord. By ... by chance I found myself, with my maid, in this district and we were followed by some men. We wondered if we could take shelter with you for a while. A hackney will come for us soon. Bess will look out for him from the window there, but if you could ... could lend us countenance? Let me come inside and leave the door ajar just until Bess calls out that the hackney's here . . .'

Sophia's voice tailed away. In the dark little hall behind the woman a man's shape had appeared. He strode briskly forward and loomed over

Mrs Craddock's shoulder, resting a hand on each side of the doorframe.

'What in hell's name is all this?'

'It's Miss Whitmead, Lemuel.' As Mrs Craddock twisted her head to look up at him, Sophia saw how extreme her emaciation was. The ligaments in her neck stood out pitifully and the skin that covered them seemed as fragile and transparent as tissue paper. 'She and her maid – I don't understand it – they want to come in until their hackney arrives; some men in the street...'

'Our driver'll not be long now,' said Bess, and made for the landing window again.

Lemuel stared at Sophia and then glanced upwards. So did Sophia. On the landing above some interested faces were peering over the banisters.

'Mind your own business, up there,' Lemuel barked at them, and the heads disappeared. He jerked his head at Sophia. 'You'd best come in where no one else can gawp. We'll leave the door ajar like you said; I heard that bit. Now then.' He drew them all back into the little hall and then stopped, showing no inclination to invite the visitor into any kind of room. 'What's all this about? How did you get here, Miss Whitmead? And why? Don't tell me you lost your way, not if there's a hackney about to collect you.'

'We didn't lose our way.' There seemed to be no point in pretending. 'I came – with Bess, of course – because I wanted to see Wagoner Street for myself. My father owns this building but I'd never seen it and—'

'You just came to have a look?'

'Yes. Yes, that's right.'

'There's a word for that,' said Lemuel pugnaciously. 'It's called slumming.'

'Lemuel!' said his mother, in an attempt at reproof, although she sounded too tired to make it effective.

'Well, I didn't intend to come here to your home!' Sophia was annoyed. 'And I am extremely sorry to be a nuisance, which I realise I must be. But as soon as Bess calls, I'll be on my way. It was only that... those men...'

Lemuel strode out to the landing and went to the window. Taking no notice of Bess, he looked out and then came back.

'They're still there. They've spotted your girl looking out, I think. Silly fools. They don't mean no harm, Miss Whitmead. They might have been a bit unmannerly but they wouldn't hurt you. You could have asked them to escort you to wherever the hackney's waiting – I take it that it's waiting somewhere? They'd have made a bit of fun of you, but they'd have done it.'

'Now, Lemuel,' protested his mother. 'How would she know that? She's a lady.'

'Oh, quite. The landlord's daughter!'

His scorn was obvious and infuriating. 'Tell me,' said Sophia, trying to imitate Horatia at her loftiest, 'how is it that you're here at this time of day, Mr Craddock? Should you not be at your place of business?'

'Place of business? That's a fine-sounding name for it,' said Lemuel. 'I don't work sitting behind a desk and signing documents to put up

274

rents to make honest men's lives a misery. I fettle horses for stage-coaches and for the folk who keep their nags at the White Horse in Fetter Lane. I *am* at my place of business as it happens, or more or less. There's a harness-maker not far off who does good work cheap and I brought him a repair job from the inn. So I called in home for a bite while I was waiting to collect it.'

'Oh, I see,' said Sophia.

'Lemuel, hadn't we best go inside properly?' His mother became aware that they were still standing in the hallway. She pushed a door open and Sophia went through into a room which was living room and kitchen all in one, with a table and four wooden chairs, and a range set back in a wide hearth. Beside the hearth were two battered armchairs, their upholstery thin with use and so dirty that all trace of their colour was gone. Mrs Craddock vaguely indicated that Sophia was welcome to sit down, but Sophia pretended not to see.

The room contained little else except a pair of vases and a clock on the mantelpiece above the hearth and two pans on the range itself. Something was simmering in one of them, and the other was a small copper in which clothes seemed to be boiling. It was from this, Sophia realised, that the washday smell had come. Mrs Craddock saw her looking.

'I do a bit of washing for folk. Big lots down in the basement laundry and little ones up here. I've always got something on the go.'

'Too much,' said Lemuel, still angrily. Sophia turned to him and saw that his odd, asymmetrical face, in which the prominent cheekbones seemed to be set at slightly different angles, was full of anger – that it was probably his normal condition. His eyes were greyish-blue and they too were angry. They were also oddly forceful. When her gaze met his, she felt the impact as though a spark had been struck inside her.

'You mustn't take too much heed of him, Miss Whitmead.' Mrs Craddock was clearly disturbed by her son's aggression. 'He's had so much worry and he's a good son. Don't you go saying to your father that Lemuel's been rude to you or anything, I beg of you.'

'But I wouldn't do that,' said Sophia, taken aback. 'You've been very kind, letting me come in here. Of course I wouldn't say anything wrong about you.'

'Ah, yes. Does your father know of this escapade?' Lemuel enquired. 'And if not, are you going to tell him?'

'I . . . no, he doesn't know. I don't expect to tell him. I . . . would just like to get home safely.'

'Quite right, too. Young ladies should stay at home with their music and their stitching, or go out only with their mothers and two footmen. Come to places like Wagoner Street and get mixed up with the likes of us, and they might find out what the real world's like and that would never do, would it?' Lemuel said.

'Lemuel, please!' Mrs Craddock, who had been stirring the copper with a long stick, swung round in alarm. 'He means well, Miss Whitmead. I was thinking, perhaps you'd like a cup of tea?'

'Miss!' Bess was calling from the landing. 'The hackney's coming! I'll just run down and meet him! I'll make him wait outside!'

'I would have liked a cup of tea but I shall have no time.' Sophia was sorry for Mrs Craddock but Lemuel was making her very uncomfortable and the poor surroundings were embarrassing. She longed to get away. 'I must go. But Mrs Craddock and ... and Mr Craddock ... thank you for letting me come in. Bess and I were very frightened down there. I'd had my reticule snatched just a moment before and it was all very upsetting.'

'Had your purse snatched? I suppose,' said Lemuel exasperatedly, 'that you've money enough for your fare back?'

'Not with me but I have some at home. I shall have to ask the hackney to wait when we get there.'

'And that'll be all right, will it?' Lemuel's tone was still hectoring, but he was serious. 'No one at home'll think it odd, you spinning about in hackneys with just your maid? I thought you young ladies were looked after more carefully than that.'

'No, if anyone at home realises Bess and I were out in a hackney ... well, I'll have to make up some tale or other.'

'Godalmighty.' Lemuel rolled his eyes. 'Here.' He caught up a jar from the end of the mantelpiece and tipped something into his palm. He pushed some coins at Sophia. 'Take those, they'll see you right. And stop the hackney short of Hanover Square. Make everyone think you just took a walk round the square.'

'Lemuel!' protested his mother. 'That's the rent money!'

'It's all right, Mrs Craddock. I can't take it. It's very kind of you, Mr Craddock, but—'

'Kind? It ain't bloody kind at all. Don't you understand? No, of course you don't. Even my mother doesn't. Listen, I'm already in bad with your father for daring to go and argue with him about the rent. If he finds out you've been here, then somehow or other he'll make out that I'm to blame and that'll be it. We'll be for the push. We'll be evicted.'

'We'll be evicted if we get behind with the rent!' Mrs Craddock's cry dissolved at the end of the sentence into a fresh bout of coughing. This time, Sophia saw to her horror that what she had taken for cooking stains on the apron were blood from previous bouts.

'I can manage it for this week,' Lemuel said. 'I've had a tip or two lately. It's best, Mother. Miss Whitmead, you'll be doing us both a favour if you take that money. And now I'd better see you downstairs. The hackney'll be waiting, presumably, with your maid inside, and adding on to the fare with every passing minute as well as collecting a crowd.'

'I'll pay you back,' said Sophia, as he thrust the money into her hand and held the door open for her. 'Please don't worry, Mrs Craddock. I'll see that every penny is paid back before the end of next week. I promise. And thank you for looking after me.'

'And don't try to lift that copper off the fire till I get back,' Lemuel added over his shoulder. 'It's too heavy for you. I'll do it, and mangle the stuff before I go.'

He hurried Sophia downstairs. As he had foretold, the hackney was standing in the street with a small gathering of urchins and loungers

276

staring at it. A chorus of whistles broke out as Sophia emerged from the building.

'Take it as a compliment,' said Lemuel, handing her into the hackney with an unexpected degree of courtesy. For the first time, his face softened into a smile. 'You're a pretty thing, you know, and all right, it's not your fault you don't know how the other half lives. I don't care for your father, frankly, but I was wrong to take it out on you. Have a safe journey home. And don't worry about the money.'

'But I must.' Sophia let him close the door on her but lowered the window and leaned out. 'Mr Craddock, I know that horses must be fed and groomed every day, but do you have any time off on Sundays?'

'Varies. This Sunday, yes. Why?'

'We go to church on Sunday morning – St George's, Hanover Square. If you were there when we came out of church, somehow or other I'd manage to slip the money back to you. Father mustn't see you, but I can drop behind the others for a minute and you could brush past me. I'll pass it to you then. I insist on repaying it. Please.'

'All right.' He smiled again and the grey-blue eyes, which earlier had been so angry and mocking, suddenly lit up in a way which told her that he found her pleasant to look at. 'Perhaps I'll see you Sunday, then. And thanks. What's your name, by the way? Are you the only daughter?'

Sophia laughed. 'No, I'm the youngest of three. I'm Sophia. There's Phoebe and Anne before me.'

'Then get home safely, Miss Sophia. Goodbye.'

He watched the hackney depart and turned back to the tenement, remarking to the bystanders that the show was finished. 'Haven't you lot got anything else to do besides stand about gaping?'

He went upstairs and back into the Craddock living room, and found his mother, as he had feared she would, trying to lift the copper bodily off the range.

'I *told* you to leave that to me.' He pushed her aside and steadied it to the hearth. 'Why don't you at least lift the washing out first?'

'It drips everywhere and puts the fire out. Oh, leave it, Lemuel. Don't waste time doing the mangling; you'll be late back and get into trouble. There isn't much here and anyway I might have someone round this afternoon with some sheets to do. I'll have to go to the basement for that and I'll need to use the mangle anyway. I'll do these things at the same time.'

'You won't. I'll do them. It won't take ten minutes. I wish my job paid more,' said Lemuel. 'I'd like to get you free of this before it kills you.'

Mrs Craddock did not reply.

Chapter Twenty-four

Lemuel

Thankfully, Lemuel pushed the linseed-oil bottle, the metal-scouring powder and the saddle-cleaning rags and dusters into their cupboard and slammed the door. That was it. He'd been here to see off the first stage-coach of the day and someone else would receive the last one to arrive. He'd rubbed down the horses that were at permanent livery at the White Horse, and settled them with their bran mashes and their full mangers. The tack had been cleaned and the yard had been swept. Unless Dick Grant the ostler managed to find him something else to do, he could go home.

Going home meant trudging from Fetter Lane, up Fleet Street and along the whole of the Strand to reach Wagoner Street beyond. Them as rubbed down horses didn't, unfortunately, have the use of them. And when he did reach home, he'd have to do some mangling for his mother. He hoped he had made it clear to her that she must stop trying to do the mangling herself.

Tomorrow was Saturday, another busy day. But on Sunday there would be no coaches in and after seeing to the horses in the morning he would be free for a few hours. He allowed himself a private grin. He'd be doing something he very rarely did – going to church. Well, not *into* the church, exactly. But he'd be hanging about outside St George's, Hanover Square, and when the congregation came out, with a bit of luck, he'd manage to bump into the youngest Miss Whitmead and she'd give him back the money for the hackney. He hoped she wouldn't make a mess of handing it over; she'd been clever enough about thinking how to do it but if anyone, such as her father, spotted them, they'd both be in big trouble.

'What's that smirk on your face for?' enquired Dick Grant as Lemuel stepped out of the harness room. 'Walking out at last, are you? Hope she's pretty.'

'We're not quite at the walking-out stage yet, but who knows?' said Lemuel cryptically, and made his way into Fetter Lane, grinning more broadly than ever, because the notion of walking out with Sophia Whitmead was such a piquant jest.

Piquant because she certainly was pretty. That pale ash-blonde was an uncommon shade and she had a skin like alabaster and as for those bright eyes . . .

Sophia Whitmead wasn't for him, which was a pity, but a man could use his imagination, couldn't he?

He used it, as he walked along Fleet Street and the Strand through the windy autumn evening. It passed the time wonderfully.

Dick Grant watched him go and then went to the harness room to inspect Lemuel's work. He often checked up on Lemuel in this way, although the young man had never given any cause for complaint. Occasionally, Grant admitted to himself that the checking-up was an attempt to find one. There was nothing apparently wrong with Lemuel, and he was said to be a very good son to his mother, but Grant didn't like him.

The fact was that although Lemuel was competent enough with horses he had no real feeling for them. He never petted them or talked to them and on one occasion, when holding a horse while another groom checked its feet to see why it was lame, he had been seen to jag its mouth because it was restless. But it was only like that because it was in pain and a good horseman would have known that.

There was nothing to criticise in the harness room. Pity, thought Grant.

Lemuel was in an optimistic mood by the time he reached the far end of the Strand. The still-blustery wind was somehow enlivening, while the imaginary scenes he had been playing with Sophia were more enlivening still. He quite looked forward to seeing her on Sunday, and not only because of the money.

There were girls in his home district who would oblige for a consideration and he had a feeling that after Sunday he'd be in need of one of them. If he shut his eyes, he could pretend she was Sophia. He swung into Wagoner Street whistling and he was still whistling as he turned in at the door of the tenement, but just inside the door he stopped short. A little knot of people, some standing and some crouched, had gathered on the stairs to the basement. Their faces turned upwards to look at him, and someone said, 'It's Lemuel,' in a voice which instantly destroyed all desire to whistle.

Then he saw the splashes of blood on the steps down to the basement, and on the wall beside them, and that the little crowd was gathered round someone who was lying sprawled on the stairs.

Cursing and shoving people aside, he ran down and knelt beside his mother. A stone stair made an inhospitable pillow but her white face was turned into it as though it were the softest down. Her mouth and the front of her dress were horribly stained with blood and a dreadful trail of crimson blotches led up from the laundry room.

'Ma? *Ma!*' He grabbed her and shook her as if hoping to rouse her. She was heavy and slack in his grasp and her head jolted from side to side against the stone. Her eyes were open but they were blank. He laid her back on the stair and, rising, walked slowly down to look through the stone arch at the bottom of the steps. Silently, the little crowd of neighbours made way for him.

The trail led where he expected it to lead – to the massive mangle. A sheet was halfway through the rollers and two baskets, containing wet linen awaiting treatment, and linen which had been through the rollers, lay close by. All were splashed crimson from the haemorrhage which must have overtaken her in a fit of coughing as she worked.

'I told her not to use the mangle! I said I'd do it for her; why didn't she wait for me to come home?' He came back to his mother's side and stood there staring round the others. 'I kept on telling her,' he said wretchedly.

'I know, Lemuel.' Mrs Bradley from number five was his mother's age and nearly as skinny, but still had her health. At that moment, he almost hated her for it. 'I used to offer to help her sometimes,' Mrs Bradley said, 'but she didn't like it. I could never do much for her and I expect she was the same with you. We're all that sorry, Lemuel. Can we help you get her up to your rooms? It's a right shame you had to find her like this. It only happened a minute before you come in.'

His mother had been alive a few minutes ago. Now she was dead, gone for ever, and it wasn't Mrs Bradley's fault, of course not. Hatred was wasted on her.

There were others a lot more worth hating than his good neighbour Mrs Bradley.

It had been Lucy-Anne who suggested that the girls should have rooms of their own. 'I have always valued my privacy,' she told Henry when Anne was twelve and Sophia seven. 'Anne should now have a separate room and, later on, so should each of the others.'

'There won't be enough to go round,' Henry objected. 'Not with the governess as well.'

'All the rooms on the second floor are of a good size,' said Lucy-Anne. 'Have the two back bedchambers turned into three. There's space enough.'

The three rooms which resulted were not large but they were adequate. The governess's room, which was now used by the infant Francis and his nurse, was considerably bigger than any of them.

But although Sophia's tester bed, bedside table, chair, clothes cupboard, chest of drawers, washstand, dressing table and stool all jostled each other awkwardly for floor space, privacy she certainly did have, and she valued it.

She was especially glad of it now, for in this quiet pause between returning from church and going down to Sunday dinner, she was free to read the note that Lemuel Craddock had pushed into her hand.

He had done it very neatly. As they were all walking away from the church, she had palmed the coins she had been carrying in her second-best reticule, and hung back to scrape her shoe against a tree, as though there were something sticky on the sole. At once, as if from nowhere, Lemuel appeared.

At this point Sophia had nearly wrecked everything by failing to recognise him, because he was dressed in a dull black suit, quite unlike the brown jacket and breeches in which she had seen him before. Fortunately, however, he muttered, 'Sophia!' as he came level with her and just in time, as he walked by, she had let him take the coins from her hand.

And felt him press something into it in return. As Anne stopped and called to her to come along, she stowed it quickly in the reticule, turning a little so that Anne shouldn't see. What Lemuel had given her, intriguingly, was a square of folded paper.

She hurried demurely after the others. What a terrible suit Mr Craddock was wearing. It wasn't just funereal, but looked cheap, too. But very likely he thought it smart. It was probably his best suit and what he always wore on Sundays. People like Mr Craddock were very different from oneself.

A square of folded paper. A note? Why on earth should Lemuel Craddock have written her a note? It was risky for them both, passing it to her like that.

And extraordinary, and exciting. She could hardly wait to look at it.

Now, at last, in the solitude of her room, she took it out of her reticule and opened it out. It was a letter, neatly written, surprisingly well expressed, with correct spelling. Lemuel Craddock's boyhood schooling had been fairly competent.

Dear Miss Sophia,

I just wanted to put in writing that I'm sorry for being so rude when I met you. I was worrying about my mother who as you saw wasn't well. I'm also sorry to tell you that she died on Friday evening. Please think of me on Monday afternoon which is when she's being buried.

I'm truly sorry I was so short with you. You're very beautiful. Do you ever go shopping in Oxford Street late in the evening, at about nine o'clock? Do you know James Smyth's perfumery or Richard Robinson's confectionery shop near it? If you were thereabouts any evening during the next week or two (except Monday next), I might see you. I'd like to.

Yours respectfully, L.C.

'Oh, good heavens,' Sophia whispered. 'Oh, my goodness.'

They did shop in the evening, now and then. Horatia liked shopping at any time of day and was always free to invite her stepdaughters to go with her. They had no need to ask permission then.

In addition, Henry himself sometimes felt like parading in the midst of his womenfolk and these were often evening expeditions since he was engaged in business during the day. On these occasions he quite often took them to Oxford Street and even bought them presents.

Such trips could take place at any season. The nights were drawing in now but this made no difference. The shopkeepers of Oxford Street, with their eyes on deep Mayfair pockets, stayed open as long as the owners of the pockets stayed awake. They lit their shops and the pavements outside with oil lamps and made a handsome profit despite the cost of the oil.

All the same, evening expeditions were not as frequent as daytime ones, and when they did occur it was very often because the timing happened to be convenient for Henry. It would be easy enough to encourage a shopping trip into being, but for Sophia to specify that it should take place after dark would be difficult.

282

She lay awake for nearly all of one night, thinking it out, and wondering, indeed, whether she ought to attempt it at all. She had that day overheard another snatch of conversation – or rather, argument – between her father and Grandmamma.

'Henry, unless you help those girls to form suitable alliances, they'll go and form unsuitable ones. I warn you!'

'Nonsense, Mother. I take far too much care of them for that and I would prefer you not to put ideas about alliances, suitable or unsuitable, into their heads at all.'

Could she, Sophia asked herself, be accused of trying to form an 'unsuitable alliance' with Lemuel Craddock?

Surely not. He was sorry he had been unkind and she was going to show that she accepted his apology by exchanging greetings with him in the street.

All right, by *secretly* exchanging greetings. But what difference did that make?

Well, she was going to do it, anyhow. And now she had begun to perceive how it might be achieved.

She put her plan into action over breakfast. A little sighing about the noticeably shortening days, and a remark that nearly all her winter clothes needed new trimmings and that her best winter bonnet was so out of date that it ought to be replaced, easily brought about the result she wanted.

'I want to buy a new cloak,' said Horatia languidly. Horatia never seemed to be more than half awake at breakfast. 'Today is as good a time as any. You may come with me if you wish. Will Anne and Phoebe come too?'

'Yes, I should like that,' said Phoebe, and Anne, after saying grumblingly that they'd only just been to Oxford Street, finally said that she would join them.

They spent most of the morning in Oxford Street, returning laden with a satisfactory amount of packages. So far, so good, thought Sophia, relieved because her first essay in manoeuvring other people had been a success. But now for the second half of the plan. In the evening she got out a blue velvet winter dress in order to re-trim it, and discovered, with loud annoyance, that she had that morning bought the wrong shade of blue ribbon. Going restlessly to the window, she remarked that she was longing for another walk and the evening was fine, and why should they not make another foray? 'I want to buy the right shade, now, at once. I forgot to get another bottle of lavender water this morning, too. I can buy that at the same time.'

It worked.

She had imagined all sorts of difficulties, from Horatia and her sisters saying they didn't feel like it and her father saying that they couldn't go without Horatia, to Anne simply telling her not to be so impatient but to wait for tomorrow. But instead everyone proved perfectly agreeable, and she had, furthermore, managed the timing well. At five minutes to nine, all four of the Whitmead ladies, accompanied by Millicent, Bess, and a footman, were approaching James Smyth's perfumery in quest of lavender water.

And Lemuel was there. Sophia scanned the street, watched a laden stage-coach thunder past, bound for the Uxbridge Road and perhaps after that for Land's End itself, and felt the usual pang of excitement, and then saw him, loitering on the other side of the street. She lingered behind as the others went into the perfumery, and turned away towards the nearby confectioners. Lemuel met her just outside.

'Miss Sophia.'

'I ... I got your note. I'm so sorry about your mother. That was dreadful, Mr Craddock. It must have been such a shock.'

'Well, it was, but she was that ill ... maybe it was better than if she'd had to go on struggling.'

'Are you alone in the world now?'

'More or less. I've some aunts and uncles somewhere but we lost touch with them long since. That's a charming bonnet, Miss Sophia.'

'You like it? I saved up my pin money for months to buy it.'

And what you call pin money, my lady, some people call a wage.

'You didn't mind me saying I wanted to see you again, did you, Miss Sophia?'

'No, oh no. Only, giving me that note was very risky; it added to our chances of being caught. But I was very touched ... I mean ...'

'You wanted to see me again. You must have, because you're here.'

'Well, I wanted you to know that ... I mean, in the note, you apologised for the way you'd spoken to me, and I wanted you to know that I understood and ... and had accepted the apology.'

'And was that all?' said Lemuel softly.

'Why, of course, Mr Craddock.'

There didn't seem to be much else to say. In spite of this, Sophia longed to stay where she was and go on talking, however pointlessly, to Lemuel, but she dared not.

'I must go now. My sisters and stepmother are in the perfumery and they'll come looking for me in a moment. Once again, I'm so very sorry about Mrs Craddock.'

'Then I'll say goodnight, miss. I don't expect you can come shopping in Oxford Street in the evening all that often, but if you can slip out of the house at about this time, some other evening, you just might find me hanging about in Hanover Square. Then we could talk longer. I'd like it, if you'd like it. Goodbye.'

He was gone, stepping smoothly back and out of sight behind a passing hackney, and Sophia, heart curiously light and pulses jumping, darted into the confectioners just as the door of the perfumery a few yards away opened. When the others came to find her, and tell her laughingly that they had got the lavender water for her, she was buying comfits and pistachios, which she distributed to them and to Bess and the footman with a lavish hand before sweeping them all off to search for the right shade of blue ribbon.

Getting out of the house was also easier than she expected. On the ground floor, the hallway was extended by a passage which led to the garden door at the back of the house. Two evenings later, Sophia withdrew to her room soon after supper, pleading a headache, put on a wrap, chose a moment when the rest of the family were round the piano in the drawing room and the servants were washing up, took her walking shoes in her hand and went noiselessly downstairs in her slippers.

Once in the garden, she changed her footwear, left her slippers in a shadowed corner, and made her way stealthily to the door that led into an alley. A left turn brought her back to Hanover Square.

It was dusk, and the sharp, disturbing smell of autumn mist was in the air. It made her feel both excited and alarmed. She had never been out in the street on her own in her whole life before. She hesitated, not sure which way to turn. Then, with relief, she saw Lemuel coming towards her. She recognised his walk and his lean shape before she saw his face, and went quickly to meet him.

'Lemuel! I mean . . . Mr Craddock . . . good evening.'

His greeting was not what she expected.

'Here, now, Miss Whitmead,' said Lemuel reprovingly, doffing his hat. 'You shouldn't come rushing at me like that. You ought to wait, looking nice and haughty, and let me do the rushing.'

'Oh. Should I?' said Sophia, dashed.

'Indeed you should.' Lemuel, however, gave her a grin as he put his hat on again, and offered her his arm. 'But I'm glad to see you. Let's take a turn – down this side street, not round the square, in case we meet someone you know. How did you get out?'

'I just walked out through the garden, but I can't be out for long. I'm supposed to have gone to bed early with a headache.'

'A headache?' Lemuel laughed. 'Young ladies like you can afford them, I daresay. My mother couldn't take time off to have headaches. Maybe she'd have lived longer if she could.'

'Oh. I . . . I'm sorry,' said Sophia, not sure if she was saying that she was sorry for his mother, or for his bereavement, or for being Sophia who was free to have minor illnesses when other people weren't.

'No, *I'm* sorry.' The arm she was holding tightened, drawing her hand close against him. 'An ill-tempered lout, that's what I am. I meant it when I said I was glad to see you; you're a ray of light in a dismal world, you are. Not too cold, are you?'

'No, no, not a bit.' The feel of Lemuel's hard, masculine arm under her hand was amazingly pleasurable. She wanted to go on feeling it there for ever. 'What happened to your mother, Lem . . . Mr Craddock? Or don't you wish to speak of it?'

'Lemuel'll do very nicely; I like hearing you say it. No, I don't mind telling you, but it'll upset you.'

'Oh.'

'And you don't know what to say to that, do you? Well, she had the lung-rot. She'd been coughing blood for a good while, on and off. She used to take in washing to help out with money and she was at the mangle, down in the basement, when it seems she had a coughing fit. Anyhow, she choked on her own blood and died trying to get up the stairs to our rooms. That's all.'

'Oh, Lemuel, how dreadful!' Sophia was glad of the deepening dusk, because she had gone crimson. 'Was Mrs Craddock worried about the rent going up?' she asked timidly.

'She was that. But don't you take on; no one's blaming you. London's a hard place to make a living in.'

'How was it that your family came to London? You came originally from Chestnuts, didn't you?'

'So you know that?'

'I was listening when you had your interview with my father,' Sophia said.

'Yes, I thought you might of been, when I saw you on the stairs. Do you make a habit of eavesdropping?'

'We all do, me and my sisters.' Sophia had decided to show some spirit. 'It's the only way we ever hear anything interesting. Our lives are very dull.'

'That I can believe. So you were listening and you heard me talk about Chestnuts. Well, the fact is, your grandfather threw my grandparents out. My grandmother asked yours to try to talk to him. I dunno if she ever did, but anyhow it didn't make any difference. My family was thrown out to make room for a lot of extra sheep.'

'If my grandmother was asked to help, I'm sure she tried. She would; she's like that. But I expect my grandfather wouldn't listen. My father doesn't listen to other people very much and I've heard Grandmamma say to my father, "Henry, you're just like your father was."'

She imitated Lucy-Anne's voice and was rewarded by Lemuel's laugh. Encouraged, she said, 'My father gives generously to charity. I'm sure that neither he nor my grandfather really understood the hardship they were causing.'

'Oh, they understood all right. Causing hardship to the poor is how people like them keep us in our place. If we stay poor, we stay respectful and they keep their power. They like us to be scared to give offence for fear they'll throw us out of our homes or our work. The parsons preach a lot of nonsense about people being called to their station in life and how they ought to stay there. Me ma used to go to church but I gave it up years back. Couldn't stand all that smug sermonising. I'd like some of them well-fed parsons to live like me for a bit; if they knew more about my station in life, they wouldn't think it was anyone's duty to stay in it. As for charity, it makes the rich feel good and keeps their consciences quiet; that's all that is.'

'Oh, dear,' said Sophia, set down once again.

'Again, I'm sorry. It ain't your fault. You're a lot different from most girls of your sort. Most wouldn't understand a word I was saying. But you're beautiful and you're kind. You oughtn't to be here with me. You know that?'

'But I want to be, I really do. Only, it's nearly dark and if I don't get back soon Ames will do his rounds and lock all the doors.'

'All right. We're nearly back to the square, as a matter of fact; I've brought us round in a circle. Here we are.'

'Oh, good. Thank you. Oh, no!' Sophia, as they emerged into the square, stopped short and clutched Lemuel's arm with both hands. They were only a few yards from her home and the alley which would be her route back to the garden, but between her and sanctuary was the Faulkners' house, and a carriage was standing outside. Footmen had come out of the house with lights, and in any case it was not yet quite dark. Mr and Mrs Faulkner, who knew all the Whitmeads by sight, were alighting from the carriage. If they looked this way they would see her as plainly as she could see them. 'They *know* me!' Sophia gasped.

'Don't worry,' said Lemuel. Pulling her into the shade of a small tree, he put his arms around her and hid her face from the world by bringing his own down on it in a long kiss.

After a moment, he lifted his head enough to mutter: 'They can't see who you are and they'll look the other way anyhow, don't you worry. They'll reckon I'm someone's groom or second footman having a cuddle with a kitchenmaid. It's the way the lower classes behave, my dear,' Lemuel added with a parody of a well-bred accent.

'You're making fun of me,' Sophia protested, hurt. Momentarily, she tried to pull away from him but he held her tightly and put a comforting palm on the back of her head.

'Sorry, sorry. It's just my way; I don't mean any harm. Don't be such a prissy little juggins. Here.' And with that his mouth was on hers again and the strong hand was stroking down the back of her neck and her spine. His nearness, the pressure of the hard body against her own and the thrilling spicy smell of stables and maleness which hung about him awakened sensations which she had never before known existed. The long kiss ended but she went on standing in his arms; with her face pressed into his chest, while behind her the Faulkners' voices retreated up the steps of the house. A front door banged, and the coachman chirruped to the horses.

She heard the carriage driving off, round to the nearby mews. She drew back and raised her face, and Lemuel promptly kissed her for the third time. 'That's just to prove that I want to, that I didn't just do it so you wouldn't be recognised,' he said. 'Will you meet me again, Miss Whitmead?'

Necessity is the mother of invention. Sophia had heard her father say that across the dinner table when his coachworks manager Mr Greenaway was dining with them and a discussion arose about new types of carriage suspension. Mr Greenaway was of the opinion that leather braces were comfortable and lasted well enough, while her father was all for experimenting with steel springs.

'I want to get ahead of my competitors. I *need* to get ahead, and necessity is the mother of invention.'

And so it was, Sophia thought as she strolled decorously round the garden, stooped to pull a few weeds from her own special patch, and let a little silver ring which Lucy-Anne had given her for her last birthday slip from her little finger to nestle under a rosebush. It was amazing, the number of ruses she had invented already.

She had now met Lemuel in the square three times. Twice she had got away with ostensibly retiring to her room after supper – on that first occasion with a pretended headache and the second time with an overwhelming desire to finish *The Mysteries of Udolpho*. She had secreted a lantern in her room, now that the nights were drawing in so quickly.

But she could not go on making excuses to leave the family circle, and besides, if she went on creeping down the stairs and out of the garden door, she would sooner or later be detected. For her third escape, therefore, she had tried a different ploy. That time, she took advantage of a particularly mild and lovely night – 'So unusual for October!' – and gone openly into the garden to look at the stars.

Lucy-Anne was interested in astronomy and an astronomer called William Herschel, apparently quite well-known, had once actually visited her, with his wife and young son. She had taught the girls a little, too. No one thought it odd that Sophia should suddenly want to stand in the garden and go into ecstasies over the Great Bear and Cassiopeia. But she didn't think it would do as a regular excuse. It would be no use at all on cloudy nights, for one thing.

So now, for this fourth escape, she was adopting yet another ruse. Dropping a ring in the garden and going out in the evening, quite openly, to look for it would do for just once. After that . . .

Being in love was the most extraordinary thing. She had wondered about it at times, because when one heard adults speak of it they gave off such oddly mixed signals.

'They're obviously deep in love, miss,' Bess had said to her when Mr Greenaway got married and brought his bride to dinner, and next day Lucy-Anne had said the same, in much the same caressing tone. But Henry had said yes, a pretty pair of turtledoves, but such a public display of affection was a sign of low breeding, and particularly undesirable in the presence of young ladies. 'If they hear talk of being in love, it can only encourage them in foolish romantic notions.'

But later that day Sophia went to talk to Lucy-Anne and found herself asking, 'Have you ever been in love, Grandmamma? What was it like?'

Lucy-Anne's answer startled her. 'It's like being completely taken over by another person. The other person fills one's thoughts and dreams. You think of him so constantly that you almost become him. You leave yourself behind like a discarded dress. It can be a very happy thing, if you fall in love with the right person. But it's dangerous to fall in love with the wrong one, so take care, my love. But I hope,' Lucy-Anne had added, 'that you will one day have the experience. Yes, I would hope that for you.'

And now the hope had been fulfilled. Sophia was in love, and everything that her grandmother had told her was the truth. She was no longer just Sophia but one half of a composite being called Lemuel-Sophia and it did not occur to her to put Lemuel anywhere except first. In her mind, she had, as Lucy-Anne had foretold, virtually become him. And she had begun to understand that the strange physical feelings he aroused in her were her body's demand to be somehow – though she did not know how – united with his.

She had also begun to see that this could not go on for ever, that the deception must sooner or later end, and that she and Lemuel must either be joined, in defiance of family and custom, or else part. But when she had the prospect of being with him soon, within a few hours, this very evening, these promptings of common-sense became unreal. She had only to think of the feel of his arms around her and the delight of his kisses, and there would be nothing else worth having in the world and she would wade through blood and fire to win them.

She discovered the loss of her ring during supper, with carefully tuned casualness. 'How strange. I'm sure I had my silver ring on earlier. Anne, Phoebe, can you remember if I did?'

'Yes, I think so. Well, you wear it on most days,' said Phoebe, not very interested. 'But if you took it off for any reason, it will be on your dressing table, I daresay.'

'Yes, probably. I'll look after supper,' said Sophia.

She was becoming really very good at deception now.

Chapter Twenty-five
Flight into the Unknown

This time, as on the evening when she went stargazing, she left her room and went down the stairs boldly, armed with a perfect excuse. 'I think I must have dropped my ring in the garden; I'm just going out to look. I've got a lantern.'

But she had no need to make the excuse to anyone, for she met no one on the stairs or landing, no one in the hall. She went unchallenged out of the back door into the dusky garden, paused to find her ring, took long enough over it to assure herself that no one had after all followed her out to see what she was about, and then she was out in the alley, closing the garden door noiselessly after her, and making her way to where Lemuel would be waiting.

He looked tired. The day's work at the stables was long. Coaches started leaving at four in the morning and were still arriving at eleven at night, and although those who were there for the early-morning ones were allowed to leave earlier in the evening, they rarely had much spare energy by then, for they had been on duty since well before dawn.

Most of the others lived over the stables, which at least meant that they didn't have to walk to work, but Lemuel did not. He had to leave home at three in the morning to be on duty in time, and in the evening he had to walk back. He had a breakfast at the inn but if he were coming to Hanover Square instead of going straight home, he would have had nothing to eat since early morning beyond a midday snack.

Sophia had learned all this by now and it worried her. She felt ashamed because she had had a good supper, and an excellent dinner earlier in the day. She greeted him with a quick hug, in the shadow of a wall, and through the cloth of his coat was unhappily aware that his bones were too prominent.

'So you got away all right,' Lemuel said. He offered her his arm and they began to stroll, taking as usual a side turning that would lead them away from the square.

'Yes. It's getting harder, though, because it gets dark so early now. I made a clever plan this time, though.'

She began to tell him about the excuse of the dropped ring. She was halfway through before she realised that he was not really listening. 'What is it, Lemuel?'

He didn't answer at once, and she had to repeat the question. 'Lemuel?'

He stopped walking and let go of her. Puzzled, she turned to face him and saw that he had turned his head so as not to look at her. 'It's got to stop,' he said.

'Got to stop? What has? Do you mean . . . ?'

'Yes, 'course I do. Us. This can't go on and you know it. Sooner or later you'll get caught, creeping out to meet me or creeping back, and then what? That 'ud be the end of it for us anyway; you'd never be let out of their sight again, especially if you let on who you'd been seeing – and they'd make you let on, I've no doubt about that. Your father'd see to that. I've been a fool, wanting to see you at all, and you've been a fool, agreeing. So it's got to stop.'

'But, Lemuel . . . !'

'"But, Lemuel!" Oh, for Christ's sake, what did you think would happen in the end anyhow? Where did you think we were going? Oh, all right, I should of done some thinking too. Trouble is, I fell in love with you, but there's no sense in the likes of me falling in love with the likes of you. Go home, Sophia, back to your nice safe house and your father who looks after you so well, and leave me alone.'

She hadn't lit her lantern but a street light showed him the sparkle of tears in her eyes. 'Now, don't start crying!'

'I c . . . can't help it!' She was trying to help it, but her eyes had overflowed by themselves. 'You're being so unkind. I know everything you say is true, but if we've g . . . got to say goodbye . . .'

Say goodbye? Say goodbye to Lemuel, the only excitement, the only chink of freedom she'd ever experienced in her life? She *had* known that it couldn't go on, but knowing something in a secret, unadmitted way was one thing, and having it flung at you out loud and without warning was like being kicked in the stomach. Her voice shook.

'. . . if we really have to say goodbye, can't we do it kindly? Can't we even have a last kiss?'

Her upturned face was pale and strained and very very pretty – the features delicate as carved ivory, the tendrils of hair on the hollowed temples and smooth brow glinting ash-gold in the lamplight. 'Sweet, simple and sentimental, that's you,' said Lemuel. 'But if you want a kiss . . .'

Lemuel's kisses were never gentle but this was harder and rougher than anything she had experienced before, and it went on longer. She tried to break away in order to breathe, but he only held her harder and ground his mouth down on hers more harshly. When he did release her, her arms and ribs felt bruised and she knew her mouth was swollen. The tumultuous feelings his embraces always produced, were roaring through her body in a storm, obscuring all reason.

In a whisper, she asked, 'Will we really never see each other again?'

'Not unless you want to come to America.'

'America?'

'Yep. I'm going to emigrate. I'll never make anything of myself here but they say there's chances over there if a man's got two hands and he's willing to use them. If he's got it in him to make his way, he's allowed to make it; the place ain't all full of rich folk keeping the rest down. So I'm off. My mother's gone, so what's to keep me?'

The answer to this was so obvious that Sophia had no need to speak, but contented herself with putting a hand on his arm and looking up at him.

'You? You think you're a reason to stay? But we've no future together. Haven't we just agreed on that?'

'Yes, but—'

'But what?'

'I just wish . . . I'm sorry it has to end, that's all.'

'I told you. It's got to, unless you run off with me to America. You've got the choice,' said Lemuel.

'The . . . the choice?'

'Yep.' She was aware that he was studying her carefully, trying to assess what her answer would be. 'You could come too. I'm going to get a ship from Bristol. Ma left a little bit of a nest egg, believe it or not – what she'd put by for a rainy day as she used to say. It's enough for the fare to Bristol and a passage, steerage. You can tag along if you like, and if you can bring your own passage money. But I don't expect a well-brought-up little bit of a thing like you to face a life like that, so I didn't ask.'

'I'd . . . I'd face anything if I could be with you, Lemuel.'

'Would you? Sleeping in the hold along with all the rest, all the poor folk; then living God knows how and God knows where in America till I get on my feet? Can you cook?'

'I can learn. And I can sew very well. I'd be useful. We . . . we'd be married?'

'Not till we're on board ship. Once we're on the sea and well on our way, we'd get the captain to marry us. Can't do it here – you're under age and there's no time for a round trip to Gretna. I ain't asking you to do it, Sophie. I reckon it 'ud be asking a lot too much of you.'

'But . . . you said you loved me.'

'So I do. What's that to say to anything? You well-off folk don't marry for love, most of the time. I don't expect it means much to you.'

'Oh, Lemuel, it does. Most of us do marry the people our parents choose but we don't always want to, and anyway my father hasn't chosen anyone, not for my sisters, and not for me. But you've chosen! You've picked me out and I . . . I . . .'

'You want me and you'd face any hardship to be with me? You're saying that and you mean it?'

'Yes, yes I would, and I do.'

'You'd better think it over. But if you're serious, if you mean it, I'm off in a few days time – next Tuesday, to be exact. I've given in my notice and I'm leaving on the stage from the Belle Sauvage at Ludgate Hill at four in the morning, going to Bristol by way of Bath. I'll be in Bath before midnight, in Bristol next day, and sailing the day after. I've got my passage fixed. The ship's called the *Bristol Pearl*. I could get a coach from where I've been working, at the White Horse,' he added, 'but I don't want everyone knowing my business.'

'But Ludgate Hill? I've never been there, and I'd have to get out in the middle of the night—'

'No, you wouldn't. I'd meet you the evening before. We'd go to a cheap inn – I can't waste money on the Beautiful Savage—'

'The Beautiful Savage?'

'That's what the name Belle Sauvage means. It was a groom who used to work there who gave me the notion of going to America. You ever heard of a fellow called John Rolfe, who married a Red Indian princess and brought her to London – oh, way back in the days of the first King James?'

'Oh yes, I've been told about her in history lessons. If you mean Pocahontas, that is.'

'That's her. She and Mr Rolfe stayed at the inn. It was called the Bell then, and the family that ran it was called Savage. After this Pocahontas stopped there, the name was changed to the Belle Sauvage, which is Frenchie for the beautiful savage, or so they say.'

'Why, yes, it is.'

'Ah well, you'd know. You've had education. Well, that's the way the place got its present name, a sort of pun, like. Seemingly, this Pocahontas died pretty soon – couldn't stand the climate here, all the damp and the smoke. American air must be nice and clean, that's what this groom I was talking about said to me. And a week or two later, he said he was emigrating, said from all he'd heard America didn't just have clean air, it had plenty of room and plenty of opportunities too. Stuck in my mind, that did.'

'And this Belle Sauvage is where we'd start from?'

'And you say it like a real Frenchie. Yes, that's where we'd start. Now, listen. Monday night, I'll be around here, like this evening. I'll wait until eleven. If you don't come by then, then all right, I'll take myself off and that's the end of it. If you come, then we're off to Ludgate Hill and to Bath the next day. But you'll have to bring some money; I've only got so much.'

'I could do that. I've been saving my pin money again, to buy Christmas presents with. I'll bring all I've got.'

'If you come. Now see here. You got to think about this, and make sure you want whatever it is you choose. On one side, you stop at home, nice and safe and warm, but you don't see me again, ever. On the other side, you got me and I'll do my best for you, but you'll have to rough it. It'll be cheap lodgings, crowded stage-coaches, below decks on the voyage and there's always the chance the ship'll sink. Then when we get there, you'll have to work, doing all the things you've always had servants to do. Maybe I'm not worth all that. Think it over. And now, you'd best say goodnight or you'll get locked out.'

'Goodnight,' said Sophia. She heard the uncertainty in her own voice, and wondered if he had, too.

There was something the matter with her youngest grand-daughter. Lucy-Anne knew it without being able to work out what it could be. She had been aware for some time that the girl was in a state of suppressed excitement. She'd seen Sophia smiling to herself, heard her humming or bursting into snatches of song, once even seen her run upstairs two steps at a time in a most unladylike way.

The symptoms strongly suggested that the girl was in love. She'd once asked about it, Lucy-Anne recalled. But who in the world could Sophia possibly be in love with? She was strictly supervised; never out of sight of her family except when she was in her room. But there was *something* . . .

Only, lately, there had been a change. A few evenings ago, Lucy-Anne had been about to go up to bed when Sophia came upstairs from the ground floor, cloaked and carrying a lantern, and had announced, unasked, that she had been in the garden to look for her silver ring.

'I missed it at supper, if you recall, Grandmamma. I couldn't find it on my dressing table and I was so upset; I couldn't bear to think I'd lost it. Then I remembered. I did some weeding in the garden today. So out I rushed with a lantern and, look, I've found it!'

'It's very sweet of you to mind about it so much,' said Lucy-Anne. 'You'd better go up the stairs ahead of me, child. You're quick on your feet and I'm slow.'

Lucy-Anne's eyesight was no longer what it used to be, and the candles that lit the landing did not in any case show her Sophia's face very clearly. But she could hear the flurried note in the girl's voice, and candlelight had a way of picking out odd details. Most of Sophia's features were a shadowed blur, but unless Lucy-Anne was much mistaken her eyelashes were wet as if with tears and her mouth, seen plainly just for one moment, looked as red as though she had been applying rouge. Or . . .

But that was impossible. No, really. Who could the girl have been kissing?

But she had been troubled enough, just the same, to look carefully at Sophia over breakfast the next day, and what she saw made her more troubled still. The undercurrent of excitement was still there, but so was an air of great anxiety. Sophia had a frown between her brows and had clearly lost her appetite. Later in the morning, Lucy-Anne called her grand-daughter to her room to ask an outright question. 'Sophia, do you want to talk to me about anything? You seem – well – preoccupied.'

'Do I, Grandmamma?'

With a heavy heart, Lucy-Anne recognised the wide eyes and the overdone innocence. She had used the same techniques in her time, when returning to the house after passionate meetings with Stephen in the folly. But she had only had to deceive Fraser and Mrs Cobham, not the acute eyes of a close and loving relative.

'Yes, Sophia, you do. You seem very unlike yourself and, if you will forgive me for saying so, you don't appear altogether happy. Now, why should that be so?'

'But, Grandmamma, it isn't so, indeed it isn't. I am very happy. I know that I am fortunate. What if I had been born poor? Sometimes I wonder what it would be like to be poor. I've been thinking about that, lately; perhaps that's what you've seen.'

'Are you proposing to take up good works? Admirable if so, but I doubt if your father would let you,' said Lucy-Anne with acerbity. 'As a

295

matter of fact, in my opinion, you and your sisters all have quite good reason not to be very happy and I intend to talk to your father and try once again to bring him to some sense of his duty towards you all. Horatia has a family with wide connections and it shouldn't be too hard to find suitors for you all. You are sure there is nothing more on your mind? If you want me to advise you in any way, about anything . . . I know a great deal of the world, my dear, more than you or your father realise. I may be able to help.'

'Truly, Grandmamma, there's nothing.'

'Very well, then, my dear. But remember, for the time being, I am here and always ready to listen.'

'For the time being, Grandmamma?'

'I'm seventy-four now, my love. No one lives for ever.'

'Oh!' Sophia's face was suddenly stricken.

'Alas, it's true,' Lucy-Anne said. 'One doesn't think of death, at your age. Well, off you go. It's a nice sunny autumn day; you and your sisters should take a turn round the square.'

'Yes, I expect we will,' said Sophia. She sounded inexplicably doleful. But, thought Lucy-Anne sadly, it would be no use to enquire further. Whatever was on Sophia's mind, she wasn't going to reveal it.

It might be worth talking to her sisters some time. But perhaps not today. One of the difficult things about growing old was that one also grew tired. One awkward interview in a day was enough. Tomorrow would do.

In the yard of the White Horse, Lemuel Craddock had groomed his last horse and picked out its hooves, filled his last hayrack, and dragged his curry comb for the last time through his dandy brush to clean the loose hairs out of it.

'That's that,' he said aloud, as he went to put his grooming gear in its place in the tackroom, ready for his successor the next day.

Dick Grant was there, with a couple of the grooms, cleaning harness. 'You off then? Finished all your jobs? We could still find you a bit of tack-cleaning to do.'

'No, thanks. I'll pick up my pay from the landlord and then I'm away. Well, it's been nice knowing you.'

'Got a new job, have you?' asked one of the grooms, and the other, with a snort of amusement, said, 'He's allus talked of bettering hisself. He's goin' to be head groom in a gentleman's stables in the West End. Ain't you, Craddock?'

Like Dick Grant, most of the grooms had reservations about Lemuel, though they couldn't have said why. Craddock did his share of the work, and no, he wasn't quarrelsome – in fact he could be quite good company over a jug of ale on the rare occasions when they had a bit of time off together and spent it in their own favourite hostelry, a scruffy tavern off the other side of Fleet Street. He could tell a good tale and although no one could say the way he talked was la-di-dah, he was well-spoken by their standards. His family had been country folk and because they hadn't dropped their aitches, nor did he. As a result, he was agreeable to listen to. But all the same, there was something about him . . .

Well, he didn't really like horses, for a start, and if a man was a groom you hardly needed any further excuse not to care for him. The result was that they all got at him in subtle ways when they could.

Lemuel regarded them with dislike. Even if he hadn't planned to take Sophia with him, which meant covering his tracks, he wouldn't have wanted to take a coach from the White Horse, simply because of this underhand needling. He wouldn't have wanted them all staring and making remarks. But he did rather fancy leaving, as it were, on a high note.

'I don't reckon I'll ever be a groom again,' he said. 'There's a thousand things a man might be, in America. I might be a pioneer there and hold land of my own.'

'America?' said Grant. 'That's where you're bound?'

'That's right.' Lemuel finished putting his things away, took his coat from its hook and prepared to walk out of the tackroom for ever. 'I'm sailing on a ship called the *Bristol Pearl*, early Thursday morning. Think of me then, with the sea wind in me nostrils and all the world in front of me. Goodbye.'

Lucy-Anne spent the rest of the day quietly, playing cards with Letty. They ate companionably in Lucy-Anne's room, and retired early. Lucy-Anne slept well, but in the morning she was awakened by someone anxiously shaking her, and opened her eyes to find Anne, Phoebe and their maid Bess beside her.

'Grandmamma? We're so sorry to disturb you,' Anne said. 'But . . . but Father and Horatia are still asleep and Bess says . . . Bess, you tell it.'

'I've just been to Miss Sophia's room with her morning chocolate,' said Bess miserably. 'But she's not there and her bed's not been slept in. Then I saw a note pushed under her pillow, and when I looked it's got your name on it, Mrs Lucy-Anne Whitmead. I took it to Miss Anne . . .'

'And then we woke Phoebe up and we all thought it was best to come straight to you,' Anne said.

Lucy-Anne sat up, straightening her nightcap. She held out her hand. 'Give me the note,' she said.

Sophia's writing was that of a well-brought-up child, painstakingly neat and quite without the individual quirks that are the insignia of adulthood. Lucy-Anne picked up her eyeglasses from the bedside table, read the note once to herself and then again, out loud, taking pains to speak clearly.

Dear Grandmamma,

I am sorry to be going away like this without a word but I can't do anything else. I'm going to be married but I know my father would never let me marry Lemuel, so I have to run away with him. We are going to America. I am going to be very happy, so please don't be anxious. I am writing this to you because lately you saw that I was

297

thinking deeply about something and you were very kind. There was nothing you could do to help, but I'm mindful of how kind you were. Thank you.
With much love,
your grand-daughter, Sophia.

'*America*?' said Anne. 'She's going to America? With someone called Lemuel? Who on earth . . . ?'

'Lemuel? Oh, God,' said Bess. 'Oh, ma'am! Miss Anne!' She put the knuckles of her right hand into her mouth and stared at them over the top, eyes terrified and filling with tears.

'Bess?' said Lucy-Anne. 'What do you know about this?'

'Yes, what?' demanded Anne. 'Don't shake your head like that, Bess; we can all see you know something. The name Lemuel means something to you. Now, you tell us about it at once, or I'll fetch Father and he'll make you.'

'We'll have to fetch your father anyway, in a moment,' Lucy-Anne said. 'But I'd like to know what we've got to deal with first. Bess, sit down on that chair. Anne, Phoebe, come here; sit on the bed. It's no good bullying the girl; you'll never get any sense out of her that way. That's right. Now then. Bess, tell us all you know, but be quick about it. There's no time to lose.'

'I had no idea, honest.' Bess had perched herself nervously on the edge of the chair. 'I haven't done anything wrong, Mrs Whitmead, not really wrong, that is. I never thought for a single minute—'

'Yes, yes, we can take all that as read. Go on, please.'

'Miss Sophia's had something on her mind, ma'am, all these last three weeks or so. She's been different, sort of smiling to herself sometimes, or far away, as if she's thinking of something else. But I didn't think anything of it, although—'

'Oh, Bess, do get on with it.' Anne snapped.

'Please,' said Phoebe urgently, but without her sister's aggression, 'please tell us.'

'I'm trying to,' said Bess, distressed, 'but it's that difficult . . .'

'All right, Bess, tell it in your own way,' said Lucy-Anne. 'But do please try to get to the point soon.'

Bess swallowed. 'There was a queer thing one evening. Miss Sophia went to bed early with a headache and told me she wouldn't want me till morning, but Fanny – Master Francis' nurse – just happened to mention next day that she'd seen Miss Sophia coming along the passage from the garden door as if she'd been out, late in the evening, and where could she have been? I thought maybe she'd got up and gone out for a breath of air for her head. It seemed a bit funny if she had, getting up and getting dressed to go out in the cold but I never thought . . . never dreamed . . .'

'I've noticed the change in her myself,' Lucy-Anne said. 'I even asked her about it – she mentions that in the letter. Didn't you girls notice anything?'

'She's been dreamy and absent-minded,' Phoebe said. 'But she's sometimes like that anyway. Where does Lemuel come in?'

298

'Yes, Lemuel.' Lucy-Anne, sitting stiffly upright in bed, became brisk. 'Who is he, Bess?'

'His name's Lemuel Craddock if it's really him,' said Bess. 'And he lives in Wagoner Street.'

'Wagoner Street? He's one of Mr Whitmead's tenants, you mean?' said Lucy-Anne.

'Yes, ma'am,' said Bess, and then, at last, told the story of the illicit visit to Wagoner Street, and the encounter between Miss Sophia Whitmead, youngest daughter of landlord Henry Whitmead, and her father's impolite but personable tenant Lemuel Craddock.

Henry Whitmead, awakened by Lucy-Anne, informed of Sophia's incredible elopement, and presented with her letter to read, fell out of bed, seized a dressing gown, ordered Horatia to do likewise, and then rushed to the morning room, shouting for his household to attend him immediately. They gathered in moments, the nursemaid Fanny holding four-year-old Francis by the hand; the maids and the footmen, inquisitive and rather excited by what was obviously a crisis, led in by the butler Ames; and the cook still wiping greasy hands and accompanied by a smell of fried bacon. Letty was there, clucking slightly because Lucy-Anne was up too early and hurrying about too much and it couldn't be good for her; and Bess, in tears, came with Lucy-Anne, keeping close to her as if for protection.

'Oh yes, it's Craddock all right!' Purple in the face and spluttering with anger, Henry looked very much as George had looked when in a rage. The story had been told again, with corroboration from Fanny, who repeated her tale of seeing Miss Sophia returning from the garden at an unlikely moment.

'Craddock's given up his tenancy,' Henry said. 'He left yesterday and good riddance as far as I'm concerned. America sounds likely enough; just the sort of thing he'd do. But with Sophie! What was she thinking of? My daughter running off with a . . . she must be mad. She should be committed to Bedlam. When did she go? You, girl – Bess – when did you last see Miss Sophia? Didn't you see her to her bed last night? Speak up!'

'Yes, sir, I got her ready for bed, about half past nine. But she didn't get into bed straight away; she said she'd sit and read by her fire till it died down. She told me I could go, that she wouldn't need me any more . . .'

The double meaning of the last few words caused them to dissolve into a wail.

Henry ignored it. 'So she could well have been gone since last night.' He was furious, but thinking logically all the same. 'We need to get to Wagoner Street. Someone there may know which port he was sailing from, or maybe the name of the ship. And you' – he turned fiercely upon Bess – 'you went with Miss Sophia to Wagoner Street in a hackney, and walked down it with her, she has her reticule stolen, the two of you take shelter in this man's rooms, and you say nothing to anyone? Well, that's the end of you, my girl. I expect absolute loyalty from my servants.' He glanced round at the rest of them. 'You hear?

There was no question of hiding this ... this disaster from the household; that is why I have summoned you here and spoken frankly before you. But one word of this whispered beyond these walls, and the offender follows Bess. And Bess, for your information, packs her things and leaves today, without a reference. Upon my word, I—'

'Excuse me.' Lucy-Anne stepped forward and used her lorgnette to rivet his attention. 'Allow me to interrupt for a moment.' She took Henry's arm and drew him out of the room, closing the door after her so that the others couldn't hear. 'Henry, this is unjust to Bess. It may be unconventional for a young lady to go off round London in a hackney with just her maid, but it really is not a crime—'

'When the young lady is one of my daughters, it most certainly is! Above all when it is Sophia. That Sophia, for whom I have always had a particular feeling, should deceive me like this! But Bess should have prevented her. Bess has done very wrong and—'

'She has *not*.' Despite her anxiety over her grand-daughter and Bess, Lucy-Anne was finding something like pleasure in this conversation. She had so often longed to challenge George's scale of values and hadn't dared. With Henry, she could afford to dare. 'Nor,' she said, 'is it wrong to be interested enough in one's father's property to wish to look at it. And if you have your reticule snatched, you're the victim of a crime, not its perpetrator. It was quite sensible to go to the Craddock rooms, because his mother was there. No one could have expected Craddock to be there at such a time of day, nor that he would afterwards pursue Sophia, as it seems he did. You have spoken of loyalty. Well, a maid owes a loyalty to her mistress and is expected to keep her lady's counsel. It can put a girl in a very awkward position. I should know. I am your mother, but there is a good deal you don't know about me. I once had a maid who was party to a ... humph! ... Shall we say, a questionable secret of mine, and I was grateful for her discretion.'

'A questionable secret? What are you saying, Mother?'

'I'm not going to tell you any more,' said Lucy-Anne. 'It doesn't affect you in any way. But if you turn Bess off, I shall make it my business to see that she finds good employment elsewhere and I'll write the reference for her. If anyone's to blame, Henry, it isn't Bess, it's you and Horatia. You've hardly done a thing, either of you, to give the girls normal opportunities of meeting young men. You actually stopped Anne from going to parties and dances. Something like this was bound to happen in the end.'

'Well, I'll be ... Mother, you astound me. That is a most offensive thing to say. I have always cherished my daughters—'

'Sometimes I think that if I hear that word again I shall be taken with a severe spasm.'

'Really, Mother, I've no idea what you're talking about. Give that wretched girl a reference if you must; I can scarcely prevent you. But go she shall, just the same. I will not have such deceptions practised on me. Oh, how could Sophia do this? What is that saying about a thankless child? Such a one is sharper than a serpent's tooth. How very true. Sophia has behaved towards me like a viper! I must get on my way to Wagoner Street.'

He had said he would wait until eleven. Ames usually locked up just before then. It would be best, Sophia decided, to pretend to go to bed, and then get up, dress, and steal out of the house at perhaps ten-forty. Most of the servants except for Ames went to bed earlier than that because they had to rise so early.

She herself commonly retired at ten, which fitted in well with her plans. But it was a nerve-racking evening. She must chat normally at supper, and after that pretend to enjoy listening while Anne played the harpsichord. Then she must chat again to Bess as she prepared for bed, and finally she had to wait, while the hands of her clock crept slowly, so slowly, round its face before she could begin the perilous adventure down two flights of stairs towards freedom.

However, dressing herself unaided took up some of the time, and then some more of it was occupied by gathering the clothes she must take with her, and wrapping them all up in a spare cloak to make a bundle.

In fact, packing was more difficult than she expected. She must have dresses, stockings, linen, shawls, shoes . . . no, it was too big a bundle and something must be left out, but what? Not so much underlinen? One spare dress would suffice, perhaps. She could wear some extra things and transport them that way. She mustn't forget gloves. And above all, she mustn't forget her money.

Last of all, she sat down to write a note to Grandmamma. It was probably unwise to leave a note at all and she had a feeling that Lemuel wouldn't like it, but she couldn't, *couldn't*, just go off and leave Grandmamma without a single word. She hadn't been able to confide in her grandmother, but Lucy-Anne had known that something was wrong – no, not wrong, just *strange* – about her, these last few days, and she had been so kind, asking what the matter was and offering to help.

She hesitated over whether to include Lemuel's name in the letter but finally did so. What did it matter? No one would know who he was and anyway, they'd soon be out of reach.

At twenty-five to eleven, she pushed the note half under her pillow, put on her cloak, took her bundle under her arm and peered out of her door. No one was about. Candlelight showed under her sisters' doors, but they were firmly closed. She ventured to the head of the stairs and saw another line of light beneath the door of her father's study. He might come out at any moment.

For an awful, craven moment, Sophia wished he would. It would be a relief to be stopped. She wouldn't then have to hate herself for being weak or timid but nor would she have to set out into the unknown with Lemuel, who was fascinating but not always good-natured. Then she cursed herself for thinking such feeble thoughts, and took extra care to make no sound as she stole down the stairs.

Her feet were silent, but her heart drummed so loudly that she half expected someone to appear and enquire what the noise was, but nothing happened. She tiptoed across the first-floor landing and down the stairs to the hall. Still no one appeared to stop her.

The front door was before her. She had always used the garden door before, because it was easier to think of an excuse for going into the garden late in the evening than for going into the street. But her bundle made excuses impossible anyway. She'd never be able to explain that away convincingly. Her hand was already on the latch. She opened the front door, crept out, drew it to behind her as softly as she could, and darted down the steps. She turned to the left along the pavement. A few yards more and there was a movement in the shadows, and then she was in Lemuel's arms.

'I've got a ring for you,' he said in a whisper as he hurried her away. 'Until we get to the ship, we'd better seem to be man and wife. You can sail as Miss Whitmead – well, maybe you'd better give a false name, but you can be "miss" then, so that we can ask the captain to marry us later. But until we get there, we'd best be Mr and Mrs Craddock, otherwise people might ask questions. Here you are; I hope it'll fit. It's a proper wedding ring; it was my mother's.'

He paused on a street corner in order to push the ring on to her marriage finger. 'It fits very well,' Sophia said, and raised her face to his, expecting another kiss or at least a few affectionate words to mark what after all was an important moment. But Lemuel merely said, 'I hope you've had some supper. I got a bite earlier, so I'm all right. Did you bring some money with you, like I said?'

'Oh yes, certainly. And yes, I've had supper.'

'Good,' said Lemuel. Grasping her arm, he set them briskly walking once again.

It was a long way on foot from Hanover Square to Ludgate Hill. Sophia, in fact, had not had a good supper because she had been too overstrung to eat much. By the time they reached their destination she was very weary and beginning to be haunted by images of her own comfortable bedroom. In the darkness she could hardly make out the entrance to the narrow lane into which Lemuel finally turned, nor see much of the house where he stopped. 'This is where we're staying the night,' he said in a low voice. 'Don't say much – you talk too prettified. Pretend you've been crying.'

'Why?'

'So as you don't have to talk. I'll do the explaining. Oh, do as you're told, for God's sake!'

He tapped on the door, which was opened by someone holding a candle. Sophia made out a fat white face above a bulging black dress. ''Oo is it? Oh, it's you, Mr Craddock. And about time too, I'd say. Keeping folk until all hours, waiting for you to turn up. If you 'adn't paid in advance, I'd 'ave locked up by now. In you come, then. This your missus?'

Sophia, who had dutifully fished out a handkerchief, blew her nose into it and nodded silently. Lemuel patted her shoulder and then pushed her over the threshold.

'Yes, this is Mrs Craddock. Come on, Sophie. Sorry it's so late, Mrs Shaw, but by the time my wife's ma and pa'd finished saying goodbye to her, it was past eleven. I'm afraid she's a bit upset. You'll be all right once we're on our way tomorrow, Sophie. You're tired now. We'll go straight up if that's all right, Mrs Shaw. You'll call us just after three?'

'You can rely on me. 'Ere.' Mrs Shaw, having shut and locked the front door, picked up a candlestick from a hall table and lit its candle from her own. 'You'll want this. You saw the room, Mr Craddock, so you knows the way. Top of the 'ouse, turn left at the top of the stairs and the door's in front of you. Nice quiet back room. You won't 'ave long to sleep but it'll be peaceful while it lasts.'

The room was right under the roof. The dancing candlelight showed a low, sloping ceiling, a floor bare except for a single rag rug, a chest of drawers, a clothes press in the corner where the ceiling was highest, and a bed with a thin patchwork coverlet thrown over it. There was a fireplace but no fire, and the room was bitterly cold. A pattering somewhere behind the walls suggested mice.

Lemuel put the candlestick on the chest of drawers and went to investigate something under the bed. He pulled out a china basin. 'All comforts provided. We can both go before we get into bed. Well, come on, Sophie, get yourself ready for the night. It's getting on for midnight and we'll be up before half-past three. And we won't be going to sleep straight away, after all. Now, what are you dithering about? We're man and wife now, to all intents and purposes. That means we do what we got to do in front of each other and don't think anything about it. You *are* a little innocent, ain't you? You've everything to learn. Oh, and what about that money you brought? You'd better hand it over to me. I'll take charge of it now.'

It was as though she had been suddenly projected into another world, one whose existence she had never suspected before. She had, of course, known that husbands and wives on occasion shared a bed. Her father and Horatia had separate rooms but nearly always slept together in Henry's. But they had their own dressing rooms. They also had fires when it was cold, and Horatia was not alone with Henry as Sophia was now alone with Lemuel. Horatia had servants who would come in response to a tug on a bellrope, a family who would certainly make representations if she were in any way mistreated. She lived, in fact, in a world where there were rules to ensure her a measure of privacy and protection.

In this cold, cramped little room there were none of these things. Sophia found herself, to her own disbelief, watching Lemuel strip and relieve himself, and being obliged to do likewise under his interested and embarrassing gaze.

All the excitement she had once felt in his nearness, his touch, had vanished. She had never seen a naked man before. When he came and pressed himself against her and began to explore her with enquiring fingers, it felt not thrilling but horribly wrong. She tried to prise his fingers away and then attempted to pull herself out of his grasp, only to have her hands knocked aside and feel herself gripped harder.

Then he pushed her towards the bed, wrenched the covers back with one hand and shoved her down. As she fell back, the candlelight showed her how his body had changed. A moment later she understood that for some inexplicable reason he was intent on pushing that enormous excrescence inside her, and was paying no heed to her attempts to prevent him. She opened her mouth to scream.

He put his hand over it just in time. 'Shut up! This is a lodging house; there are other people asleep here. Do you want them to think I'm murdering you?'

Under his palm, Sophia, wild-eyed, turned her head from side to side and made noises which might have been attempts at words. Lemuel lifted his hand a fraction. 'You want to say something?'

'What are you doing? What are you *doing*?'

'Making love to you, you silly bitch. Don't you know *anything*? This is what marriage means. This is how babies are made.'

'What? You mean my parents . . . Father and Horatia . . . ?'

'Yes, of course, stupid. You're no more than a baby yourself, are you? Well, well. Tonight's the night you grow up,' said Lemuel.

She could never have imagined this. If anyone had told her that this was the truth behind the mystery about which she and her sisters had so often speculated, she wouldn't have believed it. She tried to scream again but he threatened to put a pillow over her face and she was reduced to moaning and uselessly struggling, and then to clutching the pillow over her face herself to muffle a shriek of sheer agony when he rammed himself into her and then began sawing up and down as though he wanted to carve her wide open. It seemed to go on for an eternity, until suddenly he gasped and sighed and flopped down on her, and she felt him at last withdraw.

'There you are,' he said. 'That's your introduction to married life. It won't be so painful next time, you'll see. Goodnight.'

He rolled off her and a moment later she realised with outrage that he had fallen asleep.

She lay there, staring in horror at the guttering candle. What had she done? Was there any way back? No, hardly, not after this. She couldn't go home again after this. There was nothing for it but to go on into the nightmare of the unknown with Lemuel. Oh, God. Oh, God. If only she could be back in her own warm room. If only she had never gone out to the landing that day and peered through that lattice screen. If only she had never set eyes on Lemuel.

She then became aware that she was sharing the bed with more than just one unpleasant companion. The lodging house had bedbugs.

Chapter Twenty-six
Duel Without Weapons

In the stage-coach, Sophia sat primly upright, squeezed between Lemuel and a thin young man in rusty black who looked like a clerk of some kind. From time to time she smiled weakly at the genteel woman opposite, who had already said that she was on her way to take up a post as a governess. She wondered if she was going to feel as lost as this for the rest of her days.

'Lost' was the word for it. She had no picture of the life to which she was travelling, no trust any more in the man who was taking her there, and she had lost her sense of identity. Who was she? She was no longer Sophia Whitmead, and couldn't see herself as Sophia Craddock. She was a being detached from roots and reality, jolting on her way to nowhere.

She was also sore and bruised from Lemuel's idea of lovemaking, itchy from the bedbugs and exhausted. She could guess now why Horatia had often seemed languid at breakfast. She had had no more than two hours' sleep last night before Mrs Shaw came to call them. She wished she were dead, and if a highwayman had stopped the coach and waved a pistol at her she would have tried her best to provoke him into firing it.

But no highwayman appeared. The stage-coach rumbled and swayed on its way, changing horses at frequent intervals. From time to time the passengers got out and went into this inn or that and were given food, which apparently had been included in the fare. Sophia ate and drank and learned to push her way through the crowd in order to get warm by the fires which most of the inn parlours provided. She also made commonplace conversation with Lemuel, partly because she had been reared to keep up appearances and did not want her fellow-passengers either to pity her or to suspect that she wasn't married, but partly too because she was afraid of making Lemuel angry.

They were past the last stop now and would be entering Bath very shortly. There, Lemuel said, they would spend the night in another cheap lodging house, and tomorrow they would travel the short distance on to Bristol. The day after that they would embark on the *Bristol Pearl*.

There really was, Sophia supposed miserably, a chance that the ship would sink before it reached America. Ships were lost quite often. She wouldn't care.

The night in the Bath lodging house was not much better than the one in

London. The room was just as shabby and this bed too was infested. She knew now what to expect from Lemuel, and, having grasped that there was no escape, she endured his advances quietly, hoping that the whole horrible business would be the sooner over. But she was still very sore from his first onslaught and her body tried to clench itself against him. His forced entry was nearly as agonising the second time as it was the first, and although she bit her hand and tried to keep silent, he resented her pitiful eyes and stifled whimpers.

'What's the matter with you? You're supposed to enjoy it, or at least not to make a fuss about it. Other women do, so why can't you?'

Afterwards, as before, he rolled over and went to sleep, and again, despite her desperate weariness, Sophia lay for a long time wretchedly wakeful. She cried for a while, but did it silently, because Lemuel would certainly be annoyed if her sobs disturbed him.

When she finally did doze off it was not for long because Lemuel shook her awake at dawn, anxious to get on to Bristol. 'We sail early tomorrow morning. We've got to be on board tonight.'

'We could go round the shipping offices,' Henry said, putting the matter baldly to Tarrant and Poole, the two footmen he proposed to take with him in pursuit of Lemuel and Sophia. 'But we'll start with Wagoner Street. His neighbours may know something.'

He drove the phaeton himself, wedging the three of them into it, and halted it outside the tenement house. Leaving the younger footman, Tarrant, to guard it from the street urchins who instantly collected, and telling Poole to accompany him, Henry strode militantly into the building.

Where no one apparently knew anything, or if they did, they weren't saying. Since Lemuel had lived in number six, Henry bypassed the lower floors in order to start with closer neighbours, but in vain. He had a feeling that he might have got more if he'd been willing to say why he wanted to trace Lemuel, but he could not bring himself to say, 'My daughter's run off with him.' As it was, he had the feeling that his tenants were closing ranks against the landlord, their common enemy.

Mrs Bradley in number five said Mr Bradley talked to Lemuel Craddock sometimes and maybe Lemuel had told him his plans, but Mr Bradley was at his work as a market porter and wouldn't be home until late. No, her husband hadn't said anything to her, not a word. 'You could try the first floor,' she said, 'or they might know something upstairs in seven and eight, but I think number seven's out at work. He's a builder.'

Number seven was indeed absent from home, and number eight was a depressed-looking elderly man who at first did nothing but insist that his rent was up to date. When at last convinced that they only wanted information about one of his neighbours, he said he was thankful to hear it; he'd always been a good tenant as far as he knew and no trouble to anyone and he'd be only too glad to help them if he knew anything about Mr Craddock, but unfortunately, he didn't . . .

And wouldn't tell them even if he did, said his closed expression.

Henry cut him short and retreated to the first floor to try numbers three and four. But the nurse who rented number four was away on a case and the woman in number three, who informed them of this, didn't advise trying to track her down. 'Typhoid, that's what her patient's got. We'll none of us go near her when she comes back. She won't know anything, anyhow; spends most of her time half-cut. If you go in her rooms, watch your step. There's bottles all over the place, including rolling about on the floor.'

Number three was herself trying to cope with several tearful small children, two of whom had chickenpox; her husband, like Mr Bradley, was out at his work, and no, she'd had nothing to do with the Craddock household since Mrs Craddock, poor soul, died of exhaustion and the lung-rot down there beside the mangle.

She said it expressionlessly and no one could claim that she was saying it was Henry's fault, but Henry withdrew angrily, knowing that he had been offered backhanded insolence, knowing that Poole had heard it too, and finding it all the more offensive because he could do nothing about it.

Exasperated, he led the way down to the ground floor and as a last resort tried numbers one and two. Number one was empty but at number two, at last, they did get something, if not very much.

The sole tenant, a man, was in, because he worked at night as a doorman in a gentlemen's gambling club, and slept by day. When finally woken up by determined hammering at his door, he bellowed at them to wait while he got his breeches on, and threw the door open to confront them with an angry and unshaven face and a broad bare chest. Told that this was Mr Henry Whitmead, the landlord, and asked if he knew where Lemuel Craddock had gone, he snapped, 'No, I don't. But where he works, they might know, and that's at the White Horse in Fetter Lane. Can I get back to sleep now?'

'He'll have had workmates there, sir,' said Poole. 'Fellow-grooms. As like as not, he'll have talked to them.'

'We'll enquire. Give this man a guinea, Poole,' Henry ordered, and a few minutes later he and the footmen had crammed themselves into the phaeton again and were rattling away towards the Strand. When they reached the White Horse a coach had just come in and the inn yard was a bustle of unharnessing and unloading, while passengers disembarked, greeted people who had come to meet them and flooded into the inn for refreshment. It was ten frustrating minutes before demands to see the ostler at length produced Dick Grant, who came to attend them with a bridle over his arm and an air of only having a moment of his time to spare.

'Lemuel Craddock? Yes, that's right, he worked here up to yesterday. He was a good enough groom but I've replaced him with a better. Is he in trouble?'

'We need to find him,' said Henry neutrally. 'Do you know where he's gone? We believe he may be making for America, but from which port?'

'Does he owe you money?' Grant asked shrewdly, taking in Henry's good clothes and vehicle, and the presence of the footmen.

Henry, with rage, saw that here too was a solidarity of the poor against the rich. Grant hadn't liked Craddock but he wasn't going to set a creditor on him, all the same.

In Wagoner Street, where his identity was known, he couldn't have borne to hint at the reason why he was pursuing Lemuel. But here at the White Horse, where he had no links with anyone, it was different. 'Craddock does not owe me money. He has abducted my daughter. If you know where he is, for God's sake tell me!'

Grant recognised the note of sincerity. 'I don't know much because he didn't say much about his plans. He's a secretive sort in a lot of ways. I guessed he had a girl, though – it's easy to tell that sort of thing. And yes, it's right that he's bound for America. He did say that much.'

'Did he mention the name of the ship or where he was sailing from?'

'Not where he was sailing from, no.' Grant frowned. 'But he did say the ship's name. Now what was it . . . ?'

Impatiently, Henry waited while Grant thought it over, shook his head, called another groom, and asked him what Lemuel had said. Eventually, they agreed that the ship had probably been called the *Pearl*.

'And she sails on Thursday. I remember that for sure,' Grant said.

Henry fished in his waistcoat pocket for some more money, thrust it at Grant and turned to the footmen. 'I've never heard of her. I know enough of the shipping world to be fairly sure that she doesn't sail out of the Thames. But if he's already arranged his passage, he must have used a London shipping office. She will be listed, therefore, at one of them, and so will the port from which she is to leave. You two can go round the offices; you can divide them between you. Take hackneys and report to me at Hanover Square as soon as you've finished or as soon as you trace a ship called the *Pearl*. If you do, ask if a man called Craddock is one of the passengers, but it doesn't mean much if the answer's no. He may have used a false name. Now, Poole, you take . . .'

In a moment, they were gone, leaving Grant to stand amazed, the bridle thrown over his shoulder so that he could hold three golden guineas in one hand while he counted them over with the other. Three guineas, for virtually nothing.

He'd think more kindly of Lemuel Craddock after this. He didn't envy that silly girl who'd run off with him, but maybe her father would get her back. As for Lemuel, Dick Grant now wished him well and hoped he'd get safe to America.

'Bristol,' said Henry, striding back and forth across the morning room, while Horatia and Lucy-Anne, seated together on the sofa, watched him anxiously and the two footmen stood by, awaiting orders. 'Bristol. It has to be. No one appears to have heard of a ship called the *Pearl*, but there's a *Bristol Pearl* sailing out of Bristol – as one might naturally conclude! – on Thursday morning, and that, according to the ostler at the White Horse, is the right day. The damned clerk in that shipping office either couldn't or wouldn't produce the passenger list but that is the ship, or I'm a Dutchman. She's scheduled for a dawn departure.'

He stopped by the hearth and glared into the fire, thinking furiously. 'This is Tuesday midday. We can do it. Poole, go and organise a post-chaise. Make sure you get a good vehicle and sound horses. Tarrant, go and see that whatever you and Poole need for an overnight journey is packed ready, and tell my man to pack a valise for me. Make haste.'

'Do you wish me to accompany you?' asked Horatia. 'You should have a lady with you, surely? If you find Sophia, she will no doubt be glad of female support. It is very annoying; I was hoping to attend a card party with Elizabeth this afternoon. But I'll come if you require it. If we do bring Sophia back, Tarrant and Poole can hire mounts or travel in another chaise, I suppose.'

'I am unaware,' said Henry coldly, 'that I expressed any wish for a lady to accompany me. It is very conscientious of you, Horatia, especially as Sophia is not your own child, but you can stay at home and carry out your intended programme. I have no need of you. If and when we catch the runaways, it could be a most unpleasant confrontation and I would rather you were not there.'

'But Sophia will be there,' said Lucy-Anne. 'Horatia is correct, Henry. You ought to have a lady with you. I doubt if the confrontation will come to much.' She raised her lorgnette and studied her son's face through it. 'You are taking two men – plus at least one hired postilion – and Craddock presumably is on his own except for Sophia. Getting her away from him won't be difficult.'

'And they can scarcely be married,' Horatia added. 'She's under age and looks younger than she is. Even if Craddock has obtained a special licence, no one would perform the ceremony without asking a great many questions. Very likely marriage isn't his intention, in any case. You are in the right of it, Mother-in-law. There should be no difficulty about separating them.'

'Quite,' said Lucy-Anne. 'If you don't wish to take Horatia, Henry, I think I'd better come. I'll ring for Letty and—'

'Don't be absurd, Mother! You can't possibly come. The journey would be far too much for you. Besides . . .' Henry's voice, which had been brusque, suddenly became chilling. 'Sophia has placed herself well outside the world in which her sensibilities are something to be considered. She will have to do without female support, as you put it. She will have to do without a great many things henceforth. I have not the slightest intention of ever bringing her back to this house again. And that is all I'm going to say. I have no more time to stand here arguing. Mother, Horatia, I will see you on my return.'

He would allow no more discussion. Poole and Tarrant reappeared very quickly, with their errands accomplished, and in what seemed only a few minutes they and Henry and their overnight valises had been bundled into the post-chaise and were clattering out of Hanover Square. Lucy-Anne and Horatia's further protests were ignored, but they were swept down to the front door to witness the departure. As they returned unhappily up the stairs they saw Phoebe and Anne peering down from the second floor, and hastened on up to join them.

'We overheard,' said Phoebe, without apology. 'We overheard everything. We wanted to rush down and join in but Anne said it wouldn't be any use.'

'It wouldn't,' said Anne. 'If Father won't listen to Grandmamma or Horatia, we know he won't listen to us. He'd only have got angrier. But what did he mean by saying he isn't going to bring Sophia back here? Where will he take her instead? Grandmamma, what is he going to do?'

'I don't know for sure,' said Lucy-Anne. 'But . . .'

'There will be gossip,' Horatia said distractedly. 'Oh, you may look at me with a curl to your lip, Anne, but gossip will affect you girls and your prospects just as much as it will affect me and my place in society. It is a serious thing, I promise you. If it gets about that your sister has behaved so scandalously and has been, well, put away, we shall never hear the end of it.'

'Put away?' said Phoebe in horror.

'I fear so,' said Horatia. 'It's difficult to think of any other possibility. There are various charitable establishments for fallen women as they are called. Your father contributes to one of them.'

'But . . . oh, *no!*' wailed Phoebe.

Lucy-Anne put out a hand and laid it quieteningly on her shoulder. 'Come into my room, all of you. I've something to say to you.'

They followed obediently into Lucy-Anne's sitting room. It was a comfortable place, hung with velvet curtains to keep out draughts, and very private. 'Now then,' Lucy-Anne said as soon as the door was shut, 'Horatia has been more or less forbidden to go by her husband, and he certainly wouldn't want Anne or Phoebe making the journey to Bristol without his permission. But I agree wholeheartedly that one of us *must* be there if he catches up with Sophia, to comfort her and try to soften his mind towards her. I think I should go. I don't require my son's permission to do anything I feel inclined to do, and if any of us can exert authority over him, I can. I must tell you, my dears, that I'm not sure how much ascendancy I have, but I will do my best. I shall set out at once.'

'But Grandmamma, can you get there in time?' Phoebe asked.

'Indeed, you could not,' said Horatia. 'It would mean hard travelling and the weather's turning cold. What Henry said was true – it would be far too much for you.'

'Rubbish. I can and I will,' said Lucy-Anne. 'Letty shall come with me to look after me and I will doze in the carriage. I'll do it, never fear.'

'But what about money?' Anne asked anxiously.

'You can take what's left of my allowance for the month,' Horatia said. 'But Henry expects me to account for it.'

Anne and Phoebe looked at each other in surprise. It had never previously occurred to either of them that Horatia was as much constrained by their father's will as they were. Horatia did not notice the exchange of glances. 'I should have to pretend I lost the money at cards,' she said. 'It isn't so very much, so I don't think he'd complain. But that's the trouble – it isn't very much.'

'It doesn't have to be.' Lucy-Anne was pulling the bell for Letty, and laughing. 'I learned quite early in life how very useful it is to have a secret supply of money. I've always made sure of keeping some by me. Ah, Letty. We're going to make a journey. Kindly pack a valise with changes of clothes and toilet articles for me and for yourself, and tell Ames to send out for another post-chaise, a closed one, please. Expense doesn't matter. I want two postilions to escort us – then I needn't take any more staff away from you, Horatia. I also want the best horses.'

'But, ma'am . . . !'

'Don't cluck, Letty. Do as you're told at once,' said Lucy-Anne, and with a pleased air watched Letty go obediently away. Turning to her grand-daughters and her daughter-in-law she gave them her witch's smile. 'My husband and, later on, Henry have always given me an allowance, much like yours, Horatia. I accounted for it to my husband, just as you do, but I have always refused to account for it to Henry, and even with George I managed to falsify an invoice or two and put something by without him knowing. Over the years I have saved quite a nice little nest-egg. I have enough by me, I promise you, for ten post-chaises. Don't worry. If I can only reach Bristol in time, there is a chance that I can rescue Sophia. It is a sorry thing,' Lucy-Anne added grimly, 'that she should need saving from her father as much as from that confounded Lemuel Craddock.'

'It is a very shocking thing that she has done,' said Horatia seriously. 'There are those who would say she has brought retribution on herself.'

'You mean well,' said Lucy-Anne. 'But young people today are such prudes.'

Henry and Horatia were of course perfectly right in their misgivings. The journey would be extremely exhausting, and Lucy-Anne's talk of dozing in the carriage had been sheer bravado. The mere thought of the interminable hours on the road made her quail. But go she must. In the morning room she had got a good look at Henry's face through her lorgnette and she had hated what she saw in it.

It was an odd thing, Lucy-Anne thought – her husband George had spent years of their married life far away from her, Henry had spent years of his boyhood absent at school, and when they were at home both of them lived lives essentially separate from hers, but she knew them both inside out. Henry had loved his youngest daughter very much but that love would make his anger greater and not less. Sophia must on no account be left to her father's mercies.

The cold, exhausting journey must be borne. A closed carriage and warm clothes should at least keep the cold at bay. She had a heavy old purple brocade dress which would do for travelling.

Be there when Henry found Sophia, she must, and she would.

With a groan, Lucy-Anne awoke to find herself in an unfamiliar and depressing room. Letty, already dressed, was setting a candle and a tray containing hot chocolate and buttered rolls down on the bedside table. 'I went downstairs to fetch your breakfast and had my own bite while I was there. I'm sorry the rolls aren't fresh. The chocolate's all right – I made it myself. They're a dead lazy lot here, begging your pardon, ma'am. We wouldn't have got a thing else, and I can only hope your sheets last night weren't damp. It's half past four and you did say we was to be on the road at five. They're getting the horses out now. I can hear the clatter in the yard.'

Lucy-Anne sat up. Every separate bone in her body was aching. It was years since she had taken a drive of longer than an hour but yesterday they had set out at two o'clock in the afternoon and, except for pauses to change horses and one stop for a meal, they had kept going until nearly eleven. Ten more weary hours at least faced her today, and she strongly suspected that last night's sheets had indeed been damp. The mattress had certainly been damnably lumpy. Everything in this nasty little inn seemed to be of poor quality.

'I wouldn't have said we should put up here, except that it isn't a proper posting house and I was pretty sure we wouldn't find ourselves sharing a roof with Henry,' she said candidly. She had few secrets from Letty. 'We certainly didn't want that. There'd only be trouble and he'd try to send me home. I sincerely hope the horses were properly looked after last night.'

'Me too, since we've got to take the same ones on this morning,' Letty said. 'I think the postilions thought us mad, or up to something dubious, when you insisted they turn off the Great West Road to find a cheap hostelry.'

'I'd like to know what kind of dubious errand an old lady like me could be on,' said Lucy-Anne. 'They can hardly suspect us of being an eloping couple.'

Letty giggled. Sometimes Lucy-Anne made her feel young again, and not just because her mistress was so much her senior that even Letty's forty-nine was youthful by comparison. She had the saltiness of the older generation, before the world grew prim. She was exhilarating.

'Postilions aren't paid to think, anyhow,' said Lucy-Anne. 'They're paid to make sure we get to where we're going.' She pushed an unfinished roll aside. 'Help me to dress, Letty. Five o'clock I said, and five o'clock I meant. If that ship's sailing early on Thursday the passengers will have to go on board tonight. We've got to get there, and we've a long way to go. What's the weather like, by the way?'

'It's raining,' said Letty, worriedly.

Rumbling wheels; the sigh of the rain on the carriage roof. It was a thin, persistent drizzling rain which gradually saturated everything, turning roads into long winding bogs. The clatter of hooves; the splash and squelch as the chaise passed through puddles; the creak and jingle of harness; the incessant jolts.

'It's a fair assumption that this vehicle didn't come from my son's coachworks,' Lucy-Anne said sourly to Letty. 'Henry has introduced many improvements into the springing and suspension of the vehicles he builds and I'm quite sure this dreadful affair doesn't possess any of them. The windows don't shut properly, either.'

The chaise at that moment crashed through a series of water-filled ruts, throwing its passengers heavily against each other, and demonstrated the truth of Lucy-Anne's last remark as dirty water splashed up and in through the crack at the top of the window.

'And,' said Lucy-Anne irritably, as she and Letty straightened themselves again, 'I've always understood that roads are becoming steadily better. This is as bad as anything I remember as a girl. Where are we?'

'No more than two hours from Bristol, ma'am.' Letty was tired, too, and her voice faded at the prospect of those two hours. She was also worried about her mistress. She was fond of her and greatly admired the gutsiness which made Lucy-Anne Whitmead refuse to dress unobtrusively so that people wouldn't notice her toothless witch-face, but insist instead on brocades, out-of-fashion and exceedingly obtrusive hoops, and dyed ostrich feathers for her hair. Letty didn't like to see Lucy-Anne's face grey with weariness and cold, and with that worried crease between her brows.

'We've made good time,' she said with determined cheerfulness, 'especially since the last change of horses. These seem to be getting a move on.'

'The second team we had today certainly didn't,' Lucy-Anne agreed, remembering the frustrated rage with which she had watched twelve miles of wet countryside crawl by when despite her request, repeated at every stop, for the best horses, she found herself behind a team too elderly and poorly fettled to get beyond a jog-trot.

But the countryside was changing. She remembered how, on her long-ago journeys to Bath, she used to watch the hills grow higher and the green of the grass deeper as she travelled westwards. From these signs now, she knew that they were in the right part of the world. The journey would soon be over. She shifted position, trying to ease the pain in her joints, and prayed that her strength would hold out.

Sophia's first impression of Bristol, as the stage-coach clattered through the rain towards it, was of rows of houses and chimneys puffing smoke at the low clouds. She had seen few places other than London. She couldn't even claim to have seen Bath, since they had arrived there and departed again in darkness. She could remember passing through Guildford as a child, and recalled it as a country town with a castle wall and a market place. She could also remember, dimly, one of her governesses telling her that London was twelve times bigger than Bristol.

Which ought to mean that twelve Bristols would fit into London, but that wasn't the way it looked. It seemed huge and bewildering. When they had disembarked from the stage-coach and taken a brief meal consisting of a cup of coffee and some bread and butter and ham, Lemuel shouldered his bundle, told her to carry her own, and led her confidently off through the streets, as though he knew where he was going. She couldn't imagine how.

They hadn't made much conversation on the journey, but now she found the courage to ask how he knew where he was.

'I don't, but the port must be this way. Can't you see the masts of the ships between the houses? When we get there, if we don't find the *Bristol Pearl* by looking, someone'll tell us.'

The drizzling rain was a thorough nuisance. Her cloak was stout, but the wet still found its way through and she was cold. She had a shawl in her bundle but she didn't want to take it out and get everything else wet in the process. She had already come to realise that the few things she had brought with her were nothing like enough for the journey ahead, even if she kept them dry.

She had also, however, learned better than to complain. In silence she accompanied Lemuel through the streets until the smell of the river came to them through the rain, and they came out on to a wide quay above an expanse of grey, slopping water.

Lemuel looked to the right and said, 'There! She'll be one of those for sure,' and pointed to where three or four vessels were moored in a line against a wall. Steep flights of steps led down towards them. 'She'll be that nearest one, that's being loaded,' Lemuel said. 'Come on.'

He was right. A few minutes later they were standing on the quay above the ship he had pointed out, watching a line of dockers carrying sacks and boxes into her hold. The name on her hull was freshly painted and stood out. 'The *Bristol Pearl*,' said Lemuel in triumph. 'Didn't I say it would be easy? Well, there she is, my girl. That'll be our home till we get across the Atlantic. Quite a beauty, ain't she?'

She had certainly been recently painted and varnished – all the rest of her as well as her name – and even to Sophia's inexperienced eyes the ropes and the furled canvas looked fairly new. 'She's bigger than I expected,' said Sophia, impressed.

'You won't think so when we're aboard,' Lemuel said. 'She'll carry every bushel of cargo and every living soul that can be crammed into her and that the sails'll pull. That's how the owners make their profit and leave enough to pay the captain and crew. We'll be squashed together like kittens in a basket, and let us hope that we don't end up drowning like kittens no one wants.'

She wouldn't mind if they did, Sophia thought again. To sink into the ocean, to drown, to be free of this hellish life to which she had committed herself. To sleep on the bed of the sea and never again in Lemuel's. Bliss! 'She looks sound enough to me,' she said.

'No way to tell. A lick of paint'll hide a lot. You soon learn that working with horses. You can put a shine on the coat of any old nag and polish its harness till the sunlight on the metalwork nearly blinds you, but it's still the same old nag under all that. However, I fancy she'll do.' He tilted his head back to look at the masts. 'The day'll come when ships'll be driven by steam, you know. They'll maybe have more room in them then, when they don't need so many crewmen.'

'Steam? Imagine!' Sophia, however, was now thoroughly damp and chilled and wanted to do something about it. 'Can we go aboard yet? We ought to get out of the rain.'

'Stop here. I'll find out.'

She waited, sheltering in the lee of a small, locked hut, until he came back. He was shaking his head. 'We can't board until after seven tonight. So we'll have to find something to do until then. The man I spoke to – the first mate, I think – he told me there's a place just round the corner here where we can hire a room for a few hours and it won't cost us much, and we can get a meal before we leave.'

314

'All right. But, Lemuel, I know it's raining, but I really ought to buy some extra clothes. I need a second shawl and another cloak and maybe a dress, something in a good hard-wearing cloth,' she added hastily, sensing disapproval. 'I just haven't got sufficient for the voyage. We've enough money, haven't we, with what I brought?'

'And we'll need every penny of it. You'll make do with what you have and if you didn't have sense enough to bring enough in the first place, that's your bad luck.'

'But, Lemuel—' She stopped in mid-sentence. His face had become thunderous.

'You said you wanted to get out of the rain, didn't you? Well, we're going to.' His hand on her arm gripped her tightly as he hurried them both away from the quay. 'We're going to take a nice, dry room from now until seven tonight and you can dry your clothes while we're in it because you won't be needing them. You can guess how we're going to pass the time, I fancy. Oh, don't look like that, for God's sake! Come *on*.' He was walking so fast he was almost dragging her. 'You've got to get used to it,' said Lemuel roughly. 'Sooner or later, you will, but it can't be soon enough for me. I want to make love to a smiling face instead of a miserable one, and I'd like to begin this afternoon.'

So she was expected not only to let Lemuel do these horrible things to her; she must also pretend to enjoy it, and smile while it was going on. She wondered if he had ever tried to smile while someone hurt him as intensely as this. Enjoy it? Oh, God, what a fool she'd been. While Lemuel pumped himself up and down and her protesting body, trying to shut him out, magnified its own pain, she tried to think about America, and a new life there, but it was no use. She would still be Lemuel's prisoner; there would still be this bedroom horror.

If the *Pearl* didn't sink, could she bring herself one day, out in the Atlantic, to slip through the rail and over the side? At the thought that she had come to this, that the best thing left for her was to be swallowed up in the cold salt seas, self-pity poured over her and she began to cry. Lemuel saw the tears and read them as defiance.

'I thought I told you to smile,' he said, and hit her.

Before it was time to leave the little inn where they had spent the afternoon, Sophia had learned finally to swallow her tears, to smile no matter what her misery of mind and body. She had also been instructed in the art of rekindling a man's enthusiasm, regardless of the fact that rekindling it was the last thing she wanted to do.

Before they got up she had even won a qualified approval from Lemuel. 'You'll be all right in time. I'll make you fit to bear the name of Mrs Craddock before I'm done. Make you fit to bear my children, too.'

She would never bear his children. Her decision was made, and when the time came, when she plunged down to the unforgiving waters and they rushed into her mouth, she wouldn't cry. Anything would be better than to be Mrs Craddock and mother to another generation of that odious family.

She had made a terrifying choice, but the fact of having made it gave her strength. Meanwhile, she would make what remained of her life easier by pretending. She went downstairs with Lemuel and, over the meal of bread and cheese and ale that he bought for them, made herself talk to him, asking him to tell her what he knew of America. At seven he paid their bill and once more she put on her cloak, which was thoroughly dry by now, and comfortingly warm, took up her inadequate bundle and followed him outside.

It had at least stopped raining. It was growing dark, but low in the west there were bars of red light between the cloud. When they reached the quay, crowded now instead of empty as it had been earlier, the sunset was reflected in the puddles, mingling with the yellow of oil lamps on tall poles. 'The weather's going to improve,' Lemuel said.

'Where do we go?' asked Sophia, looking about her at the crowd. Many were clutching bundles like her own; a few, mostly the better-dressed ones, had roped boxes. Some were huddled into groups with relatives who had come to say goodbye – embracing, being wished well, promising to write, to send money home, shedding tears which were allowed to flow without rebuke.

'Down those steps there.' Lemuel pushed her forward. 'Now, watch your footing and don't fall. There's no rail. Excuse me, sir.' He stopped as a tall man in a footman's livery got in the way at the top of the steps. 'We'd like to pass, if you don't mind. We're going aboard.'

But the man, far from moving, planted himself still more firmly, feet apart, turned his head, and shouted, 'Over here, sir!' and Sophia, who had recognised him, looked round and saw a familiar figure marching out of the crowd and the dusk to join them. 'Thank you, Poole,' said Henry Whitmead.

'*Father!*' said Sophia, on a gasp of relief.

'Excellent work, Poole. And here is Tarrant to help us.' She had greeted him with thankfulness, but Henry seemed scarcely aware of his daughter. He turned from the footmen to look not at her but at Lemuel. 'And you, I take it, are Mr Lemuel Craddock? You must forgive my uncertainty but we only met the once.'

'You know bloody well I'm Craddock,' said Lemuel truculently. 'And what I'd like to know is, how did you get after us?'

'My daughter, fortunately, mentioned your first name in the letter she left for her family.'

'You what?' Lemuel turned on Sophia so fiercely that even with her father there she backed away from him in fright, and it was Tarrant, not Henry Whitmead, who said, 'Here, none of that,' and put himself between them.

'You left a *letter*?' Lemuel shouted. 'You put my name in it, you little bitch?'

'Yes, I did, and I'm glad I did!' From a position of safety, Sophia spoke the truth. 'You're a barbarian!'

'Am I, indeed? Well, my love, may I remind you that you're my wife?'

Sophia gaped, momentarily speechless, while Henry seized Lemuel's shoulder and jerked the younger man round to face him once again. 'What's this? You've married her? You can't have. She's under age.'

Lemuel laughed. 'There's ways and means. Some hard-up parsons with a taste for brandy'll do anything for a bribe.'

'It's a lie!' Horrified, Sophia almost shouted it. 'We're not married! He said we'd get the ship's captain to wed us!'

For the first time, her father looked at her directly. His pale brown eyes were without a trace of kindness. Then he turned once more to Lemuel. 'I require to see the marriage lines. If they exist, then there's no more to be said. She's your wife and I will resign her to you. Well? Where are they?'

'There are *no* marriage lines!' said Sophia desperately. 'I'm not his wife and he can't pretend I am!'

'You're wearing a ring,' said Henry.

Her first thought on seeing her father and the footmen had been that here at last was rescue, even though her father would certainly be very angry. She could hardly expect otherwise. But now, with a chill under her heart, she saw something in him worse than anger. He was prepared to reject her, to abandon her to Lemuel.

'He gave me the ring so that I could pass as his wife.' As though the wedding ring were impregnated with leprosy or smallpox, Sophia clawed it off. 'But I'm *not*, and I won't go with him. If you make me, I shall kill myself. I'd already made up my mind to, before you found us. Take the ring back, Lemuel, take it!'

She would not go near him, but threw it at his feet instead. He stooped and pocketed it. 'My thanks,' he said mockingly.

'Dear, dear. Whatever did you do to her?' Henry turned back to Lemuel. 'She seems to have changed her opinion of you very drastically. But the real point is the marriage lines. Are you married or not and, if you continue to claim that you are, where is the proof?'

Lemuel shrugged. 'I could say she'd got the lines stuffed in her clothes somewhere and it's not my fault if she won't bring them out, but come to think of it I'm not that bothered. I don't really want her along. We're not married, Mr Whitmead, though she's right about the notion that we'd marry at sea. I did have that in mind. But not for love of your girl. The fact is, your father threw my family out of their cottage at Chestnuts, and you put my rent up in London and drove my mother to her death sooner than God intended. I took your girl to get my own back on you and I didn't mean her to be happy. Trouble was, I didn't foresee that her being a misery would get me down the way it has. You take her back and welcome. I'm off.'

'Lemuel.' Sophia's voice was a whisper. She hated him and wanted to be free of him but while he still desired her she could keep a shred of self-respect. Now even that was gone.

'You can go to America and welcome,' Henry said coolly to Lemuel. 'But not without paying. Poole and Tarrant, you know what to do. Make a good job of it but don't go too far. His corpse would be embarrassing and I don't want him too badly injured to get on board his ship, either. Take him off the quay and find somewhere secluded first.'

The two footmen were already stripping off their coats and wigs, transforming themselves instantly from figures of formal dignity to a pair of powerfully built young men with menacing intentions. Lemuel stepped back, clenching his fists. 'What the devil's this?'

'Nemesis,' said Henry. 'Merely Nemesis, Mr Craddock, if you know what that means.'

As Poole and Tarrant closed in, Lemuel struck out at Poole, was neatly parried, saw that he was outnumbered and turned to run. Dodging people and luggage, he fled towards the end of the quay, where huts and warehouses provided deep shadows and a chance of cover. But they were after him at once, like deerhounds. Standing frozen, Sophia saw vague figures lurching to and fro, locked in conflict, and heard, faintly, the sound of fists on flesh.

Her father's voice, addressing her, brought her attention back to him. 'I am assuming, Sophia, that you are not in fact married. But I will ask you once more. Have you been through any kind of ceremony?'

Sophia shook her head.

'Good. Are you ready to come with me, then? We can return to my carriage, which is waiting nearby, and Poole and Tarrant will rejoin us when they have – er – finished the commission I gave them. Perhaps you would take my arm.'

'Th . . . thank you. Are we going home now?' She wanted nothing in the world now more than to be safely back in Hanover Square, back on the second-floor landing, looking at the world through the lattice, and protected by it from such savages as Lemuel.

But when she looked into her father's face she saw there no reassurance. 'Home? Oh no, Sophia. After this, you can hardly expect just to return to life as it was before. Your sisters are still innocent girls. Do you want them to become contaminated? No, no, my dear. You're not coming home.'

'My mistress can't get out and stand in the rain!' Letty protested through the carriage window, resisting the efforts of the postilion to open the door. 'She's tired and she's old and she'll catch her death out there. Put sacks under the wheels, can't you?'

'We have, miss,' said the postilion doggedly. 'We're very sorry, but the sacks just sink into the mud. We'll never shift unless we lighten the weight.'

'Stop being obstructive, Letty!' Lucy-Anne snapped. 'Let the man open that door and help you out and then give me a hand down. We've got to get moving again.'

Clicking her tongue with disapproval, Letty did as she was told. There were trees at the side of the road which gave some shelter but the rain still dripped through the branches, and it was cold.

'I've no time to waste,' said Lucy-Anne to the postilions. 'Damn this weather! We'd have been in Bristol by now but for this.'

'We'll do it now, madam.' The senior postilion had started out by regarding the crone in outdated hoops and purple brocade and her scrawny, middle-aged companion as comical eccentrics, but had by now grasped that Lucy-Anne was a lady of character, and that whatever her errand might be it was both serious and urgent. He touched his cap and went back to the business of getting the offside wheels out of the glutinous uphill rut in which they were stuck.

318

A heavily laden cart had evidently passed this way not long ago, and on this steep slope its trail was as lethal to following traffic as a gin-trap. The horses, mired above the girths, their coats glistening with a mixture of rain and sweat, and steam rising from their bodies, struggled to drag it free, heads down, hooves pawing for a foothold and continually sliding back.

But with the carriage now empty, they were making an impression at last. The men threw a further set of sacks under the wheels and this time, instead of spinning uselessly, they began, slowly, to turn. With a heave and an alarming sideways tilt, the vehicle came free. At the same moment the sky darkened still more and the rain grew heavier. One of the postilions ran to open the carriage door again and help the passengers back in, but even crossing the few feet of open space between the trees and the carriage was enough to drench them.

'There's rugs under the seats. You'd better wrap up in those and take those cloaks off,' advised the postilion as he shut the door on them.

'Oh, this is dreadful,' Letty moaned, fishing for the rugs. 'Ma'am, you shouldn't be exposed to all this, you shouldn't. Pah! This rug smells of stables! I think it's a horse-blanket.'

'At least it's dry.' Lucy-Anne shed not only her cloak but her saturated hat, and took the blanket gratefully. 'I'd rather not be exposed to this sort of thing myself, but I've no choice. We've *got* to get to Bristol, and soon. If Henry finds my grand-daughter, and somehow I'm becoming more and more sure that he will, I must be there.'

She could not herself have said why she was now so sure that Henry would find Sophia in Bristol, but if her certainty owed nothing to logic but was coming to her through some sixth sense which had no official existence, it was certainty just the same.

She felt cold and exhausted and ill and would have given almost anything to be home again, tucked up in her warm bed with a hot brick for her feet and a comforting cup of chocolate to drink, but it was her duty to go on.

Huddled in the rug, she dozed a little, and roused to find that the rain had ceased and that, at last, they were rolling into a town. It was nearly dusk. The mire on the roads had wasted, literally, hours of their time.

'Where are we, Letty? Do you know?'

'Yes, ma'am. This is Bristol.'

'Thank God.'

'Where do we go now, ma'am? If Mr Whitmead's caught up with them, how do we know where he did it?'

'We try the main coaching inns first. Then find out where the ship is and try there, and all as fast as possible. Put your head out and shout to the men, Letty. Oh, if only we had more time!' Lucy-Anne said in frustration.

The postilions were fortunately experienced and knew where the inns were. They tried three in succession, but no one reported any fracas or dispute between arriving stage passengers and any gentleman driving in by post-chaise. In the third inn, however, an ostler remembered a gentleman and two footmen who had come by chaise and gone off somewhere on foot. No, the postilions had taken themselves off; they weren't here to be questioned. But yes, the gentleman was of stocky build and yes, one of his men had enquired the way to the quay and asked about a ship called the *Bristol Pearl*.

'The quay!' said Lucy-Anne. 'Do you know where it is?'

'Certainly, madam,' said the senior postilion, slightly affronted. 'I've been to Bristol many a time.'

'Then take us there at once!'

Henry and Sophia were there. As the post-chaise halted by the entrance to the quay, Lucy-Anne saw them immediately. They were coming towards the road, and heads were turning as they passed, because Sophia was weeping so wildly, and Henry's grip on her arm was more that of an arresting officer than a father. But no one was going to interfere, and not only because the pair were being escorted by two large if oddly dishevelled footmen. From time to time quaysides, inn yards and post-houses were enlivened by stormy scenes when angry parents and guardians intercepted runaways. It was always interesting, but it was no outsider's business.

Lucy-Anne called to the postilions to halt, told Letty to stay where she was, and clambered out of the carriage. A chill wind blew around her ears and she dragged her blanket protectively over her head. Rich purple skirts swaying beneath the makeshift shawl, she hurried towards her son and her grand-daughter as fast as her elderly joints and the weight of her peculiar costume would allow.

'Henry! Sophia!'

'Good God. Mother!' Henry stopped short. 'How in the world do you come to be here?'

'I followed you,' said Lucy-Anne. 'I'd have been here before except for this accursed weather. Oh, Sophia, I'm so thankful. You're safe!'

'No, I'm not. Oh, Grandmamma!' wailed Sophia, and tried to break away from her father in order, at last, to find refuge in friendly arms. Henry, however, held on to her.

'What do you mean, Sophia?' Lucy-Anne enquired. 'Where's the man, by the way, this Lemuel Craddock you ran off with?'

'Poole and Tarrant have given him a little lesson in respect for his betters,' said Henry. 'Presently, he'll be on his way to America, somewhat bruised in body and, I trust, much improved in his morals. He didn't marry her, it appears, which is fortunate because Sophia has no wish to go with him. Have you, Sophia? Unfortunately, she doesn't seem to want to come with me either, but there, I'm afraid, she has no choice. Now, Mother, you really shouldn't be here. You look very unwell, and whatever is that thing you've got draped round you? It looks like a horse-blanket.'

'It is. What of it? Let Sophia go, Henry. Let her come to me. It's all right, Sophia; it really is all right. We're going home now and everything will be just as it was.'

'No, it won't. Father says I can't come home! He says I'm a f . . . fallen woman and he's going to put me in the Magdalen Hospital!'

320

'In the—?'

'To do what Sophia has done,' said Henry, 'a young woman must obviously be a moral defective if not completely out of her mind. I cannot allow her back into the company of Anne and Phoebe.'

'Why not?' demanded Lucy-Anne.

'Don't be ridiculous, Mother. It's unthinkable. In the Magdalen Hospital, she will be segregated from society but also safe from the danger of falling into prostitution, and her mental condition can be carefully studied and if necessary treated. In time, perhaps, Sophia, you may be released into respectable domestic employment, and you may think yourself very fortunate. I could if I wished have you confined in a private lunatic asylum. But as I have long contributed to the Hospital's finances, it will be easy to find you a place there and—'

'It's like a workhouse,' Sophia sobbed. 'I can't go there, I won't!'

'And how would you know what the Magdalen is like, Miss? Who told you? Have you, unknown to me, been mixing with others of your kind?'

'Quiet, both of you, please!' said Lucy-Anne. 'Don't attract a crowd. Henry, you can't do this.'

'I *won't* go. I'd rather drown myself. I was going to and I wish I could!' moaned Sophia.

'Quite,' said Lucy-Anne. 'Edward Harper was involved in trying to set up an earlier version of the Magdalen and backed out because he said it was going to be organised more as a prison than a refuge. Sophia is coming home!'

'Mother, much as I respect you, I am the head of the household and I can and will make what dispositions I see fit for its members. Sophia has utterly betrayed me. If I now choose to put her in the Magdalen or in an asylum, or simply throw her into the street, you cannot prevent me.'

Sophia's eyes were on her, pleading, begging for help. Lucy-Anne, now, was all that Sophia had.

Long ago, her great-aunt Henrietta had wished her power and freedom, but she had never had either. And now, at the age of seventy-four, standing chilled and weary and idiotically dressed on this damp quayside far from home, she must challenge Henry, who had them both, and win.

'Well, really, Henry,' she said. 'I'm surprised at you. If you put Sophia away in an institution, even in the Magdalen Hospital, which is supposed to be more for fallen women than for lunatics, it will give rise to the most unfortunate kind of talk, and I shall see that it does.'

'What do you mean, Mother?'

'It is quite true that in such cases people tend to think that some kind of mental affliction is involved. In this case, it will be taken for granted that the condition was inherited. You have never been prepared to admit it, Henry, but your father was completely demented, and your grandmother had an uncle who had to be kept confined. I only hope that poor little Francis has escaped the taint. If word gets about that you have a crazy daughter, people will begin to look askance at *you*.'

She paused, observing with satisfaction the effect she had had on Henry, which was very much the same as if she had grown to the size and bulk of Tarrant or Poole and punched her son very hard in the solar plexus. She also saw with pleasure that the two footmen, despite their training in impassivity, were unable to keep the enthralled glint out of their eyes. By the look of them, they were having the most exciting day of their entire careers. She followed up her advantage.

'I can tell you this: Francis is more likely to grow up normal if he doesn't hear tattle about his poor mad sister. But if you put Sophia away, he *will*.'

'Mother, this is intolerable.' Henry was acutely and visibly conscious of the listening footmen. 'How dare you threaten me? And how dare you say such things about my father? He suffered from a recurrent tropical fever—'

'He was insane,' said Lucy-Anne flatly. 'And plenty of people saw him in his fits of madness, let me remind you. It's not just my opinion.'

'Mother, please!'

'You've always lied to yourself about it and I let you, out of kindness, because it made you happy and did no harm. But it will do harm if I let you go on doing it now. Put Sophia away and it will soon become known. I warn you, I shall make sure it does. Then the whispers will start. Think of it, Henry; think of people glancing aside when you enter a room, whispering behind their hands and their fans. A mad father and now a daughter shut away? Well, well. You're the generation in between, the canal down which the madness must have flowed. It could well affect both your business and your social life. Don't imagine that you can prevent it by putting me away too, by the way. Two members of your family vanishing into homes for the inadequate would take far too much concealing. It would get known without my help and whatever would people say about *that*? Father, mother and daughter, all out of their minds? Dear, dear.'

Delving under her ridiculous blanket, she found her lorgnette and through it examined her son's face. But though he was shaken, he had not softened. Lucy-Anne tried again.

'The Magdalen Hospital will serve no purpose, Henry. What is the point, after all? Your daughter fell in love with a worthless man. Unwise, but such things happen. Girls run off with unsuitable young men, and young men fall head over ears for unsuitable young women; it's a common tale. That's human nature, not insanity or even wickedness.'

'When the girl who behaves in this way is my daughter, and above all when it is Sophia, Mother, I say that it is both.' Henry, his face suffused, pursed his lips and looked at Sophia. He was a more urbane man than his father had been, but at this moment he seemed to the despairing Lucy-Anne to be almost identical with George. She began a fresh protest but Henry cut her short, addressing Sophia.

'I have always had a particular feeling for you, Sophia, as no doubt you know. You bear so great a look of your dear mother, my first wife, who died at your birth. It grieves me, more than I can say, to find that your fair face is all deception, that in your heart you are nothing like my beloved Emma. It tears me apart, believe me.'

'And it tears *me* apart,' said Lucy-Anne fiercely, 'to hear you talk in

322

that foolish way, Henry. So Sophia looks like her mother? Well, you at this moment sound like your father! He had the unhappy knack of confusing people with one another, too! He mistook himself for an Indian prince and housemaids for dancing girls and he once took Emma for someone whom one presumes was a woman he knew in India. It was because of that that Emma had to go away to Bath, and ultimately to her death, as you well know.'

Henry turned to her sharply. 'What are you trying to say, Mother? I don't understand you.'

'Oh, yes you do.' Lucy-Anne, like a duellist perceiving victory, attacked with all the skill and force she could muster. This would do it, or nothing would. 'I'm saying,' she told him, 'that I hope you are not going to make a habit of mixing people up with one another – Emma's daughter with Emma herself, for example. I would call that a most alarming symptom.' She infused her voice with a note of grave warning. 'You should be careful, Henry.'

His face changed. She watched the doubt come into his eyes and saw his brow furrow. Relief almost made her faint, 'Come, Henry,' she said. 'You must not pile extra blame on Sophia because she has a look of her mother. Family resemblances can be striking, but what of it? Sophia is Sophia, no one else, and you are her father. She has been very silly, but she knows it. She looks to you now for forgiveness and protection.'

Her victory was there in his face but he would not give in to it instantly. Pride must be served first. He turned judicially to Sophia.

'I will consider if perhaps you should have a second chance. If so, you will owe it to your grandmother. But it would be best if we discussed this matter somewhere else. We ought to get to an inn for the night.'

'I quite agree,' said Lucy-Anne fervently. 'I've a carriage waiting, with muddy horses and drenched postilions. They all need warmth and shelter. Come. My goodness,' said Lucy-Anne, giving Sophia a reassuring smile, 'I spoke just now of Edward Harper. You know the name, of course. You know you were born when your mother and I were staying with the Harpers at Bath. Edward and Julia could have told you a tale or two. They once took in a young wife who had had a child by a lover while her husband was away from home. But the woman concerned wasn't mad; just unwisely besotted. As I said, these things happen. Now then. Which inn are we going to?'

By sheer force of will she got the choice of inn settled, and steered them all off the quay. She packed herself and Sophie into the post-chaise. Henry, Tarrant and Poole would go to the selected inn on foot. Despite the chill of the evening, rivulets of sweat were running down Lucy-Anne's temples under the absurd horse-blanket. It was a fearful thing, to have to fight without any weapons beyond those of words and ideas. For the moment she was in the ascendant but Henry was still hesitating in the name of pride and she knew her victory was fragile. Would the idea, just the mere concept, of insanity, hold Henry in check long enough to get Sophia home?

He was terrified of the stigma of madness and always had been. Play sufficiently on that fear, and Sophia might remain safe. But Lucy-Anne did not trust her son. To make sure that he didn't change his mind, she would have to play on his fears all the way home and afterwards too. Sophia must not only be got to Hanover Square. Once there, she must also be seen by friends and neighbours and Horatia's family, living and associating in normal fashion with her sisters. Once that was done, it would be hard for Henry to go back on it.

As the chaise set off, a frightening phrase drifted through Lucy-Anne's mind.

Whatever happens, I must live long enough to see that through.

Lemuel awoke at dawn, lying on a thin blanket in the steerage quarters of the *Bristol Pearl*. She was under way. He could hear the slap of water along the ship's sides and the sound of wind in canvas. Close beside him a man lay on his back snoring and at the far end of the low-ceilinged compartment a woman was trying to hush a crying child and nurse a baby at the same time.

The smell of bilge-water and crammed-together, ill-washed humanity was all about him and his body throbbed from numerous contusions placed there, ruthlessly and scientifically, by Tarrant and Poole. Mr Whitmead's footmen clearly frequented boxing establishments in their spare time. He had thrown up afterwards, when they left him crouching on his knees behind an empty hut, and the sweet-metal taste of blood was still in his mouth from the teeth he had lost. But they hadn't broken any bones and they'd left his bundle lying where it fell when they attacked him. He'd got himself and his things on board ship no more than an hour later and settled down at once to sleep off the worst of his pain. He'd live.

He wondered where Sophia was now. On her way home with her father, no doubt. Well, that smug bastard Henry Whitmead had at least been disabused of the notion that poor men couldn't retaliate when he made their lives hell. Good.

He sat up carefully, exploring his bruises with cautious fingers. In a way, of course, he'd been a fool. Sophia hadn't been worth all this. Though he might have made something of her in the end. She was sweet enough when she was smiling; it was just a pity she was always in the dismals. He wondered if he would really have done what he intended to do, which was to keep her quiet by getting the captain to marry them at sea, and then to ditch her in some American port and go off to make his fortune on his own.

If she'd improved, and learned to please him, he might have kept her by him after all, for as long as she survived. It probably wouldn't have been long. She wasn't strong enough to stand much hardship. Not like his mother. Now, his mother had stood a lifetime of it before she gave in.

He wondered whether by any chance he'd got Sophia with child but didn't think about it for long. He wasn't really interested.

Lucy-Anne was roused from sleep by grooms calling to each other in the inn yard below her bedchamber. She still ached with exhaustion, but she could face the day, she thought, and she would manage the journey home. She was also equal to making certain essential enquiries. When

Letty came to see if her mistress were awake, she said, 'I want to talk to Sophia alone. Bring her here.'

'Mr Whitmead told her she wasn't to leave her room until he fetched her to the chaise, ma'am.'

'Oh, confound Henry! Very well, I'll go to her!' snapped Lucy-Anne.

Sophia was sitting by the window in her room. She turned her head as Lucy-Anne came in. 'The ship will have sailed,' she said. 'And I'm thankful for that. I'll never have to set eyes on Lemuel again. It was unspeakable. Grandmamma, does that happen to every woman? Is that what . . . what marriage is?'

'If you mean what I think you mean, then yes.'

'And women don't mind? *You* didn't mind? I mean, you were married, so you must have . . . have . . .'

'Yes, I did. I found it disagreeable at first but one gets over that. You apparently found it worse than disagreeable and I can only conclude that Lemuel Craddock was very unkind to you.'

'He was. I was so thankful to see my father. But then . . .' Sophia's voice became a whisper and in her lap her hands were clenched, 'then Father said . . . but I am going home after all am I not? Oh, Grandmamma!' She choked, and Lucy-Anne, going to her, put her arms tightly round this hapless child who like her mother and her grandmother before her had tried to break free and failed. 'I'm so ashamed,' said Sophia. 'I can't believe I did those things with Lemuel. I can't believe I was so foolish as to run away with him in the first place.'

'Oh, my dear. Believe me, others have been as foolish before you, if foolishness is what it is. It's natural for a girl to want a man's love; you were unlucky in the man, that's all.'

'You were married, at least. You were in love with your husband. I suppose that's somehow different.'

'I wasn't in the least in love with my husband,' said Lucy-Anne crisply.

'What?'

'I'm going to tell you a secret,' said Lucy-Anne. 'No one now alive knows this but me, and now you. In my lifetime, you must never pass it on to anyone else; after I'm dead, it doesn't matter. My husband spent most of our married life in India and left me behind. I had someone else. Oh, not for very long. It soon ended. But I know all about being in love, and I know what it can really be like, between a man and a woman.'

'You . . . ?' Sophia drew back and looked up into her grandmother's face. '*You* . . . ? But . . . who was he?'

'I think I'll keep that much secret still,' said Lucy-Anne. 'I just want you to know that it happened.' She paused, wondering whether to say more but decided against it. It was best that Hugo's existence should remain as secret as the name of his father.

'I just want you to know that you're not the only one whose heart has led her into doing dangerous things. I look back and I can hardly believe, myself, in what I did long ago. Take courage from that. Now, some useful advice. I will help you all I can, but in turn I need help from you. Yes, you are coming home. After your father had sent you to your

325

room last night he told me that he had decided to permit your return, and he said it in the presence of both Tarrant and Poole. All the same, you must take care. From now on you must behave very quietly and calmly – in fact you must be the epitome of sanity and propriety, and give no one any excuse for thinking otherwise. You understand me? And there's something else I need to know. Tell me . . .'

Sophia was bewildered by the question, but answered it. 'This morning. When I woke up, I found that it had come. It was fortunate that I put what was necessary in my bundle. But why?'

'You don't know? When we do get home,' said Lucy-Anne, 'I think I'll break Horatia's neck. I didn't realise that no one had told you the simple facts of life. No one ever expected Horatia to be a mother to you, but she might at least have given you some basic information. You are not with child, that's what it means. Thank God for that.'

Chapter Twenty-seven
The Hatching

Lucy-Anne came of strong stock. She did not know it, but in her ancestry were people who had survived bubonic plague not by hiding from it but by recovering from it or being simply immune to it in the first place. Many of her forebears had lived longer than the average. And many had fought through difficult times to preserve things and people they held dear – loved ones and homes and freedom.

The chill she took on that hard, wet journey to Bristol gained on her only slowly. She began to be feverish before she reached London but on the way she nevertheless managed several times to speak impressively to Henry about the importance of avoiding any kind of scandal, and the necessity of resuming normal family life once they were home. Before they arrived in Hanover Square she was reasonably sure that the shadow of the Magdalen no longer hung over Sophia.

Once home she retired at once to bed, but got up the next day and came downstairs to send notes inviting Horatia's sister Elizabeth and her husband and Mr and Mrs Faulkner and various other acquaintances to call, and when they came, Lucy-Anne, though suffering by this time from a husky voice, was there to greet them with all three grand-daughters in attendance as well as Horatia.

Horatia abetted her. 'I agree with your mother, Henry. Sophia's behaviour has been quite shocking, of course, but I don't want scandal to touch our home or our family. I don't want people saying that there is madness in our son's blood or that his sister has been shut away as a moral defective. When Francis is a man and joins a club, he won't want that sort of gossip to be whispered over the card tables. We have warned the servants not to talk and none of them have, as far as I know. But if any rumours do slip out, well, they should die away if Sophia is seen to be living life as usual.'

'You hardly need to persuade me, my dear,' said Henry huffily. 'I have balanced the likely damage to my family's reputation against the risk to my other daughters if Sophia associates with them, and decided that I must take the risk, although I very much fear that Sophia may in some way corrupt her sisters.'

'I don't think the risk of corruption is very high,' said Horatia. 'She was so distressed by her experience that she is more likely to warn them off love affairs for ever. A pity. I can see my son one day having to support three unmarried half-sisters.'

'I trust Francis will never grudge the bread in the mouths of his sisters,' said Henry. 'I would hope, indeed, that he will always care for them and protect them. So, you feel that I am right in allowing matters to slide, do you, my dear?'

'It's the easiest thing to do,' said Horatia. 'And I feel sure that Sophia has had a dreadful and frightening lesson. She won't offend again.'

Lucy-Anne, hearing all this from Horatia later the same day, cleared her painful throat and said that she was glad that everything had been settled. She also thought, privately, that the well-defined streak of pure idleness in Horatia's temperament was a blessing. Horatia would always choose the least troublesome path, which in this case meant assuming that Sophia would cause no further disturbance and allowing normal life to resume for all of them.

It was true, in any case, that Sophia was unlikely to repeat her transgression. All too true, Lucy-Anne thought grimly. She had warned Sophie to be careful in her behaviour, but she still didn't like to see her grand-daughter so pale, or to hear her make such colourless conversation. In company or out of it, there was no vitality or originality in her now; she uttered only platitudes, in a correct little voice, and her eyes were always downcast.

But there was nothing more that Lucy-Anne could do. She was becoming a little more ill each day. Tomorrow, she did not think she would be able to get out of bed at all. She had always in the past conquered illness without too much difficulty, but she was old now and very tired. She had done her utmost and soon she must leave her descendants to lead their own lives.

Very soon. She lifted her eyes to the window. Outside was a clear autumn day, with a cool blue sky and golden-brown leaves on the trees. Each month had its own beauties and even November had, on occasion, an austere charm. Who, really, wanted to leave the world? She wondered why, now that her departure was near, she felt so little grief, so little fear. She dreaded the process of dying somewhat, but not death itself.

She coughed, flinching from the pain in her throat and chest, and prayed silently that her passing would not be too hard, but did not pray for its postponement. Perhaps, quite simply, it was time to go.

'In her sleep,' said Henry. 'She was fortunate; it was easy and without pain. You may go up and make your farewells. Anne and Phoebe, you go first. Sophia, you will follow them. But I want to speak to you before you do so.'

All the rooms were dim because all the window curtains had been closed. In the morning room, Sophia sat with her hands in her lap and waited dumbly. Her protector was gone and she was alone with her father. Was he about to say that after all she was to be cast out of the family? Was the Magdalen once again a threat?

Henry took up a position in front of the mantelpiece, feet apart on the hearthrug, coat open and waistcoat stretched over what was now an increasing paunch. He took a pinch of snuff. 'I hope,' he said, 'that you are content with your work, Sophia.'

She must speak now, because he expected it and she must do the

328

expected thing. That was one of the requirements of sanity. 'My . . . my work?'

'Had your grandmother not felt obliged to make that journey to Bristol, she would not have taken the chill that killed her. You are responsible for her death, Sophia.'

'Yes. Yes, I see. I'm sorry. So very sorry.'

And her grandmother wouldn't have come to Bristol if she hadn't, quite rightly, feared what he would do when he found the runaways. Sophia wanted to cry out: 'It's your fault as much as mine! Just because I am dependent on you, just because you have power over me, doesn't make you always right. It just means that I have to pretend you are!'

But, just because of that power, she must not. She bent her head and waited.

'Because of your grandmother's pleas, and also because of Horatia's, I have decided that it is best for the whole family if we present the world with the appearance of a household in which nothing is amiss. For that reason, you are still here and may remain so. You should thank me.'

'I do, Father. Indeed, I do.'

'You must also promise that never, in the future, will you give me cause to regret my decision.'

'Oh yes, I promise.'

Henry moved across to the window and put a curtain back just enough to let a shaft of light fall on her face. 'Look at me, Sophia.'

His daughter raised her eyes to his. Her eyes really were amazingly like Emma's. He had never forgotten his first wife. Horatia was decorative and dutiful and she had given him a healthy son, but she had never made him feel tender as Emma sometimes had. He could not look into Sophia's face and not remember that tenderness, and wish he had shown Emma more of it.

When, this morning, a stricken Letty had summoned him to his mother's room, his first reaction was fury. For ten whole minutes he had been quite determined to have Sophia out of the house within the day. And then he had come into the room where she was and found that he couldn't do it. He could have done it at Bristol, but that was three weeks ago now and his first outrage had lost its force. Now, as he gazed into the face of this daughter who so greatly resembled Emma, it died away altogether. He would miss Emma for the rest of his life and he could not in cold blood disown Emma's daughter, or consign her to the Magdalen.

But he must not appear weak.

'Say it again, Sophia. Say that you promise that I will never regret deciding to forgive you.'

'I promise, most sincerely, that you will never regret deciding to forgive me.'

'And you will never forget that, because of you, your grandmother has been called to her Maker before her time?'

'No, Father. I will never forget that, because of me, my grandmother was called too soon to her Maker.'

'Good. Well, go now and make your farewells. You could not of course foresee that that would be the outcome. You did not intend it. I

329

recognise that. You are forgiven for that, too. You have given me your promise and now I in turn promise that I will always take care of you.'

'What a relief,' Anne said, coming into their sitting room on the day after the funeral. 'Daylight in the house at last and even if we're all in black we can at least speak in normal voices. Horatia is going shopping today for what she calls more fashionable mourning. I believe she has seen a black silk gown with lace trimmings in Oxford Street, and intends to buy a jet necklace to go with it.'

'Oh, is that where she's off to?' Phoebe was standing by the window, enjoying the restored freedom to gaze out of it once again. 'She's just setting out, on foot, with Millicent and Tarrant in attendance.'

'I've become quite fond of Horatia,' said Sophia. She was well aware that Horatia had helped Lucy-Anne to defend her.

'But I wish she wasn't so lazy,' grumbled Phoebe. 'We embroider all the linen in this house; she never puts in a stitch. She says she doesn't care for doing the same bridge-over-water picture time and again but really she just doesn't want to work.'

'You're not so very fond of your needle yourself,' Anne remarked, seating herself and picking up her own embroidery.

Sophia, doing the same, observed: 'Horatia's indolent ways could be to our advantage. We used to wish she would try to find husbands for us but, believe me, it's a blessing to know that she won't want to be bothered.'

'I wish you wouldn't drop these mysterious hints, Sophie,' Anne complained. 'You've said before that what happens between men and women is a frightful thing and that we're lucky to be single and you never want to be married, but you just won't tell us what you mean.'

'That's right. It's not fair to drop hints and then not finish the story,' Phoebe said.

'I didn't drop hints. You kept *asking*.' Sophia, trying to stitch, found that her hands were trembling. Her sisters kept on pestering her to tell them what had happened between herself and Lemuel, but she never wanted to think of it again. 'It means talking about such improper things,' she said.

'Oh, come on, Sophie! We didn't press you too much at first because you looked so ill. But you're better now,' said Anne, 'and we're all sisters together and we want to know. We ought to know! Tell us.'

Sophia laid her sewing down. In a way, it would be a relief. To speak of it might free her at last from those awful dreams in which Lemuel again loomed over her, ready to take her in that dreadful assault which he said she ought to enjoy, and which Grandmamma, weirdly, had implied that one *could* enjoy. Haltingly, not meeting their eyes, she began, after all, to speak.

'I can't believe it,' said Anne at last. 'You're not making this up, are you, Sophia?'

'Would I make up something like that? How could I?'

'I'm not so surprised,' said Phoebe. She had perched herself on the arm of a chair, from which she could go on enjoying the view of the square. 'I always thought it must be something like that – something very crude and physical – or there wouldn't be so much mystery about it. But what I can't understand is why, if it's so awful, Horatia doesn't seem to mind. She and Father must have done it. After all, there's Francis.'

'I don't *know*,' said Sophia. 'It's all still a mystery to me. I don't understand any of it.'

It was true. She really would have thrown herself into the sea rather than go on with Lemuel, yet all the time, in the worst of those hateful, agonising couplings, the possibility that it could, somehow, all be quite different had been tantalisingly *there*. Grandmamma's hints had confirmed the feeling. It was as though sex were a double porch, an archway within which were two doors. One led to heaven and the other to hell and somehow she had opened the wrong one.

She was glad when Phoebe changed the subject. 'We've got a visitor. There's a clergyman coming up our steps.'

'A clergyman?' Anne was interested. 'Do we know any clergymen?'

'I've never seen this one before, anyway. He isn't from St George's.'

'Well, it's been a dull morning so far. Let's find out more,' said Anne.

As one, they rose and made for the landing, to peer through the latticework screen as Ames admitted the newcomer.

His voice floated up the stairs towards them. 'Is Mr Henry Whitmead in? I would much appreciate a few words. No, he doesn't know me, but I know of him. He's on a list I've been compiling, of influential men, especially shipowners, with charitable inclinations. I'm here to make a charitable appeal. My name? Oh yes, certainly: Richard Harper.'

'It's good of you to see me, sir,' said Richard Harper. 'I appreciate it.'

'I would hardly refuse an interview to a man of the cloth such as yourself. May I know what I can do for you?'

'You are all consideration, sir.'

Henry regarded his visitor thoughtfully. Harper's words were courteous and respectful, as befitted a man in his twenties to a man in his fifties, even when the younger one was a clergyman. But Henry was quite experienced enough in the ways of his fellow creatures to know that the cool expression in Mr Harper's grey eyes was one of assessment. He didn't entirely care for it.

'You are here on behalf of a charity, I believe?' said Henry, and allowed his glance to stray briefly to the watch in his waistcoat. 'I support many worthy causes, including the Magdalen Hospital and other institutions whose purpose is to raise the moral tone of our society.'

'The moral tone of our society could indeed do with raising, in many different ways,' said Richard Harper. 'One of them concerns the sadly low value it places upon human life.'

'Indeed?' said Henry, raising his eyebrows.

Harper had a West Country accent, not very broad, just enough in fact to be pleasant. But what he now said in that agreeable voice was to Henry's ears not pleasant at all.

'You have invested in shipping, sir. This matter should be of great interest to you. The fact is, that too many ships are being lost at sea. This has been the case for a long time and it can't be satisfactory either to the line-owners or to their insurers. But it's still less satisfactory for the sailors and passengers whose lives are lost, and for their families on shore. I speak from experience. My brother is a seaman.'

'Quite. Quite. But the sea is a hazardous place, Mr Harper. It is prone to storms, and ships that ply towards the equator, or to the Caribbean or the Indian Ocean, risk foundering in hurricanes. These things are acts of God.'

'Are they? Is it not true,' said Harper, 'that seaworthy ships which are not overladen have more chance of riding out bad weather? A vessel that goes down because her timbers are rotten, or her hold too full, does so because of the greed of men, not because of the will of God.'

'Oh, come now! It's to be expected that owners and captains will carry as much cargo as possible; profits must be made or it would become impossible to conduct overseas trade at all. Both sailors and passengers go to sea knowing the hazards. Why, precisely, have you come to see me?'

'Because, sir, you do have a reputation for contributing to charitable causes. I therefore conclude that you are a man of heart and good moral standards and I hope to secure your help in a campaign I am conducting. I am gathering signatures and promises of support for a petition to be placed before Parliament, asking for legislation to control the seaworthiness of ships before they are allowed to put to sea, and to limit to safe levels the amount of cargo they can carry.'

'You wish for my signature and my promise of support, whatever that may mean?'

'Yes, sir. And by support, of course, I mean any assistance you can give. All such campaigns require funds; and all are the better for men who will uphold them by speaking in their favour not only at meetings but also in clubs and across dinner tables. This would be a most worthwhile reform. I and my late father have been interested in this subject for a long time. Our efforts have met with little success up to now, but before my father's death, which took place suddenly, a fortnight ago, we planned a new campaign, based on a carefully prepared report, which we decided to take round to possible supporters, such as yourself. I am now carrying the work on alone. I have the report with me and perhaps you would care to peruse it.'

Harper took a rolled sheet of paper from inside his coat and, without waiting for permission, spread it out on Henry's desk, planting the inkstand, a paperweight and a ledger at strategic places to hold it down.

'This gives the history of a number of ships, including some in which I believe you have an interest, over the past five years. Here are the names of the ships and against each are written details of their voyages – destinations, cargo carried, its nature and estimated weight – and information on the age of the ship and repairs carried out during her life. Where there is a cross against a vessel's name it denotes that she foundered on her last voyage, and here' – as if by magic, Harper whisked another rolled sheet from under his coat and spread it out – 'are details of those losses, wherever they are known. Some ships, of course, have simply sailed over the horizon and never been seen again. But where there were survivors, their accounts have been summarised – the cause of the disaster and the ship's position at the time – and the survivors' names are listed. You will notice that there have been a number of losses in the last few years. Please spare a few moments to look closely.'

Interested in spite of himself, Henry leant forward. The information was carefully and legibly set out.

'You will see,' said Harper, 'that there is a definite correlation between cases of foundering and the age and loading of the ship. I must say to you frankly, sir, that there are suspicions that in some cases the overloading was deliberate, because from the owners' point of view it is more profitable to let an old ship sink, and claim the insurance, than to replace or repair her.'

Henry, who had been examining the list of foundered vessels, raised his head and snorted. 'It is normal business practice to get the most out of a vessel. That is not the same thing as willing her to sink and it is damnably insulting to suggest that it is. However.' He leant back. 'I suppose I must be prepared to make allowances for you. You say your brother is a sailor, and also, as a man of the cloth, you naturally do not live in the everyday world and do not understand that in business certain risks have to be taken.'

'With other men's lives?'

'Men's lives or even women's. Even your brother's. It is the way of the world, and I have already said that there is no avoiding acts of God.'

'And I am trying to persuade you to understand that sometimes, there is.'

There was impatience in Richard's tone, but he curbed it. His mother had always said that friendly persuasion was better than anger, and he had found it to be true, especially when backed up by some of the subtlety which came naturally to him, and which was a far more effective weapon than crude answering back.

He had not expected this to be easy. So far he had made eleven visits and obtained only one signature and, although depressed about it, he wasn't surprised. He was however surprised to find that Henry Whitmead made him want to be angry. It was as though, for some reason, he felt that this man Whitmead ought to be more willing to help him than the other men he had approached.

Which was ridiculous. He tried to adopt a more conciliatory attitude.

'My father's death, as I have said, was recent, and my grief is very real, but I would like to think that by carrying on his work I am honouring his memory as a son should. You have just said that to suggest that ships are commonly overloaded on purpose is insulting; therefore, you would presumably not approve of such a thing or want to be suspected of it. If legislation were brought in, it would become impossible and, therefore, not only would your ships be safer but also your good name—'

'My good name is perfectly safe, thank you. I find you impertinent, sir, and only the fact that I naturally feel for you in your bereavement is at this moment keeping me from expressing myself far more forcefully.

I have lost my mother within the past week, as it happens, and therefore am prepared to make allowance for your emotions.'

'Indeed, sir? I am extremely sorry; for your loss, I mean, not for your indulgence. Please allow me to offer my condolences.'

'I daresay you mean that. Well, Mr Harper. Thank you for calling on me and I can only regret that I am unable to help you. Clearly you belong to this modern Reformist movement. You will find yourself ploughing a stony furrow if you want to overturn ordinary business practice and limit the profits of those who, after all, bring prosperity into the country.'

In the course of those eleven previous visits, Richard had learned a great deal about doggedness. He drew a further sheet from his coat. 'It is not ordinary business practice I wish to challenge, sir, but cruel and inhuman business practice. I feel sure that you would not wish to defend such things. If you would let me have your signature—'

'Dammit, I will *not* let you have my signature! Haven't I made it quite clear that I do not support your absurd campaign? Your family feeling does you credit but I don't propose to pay for it! I have been patient with you, sir, but I will tell you now that in my opinion the Reformist movement is a menace. It seeks to make interfering laws which will keep honest men from getting a fair return for their labours and investments, while riff-raff are pampered!'

'A return which is squeezed out of dead men's bones, sir, is *not* a fair return!'

'And that, sir, is the outside of enough!' Henry, pushing inkstand, paperweight and ledger aside, rolled up the schedules and thrust them at Richard. 'Allow me,' he said, rising to his feet, 'to see you out.'

Richard shook a regretful head as he was shepherded to the study door. 'I have interviewed survivors from shipwrecks, and men – I am not speaking of my brother – who have had the experience of giving themselves up for lost in leaking tubs which came to the brink of disaster. If you had heard what they had to tell, you would feel differently, I know. I am saying that in the hope that although you reject my words now, they will lie like seeds in your memory and perhaps, one day, spring into a sweet new growth.'

'You are pleased to be poetic, but life, alas, is not as the poets pretend.' Henry escorted his visitor briskly on to the landing. 'I'm afraid, young man, that you've done a great deal of hard work for nothing. I suppose I should commend your industry! It could be put to better use. Do you have a parish?'

'I have.'

'Then I urge you, Mr Harper, to return to it and concentrate on caring for your parishioners. I don't doubt you will do excellent work among them, such as everyone must commend. Tell me, are you by any chance related to a Mr Edward Harper, who was once vicar at St Oswald's, near Bath? You have a West Country voice. Edward Harper was an admirable clergyman, if my memory serves me correctly.'

'Edward Harper?' Richard paused in the middle of the landing to look at Henry in surprise. 'He was my great-uncle – well, by marriage. His wife was my great-aunt. My father was . . . he lost his parents and my great-aunt and uncle adopted him. They brought him up and allowed him to take their surname. He was called Hugo Harper but—'

'Remarkable,' said Henry. 'I knew Hugo Harper when I was young. My mother used to take the Bath waters and,as she was friendly with Julia Harper – who must have been your great-aunt – she used to go and stay at St Oswald's vicarage. I stayed there once or twice myself. In fact, I attended your father's wedding. Amazing. I believe I did hear that Hugo was adopted and was not one of the Harpers' sons, but it was rarely talked about.'

'Few people knew. It was not discussed very much although great-uncle Edward was frank with my father up to a point. The Harpers were very honest people and had a dislike of deception.'

Always try, Richard's mother had said, and still did on occasion, to make an enemy into a friend. If there is an argument, dissolve it into ordinary talk before you part. Never, never part in anger if you can avoid it. Give yourself freely and never mind your pride.

'My father was actually the son of Mrs Julia Harper's brother Stephen Clarke,' Richard said, offering a confidence as though it were a handshake. 'But there was some kind of mystery about his mother. My father was almost certainly a love-child; indeed he believed that one particular woman, who visited St Oswalds sometimes and showed an interest in him, could have been his mother. But he knew nothing for certain.'

'That might well be so,' said Henry. 'My mother once mentioned that the Harpers had sheltered a married woman who had had a love-child. No doubt Hugo was the child concerned. You certainly come of a family anxious to do good deeds, Mr Harper, although Stephen Clarke sounds a dubious character. I fancy I've heard that name somewhere—'

'Perhaps when you visited St Oswald's, sir? No doubt—'

He stopped, because Henry was no longer listening to him, or even looking at him. His eyes were on a point somewhere above Richard's head. Richard moved so that he could see what had so abruptly taken his host's attention. He almost said, 'Oh my God!' aloud, but checked himself, because one must not take the name of God in vain, and because he must on no account let Mr Whitmead know that he had seen.

Henry remembered that moment for the rest of his life, for then it was that he finally knew, finally saw, how right and wise his father had been. Through fever, delirium – all right, madness if you like – he had been consistently right about one thing: women must be cherished but they must also be protected, from the outside world and from themselves. Even his own mother . . .

I once had a maid who was party to a questionable secret of mine.

They once took in a young wife who actually had a child by a lover while her husband was away from home.

And one particular woman, who habitually visited St Oswald's, could have been Hugo's mother.

The hateful tale of evidence, relentless as the schedules Richard Harper had just spread out on his desk, unrolled before his mental vision.

He had remembered now who Stephen Clarke was. The man had left Chestnuts before Henry was old enough to recall what he looked like, but Lucy-Anne had spoken of him sometimes. His name had been bandied about during that original argument over the Craddocks. He had been the bailiff at Chestnuts before Cottrell's day. He and Lucy-Anne had been together there while George was in India.

And there had been a time – again, he was too small to remember, but it had been mentioned sometimes later on – when his mother was away for a long time in Bath (oh, God, yes, Bath, where she so often stayed with the Harpers!) because she had been seized by some mysterious illness and prevented from coming home for months.

And the final proof was in front of him, there on the landing wall. There, proudly positioned, hung the portrait of George Whitmead and Lucy-Anne at the time of their marriage, when Lucy-Anne was young and good-looking and had all her teeth. It was a good portrait, faithfully reproducing the faces of the subjects.

And Richard Harper, the son of Hugo Harper, standing here in the flesh, was the image of that youthful Lucy-Anne.

'As I was saying,' said Richard, 'my ancestry is something of a mystery. I have no idea who my paternal grandmother was and I shall never know now. That is a remarkably fine portrait. My mother had – still has – a tendency to think of art and indeed of artists as, well, worldly, but my father thought that an educated man should have some knowledge of the subject and took me, on occasion, to exhibitions. That looks to me like an early Reynolds.'

'No.' Henry too was forcing a veneer of calm over a tumult of feeling. 'Although you are not far wrong. The painter was Thomas Hudson, to whom Sir Joshua Reynolds was apprenticed. He was already with Hudson when that picture was painted in 1743, so perhaps it has a few of his brushstrokes in it.'

'I see from the legend beneath it that it depicts George and Lucy-Anne Whitmead. Your parents, I take it?'

'My parents,' Henry agreed. He was trying not to let himself tremble with rage and shock. God, even in old age, his mother had had a look of Richard Harper. The colour and setting of the eyes and the shape of the nose were exactly hers. But Hugo hadn't taken after her. Extraordinary, that a resemblance could vault a generation and then appear, like the accidentally disinterred victim of a murder, in the grandson.

'A charming picture,' Richard said. 'You are fortunate in so many ways, Mr Whitmead. I imagine there are no mysteries among your forebears. I wish I did know who my paternal grandmother was, but I never shall. Well, I have several other visits to make today. Please allow me to let myself out; there's no need to trouble either you or your butler. Good day.'

Upstairs, behind the lattice, there was the faintest swish from three long skirts as Henry's daughters retreated from the chance of being caught eavesdropping. Neither Henry Whitmead nor Richard Harper noticed.

Richard was gone, stepping briskly down the stairs, never once turning his head as he went, taking with him, for ever, the answer to the question: had he seen?

Had he seen that the features of the girl in the portrait and the face he encountered daily in his own mirror were virtually the same? Had he made a connection between Mrs Whitmead who had often visited the Harpers at Bath, and the unknown woman who had also visited St Oswald's and taken such an interest in Hugo? Or attached any significance to the fact that the name Stephen Clarke sounded familiar to Henry Whitmead?

Richard, walking away round Hanover Square, had been disappointed of a signature but he had been nicely revenged for its refusal. So that was his father's mother. Oh yes, he was sure of it. She had to be, had to be. Lucy-Anne Whitmead. He could probably make certain, or nearly so. One or other of his numerous Harper cousins – perhaps Julian, who had been so good to Jimmy – might know whether there was a link between Stephen Clarke and the Whitmead family.

But he'd never let anyone know why he was asking. He would never speak of it to anyone, except that he might put it in his diary where it might be read after he was gone. Anything more would be unethical. It was enough for him to recall the sickened expression in Henry Whitmead's eyes. At this moment, Whitmead was wondering how much Richard knew or guessed, and whether he would ever gossip about it, and he was trying to absorb the horrible information that his mother had probably been less than perfectly virtuous. Poor Henry Whitmead, thought Richard cheerfully. Oh, poor fellow!

Henry watched him leave and then turned back towards his study. Once in it, he sat down at his desk and stared around the familiar room. Incredible. Between one moment and the next he had lost his mother for the second time, seen a woman he had loved and respected changed into a deceiving adulteress whose memory filled him with horror.

He wouldn't get over it. It was difficult to realise, just as the irrevocable nature of death was always difficult to accept at first, but this had changed his world for ever. He would never be able to think of his mother with affection or honour again. He found himself gripping the edge of his desk as if to assure himself that that at least was still real. The whole of his study had become weirdly misty and insubstantial.

He reached for the bell-pull and jerked it violently and, when Tarrant answered it, demanded a stiff brandy.

When it came, he sat for a long time, sipping it slowly, thinking. Once or twice his gaze turned upwards, towards the ceiling, above which was the upper floor, and his daughters' sitting room.

'This is your doing!' Horatia's poise was gone. Her nose and eyes were pink with outraged crying and her hair was wild. Her movements were jerky. She walked to and fro from window to door of her step-daughters' sitting room like something caged, caught up a workbox from the table, looked at it as though she didn't know what it was, slammed it down again, stopped in front of the mantelpiece, moved an ornament, moved it back and then, with a sound halfway between a wail and a shriek, swept all the ornaments and the clock on to the floor before rounding on Sophia. '*Your* doing, *your* fault, yours, yours, *yours*!'

'Please, Stepmamma,' said Phoebe nervously. She slipped from her chair and knelt, trying to gather up the fallen ornaments with her hands. 'They're not all broken,' she said, 'and the clock's chipped but it's still ticking. We can pretend it was an accident and the servants needn't know.'

'I should think they know already,' said Anne, turning the pages of a fashion pamphlet. 'None of them are deaf.'

'As if I care a farthing for the servants.' Horatia resumed her frantic pacing. 'Because of what Sophia's done – oh, you silly, *silly* girl, Sophia – because of her idiotic escapade, I'm to be made a virtual prisoner! Your father says no woman can be trusted out except in the company of a husband or father, or brother if he's old enough and responsible enough! His very words! You would think we were all lunatics who needed a keeper with us at all times! I can only go shopping if he's with me! I can't go out to tea unless he's with me! I can't as much as go down the front steps unless he's with me! I'm to spend my spare time with you, up here, so that we can all keep an eye on each other, I presume! I've tried to talk to him, I've tried to argue with him, but he won't listen to a word I say. He won't explain either, but he doesn't need to explain; I know why he's done this, oh yes, I know. The rules apply to you too. Did you think you were too much restricted before? You wait awhile. You won't even be able to take a turn round the square unless your father's with you. The front and back doors will be kept locked on the inside and you'll have to apply to Father or Ames to get them unlocked. None of us will even be able to slip into the garden for five minutes without permission. And that's how it will be for ever. They'll apply for ever; I know him, believe me. And it's all because of Sophia!'

'I think not.' Sophia was sitting immobile in a chair with her back to the window, and her voice came out of shadow. 'It has very little to do with me. You were not there at the time, Stepmamma, but I'm surprised Anne and Phoebe didn't see.'

'Didn't see what?' Anne asked, and Phoebe, who had retrieved a matching pair of china dogs, which had landed on a thick rug and thus survived Horatia's assault, turned from arranging them on the mantelpiece and said, 'Yes, what on earth do you mean, Sophia?'

'This . . . this virtual imprisonment that Father has decreed for us all – I don't think it has much to do with me. I've been home for nearly a month. If my running away is the cause, I'm surprised he didn't announce it before. I don't think it *is* the cause. I think it's because of Mr Harper, who came this morning. We were all three there on the landing when Father was saying goodbye to him. Didn't you understand what was going on? Didn't you *see*?'

'What in hell's name are you talking about?' Horatia shouted.

Sophia told them.

She took a certain amount of pleasure in it. It was something to have worldly experience, no matter how unpleasant, to be recognised as knowledgeable and therefore able freely to speak of such things as affairs and love-children. It was the only kind of superiority she would ever have now in her whole life – the fact of knowing more than her sisters and, in this particular case, more than Horatia. She might as well get what she could out of it. She positively enjoyed their expressions – Horatia's astonished gape, Anne's affronted air, and Phoebe's embarrassed flush.

'Grandmamma?' said Anne at the end of the recital. '*Grandmamma?*'

'I think so. She told me she had had a lover and, although I don't remember the Harpers, I know I was born when Mother was visiting them at St Oswald's. You were already six, Anne. You remember them, I know. And there was this Richard Harper, saying that his father was a love-child, whose own mother wasn't known, but who used to visit St Oswald's, and whose own father's name was Stephen Clarke.'

'Someone of that name once worked at Chestnuts,' said Phoebe, her eyes wide. 'I'm sure of it. It was before we were born, but I'm certain I've heard that name mentioned.'

'Yes, so have I,' said Sophia. 'It all fits. I was putting it together while I was listening. And then I *saw*.'

'What did you see?' demanded Horatia.

'From where I was, I could see Mr Harper and also that painting of Grandmamma and Grandpapa when they were young. I could see that Mr Harper looks just like Grandmamma. And what's more, Father saw it too. He looked at the painting and he looked at Mr Harper and he went so white I thought he was going to faint. Then, within two hours, this. These new rules that Father has made, they're not on my account, or at least not entirely.'

Horatia sat down shakily. 'They're because he's just found out that his own mother . . . ?'

'I think so, yes.'

'I can't believe it,' said Horatia.

'I can,' said Sophia.

They were all still staring at each other when they heard Henry's footsteps approaching. Instinctively they drew closer together as though to confront a common enemy. He came in without knocking and stood surveying them.

'Horatia has told you of the new rules of the household? They apply to you all equally, that goes without saying. She *has* told you? Yes or no?'

Anne spoke for them all. 'Yes, Father.'

'I have one more thing to tell you – well, specifically to tell Sophia.' Henry's gaze rested on his youngest daughter. 'This morning, I received a piece of news. A visitor called on me to discuss – some business which concerns shipping. He had with him documents which mentioned vessels recently lost. One, my dear, was the *Bristol Pearl*, the ship on which you *nearly* sailed to America. She went down in a storm off the Irish coast. A few survivors apparently escaped in boats and reached Ireland. They sent word back, presumably. All the details were there, including the survivors' names. That of Lemuel Craddock was not among them.'

He watched Sophia's face intently as he spoke. He had wondered, as he climbed the stairs, what impact the news would have on this daughter who reminded him so much of Emma, and whether, whatever it was, she would reveal it. Her eyes – eyes in which, now, was knowledge of a kind to which she had no right, knowledge which could only soil an unmarried girl – met his and he saw the horror in them. 'Lemuel is dead?'

'He most certainly is. He's now at the bottom of the sea, my love. As he treated you so ill, I felt you might be glad to know of it. The mills of God may grind slowly, but grind they do. I call this a dispensation of Providence.'

'Glad?' Sophia said.

She hardly knew what she felt. Before she was snatched away from him, she had learned to hate Lemuel and to fear him. She never wanted to set eyes on him again, still less to touch him. He had hurt her grievously, in body and in mind.

So it was absurd that she should be appalled to think of him drowning, his body now a thing to be nibbled by fish. It was incredible that she should want to cry for the harshness of his life and the waste of all that vitality, that she should be anguished by the thought of his terror when he knew he was going to die. Had he been on deck or down below when it happened? She hoped desperately that he had not been trapped below decks.

'I fancy she'll do.' That was what he had said of the *Bristol Pearl*, but he'd been wrong and he'd gone down with her. The sea had rushed into his mouth and nose and choked him, had it? Well, hadn't she been prepared to endure that herself, and would not Lemuel have been the one who drove her to it?

She had no reason to grieve for Lemuel Craddock, and she was not even sure that she truly did. Perhaps what she felt was only pity, and sorrow for the man he might have been, and for the love that he had killed. But the division between these things and grief was very narrow and her eyes filled.

Henry saw it and shuddered. She was so like Emma, so very like Emma. This was as though he were looking at Emma and seeing in her eyes desire and grief for some other man. It was unbearable.

He drew in a sharp breath and caught himself up. He must not brood on his daughter's resemblance to Emma. That way lay madness or even perversion, which was a form of madness. His father had been . . .

No, no, his father had *not* been mad. Or had he? This thought too was unbearable and he shrank away from it. He found another interpretation for Sophia's tears and thankfully seized upon it.

'You have had a narrow escape from death, Sophia, and I see it has upset you. But you have nothing to fear now. You are quite safe. Indeed, all of you are safe. My womenfolk will never again be exposed either to violence or temptation from other men, or to the perils of your own frailty.'

Indeed they wouldn't. His father, George Whitmead, had not, *not* been mad, but very wise. But in spite of all his efforts he had not sufficiently protected the females of his family. He, Henry Whitmead, would do better.

'You will remain,' he told them, smiling, 'always, now, together and under my paternal – in Horatia's case, my conjugal – eye for as long as I am here, and I shall teach Francis to look after you so that when I am gone you will still have someone to guard and cherish you.' He saw that although Sophia had remained silent her tears had begun to fall. 'Anne and Phoebe, try to calm your sister. I will send Letty with a restoring draught.'

He went out, closing the door after him. Anne went to put an arm round Sophia. Phoebe said blankly: 'It's true, then. It's for always. There'll be nothing but this for any of us, ever.'

'Thank God I have no daughters, and never will have,' Horatia said fervently. 'I am beyond being careful what I say to you girls about your father. I notice,' she added slowly, 'that Henry made no mention of Mother-in-law.'

Sophia wiped her eyes. 'Well, he wouldn't. But I know what I saw this morning. I suppose it was Richard Harper who told him about the *Bristol Pearl*. We couldn't hear what they were saying in the study this time, but they were talking about ships as they came out on to the landing. It can't have been the sinking of the *Pearl* that caused all this, though. Why should it? It must have been what that man Harper said about his mysterious forebears – and the way he looked just like that portrait.'

'If Mother-in-law once had a lover and a son to whom she wasn't entitled . . . *that* makes sense, certainly,' said Horatia. She looked around the room and then let out a somewhat hysterical laugh. 'Take a good look at your familiar sitting room, stepdaughters. It's virtually our prison from now on, except when we are taken out for exercise under guard. I am sorry I shouted at you Sophia. We had best not quarrel. We're going to be in each other's company a great deal from now on, are we not? Probably for the rest of our lives!'